MEETING JACK CASH

J. W. UTLEY

To Susan,
A woman of uncommon beauty,
The best of best friends,
My greatest cheerleader and most compassionate critic,
An amazing mother and even greater Gigi,

A perfect wife.

Grief is like wading in the ocean
when a storm is raging offshore;
some waves move you a little,
and others knock you down.
If you are to live,
you must quickly get your feet underneath you
because it is certain the enormous waves will soon come,
and when they do,
they will demand your complete surrender.

CHAPTER ONE

BANG, a loud and sudden shot rang out!

I shuddered, expecting immediate pain, even running my hands across my upper torso, feeling for a wound. Instead, a hot liquid substance pulsated down my back. Confused, I quickly turned. I distinctly remember telling her to stay behind me as if I could stop a bullet, but she didn't listen. She looked at me and then at the wound where the bullet penetrated her shoulder and started shaking her head with disbelief. It was as if dread was poured out like a thick poison, starting with her eyes and then consuming her countenance. Blood was now everywhere, as were people with guns shooting here and there, filling the air with rapid fire and the pungent smell of gunpowder smoke.

"I love you, Jack Cash, don't leave me," she whispered as I gently lowered her to the ground. What should have been a sweet moment had a certain bitterness attached to it because the shooter said the very same thing a few days ago.

But it didn't matter now.

I turned back to the shooter, who was now also on the ground, bleeding herself, wounded from another, and looking as if the last glimmer of her life was slipping away. I couldn't help her and wouldn't help even if I could because my friend was now bleeding profusely. I turned and tended to her, pressed her wound, hoping to cheat death for her, when suddenly, someone forcefully jerked me away, "We've got to go, Jack Cash, or you'll be next."

Her voice grew louder as she tugged my arm harder, "They will take care of her! You MUST hurry."

That emphatic command met with what seemed like a choreographed group of people pushing me away, tending to the wounds of my friend and her shooter. A mix of extreme sleep deprivation, the pandemonium that started early that morning, and pure adrenaline forced me to run. Even though so many emotions should have stopped me in my tracks, they would have had to contend with the woman with the death grip on my arm, pulling me to places unknown. I offered no resistance because I was on autopilot, too tired to care, too scared to stay, and too done to try to figure things out. I wish I could say that I was surprised at this turn of events, but after weeks of senselessness, nothing surprised me anymore. I figured I might as well go along with whoever was assuming leadership of my life because, clearly, I was not doing a good job at it.

A lot happened in a such a short span of time. I thought I was simply a grieving man walking on a beach trying to make sense of my life, but that was two weeks and a few wives ago.

CHAPTER TWO

(Two Weeks Earlier)

As I walked on the beach, I was numb. If I could turn back time, I would beat the living daylight savings time out of it. After the other funerals, I waited at least six months before coming here, but this time was different. It was as if something or someone drew me, but honestly, I didn't know who or why. If anything, I thought it was a divine misdirect.

The waves buffeting the shoreline, churned up by that distant storm, attempted to push me into the wash, just as the force of the battery in my soul had done repeatedly. Just a few weeks ago, I buried Marie. Someone murdered her outside a strip club, and since then, my world has turned upside down. Evidently, in cases like this, the husband is the primary suspect. The headlines in our local newspaper questioned every part of my life, integrity, and ministry. I shouldn't have read any of the stories or watched the news. But I did. The worst headline was "Serial Killer Pastor?" Someone must have thought I had it coming, that somehow, I deserved this parade of suspicion.

No doubt they felt I was responsible for what happened to Marie and the others.

Even though I was "cleared" by law enforcement (whatever that meant), I knew that until they apprehended Marie's actual murderer, there would always be questions. Probably millions of them. I had my own. I turned and looked at the action of the waves behind me as they erased my footprints. If only they could also wash away my past.

I wondered if my everyday life was over. I don't just mean my ministry. Most had walked out before Marie's murder because of her work. Now, I wondered if any of the others would stay. Even more so, I questioned if I would ever truly love again or if any woman with half of a brain would even consider a relationship with me. I was damaged goods, tainted by murder and mystery. Only women who want to date a notorious murderer would be interested in me, even though I was not one.

It was not as if I was interested in pursuing a relationship; it was too soon, but facing life alone seemed a foregone conclusion. Would I end up a sad, broken, and lonely man? I would have drowned in public interrogations without some very caring friends and parishioners. Even leaving for a time of grieving was surely going to stoke suspicion. I'm not sure if walking on the beach was diversion enough to get me through it, but at least I didn't have to worry about what people were saying behind my back. I heard enough conversations in my head of my own making.

So, if anything, this was my therapy, walking along the shoreline alone, feeling the warm saltwater move the sand between my toes as the ocean's waves roared towards me.

As tears streamed down my face thinking about my loss and abandonment, trying to forget it all, I turned to the sea and found myself mesmerized by the sea birds circling above the waves when a strangely familiar voice said, "Jack Cash, is that you?"

I turned and vaguely recognized a friend's face from long ago. Standing there, with rolled-up blue-jean shorts, cropped blond hair, hazel eyes, and a face wet with seawater, stood Kim Crane, a friend from high school. She was one of those high school friends who shared most classes, sat close to me, and always laughed at my humor, but she was never the girl I would ever want to date, marry, or be anything but a friend.

"It's me! Kim, Kim Crane, do you remember me?" She asked.

I shrieked, "Kim Crane, I can't believe it is you! Of course, I remember you! Here you are, right here, on the beach," I said with disbelief. "In the middle of nowhere, what in the world are you doing here?

In one moment, I forgot the pain that put me into this ocean of grief. Suddenly, Kim interrupted my life.

———

BEFORE I CONTINUE, my name is Jack Cash. Jack...Cash! Not Jack, and not Mr. Cash. I have always been called "Jack Cash."

I think it is a southern 'two or more syllable name' thing, where everyone has at least two syllables in their name.

We had Johnny, Mark Allen, Bob Lee, and Lisa Marie (not of the Presley variety) in our neighborhood. In school, it was worse, and once a name stuck, it became a legacy. When I graduated from school, I thought I could escape the "JACK CASH" thing, but instinctively, "Jack Cash" became my moniker once I met someone. Even girls I dated and women I married called me "Jack Cash." Not to belabor the point, but it made it difficult to determine if my mom, wife, or girlfriend used my name in anger or affection. It was all about inflection, and I became an expert at inflection.

I am also an expert at having wives. I have had seven wives. SEVEN!!!! The first one was Mandy. I met her at school. She proposed to me in fifth grade. Then there was Tamera. She was an elementary librarian who enjoyed adventures through the books she read. Number three was Veronica. She was a Gypsy. Yes, the singing, tambourine-carrying type. Gypsy was her last name which she embraced to the fullest. The fourth was Monica. I did not plan on a wife's name rhyming with the previous wife's name, but it happened. Monica worked for the FBI. My fifth wife was called many names. Most were nicknames given by some family member, but I called her "Cybil." The sixth was Callie. Callie was a missionary in Ecuador when we met. Her feet were so long, but she had the brightest eyes. But my seventh wife, Marie, is why I am here today. I decided that after her murder, I would return to the spot we met and take time to grieve alone.

Alone, like all the other times, or so I thought.

Marie's murder, the endless questions from the police, reporters, church members, busybodies, the funeral, and the endless condolences had taken their toll. I was emotionally spent and desperately needed this moment to collect my thoughts, remember a beautiful woman, and contemplate my life. The pain of this loss was profound, and like the storm that had formed just offshore brought gigantic waves, the waves of grief have pushed me down more than I care to mention. The turmoil of grief was like a familiar nemesis.

While I was oblivious to what Kim said, it didn't matter. She talked as fast as possible, with many tears. I was in the fog of grief while the storm brewed offshore. Adding to the bass rumble, the birds calling for dinner in the distance and ocean waves pounding the shore brought about a symphony of music in the background of my soul, even while I tried to listen to her. I looked at her, and her tears had given way to sobs. Instinctively, I reached out to her, and she melted in my arms. Somewhere in the moment of increasingly blubbering and blabbering, she shared her pain, her strangely familiar experience of loss. She came to this beach, too, not for the beauty but because of her pain. At least, that's what she said—a moment to remember, forget and heal. A time to mourn, but the alone part was the greatest struggle for Kim. This moment, however, was surreal. A chance meeting on this beach I had traveled to so often was odd that I would find Kim here doing the same thing.

The longer I held her, the clearer her garbled, blubbering words became. Her husband of twenty-one years had suffered a heart attack, one the doctors called a "widow-maker," which became Kim's reality.

In an instant, what seemed to be a healthy fifty-two-year-old man slipped into eternity. Spiritually, he was ready for death, but no one expected it so early. Now Kim was experiencing something I had felt all too often. The stabbing pain of grief, the sudden aloneness, pounding the soul like the waves coming from an offshore storm called grief. Her identity as "Mrs." had suddenly ended, and I felt I was about to become Kim's grief counselor right here and now. Not because I knew how to do it with a college degree but because I had walked this path repeatedly. Seven times, to be exact. If grief were a forest, my well-worn path had become a familiar trail, an enemy, but one I had wrestled with way too often.

We stood there for what seemed like hours. My arms and legs ached because of the lack of movement. Turning, I noticed several unoccupied beach chairs nearby and held Kim as I walked her to this better place. After sitting down, Kim apologized for 'throwing up her grief all over me.' Her words, not mine. We both laughed as I wiped the imaginary 'vomit' off me.

"Why are YOU here, Jack Cash?" Kim pursed her lips, twisting her head to divert the conversation away from her pain and tears.

"Well, you will not believe me, but I came here because of Marie. Marie and I were married three years, and I came here to help the process after losing someone."

"I am so sorry. Was it a painful divorce?"

"Oh no, Kim. Marie died two weeks ago."

Immediately Kim's face went ashen, and she turned her gaze toward the offshore storm. As if frozen in distant thought, Kim encountered a painful reality. Somehow, two people from a world away found their way to the same beach, experiencing the same pain, wandering through the same fog, and made it to this place to find one another.

Some would call it 'fate.' Not me and not today, and I was not sure why this "coincidence" happened now, in this place called here, in my moment of pain. It was too convenient and as I have learned in my previous times of grief, too emotionally charged.

"Wait, I thought you married Mandy. You said, Marie, right?"

I chuckled, "Mandy was a lifetime ago, and yes, we got married, but Marie is why I am here today."

"I knew about Mandy or part of the 'Mandy story,' but I had heard little about you since high school, and I certainly knew nothing about Marie. What happened to Mandy?"

"Why don't we talk about it tonight over dinner?"

"I would like that, but I am struggling with everything. Be ready for the possibility I might not be good company."

"That's all right, and I want to give you as much room and time as you need. I want to be a friend to you. Besides, I don't know anyone on this beach who can understand the pain level we both are experiencing except us. Why don't we meet at this spot at five o'clock this evening? There is a wonderful restaurant on the boardwalk just about 10 minutes away," I said, motioning towards the restaurant. "We can walk, talk, get something to eat, and talk some more. Or we can sit and watch the sunset; it should be beautiful today with the thunderheads offshore. How about it?" I asked, all the while knowing there was always the possibility Kim would not come.

Grief is a powerful, debilitating force, and it comes in waves that wash over us at the most inopportune times, even if time is when we can best heal.

"I will be here, and if I am not, call my cell phone," as she rattled off her phone number. I quickly grabbed my phone and called her cell to ensure I had the correct number.

"I will see you at five," Kim smiled gently and walked away. It would be three more hours until five o'clock, and I felt a long walk on the beach would be helpful for me.

As I walked, I thought about the chances of meeting someone I knew on a random beach, and even more so, they were walking the same path as me.

It would be easy for me to believe God orchestrates these kinds of things, but this was too much, and I didn't feel like entertaining such random thoughts anyway. Was she a stalker, opportunist, or worse, someone I would have to carry her through grief when I needed it as much or more?

It was even more remarkable because it was where I started my journey after Mandy.

CHAPTER THREE

As with most people, I remember little about my childhood except vignettes of disappointment and extreme joy. We forget mundane things because they are not important. One day, I remember so well, and it did not leave me with disappointment or extreme joy, just Mandy.

It was a typical day in elementary school. My friends and I had just started talking about girls, and that some could be pretty and some ugly. I know fifth grade is a young age to think about such things, but we did. On the playground on this memorable day, we were climbing the playground equipment and talking. One of my friends commented on an awkward girl with large glasses wandering around the playground, saying something to other children, and then running to the next group. He laughed and asked, "Who's the "weird ugly girl with gigantic glasses?"

She looked our way, ran up to me, and without hesitation shouted, "When I am older, I am going to marry you," and then ran away.

As typical protocol on an elementary playground, interaction with anyone of the opposite sex creates a cacophony of noises, somewhat like primates in the zoo when someone places a new toy in the cage, or better yet, bananas in a monkey's periphery vision.

The jumping, laughing, and overall exhilaration my friends gained from this interaction were more than unsettling. This marriage proposal embarrassed and frustrated me. We were in fifth grade, and I couldn't understand why anyone would propose at such an age. My monkey friends continued their antics, "Jack Cash and Big Glasses Molasses, sitting in a tree, K.I.S.S.I.N.G. first comes love, second comes marriage, here comes Jack Cash with a baby carriage."

Sigh! I don't miss those days.

Throughout the rest of elementary, Mandy Clark was the awkward girl with enormous glasses. She was outgoing enough to keep ridicule from stinging too severely but not anything else enough to become famous. She was also pushy enough to be a part of groups, forcing her way in but was never asked to join. I could relate to that, but that was all.

From time to time, Mandy would remind me that we were getting married. I always envisioned marrying a beautiful girl, but not so much Mandy Clark.

Our elementary school was kindergarten through sixth grade, and a combined Jr High and Sr High school. At our elementary graduation (yes, we had one), Mandy was just a few people behind me in line as we made our way to the auditorium to graduate from elementary school. I heard Mandy sing, "I'm going to marry Jack Cash someday. He's going to carry me away. I am going to be his wife, and we will have a wonderful life."

It embarrassed and impressed me; impressed she could sing and sing well and embarrassed that she was singing about something of which I had no input. Who would propose in fifth grade and continue the ruse until sixth grade, anyway? I had not decided to marry anyone anyway because my entire high school career was ahead of me. I had plenty of time to make those decisions.

Mandy kept the tune going, repeatedly, "I'm going to marry Jack Cash someday. He's going to carry me away. I am going to be his wife, and we will have a wonderful life."

Finally, one teacher, hearing singing, put her finger to her mouth and said rather loudly, "shhhhhhhh! QUIET."

Mandy stopped singing but hummed the tune for the rest of the graduation. Afterward, I left with my parents when I heard the song again and turned to see Mandy walking away with her dad, waving at me.

That summer, I thought about Mandy a few times, because she had left enough of an impression that I was looking forward to seeing her when school started back. Yes, that awkward girl with large glasses had captured my interest. The first day of the next school year started with new classes, multiple teachers, and schedules I had not known in elementary. This focus forced me to forget about Mandy for a moment, but once normal settled in, I wondered where Mandy had gone. She was nowhere. And when I asked around, no one knew what had happened to her.

Seventh grade went by quickly, and a young man's enemy brought powerful transitions in my life: namely puberty.

On the fourth day of eighth grade, Mrs. Eudy, the literature teacher in my fourth-period class, wanted us to form groups to discuss our reading that semester. It was there that I met Kim as she joined my group. As we were assembling into groups, a beautiful, frail girl with large glasses walked into the room, one who looked vaguely familiar. She walked over to Mrs. Eudy and handed her some papers, and Mrs. Eudy said, "I knew you were coming. We are so glad you are here today. Why don't you join the group in the corner," she said as she pointed in our direction. Since we were in "the corner," and we had a new member of our group, we cheered loudly, clapping our hands.

When we cheered, that frail girl with large glasses started crying and walked our way. She stood next to me, asked me my name, and when I said, "Jack Cash," she sang, "one day, I am going to marry you." I screamed out, "MANDY CLARK," and grabbed her in the biggest hug, twirling her around in the most epic form of hugging I could.

Mrs. Eudy screamed, "Jack Cash, please put the young lady down. She is very sick!"

As if Mrs. Eudy hit me with a reality stick, I slowly put Mandy down, apologizing profusely for hurting her. She smiled as she wiped away tears of joy.

Over time, I pieced together Mandy's story. In the last few weeks of sixth grade, they diagnosed Mandy with a rare form of cancer, the same one that took her mother's life. She had to undergo months of chemo and radiation therapy, making her highly vulnerable to any type of virus or bacterial infection. Because of her health, she completed all her school-work at home or in the hospital for the entire seventh grade.

The cancer was in remission, and for the time being, Mandy was cancer-free. We had a great time in our eighth-grade year, and I fell deeper for Mandy. She started coming to my youth group, so our 'dating' time was church youth group, youth group functions, our homecoming game, and a few basketball games when we would both show up without knowing the other would be there. It was not truly dating, as we never kissed, at least in eighth grade, but I enjoyed being with her.

CHAPTER FOUR

I had walked so long down memory lane I lost track of time. I looked at my watch, and it was almost four o'clock now. I had to jog back to my condo, shower quickly and prepare for my evening with Kim. I knew there was a significant possibility Kim would not show.

When I arrived at my condo, my cell phone had a missed call and voicemail from Paddy Gypsy. Paddy was Veronica's brother (my third wife). Paddy believed someone had killed Veronica, and his voicemail was like all the other times I had visited this same beach, except this time he had more information than before: "Jack Cash, this is Paddy Gypsy. Someone murdered Veronica, and I think I know who did it. We should meet because I have something for you. Don't trust anyone. Call me as soon as possible. Call me. Your life is in danger."

Paddy loved his sister, and her death devastated both of us. It frustrated us that her death left so many unanswered questions. So, Paddy took to heart the search to find out why he lost his sister. This time, however, there was an urgency in his voice, leaving me unsettled. I returned his call, but it went to voice mail, so I said, "Tag Paddy, you are it. Call me when you can. Hope you are well!" After my shower, I quickly dressed and headed out to the beach.

The wind had changed direction, pushing the ominous clouds closer to shore, promising an epic light show. Hopefully one we could enjoy from a distance.

As I made my way to the rendezvous point, I wondered if Kim would come and, if she didn't, whether I would change my dinner plans. High-minded things to consider, but in this grief journey, I have learned that planning takes a lot of effort, and abrupt changes in plans can quickly send me into waves of grief. Too often, I faced unexpected moments that went very badly; things that were not in my control made me feel like I was losing my grip, and a grieving person out of control is not pretty, so a bit of planning helps a great deal. Besides, public meltdowns were the worst experiences and sometimes caused strangers to console without context. So, this small plan was a coping mechanism I had learned well.

I was determined not to keep watching for Kim but to focus on the clouds, the storm not too far away, and the ocean waves pounding the beach. It was ominous to the soul and oddly therapeutic that such chaos gave me perspective. Eventually, I glanced at my watch and scoured the distance to see if I could see her coming, but I couldn't. She didn't reply when I called her cell phone to see if she had changed her mind. Her grief was likely too much, and I knew the feeling and the need to process things, but honestly, I would have enjoyed spending time with someone instead of eating alone.

I decided to eat at the boardwalk restaurant I had suggested. It was a short distance away, and as I walked toward it, I turned to see if Kim was following, but she was not. Once inside and at a table, I ordered sweet tea and then set out to decide on the dinner choice, "Swordfish," I said to no one but myself, mesmerized by the storm in the distance diverting my thoughts for a moment.

The lightning was almost constant by now, and no doubt anyone in the storm was feeling its power, much like Kim's grief, I was sure.

Kim's voice interrupted my storm watching, "What a storm, it's scary! Can I join you?"

"Of course, I waited for a while and called too, but I thought you might have wanted some alone time."

"I thought I did after we talked," Kim continued, "and then could not stand the thought of being alone for dinner tonight, so I remembered where you said you wanted to go, and now here I am. Before we get any further, I am paying for my meal. Like you said, we are not on a date, just time with friends."

"Agreed!" I replied with a smile.

As she sat down, her beauty captivated me. She had spent time on her makeup, dressed as if she were going out on the date of dates with sweet perfume announcing her arrival and lingering long.

Every hair was in place, and a bright-colored sundress and sandals accentuated a fresh pedicure. This reinforced the lowering of my emotional guard; lower than it had been all day. Even though I set the parameters for dinner, and she insisted on paying her way, I felt blessed to be with her, even if for a meal and conversation, and even more, if it was so curious she "found" me at this particular beach.

The waitress asked for our drink order and then recited the usual "special of the day" information.

Within a minute, we had our drink order as we exchanged the usual chit-chat about our afternoon, and then Kim broke through the mundane with a question. "I don't know how to ask, but whatever happened to Mandy? You guys were so crazy about each other, but I never heard what happened."

"I can go back to elementary school when Mandy was my grade school stalker or when she re-appeared after missing the entire seventh grade. Where do you want to start?"

"Grade School Stalker sounds like a great story; tell me from there."

I told Kim about Mandy, the early days, and her time away from school in seventh grade. Kim interrupted, "I was in Mrs. Eudy's class, and I remember Mandy coming to class for the first time. I remember the bear hug, but I didn't hear her marriage proposal to you."

"It was our thing, I guess, and technically, she did it in fifth grade when she informed me that we were getting married," I joked.

"She was crazy about you, I could tell, and I always thought you were crazy about her. I never wanted to interfere, even though I had a crush on you throughout high school."

Kim's words cleared up everything. She was a stalker in high school, in virtually every class, laughing at almost everything remotely funny that I said and showing up at virtually every event I attended.

"So, what happened after eighth grade? Inquiring minds want to know?" Kim wondered.

"Ninth grade, puberty, and not as much togetherness."

"Smart, come on, we are here. We have time. Tell me all about it."

"Ninth grade was pimples and a bit of distance. We were not seeing each other through the day because we had few classes together, but we saw each other on Wednesday nights at the youth group and on Sundays at church. Often, we would go out to eat after church on Sunday night and see one another. We'd be with a larger group and would laugh, tell stories, and were pretty much typical ninth graders."

"Tenth grade was the same, except we had one class each semester together and 'study hall.' We had study hall in the same room as the previous class, so two classes acted like a long one.

We studied together and talked. I thought I liked her before, but it got worse, or better, depending on how you look at it.

She was smart, and the enormous glasses and that awkward girl had become a beautiful girl with contacts; from the look of it, she was very healthy.

The cancer scare in seventh grade was all but a memory. She was doing great. We were great."

"The summer before eleventh grade, we both went to Ecuador on a medical mission trip our pastor led. We worked together for two weeks in the country, saw amazing sights, and while we were there, I knew I wanted to marry her, even though technically she had already proposed in fifth grade."

"After we returned, we started school, and not too long after school started, I asked her out on a proper date. Believe it or not, we never had a 'just us two kind of date.' We went to a Christian concert; not very romantic, I know. We both liked the group, and both wanted to hear them. Anyway, during the concert, one singer talked about how he fell in love with his wife and it was at a concert that he proposed to his wife. He realized the treasure God had given him in her. Then he sang a love song to his wife. The more he talked, the more I felt he was telling my story. I looked at Mandy and told her I could not imagine my life without her. We kissed for the first time at the concert after I told her I loved her. I felt like someone put helium in my body because I was floating so high. She told me she had always loved me too, but wanted me to say it first."

"That date started a whirlwind of dates until Christmas. We had made a vow to be virgins until we married, so we did everything we could to ensure we could keep the vow. It was hard to do because I loved her so much. I spent part of Christmas day with her, and she acted strangely. I said nothing but felt I had done something wrong. She told me she wanted to spend a little time apart, at least for a while. It devastated and crushed me. I asked her if I had done something wrong, what was wrong, so many questions and all she said was she needed a break. I went home and cried for the rest of Christmas break."

Right then, the waitress cleared her throat and said, "I waited as long as I could. Are you ready to order?"

We ordered, and then in curiosity, Kim leaned across the table, "She broke up with you? I never knew."

"I know. I kept it to myself because I was hurting so bad."

"The beginning of school after the Christmas break was a new semester. I thought we had classes together. At least, that is what we had planned, but she was not in any of my classes. Not one! It was like she had disappeared. I asked each teacher if 'Mandy Clark' was on the attendance roll for the class, and each one told me she was not. I could not understand. She had gone silent, quiet, invisible. So, I went to her house after the first day back. I rang the doorbell and looked into the house. I could see furniture, I could see her cat, and the lights were on, so I knew someone was there, but I could not figure out what was going on. No one ever came to the door, so I went home."

"About two weeks after the new semester started, I saw Mandy leaving the main office at school. Her head down and not making any eye contact with anyone, she walked briskly with determination toward the parking lot. I called out her name, but she either ignored me or didn't hear. She didn't respond at all. I thought she was seeing someone else for a while, but the people who knew her were getting the same treatment. It was like she was shutting everyone out of her life."

"Would you like a refill on your iced tea, sir, your hot tea, mam?" the waitress asked.

"Yes," we said in unison.

"Why was she shutting everyone out?" Kim wondered.

"That's what I wondered too, but she disappeared, even missing church was unheard of for Mandy. She loved God, loved the church, and now it seemed she was gone."

"Then, one day, my mom called me and asked me to go to the emergency room for my grandmother. She had fallen, and they thought she had broken her hip. As I rushed to her room, one of the other rooms had the curtain opened, and there was Mandy. IVs were connected to her as she lay there with a troubled look on her face. She saw me and she started crying uncontrollably. They had a heart monitor on her, which responded to her stress at my arrival."

Just then, a clap of thunder and a flash of lightning startled everyone in the restaurant with a collective scream of surprise. The storm we had seen in the distance had finally made its way to the shore. The wind started blowing, lightning flashed, and thunder rolled with a powerful reverberation on the boardwalk.

Kim was unfazed. "Why was she was in the hospital?"

"I found out that she had recently completed a routine cancer check and found something that caused concern. On December 23, the doctor called Mandy and her dad and told them they needed further tests. In seventh grade, Mandy had Hepatosplenic T-cell lymphoma. It is a cancer that affects the bone marrow, spleen, and liver. After a course of treatment, including a bone marrow transplant from her dad, it went into remission. The doctor felt like she bought five years with treatment, but there were no guarantees. So, when I found her in the hospital, her secret was out. There was pain in her body and dehydration. She told me the story and said she wanted to keep it to herself and not tell anyone, including me, just in case the cancer had returned. She felt it would be wrong to lead me on if she were about to die."

"Kim, I just stood there. The news was NOT what I expected. I blamed myself that she was carrying such a huge load all by herself."

The main course arrived; the waitress found out who had what dish, and we began eating.

"So, her cancer came back, and Christmas day was the day she decided to dump you; that was pretty harsh, don't you think?" Kim interjected.

Her question was unsympathetic and unusual, but I replied, "Well, it did hurt but after I found out what she had been facing, I didn't worry about it too much. The girl I loved so much was in so much pain. So, as I stood beside her bed, it seemed she was very ill and would not live much longer. I couldn't imagine anything but doing what I could to make her happy. I walked over to her, took her hand, and told her I loved her. She cried, and I cried, and several times, the heart monitor brought nurses to the room to check on her. I was unsure what they thought, but I wanted to be with her forever!"

"How is the swordfish? Is the steak cooked the way you wanted?" the waitress wondered. That interruption created the distraction I needed. My love for Mandy was almost too much as I recalled her story, compounding the sorrow I had just encountered. All of this made me feel that if I kept telling the story, I would end up as the blubbering man everyone pointed to in the restaurant. That would not happen if I could help it.

"It is wonderful," I replied, barely taking a bite. I looked at Kim, saying, "that was a 'by faith' statement." Then I took a larger bite and exclaimed, "Wow, this is incredible! My faith has given way to awesomeness."

Kim was very curious about the taste of swordfish, especially after I expressed delight, so I offered her a taste.

"That is delicious. Do you want to trade?"

"Not on your life, but I will give you half of it if you give me a few shrimp off your plate." I scored a few shrimp as she hauled off half of my swordfish.

Our conversation took a welcome turn away from the painful memory, almost as if Kim and I had agreed on an emotional diversion.

Small talk continued through the meal; a few laughs and recalling fun memories of high school made this evening especially enjoyable. I knew I was not on a date but could not get past Kim's beautiful eyes and smile, which I must have missed in school.

We both decided on dessert and coffee when Kim asked me, "What kind of work do you do?"

It is usually at this point that I meet the wall. People build one, hide behind it, and act like they have encountered a leper or some oddity. So,

I took a deep breath, preparing for the awkward moment, "I am a pastor."

"I knew you wanted to go into ministry in high school and felt you would do that for your life's work but wasn't sure. Believe it or not, my husband was also a pastor, so I have known ministry for a long time."

I never knew. That news immediately improved the evening, as I did not have to explain or excuse any behavior, such as not drinking an alcoholic beverage if I didn't want.

"I don't know what I would have done without God's help," Kim continued. "During the darkest times, I have called out to God, and He has helped me."

Right then, a few tears started down her cheeks, and instinctively, I took her hand and said, "I understand completely."

Another loud clap of thunder and lightning flash gave everyone pause, and a few seconds later, Kim's phone started playing a song with a great beat, and I started moving to the sound as she answered.

Kim explained to her caller she met up with a high school friend at the beach and would be back before too late. As she finished her call, she shared she had to go back to her condo. Her sister and brother-in-law were passing through and wanted to see her and check in on her. It shocked them she found someone to have dinner with and worried since she hadn't told them of her plans.

"They live here?"

"Oh, no," she replied, "but they said they were going to come sometime while I was here to have dinner with me. They just waited till the last minute to let me know. Of course, they never would have guessed I would have a date's not a date with an old friend, me either."

"Good luck with making this story believable. I can't believe it either, and I am in it."

"Well, I need to get back to the condo. I have enjoyed tonight and seeing you again."

Right then, I had a mix of anxiety and desperation sweep over me that I did not expect, like I was losing someone all over again. I did not want Kim to leave but was afraid it would sound extra creepy if I said anything, so I kept thought to myself and replied, "You too, Kim. I will pray for you. You have my number if you need anything," I said as I guarded my parting words.

"I do have your number, don't I?" Kim said slyly. "Now I can call you anytime I want. Goodnight, Jack Cash."

As Kim stood up to leave, I also stood and leaned towards Kim, and she took the hint and hugged me. "Good night, Kim."

She left, and I realized I did not know whether I would ever see Kim again. I sat down, sighed deeply and ordered another coffee.

As the storm dissipated into the night, there was a last clap of thunder and lightning as if it were saying, "all done!" The sun had set, and now the twilight was turning to darkness. The nights were always the hardest, and now I was sitting alone, drinking coffee, staring at the horizon.

As I drank, I could not shake the image I shared with Kim of discovering Mandy in the hospital bed. It was as if the remembering had dislodged a stopped-up well of emotion. Remembering Mandy was like the waves on the beach, building up in exaggeration until they crashed on my mind's shores. Some moments like that are frozen in my memory.

I hid my meltdown as best as I could as I remembered Mandy.

CHAPTER FIVE

y remembering got the best of me and I sat there recalling that hospital visit with Mandy.

"Jack Cash, you are an incredible man," Mandy cried as she clung to my hand.

I got as close to her as I could and whispered, "Why are you here?"

Mandy told me of the routine cancer check. The doctor wanted to do further tests and consult with experts at the Mayo Clinic. Out of an abundance of caution, he wanted her to stay away from school so she would not have contact with people who were ill. She was unsure if cancer had returned, but she was in pain and dehydrated, so her dad brought her to the hospital.

"I am scared," Mandy confessed. "Scared cancer has returned, scared I will not live much longer, and scared I will lose you."

Immediately, without even thinking, I started singing, "I'm going to marry Mandy Clark someday. I'm going to carry her away. She is going to be my wife, and we will have a wonderful life."

"Ahhhhh," Mandy shrieked with massive tears and increasingly garbled words, "You remembered my song." Then we laughed with tears flowing down our faces.

Mandy's dad had watched most of our moment from the hall but finally could not take it any longer and cleared his throat. I thought it was to get my attention, but it was to keep from "crying like a baby in front of God and everybody," he said as he walked in.

I turned to him and said, "Hello, Mr. Clark."

"Who told you Mandy was here?" He asked sternly.

I walked over to him and extended my hand to shake his. "No one! I came to the ER to see my Mamaw. She is down the hall, but I saw Mandy here, so I stopped. I still haven't seen Mamaw yet."

"Go check on her and come back," he suggested with a solid hint to leave for a moment, so I left.

The walk to her room was only a short corridor away, long enough for me to decide to marry Mandy Clark, no matter what, as soon as I could. I could not imagine living my life without her, even if she only had a short time to live.

Mamaw had bruised herself severely, but fortunately, she did not break her hip. I told her about Mandy's condition. My entire family knew the story of Mandy Clark, and they knew how crazy I was about her.

"Jack Cash, it seems to me you already know what you want to do, and I think you should do it. You should do it and be happy in your life. Make her happy. I think you already have prayed about this and know what God wants. So, what are you waiting for?"

I rattled off the list of things I wanted to have in place before I proposed formally, "A job, a ring, income, a house, graduation."

Mamaw interrupted, "You have forgotten the most important thing."

"What?"

"You have forgotten what you already have: Mandy, and you have God. From the looks of it, you may not have her forever."

"Mamaw, I don't have a ring, and I want to give her a nice ring, and as much as I can, a nice life."

With that, she took off her wedding band and handed it to me. My Pawpaw had died a few years before, and she was a widow. She handed me the ring and said, "I would be overjoyed to see you use this, sell it and buy what you want, give it to her as it is, have it remade into a different ring, your choice, but don't say you don't have a ring."

I think my Mamaw heard from God. I would have never moved forward if it were not for a kick in the pants. I hugged her and thanked her repeatedly.

"Your dad is coming to take me home. They are releasing me. Now go see about your girl."

"Thank you. I love you, Mamaw," I said, fighting tears.

As I walked back to Mandy's room, I had great expectancy. I wanted to get on one knee and propose right next to her hospital bed just as soon as I arrived. Unfortunately, the nurses had closed the curtain, and inside, there was a lot of talking and tears. A nurse opened the curtain and passed by me, intent on carrying out the orders from whatever the doctor had just told her.

I was so scared. Did I miss my moment? Was there ever going to be a moment? Fear gripped my heart, and my chest tightened as a wave of terror swept over me. It was then something happened inside of me changed the moment. I whispered a simple prayer to God, asking for His help. I asked for the peace passes understanding because my under-standing was not peaceful. Immediately, my heart and mind flooded with peace.

With the peace came joy bubbling up in me. I had a ring. On the other side of the curtain was the girl of my dreams, and no matter what was just said, I was ready to live life to the full.

As I waited for the curtain to open, the doctor walked out, smiled, and nodded at me. Mr. Clark followed him. He had been crying but grabbed me and bear-hugged me. "Go see Mandy. I'm going to get some coffee," he said as he walked away.

I walked in tentatively and looked at Mandy. "Are you ok?"

"Yes, better than ok. In seventh grade, the doctor told me my cancer would probably come back in five years, and when they did the routine check, they saw something that caused them concern. They do not think it is what I had before, and they will monitor it for now. I came because of pain, but the doctor thinks I have pulled some muscles. Anyway, I can go home after the fluid in my IV bag is gone."

I was so excited. I almost proposed right then, but at the moment, my saner mind won out. The doctor dismissed her about an hour later, and she went home to rest. I told my parents and my friends what had happened.

Later in the week, Mandy returned to school. The months flew by, and before we knew it, it was summer. We spent so much time together then.

The ring my Mamaw had given me was safely in my dresser drawer. I also worked as much as I could mowing yards, working for a real estate company cleaning out move-outs for their rentals, and so much more. By the end of the summer, I had saved six thousand dollars.

During the same summer, a revival at our church became the moment I surrendered to the call of God to preach the gospel. It was a profound moment for me, as I would give up any other pursuits and focus on following God's call for my life. Mandy was just as excited as I was when I shared my surrender. Even though it seemed to mean wealth would never be ours, purpose and God's blessing were enough for her and me.

Twelfth grade was the beginning of the great transition into the next phase of our life. Mandy was fantastic, and our relationship continued to grow. I knew it was developing the right way since she started confiding in me her fears about cancer returning and sharing doctor reports.

The waitress startled me, in my state of remembering, "Would you like more coffee?"

It was like the hint to stop looking back had arrived. I replied, "No, I am ready to leave. Can I have the check, please?"

She said Kim had paid the check, and then handed me a folded napkin with a handwritten note inside from Kim. It read, "It was not a date, but it was so wonderful. I am paying for dinner. You can tip the waitress."

I looked at the waitress and said, "Can you get the manager for me?" "Is everything ok?" she said with worry in her voice.

Assuring her, I replied, "Everything is awesome. I want to brag about you and the meal." She left in a hurry, and the manager immediately approached the table with a worried look.

"Sir, is everything ok? The waitress said you wanted to see me."

"Everything is fine, and I wanted you to know our waitress, the service, and the food were incredible."

He looked at me, and his worried expression gave way to joy. "Thank you for sharing. We always hear about the bad, but never the good."

"That's why I called you over, to brag a little. I am going to leave the waitress a great tip, but I wanted to share with you my enjoyment of coming here."

He thanked me again and left the table. I saw the waitress from a distance and winked and nodded to her as I left, leaving a one-hundred-dollar bill on the table.

When I opened the door, the waitress ran to meet me, hugging me for the tip and the word to the manager. "Thank you," she gushed, "you have made my day, and I have to tell you I am praying for you. I was not eaves-dropping, but I heard your story, and I am so sorry for your loss."

I thanked her and left the restaurant, knowing she had only heard the story of Mandy, not the others. Another minor meltdown hit like a wave, but at least it was dark, and no one could see the hot tears streaming down my face as I walked along the shoreline. The night air had a bit of chill, much like what darkness and loneliness felt like for me, one I was not looking forward to alone.

About halfway back, my phone vibrated in my pocket. A text from Kim read, "If you are up to meeting for breakfast, I would like to see you again. My sister- and brother-in-law don't believe my story! They want to meet you too."

I agreed to meet and suggested an excellent outdoor café, just a short distance from my condo. Then I texted, "Good Night!"

Even though I would be alone tonight, having something to look forward to tomorrow made the night less intimidating. I call it my "next mailbox philosophy."

I remembered sharing my next mailbox philosophy with Mandy. I developed it by training for a race. It was during ninth grade that I ran in a 10 kilometer event in our city. This event drew thousands from around the nation, competing for prizes, including a cash prize for the first-place runner. I wanted to do well with the race I trained for during one of the most brutal summers in our state's history.

The temperature broke the 100-degree mark daily for over thirty days, with a 110-115 degrees heat index. Because of the brutal heat and my crazy desire to do well, I pushed myself to every limit possible.

I trained early in the day and late in the evening. During the late evening runs, when temps were extreme, my endurance was tested the most, and I focused on the next mailbox.

I remember challenging myself by thinking, "Jack Cash, if you can make it to the next mailbox, you can do this." Focusing on the mailbox and pushing my endurance led me to that goal. Then I focused on the next mailbox, pushing endurance further. With each mailbox, I would think, "Jack Cash, if you can make it to the next mailbox, you can do this."

Because of this philosophy, I found myself in first place for over half the race, and since I was setting the pace, I focused on the next mailbox, or landmark, and pushed myself to achieve the short term goal. Once I arrived, I would focus on the next one. I didn't win the race but came first in the under-21 age group.

Hence the "next mailbox philosophy."

In our senior year, I shared my philosophy with Mandy—encouraging her to focus on the following important dates in her life instead of keeping the focus on cancer or the next doctor visit. Even though she seemed to carry a sense of foreboding about her cancer returning, Mandy adopted the next mailbox philosophy very well. She regularly said, "I can't wait till my birthday, your birthday, dad's birthday, Christmas, Thanksgiving, spring break, etc." She would use the following date as her mailbox and pace herself to focus on the next moment.

It helped her, and in my grief, my next mailbox philosophy had helped me run the race without losing my mind. Now, breakfast was my next mailbox. It made my lonely night more bearable.

I dreamed about Mandy during the night, which was not surprising since this opened my memories like an old treasure chest without a remedy. In my dream, I relived 'the night.' We were a few weeks away from Christmas and were preparing to go to an outdoor 'Bethlehem Walk' including a reenactment of vignettes of the Christmas story. At the end of the Bethlehem Walk, a massive Christmas light display illuminated the last part of the walk with recorded Christmas music playing in the background.

When I heard about the event, I decided this was the time to propose. My first step was to ask Mandy's dad if I could have his blessing to marry his daughter. I will never forget the tears this grown man shed as he agreed to let me marry 'his Mandy,' as he called her.

With his blessing, I contacted the church sponsoring the walk and asked if I could request a song for the end of the walk. I told them I wanted to propose to Mandy in the massive Christmas light display at the end and wanted our song to play at a pre-determined time, then drop to my knee and ask Mandy to marry me.

They immediately put me in contact with the worship pastor of the church. He was elated and asked if he could call me back. About an hour later, he got back to me and said he knew the song but wanted to know if I minded if the worship team performed the song live with an acoustic guitar. He then asked laughingly, "She will say yes, right?"

"She better. She started it in fifth grade," I remarked and told him our brief history, beginning in fifth grade, including the cancer diagnosis and treatment in seventh grade.

The plan was to walk through the display of Bethlehem and then stop at a hot chocolate stand at the end of the Christmas light display to enjoy a cup of hot cocoa. The music was supposed to start with one signal to a pre-determined person after the moment had arrived. Mandy knew nothing.

So, we arrived at the beverage stand, drank hot cocoa, and laughed. I gave the nod. Hundreds of people seemed to be standing around, talking and not moving. I was too focused on my plan that I did not notice, but when we moved, they moved. When we stopped to enjoy a particular light display, they stopped too.

I did not know the worship pastor was so excited to help he reached out to his praise team and the church pastor. They decided they would take it to an entirely different level. They learned the song and then enlisted a group of over sixty 'choir' members who became backup singers including members of our families.

We walked to the display, and I reached into my pocket to retrieve the ring. Then, without warning, the lights went dark, and the crowd began clapping. Then the worship pastor began strumming, and I pulled Mandy close and held her. The lights came on, and she realized he was playing our song. Then the worship pastor started singing, and Mandy cried. I gently kissed her on the cheek, and she put her cheek to mine. When he got to the chorus, the entire crowd joined in with him, with what sounded like a chorus of angels.

I pulled her away so I could see her face, whispered "I love you," and as they were finishing the song, I dropped to one knee and shouted, "Mandy Clark, I love you and can't imagine living my life without you, you make the days filled with sunshine and my nights like shooting stars, full of wonder. Mandy, will you marry me?"

Everyone watched and waited as she screamed through tears of joy, "YES, JACK CASH, I WILL MARRY YOU!"

The crowd went crazy in celebration, then they started singing, "She's going to marry Jack Cash someday. He's going to carry her away. She is going to be his wife, and they will have a wonderful life." That moment is forever etched into my brain and is probably why I had the dream.

When they sang the final 'Mandy' song, I cried. It was the most beautiful experience ever.

CHAPTER SIX

"WONK, WONK, WONK," sounded my very loud alarm clock as it woke me from my most beautiful dream. It was so real that my face and pillow was wet with tears. It was the day after I met Kim on the beach. My phone also sounded an alarm. As I turned it off, I noticed a text message from Paddy, "Jack Cash. I know who killed Veronica, and you are in danger. Please call me ASAP. I have to go into hiding."

I tried to call him back, but again, there was no answer. I quickly showered and prepared for my breakfast date with Kim, who was dressed like sunshine and joy, with light makeup, wearing a beautiful yellow sundress with large flowers, a huge white hat, and sandals. "Good morning," she said with a sing-song melody. "Good morning," I replied. "How did you sleep?"

"Very well, I had a wonderful dream," Kim replied. "Oh, I invited my sister, Christy, and brother-in-law, Jeff, but they are running late, and I didn't want to keep you waiting and wondering if I was coming, like last night."

"I look forward to meeting them," I said, but then a realization hit me, "don't I know your sister?"

"Yes," Kim chuckled, "we did a few youth outings together, and she was like me, always around Jack Cash."

Again, I focused on Mandy for most of my high school days and very little on any other girl. I vaguely remembered Christy; when she arrived, she looked like she did in school. She was as brash as I remembered, wearing a white top and bright pink shorts as new as the day she bought them.

"I did not believe Kim when she told me she met Jack Cash on the beach, of all places, and then had dinner with him, but here you are," Christy thundered as she walked up to the table with her husband Jeff, not far behind.

I stood, hugged her and said, "Hello Christy, it's been a long time."

"Jack Cash, I want you to meet my husband, Jeff," Christy said as she held her husband's arm tightly.

"So glad to meet you, Jeff!" I replied.

"I am glad to meet you too, Jack Cash, and I don't know if you know it or not, but you are a legend with these women," Jeff said as he motioned to Christy and Kim. "They talked most of the night about you and your legend," he continued. "In fact, your name has come up a lot over the years."

"Oh, a legend. I did not know," I replied with curiosity, but Jeff's last statement caused a momentary shudder to sweep over me.

"It was all good," Christy offered, "In fact, we talked about how crazy you were about Mandy. I hope was ok."

"Of course, Mandy was a long time ago, and remembering the good times with her has been good for me this week," I replied.

Jeff said, "I hope you don't mind us joining in on your breakfast date. We are hungry and have shopping to do today because you can't get enough cheap t-shirts from overpriced souvenir shops."

"No problem, Jeff. Glad you guys came."

The breeze was just enough to cause the napkins to creep across the table, but this morning was perfect to be outside. The waiter took our drink order and then went to find the fresh coffee we begged for.

"Jeff is into derivatives," Kim said. "Tell them what you do, Jeff."

Jeff said, "I will share what derivatives are until Jack Cash's eyes gloss over, then I will stop." I felt I was in for a long morning of stocks, bonds, derivatives, and some infused sales pitch to buy something, so I tried to stay on point.

"What are derivatives?" I asked, knowing I needed to buckle down for the long haul.

"Get ready to gloss over," Jeff laughed, "they are like gambling, where the risk is great, and the reward is greater."

Honestly, I was in no mood to talk about stocks, bonds, risk, rewards, contracts, futures, options, forwards, and swaps. These were some words I heard as Jeff tried to explain what derivatives are and how people can lose everything or become instantly wealthy in the field. He was undoubtedly passionate about his work, so much so he paid no attention to Christy or Kim's side discussion or my glossed-over eyes.

That happened when he said, "the reward is greater." Sometimes risk brings a substantial reward, and with Mandy, the risk of asking her to marry her was worth the great reward I found in her.

As Jeff continued talking, I decided that my only choice was to doze off while he talked or open the memory banks again. I drool when I sleep, so remembering Mandy was the best choice.

It took me back to the Saturday morning after the proposal. I was asleep, but at seven o'clock the phone rang with Mandy at the other end, excited to start a day of wedding planning. While we were in the moment of joy over the proposal, we did not talk specifics such as dates or places, so, in Mandy's thinking, wedding planning is best done at seven o'clock in the morning after the proposal. Did I mention she called at seven o'clock on a Saturday morning? I did not know they even made that time of day when I was that age. Her excitement was too much to contain.

For most young men, planning a wedding is not nearly as much fun or nearly as important as it is for young women. I should have known. Mandy had been thinking about our wedding since fifth grade, at least to some level. Now, her fifth-grade desire was about to be fulfilled, and she was not wasting any time to start the actual wedding day planning.

"Sir, what do you want for breakfast?" the waiter wondered, interrupting my brief travel back to another time.

It was true, Jeff's discourse on derivatives had transformed me from a fifty-year-old man at a café into a teenager, preparing to marry the girl. So, while my eyes glossed over, my memory banks whisked me away to another time. It was a welcomed trip, but now, I had to return to reality.

"Eggs and toast," I informed the waiter. He began a series of other questions: how do you want your eggs, what kind of toast, and do you want hash browns, fruit, oatmeal, bacon, or ham? I felt like my eyes were about to gloss over again. During grieving, sometimes even the most mundane questions take a toll and beg for mercy.

After answering five hundred questions from the waiter, more questions from those at the table arose. Again, the first question about Mandy took me back to reliving most of my dream with Kim, Christy, and Jeff.

"Wait," Jeff interrupted. "You were THAT couple at the Bethlehem Walk? I WAS THERE, and I remember the day clearly because the worship pastor called my parents to join the choir for the proposal. They talked about it for days before, and days after, they thought it was the most incredible proposal they had ever heard or witnessed."

It amazed me my dream proposal had made such an impact on so many.

Kim, a little annoyed, spoke up, "You proposed, and then what happened?"

"At 7 a.m. on a Saturday, my phone rang, and for a senior in high school, there was no such time as 7 a.m. on a Saturday," I shared as they laughed. "We met for breakfast and then started a day of planning. Mandy wanted to shop for wedding dresses but knew I could not see her in it until our wedding day."

"We talked, shopped, and talked some more all day long. Before we had finished, we set a date, place and had pretty much decided on everything. I say 'we' loosely. Mandy had already planned the colors of bridesmaid dresses, who her maid of honor would be, and what type and color of tuxedo I would wear. I think she had planned in fifth grade on the playground."

Everyone laughed as I continued, "We had all the plans, but God had a different one. We had a great Christmas together, and after Christmas break, word had gotten out about the proposal. It seemed everyone knew we were a thing, and Mandy, never popular before, suddenly became very popular. It was kind of funny.

Mandy had become a gorgeous young lady, but it wasn't until I proposed guys started taking notice of Mandy. And take notice they did. She turned down more date offers in the second semester of her senior year than ever before, and that was as an engaged woman.

The attention she was getting did something for her that I never saw coming. It made her glow even more so, and instead of creating jealousy in me, I felt like I had truly gotten the girl. We had planned for our wedding to take place in the late fall after graduation.

There was an outdoor park that was beautiful all year round, but when the leaves turned, it was simply amazing. She told me she always wanted to get married and then have a horse-drawn carriage to take us away from the wedding to the reception. It always amazed me at how much time and thought she put into the wedding details."

"By spring break, our love for one another was at a level that was hard to imagine. We wanted to be together all the time. On weekends, we woke up early, spent the entire day together, and only going on a few dates that cost money, as we were doing our best to save money for our wedding and married life. Sundays were days at church and a meal with my parents and her dad. He came over every Sunday after church to eat and fellowship."

"Who had the fruit plate?" the waiter questioned.

After a few exchanges with the waiter and the beginning of the meal, I asked if we could say a blessing over the meal, at which Jeff spoke up and said, "I will."

After a few idle moments of random chatter about the area's beauty, they planned their day. Jeff spoke up, "I am piecing together that this story is not taking a turn for the better."

"I have been down this road internally many times, but hearing it from someone else makes it even more surreal. God never asked me to figure it all out, and believe me, I have spent countless days on this beach trying to do just that. Instead, I have come to the understanding that I need to trust God with everything and everyone."

"I am sorry," Jeff replied as if I had rebuked him.

"Oh no, no apologies needed, Jeff. This has all been a journey, one few can understand. God has given me seven tries, and I am still trying to wrap my feeble brain around it all," I replied with a grin.

"Ok," Kim interrupted, "please continue this story."

"Until spring break, it was like heaven. Mandy and I grew closer and talked about everything. You know how some people talk on the phone but reach a point that all they do is listen to the other breathe," everyone laughed, nodding in affirmation. "Mandy and I never did. We talked and talked, and then, after the evening, I called her to let her know I had arrived home safely, and then an hour or two later, we were saying good night. Honestly, I slept very little during my final year of high school."

"We had spent spring break taking long walks at several state parks. One had a mountain on it, and a second, a not-too-steep hill. It took about two hours to climb because of the rocky path. We went to the base of the hill and were talking and laughing as we started on the upward trail. There was a bench to stop and rest every so often, and about twenty minutes into the climb, we came to the second one. Mandy wanted to stop and catch her breath, so we sat down. I leaned over to kiss her when I saw something in her eyes I had only seen in the hospital. It was the look of dread and fear.

My immediate concern was heard in my voice, 'are you alright?'

Mandy said something was wrong. She did not know what but had a feeling of impending doom. I asked her if I needed to get an ambulance, but she felt it would take too long, but she knew we would pass the fire station on the way to the hospital. Knowing that she had noted that helped me to know this was serious."

"I carried her as far as I could, and she melted in my arms, almost limp. About halfway down, some hikers asked if they could help, and they helped carry her down the rest of the way, loading her into my car. I drove at incredible speeds to get to the hospital. I kind of wished for a police officer to pull me over and question my high rate of speed, but none were around."

"Why a police officer?" Christy wondered.

"In my thinking, he could have led us to the hospital with sirens or at the least summoned an ambulance. Remember, these were the days before cell phones. When we finally arrived at the hospital, I pulled up to the emergency door and began blaring my horn for help. I jumped out of the car, ran inside and found someone, yelling that my fiancé was very ill. Immediately, a massive group of medical professionals appeared and ran to the car. It was as if someone had called up angels to motivate a rapid response team with a gurney. There were people with stethoscopes, yelling highly technical medical codes. More than anything, it showed me that her situation was grave."

"While she was in the car, unresponsive, they began checking her vitals, opening her eyes and shining a light to see pupil response, and calling for a gurney. I later learned they were doing a 'rapid response' drill to ensure they were ready for a mass casualty event. Since the emergency room was fairly slow, they relied on actors and actresses to help them pull off the drill. When Mandy presented a need, the drill went into full force. It was incredible and scary at the same time."

"Would anyone like a refill on coffee or some orange juice, freshly squeezed by the freshest squeezer in all of Florida?" the waiter joked, "We call him squeezer, but you can call him Phil."

I fell for it. "Is his name Phil?"

"No," the waiter laughed, "Phil is the name of the guy who ran off with his wife. We call him Phil because it makes him get the very last drop of juice out of the orange. Lately, though, he has been sharpening the knives in the kitchen, so we would rather the customers call him Phil, not us."

We all laughed, and I took it as a cue to wrap up the story quickly.

"Mandy was severely dehydrated, anemic and had an enlarged spleen and liver. All were classic signs cancer had returned."

"The doctor admitted her immediately and called her oncologist. He came later that evening and ordered a battery of tests for the next day. After a few days of waiting, our worst fears were our reality. Mandy's cancer had returned. She was extremely ill. I did my very best to keep up a strong façade, but it was fake. When she slept, I quietly wept. When she was awake, she was reticent. All the news had brought her to a resolution I had not seen in her before, a resolve that the battle may soon be over, and she was not strong enough to fight anymore."

"It devastated me, as the woman I fell in love with was fighting an enemy I had no power to overcome. In just a few days, Mandy went from a beautiful, bright-eyed woman to one who looked ashen and hopeless."

"The oncologist consulted with the Mayo Clinic about new protocols and treatments for this type of cancer. We were in a holding pattern for a day or so. One afternoon, late in the week of spring break, Mandy had been sleeping, while I maintained a vigil beside her bed. She woke up and said, 'Jack Cash, you deserve better than me, and I am going to have to let you go. I love you, but I am hurting you, and I don't want to continue to do that.'"

"No way," I protested. "You can't get rid of me like that, do you know why?" Mandy shook her head no. I started singing, "I'm going to marry Mandy Clark someday. I'm going to carry her away. She is going to be my wife, and we will have a wonderful life."

Mandy smiled and went back to sleep.

"This sounds like a Hallmark movie," Kim insisted.

"I wish it had only been a movie," I replied, "because it was the richest and hardest experience of my life. The storm she was facing was a shared experience that made it hard for her. I was determined to marry her, even if it meant we were married in the hospital."

"Did you? You know, marry her in the hospital?" Jeff asked.

"No, but once they began a treatment protocol, we had a little relief. The hospital gave Mandy platelets and began treating some symptoms. They had a new treatment they tried on patients with this type of cancer. For some, it gave them a year of additional life. My goal was to marry her as soon as possible. I hoped to move up our wedding date. I told her I believed God would give her years and years of life and I could imagine nothing better than being her husband as soon as possible. Mandy wanted to finish high school and then get married, so we married one week after graduation. This pushed up our time clock, but we found out later it was perfectly God's timing."

"Ok, that explains a lot," Kim interjected. "I had heard you got married on spring break, then I heard you got married the last week of school but never knew. There were a lot of rumors flying around school."

"Rumors, what rumors?"

"Just that you got married, but it was a secret," Kim continued, "You guys were married during spring break and it was because of her cancer."

"No, Mandy insisted she finish high school. I think it had to do with my 'next mailbox philosophy.'"

Jeff spoke up, "I must have missed your next mailbox philosophy; what is it?"

I explained my race and life philosophy with the group and then said, "You know, I think if we had married, she would have finished what she wanted in life, so she wanted to accomplish graduating high school first.

So, we set the wheels in motion with the blessing of her dad and my parents, and although both of us had turned eighteen years of age, we still wanted our family's blessing and support. They not only supported the decision, but pulled out all the stops to make it happen. They rushed the invitations, secured the venue, even set up pre-marriage counseling with our pastor. Things were flying by, and even though things were grim, everyone was so excited. Looking into Mandy's eyes revealed both realities. One life may not last too much longer, and two, she may yet get to marry Jack Cash, a dream since fifth grade," I opined. "We studied together, prayed together, finished high school together, and were in the top ten percent in our class. I will never forget the night of graduation. It was only a week away from when I would marry this girl, and now, I watched her walk across the platform, reaching her 'next mailbox.'"

"Before she walked, the valedictorian spoke about the principles that bring about success in life and how success not measured in dollars or possessions but measured in dedication, loyalty, love, and devotion. He said, 'It's measured in tenacity. It never quits, even when faced with the impossible.' I thought to myself, 'He is describing my beautiful fiancé. She is all that and so much more.'"

"They called my name before Mandy's, so I walked across the platform and received my diploma. When I reached the other side, I turned to look back to see Mandy walk across the platform to receive her diploma. She smiled, and for a moment, looked the picture of health and vitality. We both knew, however, she was neither. As she exited, I took her by the arm and walked her to her seat, and waited for the moment we could move our tassel, graduating high school."

The waiter interrupted, "Hey guys, Phil in the back wants to know if you want any lemonade. We gave him lemons and said, 'Phil, when the waiter hands you lemons, make lemonade, and because we called him,'Phil,' the lemonade is extra tart, and somewhat sweet, any takers?" We laughed and ordered four glasses of extra tart, somewhat sweet lemonade.

Christy said, "Wow, she made it to graduation. Did you guys get married a week later?"

"Yes, we did," I continued. "The week was a blur of activity, and even though Mandy seemed to take it in stride, it took its toll. We tried to do as much as we could without her, but she was the bride, and everything had to be just right."

"Bridezilla?" Jeff questioned.

"No, more like Bride beautiful," I replied to a collective 'aww, how sweet.'

"Everything was ready, and we went to rehearsal and went through all the parts of the ceremony, but towards the end, Mandy suddenly felt extremely tired and wanted to go home and sleep. We all insisted she get checked out, but she did not want to go to the hospital, fearing a stay could ruin her wedding day. Looking back, I have always maintained Mandy knew the end was near, and she was doing everything she could to make it to the 'next mailbox.'"

"The wedding day finally arrived, and the plan was to marry at 11 a.m. and then travel by horse and buggy to the reception hall about a half-mile away for a luncheon reception. I called Mandy's house at 7 a.m., and her dad told me Mandy was still asleep and he would have her bridesmaid wake her soon. That alone concerned me because this was THE day, and she was still asleep. About an hour later, Mandy woke up and began preparing for the big day. They had a light breakfast, and took Mandy to the wedding site by limo. It was an outdoor venue with a staging area for brides. They arranged for someone to fix Mandy's hair, help her with makeup, and then helped her put on her wedding gown. It seemed time was both slow and fast, and before I knew it, I was preparing to walk out in front of witnesses and marry the girl. It was then the pastor said, 'Jack Cash, take a moment when you first see Mandy because it will be forever etched into your memory. She will be your bride, and she will be radiant with joy.'

The pastor was exactly right! Mandy was stunning, standing there with her long white wedding gown and a face expressing pure radiance. This was Mandy's moment. Then the wedding march began, and Mandy and her dad started walking toward me. I cried. Her dad cried, and Mandy cried. I think her beauty and our story moved everyone."

The waiter, with impeccable timing, said, "Phil likes you guys and made your lemonade less tart and sweeter. I hope you enjoy it." He placed the drinks in front of us, and I continued.

"We said our vows, and then the same song the choir did for us when

I proposed played. We held each other so tight, whispering our love for each other during the song. In the end, the pastor pronounced us husband and wife and then gave me the green light to kiss my bride. I did, and the place erupted in celebration. It was simply the happiest moment I think I had experienced up to that point in my life."

"The recessional began, and after greeting those who came to the wedding, I helped Mandy get into the buggy. When we were inside, Mandy kissed me and said that I had just made her the happiest woman in the world. She then sang, "I married Jack Cash today. Now He's going to carry me away. I am his wife, and we have a wonderful life."

I replied, "Mandy Cash, you have made me the happiest man in the world," and then we kissed for the longest time. The buggy driver said, "Ok kids, the honeymoon has not started yet, don't get too carried away." Mandy just smiled.

She pulled as close to me as she could as I wrapped my arm around her, holding her tightly. She said, "Jack Cash, I love you," and kissed me again. Then, she laid her head on my shoulder, sighed one time, and then, she died. She died right there in the buggy," I said with hot tears streaming down my face.

CHAPTER SEVEN

Kim stood up and walked around, put her hand on my shoulder, "I am sorry, Jack Cash," apologizing for insisting on hearing the entire story. "We did not know what happened. I am sorry we brought up something so painful."

As I wiped away the tears, I replied, "It's something I have gotten used to."

"Wow," Jeff said, "That was a heavy load to carry a week after graduation."

"Yes, it was for everyone, including her dad. He had just given away his daughter, but then, in a moment, she was in eternity. I know one day I will see her again, but honestly, it was a day of wonder, beauty, and blessing, but also despair and profound loss."

"The next few months were a blur as I tried to make sense of Mandy's death and deal with the profound loss I had just experienced. That brought me to this beach. A friend in the church offered to send me here for a couple of weeks in the fall when we had originally planned to marry. So, I came here to deal with my grief."

"Whew," Christy said, "Jack Cash, thank you for sharing your life, but it was NOT what I expected to hear." After an awkward silence, I spoke up, "So, what are your plans for the day?"

"Kim, Jeff, and I are going shopping. Would you like to come along?" Christy offered.

"Not today. I am not much into shopping at overpriced souvenir shops," I said while laughing as I stood to leave. "Guys, breakfast is on me," I said amidst protests. "You guys have a great day shopping."

"We hope we can see you again, Jack Cash," Christy said, looking Kim's way and nodding is if she were showing me that she wanted me to see Kim again.

"Me too," I replied. "It has been a pleasure drinking Phil's fresh-squeezed lemonade with you guys." I then went to pay and waved at everyone as I walked to the condo.

The morning was all but gone, and the wind started picking up to have a few powerful gusts from time to time. Those gusts caused some chairs and umbrellas to start "walking" across the beach or turn side-ways. I found my way to one chair and sat for a few minutes to catch my emotional breath. I had just told what seemed like strangers the most intimate details of my life. It was causing my memory banks to open without warning. Meltdowns were regular in such cases, and I had over-drawn my emotional bank. I needed time, and the storm of grief was sending waves of emotion.

The sudden gust of wind taking a woman by surprise helped break my depressing moment. Her hat blew off of her head, and I sat watching her chase it, laughing, falling, and chase it some more. It was all the comedic relief I needed. Her enormous hat also caused me to remember this same beach when I met Tamera.

Mandy's death had taken a toll on me earlier in the year, so someone suggested I come to this beach, one they thought would be therapeutic. A few days after arriving, I had found no one to talk to at all. Honestly, I was getting conversation hungry, and even though I was sitting near others, I struck up a conversation with the next person who came my way. A young woman with a huge beach hat, flowery top, and white shorts found her way to a beach chair reasonably close to me. She had four big floral bags. One had snacks in it, another had a plethora of lotions, sunscreen, sunglasses, and such, the third bag, filled with books and magazines, and the fourth bag had towels, wash-cloths, etc. I wanted to call her the 'bag lady,' but my humor would likely offend, so I held my thoughts in check. When she first set her bags down, she sighed and started arranging her nest. "Nest" was the first word that came to mind, and I smirked a little at the thought. I watched her out of the corner of my eye, struggling to keep her towel on the chair. It had to be perfectly aligned on the chair, as if someone were coming along to inspect it for neatness. One corner kept moving when the wind caught it, disturbing her world. She grabbed it and prepared for the other corner. The wind caught the first corner and folded it up. With frustration, she looked at it, pointed, and shouted, "Stay," and then got into the chair as quickly as she could before the towel moved again. She was too late because she realized the towel folded underneath her when she got arranged. "Are you serious?" she screamed out.

I laughed. "Can I help you?" I asked this damsel in distress. She seemed as perturbed at my offer as she was at her towel. "No, thank you!" she replied, then rose from the beach chair to attempt the battle again. She moved everything just so, and then, as she stood admiring her prowess, a puff of wind came up and blew her hat off her head and the towel off the chair.

She shrieked and started talking to herself in tones not loud enough for me to distinguish what she was saying. I almost felt she wanted to be alone, and every vibe she gave off was just that kind of vibe. But I could not shake the need to talk to someone, even if I was a source of their frustration.

"Please let me help you," I insisted as I helped her retrieve her hat and position her towel just right on the chair. I noted the direction of the breeze and stood guard on the end of the towel, keeping it in place until she was safely on her beach throne. That was what I was thinking. After she sat down, she started digging around the 'book bag' for a book to read. No doubt this was to signal me to leave her alone. I just couldn't help myself.

"Hello, my name is Jack Cash." I held my hand out to shake hers, but she just looked at her book and read. "Do you come here often?" I asked out loud. It was becoming clear she did not want to talk, and she wanted some alone time. Again, I couldn't help it. I just wanted someone to talk to, and there were no other people around, looking my way, except for a few people just shy of 100 years old or young families were more interested in keeping their children away from the 'shark-infested waters.'

"What is your name?" I asked.

"Look, I am at the beach on the only day that I have free from my conference, and I really would like to enjoy it. If you don't mind."

"No problem," I said. "What kind of conference?"

She let out an enormous sigh and said, "It is a conference for librarians."

My mind went racing, and before I could hold back my words, "A conference for librarians, I had no clue there was such a thing! What do they talk about at a conference for librarians? The Dewey Decimal number system, adding new, even more confusing numbers, or how to yell 'quiet' quietly?" Then, jokingly, I said, "Do they have fashion shows of the latest in librarian eye fashion? I mean, those half-moon glasses are the bomb!"

She smiled.

Then I continued, "you know, I can think of another thing a librarian convention should teach. They should advocate capital punishment for those who check out the most important books and never return them. Maybe burn them at the stake, or take away their license to drive, something!"

"I am an elementary school librarian," she replied. "They don't drive at my school."

"Then, you could take away nap time or recess! Hit them where it hurts."

She smiled again.

Then, I got to thinking out loud, "You know," I continued, "my mind is racing thinking about a librarian convention. I once knew an English teacher who went to a convention. I told her they should have different seminars for different English teacher needs, such as one called, "What is a participle, and how (and why) should you avoid dangling them?"

She laughed out loud. I said, "the other one should be 'Beowulf' in a postmodern society,' they reserve that seminar for insomniacs."

"Ok," she surrendered, "my name is Tamera. I really want to read my book."

I looked at her book and said, "I have read that book, and he dies in the end."

She threw the book at me and said, "Thanks, whatever your name is…"

"Jack Cash," I replied, "and I was not serious. I do not know what the book was about or if anyone died in it. I just wanted someone to talk to because this beach is lonely."

"Well, you have ruined my beach time, so thank you for that, and you have had someone to talk to, so you got that too. Is there anything else you want or need to do to me to mess up the rest of my day?" She said, with a smile that made me unsure of whether she was frustrated or flirting.

"Well, I would like to make it up to you and buy you lunch," I replied.

"It better be a good lunch, librarians have a healthy appetite and only like expensive places, because we read about them, all.the.time!"

"I have just the place, so why don't I leave you alone for a bit and come back around noon and take you to an expensive place for those with healthy appetites? That way, you can read about the butler killing the maid, and I will come back to show you the way to the eating place. How does sound?"

"It sounds like something I would like, by the way. You are not married, are you? Because I am not interested in going on a date with a married man," she wondered out loud.

"I was married, but my wife passed away in May."

"Oooookaaaayyyyy," she said nervously, "well, I will meet you back here, Jack Cash, at noon. Now leave so I can read my book."

I left for a later date.

As I sat there, I thought, 'this beach brings back so many memories, first Mandy, then Tamera, and, well, everyone.' With so much loaded in my memory banks, this place can often be too much for a grieving man to handle. I thought better about dwelling on everything too long. Kim texted me and wanted to know if I had dinner plans.

I wasn't sure what she was thinking or how she viewed the relationship, but I did not want to eat dinner alone. I agreed and decided just to let the moment be whatever it needed to be.

I texted back and told her I would be ready around five. As I walked, I received a text from the owner of the condo, Ilean. She texted that she had contacted the police to do a welfare check on Paddy and to please call immediately.

I called her and asked her what was happening with Paddy. She said that the last call she had received from him caused her to be very concerned about his life. He rambled about knowing who killed Veronica and that they were after him. She said, "Jack Cash, when they checked on him, they found him murdered." I fell to the ground in disbelief.

"Ilean, he always said he was close to finding out who killed Veronica, but..."then I just wept.

"Jack, I am so sorry. There are no other details, but you might want to be very careful."

"Careful, why?"

"Because evidently, this is tied up in Veronica's murder and it happened when you were married to her, it might be something that you need to be aware of who you are around. I don't know if it means that people are coming after you or not."

"Ilean, I don't know how much more of this I can handle. Marie died a few weeks ago, and now my former wife..." I started crying again, trying to catch my breath between words, "I... have... to... go..., I'll... call... later."

I had a few hours to compose myself, and maybe reach out to the police to see what had happened, but I didn't have the emotional strength to do anything but go to my condo and sleep.

I slept for three hours, waking up to my loud cell phone alarm. I quickly showered, trying to prepare myself for an evening time with Kim. I felt like I could not be alone, but also didn't want to have too much interaction.

An hour later, I met Kim on the beach. She wanted to try another place to eat, one I had eaten at often, so often that everyone knew me. I did not tell her, so the many "JACK CASH" greetings from waiters and waitresses took Kim by surprise when we arrived.

I looked at Kim, shrugged my shoulders, and said, "I've been here a few times."

"How often do you come to this area?" she questioned. Sighing loudly and looking around, nodding to the owner, "Too often."

As we sat down, Kim told me about their excursion into the area and some sites they found. We placed our order, and there was a sense Kim had something on her mind.

Kim confided in me she was curious about Mandy, and when they returned, she did an online search and found her obituary. Along with it, she found Tamera's story, so she asked me how I met Tamera. "We met on the beach. She had taken some time off from a convention to come to the beach. It was a librarian convention."

I then told her how we met, then I said, "Believe it or not, I found this restaurant and brought her here on our first date. We hit it off right away."

"It was a whirlwind of a relationship. I guess I wanted someone to spend my life with, and Tamera was a beautiful yet staid person. She was an avid reader and lived out her life through the stories she read. We dated every evening. She was in the area for her convention until she went home to Missouri. After that, we had a long-distance relationship. We talked every day, and then it became twice a day. Before long, we met family, went to events together, and looked for ways to be together. By this time, I was a pastor of a church, attending a Bible College and Tamera felt she could fit the role of a pastor's wife and still share her passion for reading with the children in our area. So, after about nine months of dating, many prayers, and some pre-marriage counseling, we married. Life was wonderful, and she was an incredible pastor's wife and an amazing librarian."

"So," Kim confessed, "I read online that she was working at the school library when a parent came in to get their child?"

"Yes, there was a little more to the story."

Suddenly our waitress interrupted us, "Jack Cash, it is so good to see you again. How in the world are you doing?" I always thought of Flo from the 70s show Alice when Marcy waited my table. Her hair was frazzled-red, and her demeanor was sassy sweet. She was the type at any minute could say, "Kiss my grits," but I never heard it from her. Too bad, though, because she was just like Flo.

"I am doing my best, right now, Marcy. I want to introduce you to Kim, a friend from high school."

"It's so nice to meet you, Kim. Jack Cash has been coming here for a long time. He is like a legend, but neither of you is young enough to still be in high school," Marcy joked.

"Marcy, Kim saw me on the beach yesterday and remembered me, and now, here we are, having a meal in this restaurant."

"Well, Kim, what can I get you?" Marcy took Kim's order, then mine.

After leaving, Kim leaned across the table and said, "She reminds me of Flo on the TV show, Alice."

"Thank you," I said, holding my hands up as if my team had got a touchdown. "I have always thought that, and now you have confirmed my thinking."

"So, tell me the story about Tamera."

"We were married about a year and a half, I was pastoring a church in Illinois, and Tamera was a librarian at a local elementary school. She loved the profession because she loved to read and wanted her students to share love. She would always say, 'leaders are readers,' and would do her very best to create mystery, joy, and wonder in reading."

"Tamera enjoyed living her life vicariously through the books she read. She read her books to travel to faraway places and live incredible adventures without leaving home. She was good at sharing her reading journey and some at-risk students were responding to her love for reading. Their grades rose, and the school finally saw that the librarian as more than a keeper of periodicals or the Dewey Decimal system. She was making a difference."

"There was a family in our community that was very poor. The father was abusive. The kids came into the library and read as long as they could, and Tamera kept the library open after school for those kids to come and read until their mother picked them up."

"Eventually, the mother and the children left the father later in the school year. He was always strung out on drugs and drinking, a regular in the legal system in the county, and she got tired of it. She also got tired of the abuse, which was very physical for her and the kids."

"Tamera took to these kids and their mom and showed them the love of Christ. They responded and began attending our church. The father got arrested for driving under the influence and eventually someone bonded him out. We think it was a girlfriend who bonded him out, but after they released him, he went on a binge and talked himself into coming to the school with a gun to take his kids back."

"The wife had filed for divorce and got a restraining order, but those are simply pieces of legal paper that don't hold up to a gun. Anyway, he came to the school to get his kids. No one knew he had a gun, but the kids were so afraid they ran to the library to hide from their dad. Someone called 9-1-1 and reported an angry man who had a restraining order against him was there to pick up his kids. They called it a non-custodial parent. The police came, but by the time they arrived, it was too late."

"The kids ran into the library crying and in sheer terror. Tamera took them, hid them in a closet, and locked the door, hiding the key. Someone told the dad the kids ran into the library, so they tipped him off Tamera was hiding them. He had been in some confrontations with Tamera, so she told him to leave anyway, and he went closer to the closet. When he did, Tamera stood in the way of the closet door. The dad decided he would shoot the doorknob to get to the kids at the same time Tamera moved in front of the door know, and he fired his gun and shot Tamera in the abdomen. When he realized he had shot someone, he froze."

"She told the police who shot her, and then," suddenly there was a massive lump in my throat and tears started streaming down my face, and through a voice shaken with emotion I said, "and then, she told the officer to 'please tell Jack Cash I love him, and I am sorry it's ending like this.'"

"Then, she died. The father never left the scene. He put his gun down and just stood there as everyone worked to save Tamera. The police took him into custody immediately. They sentenced him to life without parole after He pleaded guilty. They named the library after Tamera. The police never determined who sold or gave him the gun or who convinced him to do whatever it took to get his children.

Kim grabbed my hand. "The online article did not tell the back story. I am so sorry. What happened to the children?"

"There are all in college. One wants to be a doctor, another is in seminary to be a minister, and the youngest made a statement to the police and me at Tamera's funeral. She said, 'when I grow up, I want to be a librarian to teach children to read, and if they are scared of someone, I want to protect them as Mrs. Cash did for us.'"

"That is quite a story," Kim said, "I'm sure it was hard."

"Yes, I was driving to an appointment when I heard there had been a shooting at the elementary school, so I drove there immediately. Police were everywhere, and when I tried to see about Tamera, they stopped me and escorted me to the school office. It was there they told me about Tamera. I will never forget the moment. Anyway, I have talked about my life a lot, but tell me about yours. If you want, I mean, it is up to you," I said to Kim.

Kim told me about how she met her husband, salient points from their lives together, and then about his death. She never knew he had a heart condition, and because of that, his death was even more of a surprise. She had friends who had a condo in the area and offered it to her to begin the process of grieving.

After dinner, Kim and I walked along the beach holding hands. The sound of the seagulls, the waves lapping the shore, and the setting sun made the night memorable and romantic. I felt any move at all would make Kim vulnerable and hinder her grief experience. If anyone knew about grieving, I thought I did.

We were staying within hours of Orlando, and Kim invited me to go to Orlando the following day and spend the day at one of the theme parks as a diversion. I was a little reluctant, since a diversion one day could lead to addictive behaviors. But honestly, I could not pass up time with Kim.

I agreed to go and then, with no warning, Kim spontaneously kissed me. It was the kind of kiss so spontaneous no one can prepare for it. Kim did not, and her dinner included a heavy amount of garlic, which I noted when she kissed me. "That was very nice, with a copious amount of garlic, but very nice," I said, causing Kim to break out in laughter as she leaned in again to kiss. It was more intense than I imagined. She gripped me. The smell of her perfume and the softness of her body were almost too much for me to handle.

I pulled away and took her by the hand and led her to some of the stacked beach chairs, put away for the evening. We unstacked two and pulled them closer to the water's edge, side by side, and sat down together. I did not know what to say because I did not want to lead her on but did not want to push her away. Either way, it would lead me to some regret I was not wanting.

So, turning to her, I broke the silence, "Kim, I like you, I mean I really like you. I want to go to Orlando with you tomorrow, but I don't want to lead you on because both of us are very vulnerable right now. It may seem right, but it will be an emotional high after an extreme emotional low. I want to be with you, and honestly, I really, really liked the kiss. Not the garlic, but the kiss." Kim laughed and chimed in, "Or the fish, but I liked the kiss, too."

I laughed and continued, "I was afraid you would notice the fish. Look, I could fall for you and probably already have, but I want to go slower, so I am making good choices, and you are making good choices, not emotional ones. Is that ok?"

Kim shook her head, yes, and then, once again, kissed me, but this time on my cheek. Pulling away, Kim spoke up and said, "Jack Cash, I like you too, and I understand what you said, and I agree, but promise me this, you will keep your heart open to what God may want, and the possibility it could be us together."

"I promise, if it is God's plan that would be awesome," I assured her, even though my reply felt like I had crossed the line of no return. We both turned and watched the waves come in, and then, like someone switched on a switch, biting insects swarmed us.

"I think it is time to leave the beach."

"I will walk you to your condo."

When we arrived, she turned to me and once again kissed me and told me goodnight. I knew best not to linger in the moment and told her goodnight and agreed on a meeting at 7 a.m. so we could grab breakfast and head to the theme park.

CHAPTER EIGHT

eading back to my condo, I heard loud music, or more like a pulsating low bass tone. Not too far away, a bar had a disco night, and I could hear people talking, laughing, and just a general loudness. I did not want to listen to the sound all night and hoped it would not keep me up.

When I arrived at my condo, I noticed a voice mail was waiting. I picked up and dialed to retrieve the voice mail.

"Jack Cash, this is Ilean; look, they are asking me and Richard a lot of questions about Paddy. If you get this, could you call me? They want to question you about him." I couldn't believe Paddy was dead. Paddy was one of those guys who loved to fight. He would fight anyone, anywhere, for any reason. The first time I met Paddy and Veronica was amazing.

After Tamara's murder, I waited six months, and then traveled back to this beach to grieve, and there I met Paddy and his sister, Veronica. I had stopped at a souvenir shop to buy sunscreen. Next to the shop was a small, pop-up t-shirt stand with a sign said, "T-shirts & Sundries."

I walked up to the counter, "Hello, I am looking for sundries." Paddy laughed and replied, "My name is Paddy Gypsy, and I am happy to help you. What do you need? A cheap, worthless t-shirt that will make it through one or two washes, one may even leave you with whelps all over your body, or an overpriced t-shirt you can wear for the rest of your life?"

We both laughed.

"I just need some sunscreen."

"Veronica, my sister, is in the souvenir shop, and she can show you the sunscreen, but watch her. She is a gypsy," Paddy warned with a smirk.

"Like a long-haired, flowery dress-wearing, tambourine playing, earrings as big as the moon gypsy woman?" I wondered out loud. " That sounded racist! I am sorry."

Paddy laughed this peculiar laugh that began deep in his belly, sounding like, "HU,HU,HU,HU, no, our last name is Gypsy. We are not ashamed of our name, or our heritage, even though it is derogatory to some, my name is Gypsy, so why not embrace it and make money? It has worked."

I nervously laughed and headed to the store.

When I walked through the door, there was no one in the store except a beautiful long-haired, flowery dress-wearing woman holding an over-sized loop earring in one hand, and something else in her other hand, holding it behind her back.

"Veronica," I said laughing, "Paddy said you were a gypsy, and..."

"What do you want?" she asked in frustration.

And then, she turned and placed a tambourine on a display rack. I started laughing. Laughing so hard as my 'prophetic' but racist question to Paddy came to pass right before my eyes, and it was only a joke. I don't know why I laughed so hard even though she was not amused. Through my tears and extreme laughter, I tried to explain that Paddy said that she was NOT that kind of gypsy, but in reality, she was that kind of gypsy, and then I wondered out loud if her name was really "Gypsy."

Matter-of-factly, she replied, "what did you expect coming to 'Gypsy's Shell Shop and Souvenirs,' finding me dressed up as a pirate?"

"Gypsy's, now that clears that up nicely. Your name is Gypsy, you have a shop for shells and souvenirs, and you dress up because your name is Gypsy, not because you ARE a gypsy. Are you a gypsy?" I asked, laughing again.

"So, now that you have seen a gypsy, what can I help you with?" She wondered out loud with frustration bordering on anger.

"I need sunscreen. I am going to the beach." She showed me various levels of sunscreen and a hat to help with the sun on my head. I bought the items, and she asked, "Have you been here before?"

"Not to this shop, but the beach and a condo on Beachway Court," I offered.

She mentioned the condo owners, Richard and Ilean Orr, and said they had shared Christ with her and her brother. Because of their witness, Veronica and Paddy started their walk with Jesus several years earlier.

I said, " That is so wonderful, I am a minister and…," she interrupted, "Wait, are you Jack Cash?" I nodded affirmation as she grabbed me in the tightest hug. She went cold to hot in three seconds flat. I thought, "It is true. She IS a gypsy."

As she was holding me, she said, "Jack Cash, Paddy, and I pray for you every night, especially after we found out about your wife, Tamera. We are so sorry you had to go through that, and from everything Richard and Ilean shared, she was an amazing woman."

That brief exchange set off an intense wave of grief that startled me. I went from being amused to crying in three seconds flat. I was sobbing with mucus pouring from every pore on my face. Veronica held me for what seemed like forever, and her warmth and care felt like I was in the arms of God. Eventually, she pulled away and found tissues. She offered that to me as I excused my tears and thanked her for praying for me. Wiping away my grief, I told her I had planned on spending two weeks at the condo while I processed everything.

"You know," she interjected, "sometimes grieving is like standing on the shoreline, with waves coming and going. There will be times when the wave comes in, and you will want to be alone, and there will be times when you will want someone to talk to; if you do, while you are here, call me!"

Her words almost sounded like a romantic interest, and fresh off of my trauma, I feared this moment the most. But then, she added, "Call me, and I will tell Paddy to spend some time with you."

I laughed and said, "It's a deal."

"Wait here while I tell Paddy that you were the one we have been praying for; he will want to know."

She walked me out to the T-Shirt shack and told Paddy I was the minister they had been praying for. Paddy started crying the same belly cry that sounded a lot like his laughing, just backward, "UH, UH, UH, UH," as he ran to the store. Upon arriving he said, "We have been praying for you, preacher and I am so glad to meet you. If you need anything, except a high-priced t-shirt, let me know." He bear hugged me with the tightest hug I have ever had, in fact, so tight bones in my back popped.

"Paddy, you are like the best chiropractor I have ever had."

He wiped away his tears, and I noticed that Veronica had been crying, too. From there, I headed to the condo.

That jog of memory of meeting Veronica and Paddy overwhelmed me. I couldn't believe Paddy had been murdered. Coupled with compounded grief was fear. I didn't know who had murdered Paddy and almost felt that if I didn't deal with it right away, I didn't have to worry if they were after me or not. I just did what I did a lot...stuffed my emotions into a closet full of grief and quickly shut the door. I worried that someone would unintentionally open the door and then a flood of emotions would bury me. So, I tried to stuff as much as possible, and ignore it. That was a bad idea. I decided to wait until morning to return Ilean's call.

My dream that night was about Veronica. She was standing on a small island, with just a little water between us. It was a beautiful day, with about as blue of a sky as it could get, and wispy white clouds accenting the blue. The water was as crystal clear as any water, and when I looked at the water, I noticed Veronica's reflection. She was smiling, and when I looked up at her face, she was laughing as if she were so full of joy that her face could not contain it. I looked at the water again and not only saw Veronica's but my previous wives' faces, and then a wave crashed over me, pushing me deep underwater.

I woke up with a pillow wet from my tears but also with a deep sense of peace. Almost like I had passed a stage of healing with a little bit of pain, but a whole lot of healing. I only wished that was the case. I had been down this road of grief too many times to believe that this momentary peace was something that would sustain me long term. But, I was refreshed after my third day since meeting Kim. I was looking forward to the diversion in Orlando. I showered and dressed and splashed on some cologne. I think I must have done a lot because I felt like a cologne factory from that moment on.

It was the third day since meeting Kim, and I because I had visited this area so many times, I knew every great restaurant and most of the terrible ones too. I met Kim at a Victorian-looking restaurant that had the very best French toast and crepes. After we sat down and ordered coffee, Kim said, "I dreamed about my late husband last night, is that normal?"

I laughed, "I dreamed about my seven late wives last night, so I guess it can happen."

She chuckled, but her voice broke as she said, "I guess I have a lot to learn. I need this day."

I realized she was more in the thick of grief than I knew. I was so focused on her that realizing I was in the same wave of suffering was not as clear. I tried to ignore the latest death as long as I could.

"Let's just have a great day," I suggested. "Let's get our picture taken with Mickey and Cinderella and the whole crew, let's buy Mickey Mouse ears and eat ice cream and let's start with the best crepes this side of France. Let's enjoy a beautiful day together."

Kim stuck her hand out to shake mine and said, "You have a deal."

I almost wanted to back up what I had just said because I didn't want Kim to think I was minimizing her pain or acting as if we can ignore it, really ignore the pain when we need to ignore it. Such as it is with grief, second-guessing everything, feeling awkward even when making a wise choice. So, I said, "But, if at any time you want to talk, laugh, cry, or get a high priced souvenir. Do it!"

"That sounds great."

My phone rang; it was from Ilean. "Answer it," Kim encouraged.

"Hello!"

"Jack, this is Ilean. You need to call a detective about Paddy. They are investigating his murder, and it sounds like it is bigger than I knew last night. The detective called me late yesterday and twice this morning. He wants to talk to you. What are your plans today?"

"A friend and I are going to Orlando today. Do they have any idea who killed Paddy?"

"I'm not sure, but they think it is associated with the cartel. Jack, the detective asked about a document they believe Paddy had, which must be a big deal. They want to find it right away, but they have no idea where it is located."

"What kind of document?"

"I don't know, but whatever it is, it is worth killing someone over, please call him back as soon as you can. I will text you his number."

She texted his name and number, and we hung up. I called the number immediately, but it went to voice mail. "Hello, my name is Jack Cash. I am calling regarding Paddy's murder. Ilean Orr gave me your name. Please call my cell number." I left my cell phone number and hung up.

I ended the call, and Kim said, "Paddy is a strange name. Where did Paddy come from?"

"It is a gypsy name," I replied. "Paddy was my brother-in-law. He was my third wife's brother. Their last name is Gypsy."

The waiter brought us coffee and took our order. The waiter was a familiar face, but I just couldn't quite remember how or where I had known him.

After he left, I told Kim how I had met Veronica and Paddy.

Kim started shaking her head, like someone who can't believe a story. "What are you shaking your head about?" I wondered out loud.

Kim said, "This is all too crazy incredible. You met your first wife in fifth grade, and she proposed. You met your second wife on the beach, right here while she was at a librarian convention. You met your third wife here, too, because you stopped at an overpriced souvenir shop. And she was a gypsy too?"

"It is like a fairy tale, filled with characters that are too hard to believe and too easy to dismiss."

"I guess you're right," I said aloud. Kim only knew about three of my seven wives.

We talked about what we wanted to do at the theme park when the waiter started putting the food on the table. I looked at him and said, "I know you but can't remember from where."

The young man said, "I am related to the Orr's. You are Jack Cash, right?"

"Yes."

"I met you years ago when you were here after your wife died. I was at Uncle Richard and Aunt Ilean's house."

I looked at Kim and said, "Kim, I am sorry; Richard and Ilean Orr are the people I have rented my condo from for years. They are incredible people and have helped me so much. Funny story, Ilean likes to tell it. Her name is Ilean. When she was born, one leg was shorter than the other. Noticeably so, and her dad decided her name should be I Lean because she would 'lean' the rest of her life. He even spelled it I.L.E.A.N."

"How cruel," Kim replied.

"Yes, cruel, but after a life of living with this problem, she has an attitude that will blow you away. She will tell you the story of her name and then say, 'I lean towards happy.' It truly is her testimony."

I looked at the waiter and said, "You have a wonderful family."

We finished our breakfast with very little else said, other than the obligatory comments about the wonderful flavors and ambiance of the restaurant.

We got in my car, and Kim said, "I needed this time away. Jack Cash, you don't know how therapeutic this has been. Thank you!"

"It was a good restaurant," I suggested.

"Stop it," hitting me in the arm, "I mean meeting Jack Cash out of the blue and then, hearing the stories and beginning the process of healing. And now going to a theme park, this has been so good for me." She turned her head away from me as her voice trailed off into tears.

I let the moment sit while she regained her composure, and then I said, "Let's go to the theme park."

She raised her hands up and tearfully but weakly cheered, "Woohoo."

That phrase, "meeting Jack Cash out of the blue," hit me funny. I guess it was the lack of good sleep, maybe the fantastic breakfast or the gentle bump of expansion joints in the pavement lulled me into a zone of wondering. What did 'out of the blue' even mean, was it a reference to happenstance, do Sea Monkey's look like real monkeys, or are they something so much more? My mind wandered from this to that.

"Can we take an exit soon; I need to see how clean the restrooms are?" Kim interrupted my thought stream.

I hadn't taken too much thought of where we were on the highway but instinctively took the next exit. The long bend in the road opened up to a potpourri of choices for Kim, and just as I was preparing to turn into a convenience store, I saw the sign in the distance, "Gypsy's Shell Shop and Souvenirs."

It had been years since I had seen Paddy, and now his murder caused my mind to stay fixated on Veronica. Paddy always talked like a conspiracy-minded madman. I was too overwhelmed with emotion to deal with that particular kind of drama again. I regretted not calling him back.

The Orr's introduced Paddy and Veronica to Jesus. Veronica and Paddy were special people. When I met Veronica, she had been clean for a while. Her past drug addiction had taken a toll on her life. She had struggled with prescription drug addiction for several years and legal trouble due to its power in her life. She was a free spirit, and meeting her was like that thought of 'out of the blue' too, kind of like a divine appointment directly from God.

She didn't say as much, but Kim mentioned she needed time with me as therapy. When I met Veronica, she was that for me: free-spirited diversion therapy. Veronica traded her addiction for Jesus and eventually for me.

But she was the kind of person that had to have everything in a chaotic order, part gypsy thinking and part ordering her world. If anything was out of her chaotic order in her mind, she launched into a deep panic. I learned that her organization of things seemed haphazard to the untrained eye early on, but she knew what stack had the bill, letter, or essential piece of information. If anyone moved or tried to "organize" her stack, she felt that organization forced on her was chaotic. I was never sure if drug use caused this or if it was her style.

Regardless, I learned early on to leave things alone except for Veronica. She was overly flexible but intense on connection. Once we began dating, she always wanted me near. She even tried to work out a pastorate near her so I could be closer. I don't think it was because of jealousy or fear she would lose me to someone else. It just felt I was a necessary part of her chaos.

"Restroom, hello," Kim's emphatically called out as I was oblivious to my surroundings. I quickly turned into the Shell station. As I parked, I noticed a T-shirt stand next to the "Gypsy's Shell Shop and Souvenirs" building, set up just like the one where I meet Paddy. As Kim went inside, I decided to walk over to the T-shirt stand. The entire business was closed, no doubt because of Paddy's murder.

Kim called out, "You getting a T-Shirt?"

I shook my head no and started walking back to the car, shrugging my shoulders... "They are closed, so I can't get you a high-priced, wear once t-shirt, sorry." When I got into the driver's seat, I was overwhelmed with the aroma of jasmine as Kim began to lotion her hands. Jasmine was Veronica's favorite fragrance.

"Was there a note on the door at the T-shirt shop?" Kim wondered.

"Nothing, this is Paddy's business, they are likely closed due to his murder," my voice trailing off again, as the lump in my throat matched the volume of tears streaming down my face.

She shrugged her shoulders as if she didn't really care about the fact that someone I knew had been murdered. She began searching for a radio station as we left the store. The first station she found on was a country station and belted out a few verses of the song that was playing, then changed to a classic rock station, singing along with the band, and then, finding a Christian station, started singing along with it as well. She could sing beautifully and had an amazing range. "So, what is your favorite genre of music? You seem to know verses to a lot of different types of music."

"I like it all, except rap. I don't like rap. And I am not fond of classical music."

"Well, what about yodeling?"

"No, I don't like it and can't do it," as she laughed. The rest of the trip was the same, station searching until the right song came along, then loud and lively singing. Suddenly a new song began, and Kim experienced a full-blown melt-down. It was a song full of joy and very lively, but that was not what Kim was feeling. I knew the feeling well. Out of nowhere, grief can pick you up, body slam your heart, grab a chair like a professional wrestler, and hit your head repeatedly until you are a blubbering shadow of your former self. It's hard to witness, more brutal when you are the one going through it, but worse when you need a moment to process life in light of a loss while trying to help others do the same. Now, I had to be strong while Kim had her moment. It could ruin her day, and I prepared to turn around and head back if needed, knowing this moment could strain the remainder of the day.

I took the next exit and found an abandoned convenience store, and parked. I leaned over, put my arm around her, pulled her as close as I could, and started making random noises for some reason. I don't know why I started making bird sounds, squeaks, creaks, and other sounds, but through her tears, Kim said, "Why are you making those sounds?"

"I am comforting you in Khoisan. It's a click language!" I replied matter-of-factly. Then, as quickly as the melt-down started, Kim was laughing as hard as her sobs were earlier.

"Jack Cash," she signaled as much as she could between her laughs, "you have got to be the best melt-down helper that never helped anyone, but now I can't help but feel better. Is it really a language?"

"Yes," I replied, "but I made up the sounds, and I added the clicks hopefully to sound a little like the real language. I just hope I didn't say anything bad."

"Oh, you did, you said something awful," she said, "you said," as she tried to find traction with words through her laughter, "you said," and then the phone rang.

While Kim was still laughing, I answered, "This is Jack Cash." "Mr. Cash, this is Tom Cole, a detective with the Sheriff's office. I need to speak with you. When can we meet?" The meltdown ended, and the grief would have to wait.

CHAPTER NINE

"Well, I am on my way to Orlando for the day. Is this something that can wait until tomorrow?"

"Mr. Cash, I need to speak with you as soon as possible. Where are you now?"

"What is this regarding?" I asked, even though I knew it likely involved Paddy.

"Mr. Cash," he replied, "I need to talk to you as soon as I can." I was approaching an exit, "I am on I-95 about to take 192 to Orlando."

"Perfect, Mr. Cash, there is a western store just off of I-95. Pull in the parking lot, and I will be there in a few minutes."

I took the exit and turned left, and immediately found the western store.

I wondered out loud, "I bet this about Paddy, but why couldn't we talk on the phone?"

Kim said nothing and pretty much looked ahead the entire time.

A few minutes later, an unmarked car pulled into the parking lot. A man stepped out wearing blue jeans with a badge attached to the belt on one side and his service weapon on the other. Walking up to our car, the detective asked, "Are you Jack Cash?"

"Yes, what is going on?" I replied.

"Can I see your identification, Mr. Cash?" I pulled out my driver's license, and he took it and radioed my name, date of birth, driver's license state, and number. A few minutes later, he received some type of confirmation and said, "Mr. Cash, do you know Paddy Gypsy?"

"Yes, I know him. He's my brother-in-law. What is going on with Paddy?" I asked, knowing full well that he had been murdered.

"When was the last time you saw or talked to Mr. Gypsy?" he asked while writing things on a notepad.

"Well, he left a voice mail at my condo the day before yesterday. It was his usual stuff. He told me I that may be in danger, but he has said that about every time we have talked since his sister died. She was my wife."

"How long have you been in town, Mr. Cash?"

"I have been here a few days, what is going on?"

"Mr. Cash, where were you the afternoon and night before last?"

"I was with Kim until late, and then alone at my condo."

"Who is Kim?" the detective questioned.

"She is right here. Her name is Kim Crane," as I motioned towards her, "we were together." Kim waved at him.

"Where were you together?"

"We went to dinner and then walked on the beach at sunset."

I got a sick feeling when he asked, "Can anyone verify your story? What restaurant, and exactly where were you at the beach?"

I told him where we dined and the approximate area we were in on the beach.

"Mr. Cash, I am sorry to have to tell you this, but someone murdered Paddy some time day before yesterday." His voice mail to you may have been the last thing he said to anyone.

Detective Cole continued, "Do you know his family?" My mind was racing, and I felt fear I had not felt since Veronica's murder. "Did he say anything else on the voicemail? I need to know exactly what he said," he continued. "Think, is there anything he told you lately that may have led to his murder?"

This line of questioning was precisely what I heard after Veronica's murder. Veronica was in the drug scene for years but was deeper into it than just using drugs. She knew the key people in the drug trade in Central and South America. Not only using drugs but so involved, she knew the people, places, and money drops. That information alone put her in a position of power. It also jeopardized her life many times, especially after she met Christ. Her conversion was epic, and everything changed in a minute. She truly had a come-to-Jesus moment, and it was a radical change.

The DEA, FBI, and US Marshal service approached her, wanting her to turn on her employers. She did, and because she knew so much, they were able to put many people in prison for the rest of their lives. She felt that even the suggestion of turning people in was enough for those in the high positions of the drug cartel to seek her immediate death.

For her, it had the feel of a race that whoever moved first won. If she made her move first and revealed the incredibly sophisticated underbelly of the drug trade, her life would be spared, at least for a while. If the cartel got wind of an offer from the government, even if she disagreed, she knew the principal leaders would silence her just for knowing what she knew.

So Veronica turned in many high-profile people, and they implicated even crooked politicians and law enforcement officers in the case against the cartel. They arrested the highest-profile people first. The cause and effect advanced many careers of law enforcement officers.

The money seized was in the tens of millions of dollars, and the drugs seized brought down a half a billion-dollar cartel operation. Assets was so large that it took a team of agents just to catalog all of the cars, planes, houses, yachts, islands, and submarines. Needless to say, one lady, my third wife, Veronica, was the key witness and had such intimate access every charge the government brought against this cartel quickly progressed through to conviction. The government offered Veronica and Paddy witness protection, and they refused. They got protection and guaranteed income as a reward for the information, but they steadfastly refused any type of relocation or name change.

The protection eventually slacked off and after our marriage, pretty much was a phone call from some government agent checking in to see how she was doing. Since nothing had happened, those charged with her protection felt they could slack off their work. As far as they knew, she destroyed the cartel because so many went to jail, underground, or simply disappeared.

The only lingering concern was that Veronica knew every cash drop, some drops totaling millions of dollars, for massive drug deals and there was always a possibility the authorities had missed any or many. There was also a wealth of knowledge Veronica held she never shared with me. She knew that people in the highest places of government would never see freedom again should their association with the cartel become known. That revelation would destroy countless careers and families. There was still a lot of money unaccounted for, so the question was always, 'where is the missing money, and did Veronica know where?'

Her life was in constant danger. Some people in the cartel were still free but were afraid she would turn them in to authorities as she had their bosses. Eventually, however, Paddy believed they found her, bound her, and injected drugs in her body. The coroner report noted the amount of heroin injected in her would kill ten people. No one knows if she was tortured for information or as punishment, but it was always a lingering question law enforcement wanted to know.

Paddy knew most of the information since she confided in him many of the details, fearing members of the cartel would attempt to extract information from him should something happen to Veronica. His concern about my welfare was that somehow people might think I knew where money drops occurred or had other information that could implicate them. I passed it off as meaningless because it had been a long time since the court cases when I met Veronica. But Paddy kept up vigil for the both of us. All of this questioning felt so similar.

The detective pressed harder, "THINK, there has to be something he told you. It could tell me who killed Paddy and what they wanted from him."

I started to panic because he asked me if I knew what they were looking for, something that only those intimately involved in Veronica's death and court cases would know, not a detective investigating a murder that took place thirty hours before. His phone rang, and he answered utterly unhinged, with his one-sided conversation sounding suspicious, "WHAT," he screamed into his phone, "I am asking, but he is not telling me anything, look, I am doing my best. I will find out what he knows." Then, an emphatic gutterly, "I said I would take care of it," he yelled before he ended his call.

His phone rings again, and this time, he goes to his car speaking in hushed tones and that is when my phone rang.

The callerID noted, "UNKNOWN" but I answered anyway, "This is Jack Cash."

"Mr. Cash, this is Phil Townsend with the U.S. Marshal's office. I think we may have spoken years ago after Veronica's death."

"Yes, I remember you. How can I help you?"

"Mr. Cash, Veronica's brother was found murdered, and we believe your life may be in jeopardy. Where are you now?"

"I am in a parking lot talking to a detective with the sheriff's office. He called me and told me to meet him here."

"Jack Cash, no detectives are working this case from the sheriff's office. This is our case, and we have not included local LEO's in the case. We were Paddy's handlers; they were not called in at all. What is his name?"

"Tom Cole with the sheriff's office, that's all he said, I didn't even ask what sheriff's office, but he knew Paddy was dead."

"Mr. Cash, your life is in danger, and you need to leave now."

Kim is about as panicked as a wild, caged animal by this time, and she screams, "He's coming back with his hand on his gun. Leave! go! Go!"

I looked in my mirror and saw that he was coming towards my side of the car, and I put the car into drive and put the gas pedal to the floor, turning onto 192 towards Orlando. I didn't know what else to do.

Phil spoke up, "You did the right thing, Jack Cash. Where were you going today?" "We were going to Orlando."

"Who is with you?"

"Kim Crane, a friend I knew in high school, we met again on the beach."

"Listen to me very carefully, Jack. You are in grave danger. You need to go to Orlando where you can be around many people, where you can disappear in a crowd. I will work out the details, but I need for you to go to a theme park." Interrupting him, I asked, "Why a theme park if we are in danger?"

"Because there are a lot of people there, and you can disappear easier than an uncontrolled environment. Go to the ticket counter, and I will have tickets for you and Kim to get inside. I will send you a link to the specific park by text. After you are inside, I need for you to stay aware of those around you. Someone may be following you. The man that met you has your car information and may try to track you by another means. Is it your car or a rental?"

"It is a rental."

"That's worse because he might be able to track you through the rental car company if he has access to their system. Is he still following you?"

Kim kept scanning the cars behind us and said, "I don't see him." By this time, my speed was consistently 90 miles an hour, and it was clear no one was traveling at such speeds behind us.

"It doesn't matter," Phil noted, "he might still know where you are regardless of your speed. When you get to the theme park, go inside, and to your left is a place called the Emporium. Tell the cashier you lost your wallet in the park. They will ask your name and tell them, 'Jack Cash and Phil sent me.' They will take you backstage and keep you there until one of our agents, Cynthia Baker, arrives. Do not leave there until she arrives. She will have her US Marshal identification with her. Do you understand everything I just told you?"

"Yes, go to the theme park, to the emporium, tell them I lost my wallet, my name is Jack Cash, and Phil sent me. I think I have it."

Phil said, "Perfect, Jack Cash, how well do you know Kim Crane?" The question was awkward because she heard everything Phil had told us.

"Well, first, I knew her in high school, and we have spent the last few days together, and second, she has heard every word we have spoken, so if you have something you want to say about Kim, please keep it to yourself because we are both scared to death and don't know why we are in danger."

"Just be careful, Jack Cash," Phil sighed, "and call when you arrive. I am alerting Cynthia to meet you, so go there now!"

My heart was racing, and then it dawned on me, Kim and I had agreed to take a diversion day, but neither of us could have imagined this kind of diversion. "Well, how are you enjoying your diversion day?"

Kim replied, "Well, for one thing, this is the worst diversion day ever in the history of the world, and second, I am scared to death, Jack Cash!"

"I am so sorry, Kim! I never envisioned anything remotely like this happening to me, or us, or today. Nothing. I feel like I have gotten you into something I didn't know I was into, and I am scared too."

Kim had kept a vigilant watch for any cars following us. We started to come into heavier traffic, and I had to slow my speed to just above the speed limit.

Phil called again, "Jack Cash, where are you now?"

"I am just coming into the Orlando area."

"Good, stay on 192, do not get on I4, there is a wreck, and the police are stopping traffic while they work it. I know because Cynthia is stuck on I4 heading your way. She is running late, but the plan is the same. Do not go anywhere else. By the way, I verified that no detective in any Florida agency is named "Tom Cole." I did check, just in case someone was attempting to bypass federal agents. Mr. Cash, you and your friend are in danger, and the extent of the network Tom Cole, or whatever his real name is, is unknown. They intend to get information from someone who knew Veronica. Do not give anyone any information, if you have any."

"No worries, Phil, I don't even know what kind of information they want to know from me. We are at the exit now."

"Perfect, as quickly as you can, find a parking place near the tram pick up, but do not get out of your car until the tram is near, then immediately get on the tram to the front entrance. Once there, go to the ticket booth and tell them you need "will-call tickets" with your name and then go to the Emporium. You remember the rest, right?"

"Yes, we have got it. We are looking for a parking place now, and I think we found one. We will gather our belongings and head to the tram pick-up as soon as it is near."

"Text me when you are backstage, talk to you soon."

Kim grabbed my hand and said, "Veronica must have been a unique, crazy drama queen if this situation today is any indication."

"Yes, kind of like if cupid and a hurricane had a love child, that girl would have been 'Veronica,' but not every day with her was a 90 mph chase," I said as I continued scanning our surroundings. "Kim, I am so sorry this is happening. I promise I will do everything I can to keep you safe. There is the tram. Let's go."

With that, we grabbed our belongings and walked as fast as we could to the tram. We both kept looking back, around, and at people to see if anyone looked like Tom Cole. Secretly, I also looked for anyone out of place, not looking like someone excited to go into a world-famous theme park, such as a single person without family, someone in a suit, mainly anyone out of place. Our diversion day had turned into something entirely different. It would have fit Veronica nicely, though. She loved spontaneity, and planning a solid itinerary was not her at all. A 90 mile an hour chase would have made her happy. A mission of chaos filled with drama and intrigue was always her happy place, and for now, I could see Kim was not the same.

The tram sped us to the gates and ticket booth, where we exchanged our names for tickets to the park. "These are unique tickets," declared the woman who gave them to us, "they will get you places. Just show them at the Emporium."

Kim and I set out immediately for the Emporium. It wasn't too far, and when we arrived, we took our tickets to the counter. "Hello, I lost my wallet. My name is Jack Cash, Phil sent me."

"I am sorry, Mr. Cash. Lost and found is just outside our door, towards the entrance," the attendant said.

"But Phil told me to come here, tell you I lost my wallet, and my name is Jack Cash."

" Phil. He tells people all kinds of things, right. So, I would check lost and found, show your ticket and your identification, and they will help you there."

"But he said that you would take care of us," I felt a sense of panic sweeping over me, "and he told us to come here."

"Don't worry about it, Mr. Cash, everything will be fine. Just go to lost and found and tell Cynthia I sent you."

"Oh, Cynthia is there, ok, now I feel better." Kim spoke up and said, "Wow, I was getting a little worried." When we left the emporium, I tried to call Phil, but the cell service noted, "All circuits are busy. Please try again later." So I texted him.

We didn't walk to lost and found; we ran. Instead of feeling any sense of relief, we both felt things could go sideways in a second, and even this momentary change of plans was unnerving. At lost and found, we asked for Cynthia, and they called for Cynthia to come to the counter. A woman who could as well pass for Cinderella as Cynthia went to the counter. "Can I help you?"

"Yes, I have lost my wallet. My name is Jack Cash, and Phil sent me."

"Well, you have a good friend named Phil, if he sent you to "lost and found" because we find lost things. Your name is Jack, "J-A-C-K," spelling out my name as she is completing a lost and found form, "Is that right?"

"Yes, but…"

"C-A-S-H, last name, right?"

"Yes, but, we came here!"

"To find your lost wallet, I know, we get this all the time, people losing things, and they come here to find them. You came to the right place but, do not, I repeat, do not, mistake us for a cruise through the jungle, no pirates here, only people charged with making sure whoever finds your wallet does not charge your credit card."

"Cynthia, look, on any other day, I would enjoy the banter, but today is not that day."

Cynthia, with pouty lips, pitifully said, "Is Jack Cash having a bad day? We have come to make your day happy. Give me a minute to look through the thousands of wallets, walkers, raccoons, scarves, combs, defibrillators, hairbrushes, whozats and whatzits galore in the back. Have you ever seen Indiana Jones running through the cave when the rock starts rolling towards him? Get that picture in your mind as I get ready to go to the back," belting out the tune to Raiders of the Lost Ark, she starts going to the back, and turns to Kim and me, "Aren't you coming? You can't find your wallet standing there." Kim and I look at each other, now apprehensive because the order of events has given way to the love child of Jack Sparrow and Cinderella, which is fitting for the surroundings. We both shrugged our shoulders and followed Cynthia to the back of the lost and found and out the back door.

Cynthia continued down a flight of steps and at the bottom, in hushed words, said, "I was trying to lighten the moment up there. I hope I didn't scare you any more than you are already scared. I am Cynthia" (she extends her hand to shake mine), I don't work here, but in a pinch, they can make a quick badge for a U.S. Marshal, we know a guy. Anyway, my job is to get you to a safe place. Were you followed into the park?"

"No, not as far as we could tell."

"We will go over details soon, but right now, we ask you to comply with our instructions. So, I have met Jack Cash, but I haven't met you (extending her hand to Kim). What is your name, and how do you know one another?"

"My name is Kim Crane. I came to Florida to spend time grieving. My husband died, and I came here to regroup. I was walking down the beach, and out of the blue, there was Jack Cash. I knew him in high school and remembered him after all these years. We have had several meals together, and today was a diversion day for both of us."

"Diversion day, what is that? Let's keep walking."

"A day not to talk about the heaviness grieving leaves with you."

"So, you came to Florida to meet up with Jack Cash or happened to see him as you walked on the beach?"

"Walking on the beach."

"Of all the beaches in all the world, what made you choose, what was the name of the beach again?"

"Vero Beach."

"What made you choose Vero Beach?"

"I don't know. It was the place a friend recommended to me."

"What friend?" Cynthia asked as she looked both ways in a crosswalk in the tunnel, unsure which way to go.

"I don't know, a friend back home mentioned Vero beach, and I went online looking at condos to rent and places to stay."

"Did you know Jack Cash would be there?"

"What?"

Cynthia stopped and intently looked at Kim, "Did you know Jack Cash would be there, at Vero Beach, where he always goes after a wife dies?"

"Umm, no, I didn't know for sure that Jack Cash would be there. Am I in trouble?" Kim wondered aloud.

"No, just trying to figure out what is going on, and we need to know everything going on right now. Veronica's case ended years ago, but why it resurfaced this week, why someone murdered Paddy Gypsy, and other details I can't share with you. Detectives that aren't detectives questioned Jack Cash, I think we need to know everything there is to know, and right now, I only have two people to ask about the past few days, and they are on the run from someone who wants to harm them. This way," Cynthia motions as we follow a pace that is becoming brisker, "besides, small talk is not my forte."

"Where are we going?" I asked as we started down another leg of a tunnel.

"We are going to a boat ride if I can remember the right place to go up."

Breathless, I asked, "Is there some secret tunnel or rendezvous there?"

"No, I just love to ride. Besides, I heard Johnny Depp loves to dress up and hide, and I want to see if I can spot him."

Now I was becoming frustrated, "We are running for our lives, and you want to take time to see if you can get a glimpse of Johnny Depp, or some robot that looks like Johnny?

"No, I am wasting time. We are putting things in place for your safety, and I have become your handler until I get the call. There are the stairs," Cynthia said as we began the climb up the stairs back onstage.

As we ascended the stairs, Phil called. "This is Jack Cash."

"Mr. Cash, Cynthia is still stuck in traffic and won't be able to meet with you for a bit longer. Stay at the Emporium." With that, my heart ended up in my feet. Who was the person leading us through the tunnels at the park? "Are you and Kim ok?"

As we approached the top of the stairs, I didn't know what to say. I didn't want to tip Cynthia off that I knew that she was not the Cynthia we were looking for and didn't know how to let Phil know.

"Are you and Kim ok?"

"Well, we are on our way with Cynthia to ride a boat." The silence on the other end of the phone was eternal.

"Did you say, 'Cynthia'?"

"Yes, they told us at the Emporium to go to lost and found to find Cynthia. She led us through the tunnels and climbed the stairs. We are here with her now."

"I will call you back," Phil said. I was about to panic for the fourth time today when Cynthia's phone started ringing.

"This is Cynthia, hey Phil, well, you called me a long time ago, and I was able to get off of the interstate and arrive faster than I thought. I called ahead and told them to come to lost and found, which was closer to the tunnel entrance anyway. We have some time, so chill, Phil. We are going to ride some rides until we can leave. Yes, you can talk to Jack Cash, here Jack Cash, Phil wants to be real with you."

"Mr. Cash, I am so sorry to have led you to believe that she is on her way. She is the right one. Effectively, she is your handler for the next few hours. Go along with her and let her buy everything."

With that, Kim and I rode with a handler that acted like Cinderella but engaged us like Jack Sparrow, and we all looked for Johnny Depp while on the ride. I put my arm around Kim and said, "Bet you didn't think we would end up with a babysitter today, did you?"

"There was absolutely nothing about today I thought would end up this way," and then she sighed sadly.

For an hour or so, we darted around the theme park with Cynthia, who somehow led to the front of every line with some credentials that she showed the workers. We also ate at the best places the park had to offer. There were times when Kim seemed to enjoy herself and other times when I couldn't tell if the events were bearing on her or just the grieving. Probably a lot of both, but I certainly would have felt better if it were only the latter. And Cynthia was a piece of work. At times, she questioned both of us about how we met, and then at other times, she acted like a kid at Disney for the first time, giddy and enjoying every single moment. It was a beginning to become a long day, and I finally said, "Cynthia, what are you working on for us, while we are walking around the park?"

"What do you mean?"

"While we are having a blast, I have to ask, what are you waiting on? Are you waiting for the clock to strike at 10 p.m. to see if I turn into a prince and Kim turns into a princess? You are our handler, but what are you handling?"

"Well, first, I have to take my phone off of silent mode," she said cheekily, "then, I have to see who all called while I was handling you and

Kim." She flipped the switch to take her phone off of silent. Then she looked at a long list of missed calls and voice mails. As she glanced at the phone, there was a noticeable shift in her demeanor. "Hey, Mr. Cash, why don't you and Kim go to the Haunted Mansion and ride it. I, I need to return a call."

As we walked away, we could tell something wasn't right, so we got outside Cynthia's view and watched her as she made her call. While we couldn't read her lips, her body language and facial expressions let us know the news she was receiving shook her to the core, and immediately her situational awareness became acute. She continued to look around while she talked, not for us but looked as if she were trying to determine who could jeopardize her assignment. She was noticeably upset the more protracted the call lasted, and after about 10 minutes of pacing, shouting, furrowing her brow, and moving her hands in destressed motions.

"What do you think is going on?" Kim asked, noticeably distressed for the hundredth time.

"I don't know but it looks bad."

CHAPTER TEN

All of this drama took me back to dating Veronica. The dating went well, with moments of drama, and a slow revelation of her past, dispensed over months as I gained greater trust with her. As our love grew, so did the understanding in my heart that Veronica's life hung in the balance of evil people and a government that gave a semblance of protection, but only those who cared about Veronica took the measures of her safety to the level that felt safe. There were junctures where I had to decide if I was willing to date or possibly marry someone with such a past.

I didn't consider how it would look to others. I didn't worry about it since I had lost two wives. I only thought about how much drama I would endure with a gypsy who should be in witness protection. So, as I watched Cynthia walk back and forth with the news she was receiving, I transformed into Veronica's husband again, watching another phone call filled with information, pacing indicating the severity of the conversation, exactly how it was with Veronica. It was always something from someone wanting to find her, someone wanting more information, someone checking in, it was always some...thing, a veritable Veronica hurricane, an all-consuming vortex.

By this time, Kim had slowly started massaging my shoulder, leaned forward and kissed my cheek, and whispered, "Let's go to the "Haunted

Mansion. At least we can be scared out of our minds in a make-believe world and we can come back to the Cynthia show in a minute."

I couldn't believe she was taking this in stride, completely nonplussed. We started toward the ride when Cynthia found us.

"Things have changed. A couple of events have happened in the last few hours, letting us know there is tremendous movement in the cartel. The family of the cartel members we put in jail have been rebuilding the network with one aim: to make those who put their family members in jail pay for it. That is why someone murdered Paddy. You talked to Phil earlier. He was driving this way to help get you two to a secure place when he was forced off of the road and rolled his car. He was able to make a call to our office after he crawled out of the wreckage.

The people who forced him off the road ran to him and started hitting and kicking him, demanding he tell them where you were. He refused to tell them, and then the line went dead. No one has heard from him since, and we don't know if he compromised this location. The safe house we were preparing for you has had a drive-by shooting. Someone sprayed several houses with bullets, so this may be random, but we can't trust that they don't have the information about every-thing after the events so far. There's also more I've learned. They killed Paddy the same way Veronica died: restrained with a lethal dose of heroin administered through a needle in his arm. We don't know if this was a copycat murder or if the person who did this was Veronica's murderer."

"If our location is compromised, what are we going to do?" I asked.

"We can't panic but have to map out a strategy to get you to a safe place. We can't use forms of communication we have used in the past. Do you have your cell phones with you?"

"Yes," Kim and I answered in unison.

"We have to get rid of them now. Someone could track you with the phone. I have to get rid of mine too. We don't know if Phil compromised us with tracking. We can't use our cars or go to the parking lots like before. I can't even call for a car to pick us up. Any connection to any of us right now is dangerous."

"Ok, I don't understand. Is this about revenge? I didn't put anyone in jail, and I certainly didn't know anyone. Veronica is dead, and they killed

Paddy, and they were the ones that had the information that shut down the cartel. I married her after all of that."

"It's not just about revenge," Cynthia answered, "they believe you have some documents that will reveal a lot of information, some about criminals and some about assets. The court cases devastated the cartel financially, and the feds seized their assets, but not all. Veronica knew the precise locations of everything, including assets."

"She must have kept a log, a diary, or something we never received for our investigation. It may have been a sort of an insurance policy for her she kept locked away. If she didn't have it, they certainly believed she did and are not stopping until they find it. It could mean tens of millions of dollars to their criminal enterprise, maybe more. That's why they are after you, Jack Cash. They believe you have this information."

"I don't have anything like that," then I felt a sense of panic, "will I spend the rest of my life on the run from people who think I possess some type of mystery documents?"

"Let's just get through the next few days before we worry about that," Cynthia suggested, "right now, that is the priority. Kim, how are you doing through this? You have been quiet."

"Well, I wanted a day to forget about my grief, and I guess I got what I wanted. I wanted to spend the day with the amazing Jack Cash, and I got what I wanted. I didn't count on car chases, missing persons, and murder."

"We need to go, but I need to think about our exit strategy," Cynthia noted as she pulled out a map of the park, "I think we need to head to a resort. We can go by boat, yes, let's go by boat to the nearest resort. We can get a ride to the airport and then get a rental car and then go to a safe house that is not compromised. I know a place completely off the grid."

With strides like a cheetah chasing its prey, Cynthia began walking towards the exit. Kim and I just stood there and watched her walk away, disappearing into the crowd.

"Do you want to go with her?" Kim asked me. As I stood trying to form the words to convey the reality of Paddy's murder had just now sunk in, tears started down my cheeks, then overwhelming grief, like the waves of the ocean from an off-shore storm, swept me into the wash. I knew better than to talk now because at the theme park, the only blubbering, weeping people are toddlers too tired to continue their theme park adventure and need a nap.

I just lost Marie, my last wife, mere weeks before, after losing six others, and then, the one that warned me about a plot to find me has been murdered by the same people. The last thing I wanted to do was to do anything. I just wanted to stand and cry. I wanted to punch a wall. I wanted to scream at the top of my lungs. I tried to run away from the grief, but it was not happening.

Not today, not ever. It was my reality, and now I had to decide if that reality would debilitate me to the point of capture, giving in to my fate, or if somehow, Kim or Cynthia would just kick me in the pants to get me moving. Kim was stuck too, not grieving over Paddy, the one she didn't know, but suffering over the moment that caught us unaware.

"I think we should find the gazelle by the name of Cynthia and leave the park," Kim said, trying to do her best to kick me into action.

At about the time, Cynthia doubled back. She ranted about the dangers that lurked everywhere and that we had to leave. She was unaware that her elevated speech was beginning to concern other park goers. Most had stopped talking, gawking at this adult almost in tears spouting about dangers everywhere.

Knowing this outburst could alert park security, with a raised voice everyone near could hear, I said, "Cynthia, it's just a ride, the Haunted Mansion is just a ride! It's going to be ok! There are no ghosts out here, nothing to fear, it's just a ride."

Then I turned to some of the closest ones near me, "she gets a little dramatic in haunted houses." They laughed, and by this time, Cynthia realized what had just happened, "I know it's just a ride but it is so real, now, let's go." We then followed Mrs. Tiger on the hunt as she chased after the prey called "the exit."

Bobbing and weaving through the crowd, trying to keep up with one another and not lose sight of the goal felt a lot like my life with Veronica. She was the life of the party, and on more than one occasion, caused us to have to hurry to some event because she had lingered too long somewhere else.

On our honeymoon, one day we took an excursion offshore. Time was drawing near for us to be back on the boat, and our guide had listened to

Veronica one time too many to stop and let us browse in a small popup shop on the way to the ship. He did, but the ensuing moments created chaos for everyone but Veronica.

Every entrepreneur on the island converged on our small spot when we stopped. They desired to sell purses, trinkets, fruit, souvenirs, t-shirts, you name it. And each of them had rock-bottom prices made by the feeble poor older women of the island, who had twelve kids to feed. Most items had tags that said, "Made in China," but they insisted these were local items. I know this because that is what caused a stir with the sellers and Veronica. She was poised to purchase, but only if it were truly locally sourced items. The chaos was something the tour guide did not want, making us severely late for the departure. He finally said, "If you stay longer, the boat will sail without you. We must go, NOW!"

Pulling Veronica away from the shop wasn't easy; neither was trying to navigate the crowd to get to the ship. The tour guide had left us, and though it was not far to the boat, we had to bob and weave through the eager sellers of wares of the island to get to the ship. Veronica didn't mind it at all. When we got near the boat, some problems caused the ship to spend a little longer in port. This delay allowed us to catch our breath and Veronica a moment to buy something one of the young men who followed us somehow knew she would eventually give in and buy it. She bought it, and like a prize won after much work, declared she had found the best souvenir of the island. Those around were also eager to score a good find, and that the young man could smell a sale from a mile away had found the motherlode of eager purchasers.

Veronica knew souvenirs, as she was in the business, but any loud and wearable type was just to her liking. It didn't matter if someone created it on the island or not because for Veronica, a loud and wearable necklace made her extremely happy. It didn't take much to make her happy. I think she created "happy" out of the junk of life. She knew junk, and she could take it and make it so much better.

Our marriage wasn't long, and we were about as compatible as peanut butter and olives, but she made it happy. She was the 'fly by the seat of your pants experience life' kind of person, and I was a planner and hater of chaos. Drama was good for me on television and in movies, but not in real life. Veronica thrived on it, and if there were no drama, she would create it, and I always thought she would try to turn the drama into happiness somewhere along the way. Paddy was a toned-down version of it, and his death combined with remembering Veronica was becoming more than I could explain.

I was at a board meeting when Paddy called to tell me Veronica died of a heroin overdose. He found her with a needle in her arm. The autopsy discovered there was so much heroin in her body that she could not have injected so much at one time. They restrained her, perhaps while they tortured her.

We finally meandered our way through the crowd to find the exit. At this time of day, there are many more people coming into the park than leaving, making an exit and the ability to scan the people easier for Cynthia. She could profile people in a minute, reading many people as she is also attempting to find a safe place. We found the boat to the resort and boarded. Everywhere we went that offered any resistance, Cynthia flashed her US Marshal badge and said that she was on official business, and we could go. It seems as if Cynthia had been here before and knew people, which created an urgency in my mind, "Cynthia, how do so many people know you?"

"Well, I have helped other people that were in protective custody and those with kids loved theme park day. Some had kids, so to make it safe, I surveilled people, got to know them, flashed them my winning smile, and have pretty much been able to do what I wanted. Plus, I have a couple of perks that enable me to bypass lines, get access, and do other stuff others can't do. My line of work requires me to do this, and besides, having a US Marshal badge doesn't hurt either."

That cleared stuff up nicely and made a lot of sense because, after Veronica's death, the lead investigator was Monica Simmons, and she loved to flash her badge too. It opened the door when other doors were closed.

Monica worked for the FBI and spent a lot of time investigating Veronica's death. Since several federal agencies were involved in the cases successfully prosecuting many in the drug cartel that Veronica had implicated, her death was a priority for the feds.

Everyone was a suspect, and my marriage to Veronica had been watched closely by Monica. Unbeknownst to me, Monica had taken a keen interest in surveilling us as we dated, married, and up until to about a month before Veronica was murdered. She was taken off work for two months while completing additional training and a short-term assignment. She didn't blame her superiors for Veronica's murder, nor the person tasked with following us, but on several occasions apologized for her death, thinking that she could have prevented it if she had not had to do the additional training and work. It always felt very convenient for someone so entrenched in our lives to "need" to train and take another assignment at the time when we needed her most. That kind of thinking was conspiracy-minded, something I never could afford to do.

CHAPTER ELEVEN

The boat landed, and we disembarked at the resort. Cynthia made her way to the concierge desk to enquire about the next trip to the airport. He noted that the van runs every 15 minutes to the airport and the next one would arrive soon. Cynthia then approached registration, spoke to them quietly, flashed her identification, and waited for a manager. Once the manager came, again, she talked to her. The manager made a call, and off we went to a lounge for a meal. We were ushered to an out of eyesight table and offered a drink and food menu. "Order what you want. The government is paying," she insisted, "do you or Kim like wine or anything off of the alcoholic beverage menu?"

"No," we both said in unison. "We don't drink."

Cynthia look bewildered, "why not?"

"My grandfather was an alcoholic and growing up, I rarely knew him sober. He ended up in and out of jail, drinking and driving and pretty much spending all of his money on drinking. I don't drink because of what I saw, plus, I just don't need to drink. I have found other ways to feel good, have a good time, and even enjoy life. It's my conviction, and my choice."

Cinthia shrugged and said, "Well, in light of our need to stay agile and alert, I won't either, but if you change your mind, you can also order something off that menu. The waitress brought us menu's from the other restaurants to order pretty much anything offered in the resort. I don't know what Cynthia told the manager, but they pulled out everything to offer us dinner. Kim and I both ordered. Our excursion on the run felt like a date, with a babysitter in tow, but a date nonetheless. Cynthia must have gotten the vibe because she excused herself to freshen up in the restroom and left us. I took Kim by the hands and kissed them. "I am sorry a former wife has hijacked our diversion day and that we couldn't just enjoy our time together, just the two of us. Can we plan on something that would not include a babysitter next time?"

"I would like that," Kim answered, "I would like that very much. Do you think we will be able to shake the babysitter, though, because she is pretty intense?"

"I don't know. Kim, changing the subject, I have remembered things about Veronica in the past few hours, small things that have triggered memories. It has added to my grief and is helping me understand why these things are happening to us. I never dreamed we would be going through these things right now, and it makes me wonder if there is something Veronica shared with me that I missed, something that has caused people to hunt and kill Paddy and come for us. Although I don't think they are after you, they are after me. You know, I just thought about it. They are after me. Why don't you go back home and forget about all this? Whoever may be coming to me will not treat you as anything but collateral damage, or even someone they can use to harm me further or extract information from me. I think for your safety, it would be good for you to get on a bus to the airport, get a rental car and go home. Maybe, even leave your stuff at your condo and let me ship it to you. I don't want you to get hurt."

By this time, Cynthia had made it back to the table. "Well, Jack Cash, you didn't propose while I was gone, did you?"

"Propose," incredulously I responded, "we are running for our lives, and you think I am thinking marriage right now. I am thinking of living right now, and 's why I just told Kim it would be good for her to make a run without me. She could be in danger by being with me, not by anything she has ever done."

"Not a good idea, Jack Cash. Kim has become a part of your drama.

The people who sent a fake detective have already noted Kim is involved. Regardless of what they think or are doing to find you, Kim is a part of it now."

A question hit my mind at that point was, 'How did Cynthia know we told the fake detective Kim's name?' I didn't say anything out loud because I was already following conspiracy threads in my mind and didn't want to entertain them openly. I might have already mentioned it to her. I couldn't be sure unless I plainly said it. Right then, I didn't want to open a can of worms or help Kim start that line of thinking.

"I am not leaving Jack Cash. Even if no one knew I was with you, you can't get rid of me easily. I am staying unless you run me off, and you are not running me off, are you?"

I smiled, "No, but don't blame me if we are running down some long corridor with a giant rock rolling our way and a whole tribe of voodoo doctors throwing spears at us."

We settled on Kim's continued journey about the time our food arrived. From that moment, we decided on the original plan of riding the bus to the airport and securing a rental car since we didn't know how vast the network had developed for the cartel. Cynthia mentioned a tiny decision could impact all other choices. That was something Monica often said, along with "decisions, no matter how small, determine destiny."

That thought stream would have to stop for now because of pressing matters of eating, then fleeing to a safer place.

CHAPTER TWELVE

The meal included a lot of small talk until a buzzing sound from Kim's backpack broke the moment. Suddenly Cynthia flew into a frenzy. It had just dawned on her that Kim had her cell phone, and so did I. "What are you people thinking? Someone could track your phones; we have to go right now; you have compromised our position." We had finished about half of our meal and had settled into a peaceful moment, which now was no longer comfortable. Kim started crying, the "I am overwhelmed and can't take much more" kind of cry. I leaned over and put my arm around her. She melted into my arms, sobbing uncontrollably. "Get her calmed down," Cynthia ordered, "we can't draw attention to ourselves any more than we already have. I will find the waiter and pay for our meal. When our ride arrives, we have to go."

I held Kim as tight as I could as she continued to weep. It was almost like the initial meeting at the beach where parts of my body began to feel numb, and standing in one place was taking its toll on my arms, but fortunately, it was while we were seated. I whispered in her ear, "it's going to be ok, and if everything goes downhill from here, I can't think of anyone I would want to go downhill with than you."

"Well," Kim said through sobs, "at least you are not clicking like a cricket to console me like you did earlier. Look, I am having a hard time, and I know you are trying to help me, but nothing you can say or do will change how I feel. You are a wonderful man, Jack Cash, and I like you a lot, but nothing is going to work right now.

Cynthia returned and said, "Wow, I am gone for a few minutes, and Jack Cash has started making moves right here in the restaurant. We must get rid of your phones. Have you backed them up lately?"

"I don't know," Kim replied.

"I think mine automatically backs up," I shared. We both fumbled around with our phones until we figured out whether they were backed up, how to back them up, and did. Once completed, Cynthia asked for our phones and walked to the boat that brought us over from the park. She went to the captain and said that the people who owned the phones would retrieve them from the boat station on the other side. He took them and any means to contact local law enforcement, family, or friends. We had to rely on Cynthia to maintain contact with others, giving her higher trust than at any other time.

"How often will you hear from your people at the US Marshal's office about this situation?" I pressed Cynthia.

"Well, we have gone dark. No one will contact us until we have found shelter. I will not take phone calls until we have arrived at a safe place. We have to assume the office is compromised until we know for sure. One small mistake can cost us our lives."

It was then I felt most vulnerable and felt like someone was replaying the drama of Veronica and her death in my heart. It also opened up the case in my memories. Following Veronica's death, Monica made her case personal and became the lead investigator. Monica was beautiful, with long flowing blond hair, always dressed smartly in a dark blue government pantsuit, turning heads while taking names. Her first call was to gain more insight into who Veronica was and to try to determine who may have murdered her.

I never felt I was a suspect but knew that everyone is a suspect in the eyes of law enforcement. Our first meeting was over coffee, and honestly, one look into her turquoise eyes was like looking at the waters of the Caribbean for the first time, as blue-green as you could ever want, warm but ready to freeze you in your tracks in a moment.

I quickly learned she had a belief somewhat like the butterfly effect.

The butterfly effect is when a butterfly flaps its wings in Argentina, and through cause and effect, a hurricane is born in the horn of Africa.

It wasn't as dramatic, but once, she told about a woman running late for an appointment who missed her exit. She took the next exit, intending to backtrack when a detour took her to a very rough part of town. She was pulled from her car in a carjacking and murdered. That course of events started because her cat vomited on the blouse that she planned to wear to her appointment. The delay and the ensuing frustration changed the course of her day, with the end as the worst possible outcome. When she told me the story, she asked me, "Was it the cat's fault she died?"

I said, "No the cat did what cats sometimes do, but the cat was not the one who murdered the woman." "True," she replied, "but you can see the course of events can change everything, and that one decision can alter the trajectory of a life." She told me those kinds of stories often, where a criminal makes one life choice, and it alters their destiny, for good or bad. Sometimes the choices are enormous life choices, and sometimes they are minor and seemingly inconsequential. In the end, they were the pivot points for destiny. Kim and I were at such a pivot point.

Cynthia's phone rang with our ride, noting where we were to go for the pick-up. We were now without phones, going with someone we did not know, someone who was not with US Marshal's office, which meant we had no idea what or who was looking for us. At that moment, something came over me, a deep feeling of apprehension and foreboding. Kim must have felt the same thing because when Cynthia took the call for the location of the pickup, Kim leaned in and whispered in my ear, "I don't like this at all; something's not right." Her reluctance and my apprehension went on a date, and they were about to make out.

I looked at Kim and whispered, "What do you want to do? We have no phone, senorita is having an untrained cousin pick us up, and she has no idea what is going on with Paddy's investigation. For all we know, she could be with the cartel."

"That's what I am afraid of; let's test her and see if she is interested in knowing information about Veronica."

"Remember, she is a trained interrogator. She will smell this a mile away, we will have to see if she takes the bait, but she may be interested in it because it is a part of the overall case. Besides, I don't know anything."

In hushed tones, we continued arguing the point to one another when Cynthia looked over at us and said, "Are you guys ok? What are you arguing about?"

"Nothing, we just are talking about wedding dates," Kim replied. I tried to hide my complete surprise, wondering if Kim had that in mind or it was something to throw Cynthia off. Regardless, now my mind was racing, and for a minute, Cynthia seemed to want to press for answers to the question, but her brother/cousin started talking in a way that Cynthia had to calm him down. She took a few more steps away from us, with her back to us, and spoke to him so quietly we couldn't make out what she was saying at all. But it was perfect so we could continue our discussion.

"Wedding dates?" I asked Kim.

"Slow your roll Jack Cash. It was to get her off our scent."

"But that was the first thing out of your mouth to throw her off?"

"Yes, and it worked, so don't worry about it. We can talk wedding budget later," Kim said as she nervously laughed.

Since I have had seven weddings, I wasn't sure I wanted an eighth, especially in these circumstances, so I was a little taken aback by the line of thinking.

"Jack Cash, I think we need to get away from Cynthia. I think she is up to something."

I took Kim in my arms and whispered in her ear, "I am going to whisper in your ear, and you can giggle twice if you are answering no, laugh if you are answering yes. People are uncomfortable with displays of affection. We can use it to carry on our conversation, and she will get further away from us. Are you ok with this?"

Kim laughed. Cynthia looked at us as she continued her phone call and took a couple of steps further away. "It's working. That's amazing, Jack Cash; where did you learn that?"

"Monica. She was an expert in interrogation and told me things about human nature that helped me pastor people better, and understand why people do people things. Anyway, she once told me people were uncomfortable with displays of affection, so to throw people off, get affectionate. They will want to give you a private moment. We used it a few times to get people to step away from us. It worked well after church when someone wanted to hijack my Sunday afternoon with some craziness. Monica would come up to me and hold me real tight. If it were truly an emergency, I would kiss her cheek, and she would turn and engage them in conversation. She was fantastic at it."

"Monica? Who is Monica?"

"Monica was my fourth wife, after Veronica. She worked for the FBI and worked Veronica's case."

"I am sorry, I forget you have been married seven times, now what should we do?"

"I am going to plant some seed, and I need for you to water the seed. In other words, I will mention the notebooks at my condo that had Romani in them. Romani is the language that gypsies use, something Veronica used from time to time. So, I will casually mention the notebooks the FBI has investigated. I need for you to ask questions until Cynthia gets wind of our conversation to see if she takes the bait."

"Ok, I am ready."

By this time, Cynthia hung up the phone with her cousin, who we finally determined was named 'Brian.' "Where are we meeting Brian?" I asked.

"He is going to call back in a while. We might need to relax for a bit. Do you drink? I think I need a drink?"

"No," I said, shaking my head along with Kim, "we said it before, neither of us drink."

"Well, too bad for you, I need something to take the edge off," and with that, Cynthia headed to the bar and immediately ordered her mixed drink from the bartender. She motioned for us to sit at a nearby table, and we sat down, waiting for the bartender to create her drink. It was the perfect time for Kim and me to decide our next move, and it didn't take long for the alcohol to loosen Cynthia's inhibitions and information. At first, she was reluctant, but it was clear Cynthia had motives other than our protection and that Brian was possibly more than just a cousin. While we couldn't know for sure, we felt uneasy enough to wait for a moment to talk more. Brian gave us that with a phone call. Cynthia didn't want us to hear what was said, so she excused herself from us to talk to him privately. When she walked away, Kim said, "I am going to see where she is, and if possible, listen, besides, I need a restroom break."

One of the waiters noted they had drinks that were non-alcoholic and thatI looked thirsty. I ordered us a sweet-iced tea and lemonade mix, while Kim went on her mission. After about five minutes, Kim ran to the table, "We've got to go, this is not what we think it is," but suddenly Cynthia came within view, still talking to Brian, so Kim sat down, trying to hide her anxious breathing. I knew something was wrong, but I couldn't find out what Kim knew with Cynthia coming to the table.

Cynthia was finishing her discussion with Brian, but she thought she was quiet. It was clear that the alcohol kept her from judging her loud-ness, so we overheard her say, "just hurry, we can't wait much longer, they are getting antsy, just hurry." She hung up her phone as she neared the table, and just as quickly as she ended her call, her phone rang again. I could almost make out the name on caller ID: "Deputy U.S. Marshal" or something similar. She immediately sent the call to voicemail.

"Is that your office calling?" I asked, hoping she would be aware of our interest in others as part of this process. "No, probably spam, or something like it," She answered. After she sat down, her phone sounded, indicating a message. She looked at it, and again, I could see what looked like a voice mail from "Deputy U.S. Marshal."

"Sounds like spam left you a voicemail, do you want to check it?" I offered, thinking it could be more information or that we were no longer alone.

"No, no need, it's just spam," and then her phone rang again with the same caller ID. "Just leave me alone," she yelled at her phone, "I don't want to talk to you."

About as quick, Cynthia's phone rang with "Phil Townsend" on caller ID. Cynthia quickly sent the call to voicemail. "Was that from "Phil Townsend?" I enquired. By this time, I suspected that Cynthia was not telling us the truth about anything at all.

"What? No.!!! Phil Townsend was in an accident, and we have lost contact with him," she said as she put her phone in her pocket. Just as soon as she did, her phone sounded again with a voice mail, but she refused to look to see who called her.

Sometimes when fear is at its height, people feel the need to "fight or flee," and now, these two were mixing inside of me with the strong desire to run. Cynthia's actions were adding up to many things that didn't add up, but I couldn't run now or else it would tip her off to my angst. Besides, something upset Kim, but the last few moments did not allow any collaboration.

Cynthia's phone rang again, and she pulled it out of her pocket far enough to see it was Brian. "I've got to take this," she said as she walked away from the table.

"She's going to the restroom to talk to Brian. She has lied about a lot of stuff. We've got to go," Kim said as she took my hand and started for the door. We can't wait." Almost pulling me to the door, she quickly noted, "Brian is working on a place to interrogate you, they want the information you have about Veronica, and for some reason, they believe you know things. Our lives are in more danger with Cynthia than without her," Kim said.

"Wait, Kim, let's think about this. We can't go to the car to leave; we've got to come up with a plan to throw Cynthia off."

Kim quickly thought about it, "I've got an idea. Go inside and ask the host where to catch the bus to the airport. When he tells you, come out quickly, and head to the bus. We won't get on it but will hide and watch for Cynthia."

I asked the host where to catch the bus to the airport. He motioned the direction near the entrance to the resort. I thanked him, gave him a tip, and left. Kim and I ran to the front of the resort. As we neared the entrance, a bus was just leaving. We quickly hid near it so we could monitor Cynthia. About ten minutes later, she came running out of the doors near the host stand. The host must have told her we were on the bus because she ran where the buses load for the airport. As she arrived at the bus stop, another bus pulled up, and she jumped on. We could tell she was very animated as she inquired likely whether we had departed on the last bus. The driver tried to radio the other driver, but he didn't respond quickly enough. She made a call, clearly anxious and frustrated. While talking on the phone, she turned and asked the driver something. About that time, a vintage Trans Am pulled up, and Cynthia ran to it screaming, "The bus driver thinks they may be on a bus on its way to the airport."

"The airport?" the driver replied, "Why the airport? Do you think they made you?"

"What do you think?" She said sarcastically as she jumped in the car. "Let's see if we can catch them, and I will try to talk them down," and then the driver of the Trans Am punched the gas, and the tires squealed as they left to find the bus.

"We need to ride the boat back to the theme park and get our phones if Cynthia sent them there," I said, "or at least get our cell phones from wherever they were sent. We need to contact someone that can help us. Let's see if the resort can call lost and found to see if they have our cell phones."

We went to the desk, and they informed us that our phones were at the entrance to the park. So, we boarded the boat and set out for the park. As the boat began pulling away, Kim pulled me down low, "Cynthia is near the boat ramp." Sure enough, she and a man were talking to someone near the boat departure ramp. He motioned towards our boat. We got as low as we could but peered over the edge to try to see what they were doing.

"Are you hiding from someone?" one of the crewmen asked. "Yes, friends. We told them we were going to the pool, but we wanted to go ride the rides," Kim said.

"What is the fastest they can make it to the theme park from there, through any means?"

"Oh, probably 10-15 minutes, depending on what someone uses for transportation. But, you can walk from the resort to the park. It's about a mile, so it will take them as long as it takes to walk or run."

We looked, and Cynthia and Brian were running to the park. It looked like they might make it to the landing about the same time as our boat, so we thought Cynthia would catch us. The crewman must have been aware of who we were watching and said, "You know, sometimes we need to duck out of being with someone and it looks like you need help. Why don't you stay on the boat? And I will get off the boat and ask them if they want to ride back over. I will make you honorary crew, telling them only the crew is on the boat. So, you are now, honorary crew! For, oh, ten minutes, and I hope you are not a fugitive from justice. You are not, are you?"

"No," I assured our new captain, "they want us to go other places with them, and we just want to enjoy this happy place."

"I understand. Consider it done. I'll be right back after tying up the boat while others disembark."

Kim and I stayed out of the line of sight for Cynthia. Someone left a hat behind, and Kim grabbed it and put it on, told me to turn around, and took her top off, turned it inside out, and put it back on, changing the color of her top. Then she turned be back to her. With the hat and the change of her blouse color, all of a sudden, she was someone else. She told me to keep Cynthia in the line of sight behind her head. We heard the captain ask if Cynthia and Brian wanted to ride the boat back. "No," she replied, "we are looking for someone. Is everyone off of the boat?"

"Yes, only the crew is left."

"Did you see a blond woman and brown-headed man ride the boat, they are friends, and we need to find them."

"Yes, I saw a blond woman and brown-headed man ride the boat, All, day, long," he said, laughing. "Ma'am we get blond women and brown-headed men all day. We get tens of thousands of guests each day. They all become a blur after a while, so if you want to find someone, I guess you need to go look for them. I wish I could help you more."

"That's ok, we will go looking for them," she told the captain, then looking at Brian said, "let's find out if they got their phones. If they did, we would know they came over and are in the park. If not, I have no idea." She looked at the captain and said, "Could you tell me where I could find phones that were sent over on the boat earlier today?"

"Try lost and found at the gate. That's where everything ends up."

"I know where that is," Cynthia told Brian as they started walking toward the park entrance.

"We don't need our phones now," Kim whispered to me, "we just need to go." The boat started loading with passengers ready to head back to a resort. The captain asked us, "Do you want to go into the park or go back to the resort?" I looked at Kim and said, "Back to the resort?" as she nodded her head yes. On the trip back, we both kept an eye poised toward the distant park, scanning for any hint of Cynthia or Brian.

"You guys know that there are multiple ways for people to get from the park to the resort, right? There is the boat for which you are now traveling. There is a walking path for which you have already familiarized yourself. There is a bus that stops at the bus stop. Finally, there is the one and only, most exciting way of all, the monorail. All of these are potential places where one might find the way back to the resort." Suddenly the words of our captain ramped up our urgency.

"Thanks so much. You have increased our anxiety times four," Kim told him, then looking at me whispered, "We have got to find a way out of here."

"What about your sister and brother-in-law?

"They are home, not even close."

"What about one of your in-laws. You should have about seven sets of mother/fathers-in-law, and siblings, probably numbering in the hundreds!"

"Not fair, there are not hundreds," I said, correcting Kim, not sure if this was a dig or simply the truth I had come to know.

"What about Monica's family? She was in law enforcement; maybe someone also followed that path. What about her brother? Where is he?"

Suddenly this question took a turn in my heart. "How did you know about Monica's brother?"

"I mean, she did have a brother, right, um, did she have a brother?" With every response, she grew increasingly nervous. It was evident Kim knew Monica had a brother and divulged a piece of information very few knew.

Monica's brother was an undercover officer doing high-level drug interdiction. For the last eight years, he was undercover in some of the highest levels of cartel activity in the Miami and South American drug trade. Monica didn't talk about him much because his cover was so deep they only heard from him around Christmas time and on Monica's birthday. He always remembered his sister on her birthday. Any word about him would jeopardize the operation and his life. Other undercover officers simply disappeared, and no one ever heard from them again. They simply vanished without a trace. Monica knew the potential for her brother, and now his cover is blown if he is still alive. I had to think. It was clear Kim had information that came from somewhere. Now I didn't know who I could trust, but right now, I couldn't afford to let my guard down for anyone, including Kim.

"Monica's brother is no longer available," I said, diverting her attention away from my suspicion, "let's talk through a few things. What is the worst thing that can happen if we go back to the rental car?"

"They can track us and may even be waiting at the car."

"Ok," I continued, "what if we took the bus to the airport?"

"They might be on a bus or on their way to the airport."

"What if we took a taxi to another hotel, checked in, and waited it out?"

"That might work, but we will have to call a taxi, and we don't have a phone."

"Ok, let's get on the monorail and take it to another resort. We can find a restaurant, drink, determine what we need to do next, and maybe catch a bus to another place.

"Ok," Kim said, pulling the map of the park, "it looks like the monorail will take us to the next one...look here is the resort."

I looked at the map and took Kim by the hand, and said, "Let's hurry to the monorail. I think it is coming soon." We started running toward the monorail station. As we ran up the stairs, we were so excited to get on that we didn't see Cynthia and Brian getting off of the monorail at stoping point. As soon as we got on, Cynthia saw us, pointed at us, and started yelling to the workers. They tried to get back on, but the doors closed before they were able.

As we pulled away, they were screaming to stop, but the monorail continued. They ran down the stairs towards the next monorail stop and resort.

"They are running to the next stop. Let's go to the park and see if we can get our phones. If they are still there, we can retrieve them, call for a ride, and then find a store to buy a phone we can activate and ditch ours," I suggested to Kim.

"Why get our phones if we are going to ditch ours?" Kim asked.

"I have contacts in there that might help us, and I can retrieve them before we get rid of the phones. We won't have to retrieve the backed-up data, giving away our location."

"Didn't they say they were going looking at lost and found for the phones? They probably have already retrieved them. I am scared they will find us. I don't think they are going to take us to a safe house. I like your idea, but I am not sure what to do."

We stayed on the monorail to the park. Since we still had our wristbands, we could get through the gate, but deep down, I wondered if they could track us. Cynthia had some access that enabled us to get in, move to the front of the line for rides and pay for food.

When we were ready to proceed through the turnstile into the park, my wristband wouldn't work. Kim's didn't either. "She must have deactivated our bands. Now, what do we do?" Kim wondered.

I had planned on paying for tickets anyway, and then we could go inside. But when I went to purchase a ticket, my debit card was declined. So were my credit cards. I only had $200 in my wallet. I ran to Kim and told her I only had enough money for one of us to go inside. Kim stayed on watch to let me know if she saw Cynthia or Brian.

"You go," Kim insisted, "I will see if I can find a hiding place somewhere near here." She looked around and went behind a building, peering around the corner as I went to the ticket center.

"I need to check lost and found for my cell phone and my friend's cell phone. How much for a ticket to get inside just for that?"

"You don't need a ticket for lost and found. It is inside the ticket center," a distinctly Ariel look-a-like mentioned, "I can have someone lead you there, or just go to the far right, and you will see it."

"Thank you so much," turning to look for Kim. I couldn't see her at all. I had lost my overwatch, at least it seemed that way, and now I felt very vulnerable. I didn't know if Cynthia or Brian would show up at any moment, so I darted behind buildings, hiding, looking around, and attempting to monitor everyone. It was so hard since so many people were coming into the park. I walked behind a family when a seven or eight-year-old boy suddenly took me by the hand. He must have thought I was his dad, and grabbed my hand. I panicked. Any attention right now was unwelcome, but he started pulling me. "I am not your dad; where are we going, hey kid, let go of my hand!"

"Daddy, I need to show you something, I will show you!"

"Let me go, hey kid, where are your parents? Let me go…"

"Daddy, mommy says stop playing games and come with me; mommy is waiting in lost and found."

Suddenly it dawned on me, Kim, Cynthia, or Brian could be inside the lost and found, or this was some crazy kid prank. The boy kept pulling me toward lost and found, but I thought I needed to start pulling instead of being pulled so that it wouldn't make too much of a scene.

"Ok, son, let's go find mom," I said as I started to pull my 'son' briskly. We walked through the door, and I scanned the room as my eyes refocused from the bright sun.

"Are you Jack Cash?" a cast member from behind the counter asked, "because I have a cell phone that if you can unlock it, you can retrieve it? Kim has hers!"

"Where is Kim?" I asked the cast member as I unlocked my phone, "Can I take my phone?"

"Yes, it looks like it is your phone. Kim had to leave. She said she would be back in a few minutes. You are welcome to wait in here."

"She has her phone, right?"

"Yes, she was able to unlock it before it died. She took it anyway, even though I offered to charge it."

"Any idea where she went?"

"No, sir."

"Thank you for your help," I said as I started towards the door, "by the way, who was the kid?"

"I don't know about a kid," he replied, "Enjoy your day in the park."

"Thanks again," I said as I left lost and found.

CHAPTER THIRTEEN

Outside of lost and found, I had to adjust my eyes and scan for Kim because the sun was so bright. People were everywhere, and in the mix of people, I saw Cynthia and Brian. They were within 50 feet of me but were looking at the parking lot, pointing towards one of the lots, as if they saw someone.

I quickly darted behind the building, looking for some way out. I had no clue where Kim was, but knew I had to run. I looked toward the vacinity to see if I could determine what Cynthia was pointing toward, and I couldn't see anything. I wanted to see if maybe they saw Kim, so I tried to get to a higher place, but I had to know if I could see where Cynthia and Brian were pointing before doing anything, and I couldn't let them see me. Just as quickly as I turned, they disappeared.

I scanned everywhere and then looked up at the stairwell going to the monorail. Cynthia and Brian were using it to get a better view of the parking lot, but about the time I saw them, she looked my way and saw me. They were still a reasonable distance away, but the urge to flee over-whelmed me, so I ran towards the parking lot. The only thing I could think about was getting to the car. I hoped Kim would get her phone charged, and somehow she would call me, but now I had to focus on getting to the rental car. I ran through people and looked back a few times, and they were running through people as fast as they could.

I could hear them yelling, "Hey, Hey! Jack Cash! Stop!" I had hoped their voices were getting distant, but they were not, and I was running as fast as possible. Turning back one more time, I saw them closing in; And then I fell.

People started running towards me to see if I was ok, but I got up and ran. Blood was running down my leg, and I completely forgot where I had parked.

Someone yelled, "Jack Cash, over here." It was Kim. She was by the rental car, "Hurry; they are coming fast."

I pulled the keys out of my pocket and unlocked both doors. Kim got in the passenger seat as I ran to the car, jumped in, pushed the start button, and backed out of the space, just as Cynthia and Brian came to the back of the SUV. I took off as fast as I could, with both of them banging on the car.

"Hurry, Jack Cash, faster," Kim screamed.

"I am going as fast as I can," I screamed back, "keep watching for them." I was disoriented and ended up on a loop trying to get out of the parking lot and onto the freeway, "I need help, please get me out of here."

"Ok, go that way," Kim said, pointing to the exit sign to I-4.

We got on I-4, and I had no idea our direction. "Kim, we have got to get somewhere safe, but I only have $200, and we are running out of time. They might be tracking our car right now; my debit card and credit cards are blocked, we've got to get...."

At that point, I remembered Ilean Orr. Ilean and her husband Richard were instrumental in sharing Christ with Paddy and Veronica. I knew calling them would upset them, but they were who I thought of first. "Kim, I just thought of Ilean, remember me telling you about them?"

"Yes, she leans towards joy, how can I forget?"

"Well, she leans towards happy, but that's ok. They also own the condo where I am staying. Call Ilean's number on my phone; maybe they can help us.

The phone started ringing. When Ilean answered, her voice was shaky, as if either in pain or afraid, "Hello."

"Ilean, this is Jack Cash. I can't explain."

"We are busy right now, so I can't talk long," Ilean interrupted. "They have torn our house apart. Someone ransacked that nice pastor's condo, his name is Jack Cash. We don't know where he is, and people are looking for him."

"Ilean, are you ok?"

"They beat Richard up, and Paddy...Paddy," her sobbing became almost uncontrollable, "Paddy, is dead. Someone murdered him."

"Ilean, listen, this is Jack Cash, you've already told me about Paddy. I am so sorry about all of this. Are those people there now?"

"Yes!"

"What are they looking for?"

"I've got to go. They are still asking questions," and then Ilean hung up.

Kim heard every word of our conversation, "She doesn't sound happy. She sounds greatly distressed. Now I wonder if they went through my condo too."

"I don't think it is safe to go back there."

"I need to call my sister and brother-in-law; maybe they can help."

"Do that now; we have got to get rid of these phones, and this car. I will take the next exit, it has some type of store where we can buy two burner phones."

Kim dialed her sister's number, with the phone to her ear, "Hey, it is me!"

I couldn't hear her sister's part of the conversation and didn't have to, "Who called you?"

Then she began a series of questions, "What did theeeyyy want?"

"What are they looking for?"

"Did you tell them where we were going?"

"How did they get your number?"

Then Kim didn't say anything for a long time, then turning to me, she said, "We've got to get rid of these phones now."

"Look, Christy, we are on the run. I will have to call you on a different phone."

"Listening? How do you know they are listening?"

"Who froze your bank accounts?"

"I love you, I will try to get back to you later," and with that, Kim hung up.

"We've got to get new phones as soon as possible, and we can't wait much longer. They are going after everyone we know looking for us, looking for you, Jack Cash."

"We can buy a prepaid phone at most big superstores. Let's find one as soon as we can. Turn off my phone."

We continued to scan exits for a hint of a large shopping area and knew that someone probably tracked us. There was a sign for an exit with many restaurants and gas stations, including those tied to large superstores, so we took the exit. It took only a few seconds to see one, and we pulled into it quickly. Kim insisted on going inside, fearful something would happen outside and with no way to communicate with me, she would feel vulnerable. Besides, we still had the rental car that was likely being tracked too.

We walked briskly to the electronics counter and started looking for the cheapest phone we could find. We found one for $35 and an "unlimited data" sim card next to it for $10. It had unlimited minutes, so we thought it was about as good of a deal we could find. As we were paying, someone came on the loudspeaker and said, "Tim Sands, Line 9! Tim Sands, Line 9!" The person checking us out said, "well, you might want to find a comfortable place. There is a security threat outside the building, and no one can go outside or come in. Because of that, we have to round everyone up and shelter in place until authorities tell us it is safe. Folks, I need for you to go to the back, where it says, "Layaway and Restrooms" and wait there while I tell other customers."

I looked at Kim and whispered, "Either there is something else going on, or our position is compromised."

A manager walked by the clerk and told him to get everyone to the safe room as he quickly walked away. "What's going on? Has there been a robbery in the area? I called out to the manager.

"We don't know. The US Marshal's office called and said there was a fugitive in the area, and we had to lock down so the person didn't get into the building. You folks need to go to the safe room. We will meet in the layaway area. Go there now," he called as he briskly walked away.

"It's Cynthia; she must be tracking something. We've got to hide." We looked around for a possible hiding place, and the clothing area was the only place that looked as if it would work, especially the changing rooms.

As we headed there, another worker walked by us and said, "Folks, we need to go to the layaway area. There is a security threat outside the building, some type of fugitive from the feds. They tracked the person to a location near here."

"How do we know we will be safe in the safe room?" I called out with the employee, answering, "well, the fugitive is not in the store, and all of our security team is monitoring entrances and exits," as she walked away, saying, "go to layaway."

I knew we only had a short time to leave, but it seemed like every step we took had consequences.

In that moment, I was reminded of Monica's mantra of "decisions determine destiny." We just had to make the right decisions. As we made our way to the dressing room, my mind wandered to Monica again, not just her beauty and words of wisdom but her training and tracking ability.

When Veronica died, it impacted Monica profoundly. She was intent on finding Veronica's killer. When she requested a meeting, it was at her office. It was a sparsely decorated space, but a sign behind her desk offered her philosophy of life, "Decisions Determine Destiny." She asked me many questions, especially finding out that my previous two wives were murdered and my first wife was dead. I couldn't tell if she was interrogating me, ruling me out as a suspect, if she felt I was suspect number one, or truly wanted to find the killer, and I might offer something that may help in the search. She was thorough in her questions, and my time with her lasted hours. So much so, I was getting hungry and thirsty.

"Can I get something to eat and drink, I am hungry and thirsty."

"That sounds like a great idea. There is a Tex-Mex place near here, and we can go there and continue our discussion."

It dawned on me that my interrogation was turning into a date. I didn't know it until later on the initial meeting was also a date, just Monica's way to getting to know someone and part of her love language. As we sat down, it was apparent that Monica liked me and was trying to figure out a way to let me know. My grief was still very fresh. Even though I thought Monica was very nice, it was too soon.

As we were preparing to order, Monica spoke up, "Jack Cash, there are a few things about me you probably don't know. First, I don't drink alcohol at all. Second, I don't have sex with someone I am not married to, and finally, I don't like wasting my time with people that don't feel the way I feel. In other words, I don't mess around. I get to the point right away."

The deer in the headlight look on my face was probably my most prominent feature at the moment.

She continued, "I like you, Jack Cash. I want to find Veronica's killer, but I like you. I have read your story and, well, I like you! There are no more questions, I just wanted to meet you, and well, see if there was anything," she said as she took my hand, "you know...anything like with us."

"With us?"

"You know, if there is any interest, and I thought, well, here I am with Jack Cash, a pastor who lost his wife and I like him. I really like him."

"Monica, you are a lovely woman, but would it be possible to slow this up a bit. I just lost my wife, and falling for you will feel like a rebound more than true love. Let's just walk slowly through this."

Even though I told Monica to slow it down, as it turned out, I couldn't heed my own advice. I was scared, lonely and the need to know what happened to Veronica probably drove me into her arms more than anything. Not only did I fall in love with Monica, I learned a lot about the way criminals think and the way those trained in law enforcement think.

CHAPTER FOURTEEN

"When Cynthia arrives, she will first go to the group huddled in the safe room. That makes the task of finding one or two people easily. She will use the ruse to get everyone together and move on if those she is looking for are not in the group. Then, she will look at the security footage to see if she sees us," I told Kim, "so that will buy us some time to get out of the store and on our way, but we have to ditch our car and find other means of transportation."

We found the dressing room and looked around to see if we could see others. People were heading to the layaway area at the back of the store, so I was sure the employees were still sweeping the store for the final shoppers. Someone had locked the door, but I found a key near the register. We quickly but quietly closed and locked the door when we heard people walking by the dressing room. "Did you check the dressing room?" one asked the other, "Yes, and I locked the doors," she said as she tried each doorknob, "still locked."

"Good, this is the final sweep. The federal agent will be here any minute."

Our rush to find a hiding place paid off. Cynthia was due in the store at any time. Our only problem was knowing when, so we could make our escape. I looked at Kim and said, "So, how does it fit? You look very nice in your fugitive outfit." She almost laughed out loud, but then a few tears flowed down her face. "I am so sorry. I was trying to lighten the mood."

"It's just that we are in a tight spot right now. I am nervous and scared, and I have to go to the bathroom."

In all our running, I realized I needed a bathroom break too, but the events of the moment kept us from realizing relief.

Suddenly, I heard Cynthia's voice, "Brian, I am going to the back to see if Jack Cash and Kim are in the mix of people. Walk around the store to make sure no one leaves. We've got to find them as soon as possible. A lot of people are becoming a part of the investigation, and they will eventually tie me to it, and I can't have that."

"Ok, I will look."

I looked at Kim and shook my head as if to say, "There is no way we are getting out of here."

Just then, someone tried to open the door to the dressing room. "Is anyone in there?" Brian said, as he knocked on the door.

He went to the next one, "Is anyone in there?" knocking on it as the employee that secured it earlier walked by the dressing room.

"Can I help you? Everyone needs to go back to Layaway and wait for the federal agent."

"I am with the federal agent, Cynthia, she has made her way back there."

"Where is your identification?" the employee asked Brian.

"I don't have federal identification, but you can go back to check with Cynthia, and she will verify I am assisting her with apprehending this fugitive from justice. I must get into the dressing room to confirm it is empty."

"Let's go back to the back, hotrod, and verify who you are."

"I will go with you, but then I need the key to get in immediately," Brian said as his voice trailed off in the distance.

"I checked the dressing rooms and locked them so no one can get in," she said as they walked away, "you're wasting your time."

We couldn't hear anything else but didn't need to hear anything to know we had only one or two minutes to escape. Kim wrapped our cell phone purchase as tightly as she could so it wouldn't make noise as we left. I opened the door tentatively and peered out. The creaking of the opening door seemed like it sounded over the loudspeaker, calling attention to our exit. I finally got it opened enough to go out with Kim locking it back, hiding the key under the attendant station, then walked through the clothing area to the backside of the dressing room.

Now we had put the dressing room between us and the layaway area, hoping it would be enough to hide us for a minute.

We heard Brian and the employee returning, with a little bit of bickering between them. I couldn't make out what the fuss was about, but it didn't matter.

We had to leave right away. We went from clothing rack to clothing rack, hiding along the way. When we got near the front of the clothing racks, we couldn't see anyone, although we could hear two people near the exit, acting as security to keep people in and information sources to keep people out.

They talked to someone at the door who was agitated because they needed their prescription from the pharmacy. It was getting pretty tense, which bought us a pleasant diversion. The store had a pizza kiosk at the front, but no one was there. We went inside the booth, winding our way through the small area to the door used by incoming stock and employees. If we opened the door, an alarm would sound. I looked around for something that would keep our exit quiet, some type of credential or means to disable the door alarm but couldn't find one.

We heard someone talking on a phone while accessing the door mechanism. Kim quickly hid behind a rack of cans of tomato sauce. I hid behind the soda rack that contained all of the syrup for the soda machine. She opened the door and came in, still talking on the phone with what sounded like a boyfriend who wanted to spend the day with her, so it was a heated conversation, keeping her from paying attention to the slow closing door and our exit. After we slipped out of the store, we quickly ran to the rental car. We knew we had a limited time with it but had no other means of transportation at the time. We got in immediately and started to leave.

"I've still got to go the bathroom, and it is getting pretty critical."

"Let's find a convenience store, but not near the interstate," I suggested to Kim.

"Ok, hurry, I can't wait much longer."

I turned towards the central area of commerce and looked for a small convenience store that had parking in the rear. It took about five minutes, but I finally found one where I could pull around to the back of the station, and Kim jumped out of the car as quickly as I put it in park. She ran in, and I followed her. The store owner noted that we had to purchase something to access the restroom, which was easy since we were thirsty. I assured him we would buy something, and both went to the bathroom.

Kim finally came out of the restroom, and we grabbed a few snacks, purchased them, and left. Every penny we spent had to be intentional, so we tried to find the cheapest things and get the most out of our dwindling cash reserve.

When we entered our rental car, Kim started tearing open the burner phone package. She started transferring phone numbers from her cell phone into it and then took my phone and asked, "What numbers do we need right now?"

I thought and thought. I couldn't call Monica's brother, although I believe he would have dropped everything, including his deep cover, to help. Everything Monica told me about him let me know that the smallest thing could blow his deep cover, and that would jeopardize his life. The last thing I wanted was another body.

Besides, he loved his sister so much that her death was almost too much for him. Monica died during a trip to a training exercise at Quantico. She was a fantastic FBI agent, and her superiors knew it and looked for every opportunity for her career advancement. At the same time, Monica was an amazing pastor's wife. She could love people, lead people and help people and, at the same time, know what the real story was that they shielded from the pastor. We had a saying, "If they came in with a Sunday morning smile, Monica would see right through it, and like taking off a mask, help the person find freedom after becoming real. She could speak so directly into lives in ways I never could."

We had arguments every time she left, mainly because I felt I needed her to stay home. She was not only a great help at church. I loved her so much. I fell hard when I fell for her, and because I had lost my previous three wives, I struggled anytime she left. I tried not to suffocate her and worked hard on any anxiety I felt when she left. Unfortunately, it included simple trips to the grocery store or to meet a friend. As a pastor, I knew too many men who would not let their wives out of their sight, and I didn't want to be that guy who called his wife constantly when she left the house. Sometimes the insecurities and fear were overwhelming, so I started talking to a counselor to help me walk through the fears.

But on the day she died, all the counseling didn't help. Our arguments were not screaming matches, where one out screamed at the other. They were more like power plays for who would dominate the moment. After about ten minutes of watching her complete packing for her work trip, I started it.

"Monica, I am so excited you get to do this training, and it is a tremendous opportunity, but honestly, I struggle when you leave. I worry while you are gone, and every time it feels like I am losing someone all over again."

"We've been through this before, and if you are having a hard time, you need to call your counselor. I am not leaving you, I am going on a training exercise. We will not use live rounds. We will learn new tactics and interrogation techniques. I love you, and I am not going to be with someone else."

"Wait, what??? No, I am not jealous. My struggle has never been about jealousy or worrying about you being with someone else. I am worried you won't come home. That's what I always worry about."

"Well, you will have to deal with it. Look, I am sorry you have lost people you love, but I will be fine. I will be back in a few days. Until then, we will video chat in the evening. Besides, I will be back in a few days. I WILL BE BACK IN A FEW DAYS. Call your counselor today!!!"

Monica moved towards me and hugged me tighter than I could breathe and started kissing me with the deep kind of kisses that usually lead further than she had time for, "I don't want you to forget me, or not miss me much," she said as she pulled away.

"That's not fair, and you can't leave me this way," as I grabbed her hand, "You need to stay just a little longer."

"I am late now, the drive is long, and I will just have enough time to get there, get checked in to the hotel and training. Just don't forget the kiss. I love you, Jack Cash."

"I love you too. I am sorry I have issues," as I took Monica's suitcase to the car, "I will be alright."

We embraced and kissed one more time. "I love you," she whispered.

"I love you more."

Then, she got into the driver's seat, started the car, and blew me a kiss.

That was the last time I saw her alive. On her way to training, she stopped at a coffee shop to get coffee. Investigators knew she walked into the coffee shop, waited for her order, and left before sipping her coffee. She wasn't too far down the road before she started drinking it and then had a seizure. Her heart stopped, and she died as she merged onto the freeway. Fortunately, if there was anything good, they determined her coffee had been spiked with tetrahydrozoline, constricting her blood vessels. Its effects were immediate.

Being an FBI agent, the local FBI team was heavily involved in the investigation into her death. They combed through everything, including our bank records and texts between us. Because of my history of losing wives, they spent a lot of time questioning me, requesting me at several interrogations, and having other teams question me. They never said I was suspect number one, but I certainly expected I was at the top of the list. They also interviewed everyone at the coffee shop and pulled their purchase history from every rewards card with the information. They searched through our computers, web histories, and more. They never determined who killed her. I knew I had nothing to do with her death, but I was afraid they would charge me and call it a day because of their frustration. Eventually, they cleared me as a suspect but left her case open. Because she was an investigator in Veronica's death, they determined it may have had something to do with the case.

"What next, Jack Cash?" Kim broke through the memory, "We need to decide what to do next. We need a vehicle and need to get rid of this rental car."

A shudder came over me. It was one of those, you need to run kind of feelings, and I almost froze. It was a good thing I didn't. I looked at Kim and said, "We need to go."

"Where?"

"I don't know, but we can't wait to figure it out."

"What's going on?"

"I don't know, but suddenly I feel like we need to get out of the parking lot and go."

As we pulled out, Kim looked back and saw a police officer go through the front door of the convenience store. He had activated his flashing lights and was going inside. He didn't look our way, so we didn't know if the officer was at the convenience store for something unrelated to us but couldn't take any chances.

"Was he city or county?" I asked Kim.

"It was city."

"We need to get out of the city. Maybe find some backroads to travel until we can figure out what to do. I don't think we can afford to stay in one place long, though. I've got an idea. We are fugitives. I need to call my lawyer, Cass Stein."

Even though my lawyer was out of state, he might be able to help me know what to do. Kim found his number and put it in our newly acquired cell phone. "We need to get rid of our old cell phones," Kim noted, and called Mr. Stein on the new phone.

Mr. Stein answered the phone, which was highly unusual. His administrative assistant, Julie, was a gatekeeper of gatekeepers. She would not let anyone speak to Mr. Stein without a million questions, even when we had appointments and legal issues at their peak. She so furiously guarded his time that everyone called her the dober-dame, but Julie didn't answer this time.

"Hello, Mr. Stein, this is Jack Cash. I need help."

"Mr. Wardlow, this is not a good time. Julie is busy with some people, and I don't have time to talk. We need to go over your case, and I think we need to discuss some loose ends. Can you call back later, maybe sometime tomorrow?"

"You did hear me say, 'this is Jack Cash,' right?"

"Yes, that's right. I heard the other side has some interest in settling out of court. Look, I can't talk much more. We can talk tomorrow, yes?"

"Should I be concerned about someone at your office now?"

"Yes, I will talk to you tomorrow. Have a quiet evening Mr. Wardlow," and Mr. Stein hung up the phone.

Kim spoke up, "do you think he knew it was you?"

"Yes, I think he meant for us to lay low. Julie, his administrative assistant, always answers the phone. She guards his time like no one I have ever met, and he never answers the phone, so something is up. I think we need to find a way to get rid of our phones.

"Turn right, here on this highway. It looks like a road that leads to smaller towns."

As I turned, there was a small convenience store on the corner. I pulled in and parked on the side of the store. "Take our phones and put them in the back of that pickup truck, the one at the gas pump."

Kim got out and started towards the pickup truck when the owner of it exited the store. "Excuse me, my boyfriend and I are not from around here, and we are looking for backroads that will take us to nice places to see. Are there any out-of-the-way places down this highway worth seeing?"

"Yes, if you keep going down this road," he said, pointing down the road, "there is a great seafood place, just go to the end of this road to Duette, and turn right. Hold on, let me call my wife and get the name of the place."

When he reached for his phone, Kim put the cell phones in the back of the truck.

"Hey honey, what is the name of great seafood place past Duette?" There was a slight pause, "Because I want to tell a couple about, oh, I didn't realize they closed. I am on my way, I had to stop and get gas. Ok, stop yelling," he yelled at the phone, looking at Kim, and then abruptly hung up. "Well, sorry, the place is closed. If you turn right, it will take you to Bradenton. There are some nice places to eat there. I'm sorry, I am late for dinner, and my wife is mad."

"Thanks," Kim said as she started walking back to our car, "hope your wife is not too angry."

As he got into his truck, I noted that he left going north, and we were going south. His direction may buy us a little time as he took off with our old cell phones.

"He said that if we go south, turn right. It will take us to Bradenton. Maybe we can find a way to get rid of this rental there."

My mind was racing to think of something we could do in Bradenton on a limited budget and needing to ditch the rental for another vehicle, wondering what was going on with Mr. Stein. He represented me on so many legal issues, including working on each estate, as much as there was.

Mandy did not have an estate, although her dad told me I would have some type of inheritance. He was still living, so there was no estate for Mandy. Tamera had a small life insurance policy as a part of her benefits package. The school also provided insurance because of workplace violence, and we settled out of court for her pay for fifteen years. They paid her salary, or what it would have been if she were still alive, every other week. Veronica had a small life insurance policy, but it only covered her funeral expense. Monica had a $100,000 life insurance policy the government provided, plus an additional amount, but because of she was murdered, they did not pay it. Mr. Stein took care of everything. After Monica's death, I determined not to carry life insurance on a wife because the questions after each death were about as crazy as one could imagine, and not just from law enforcement. Select family members and friends felt comfortable sharing their belief that maybe I killed them for the insurance money. All of it meant absolutely nothing right now because every penny I had in any account was completely locked down, and from the sound of it, Mr. Stein was not in a position to help.

I looked at Kim, and she was falling asleep. It was getting late in the day, and many things happened to wear both of us completely out, but getting a hotel room was too expensive.

She woke up long enough to say, "I'm getting sleepy and hungry. Our little snack didn't last long. Where are we going to go to sleep tonight? We can't stay in the car because they will track us."

"We can't get a hotel because it would be too expensive for our limited cash." Then it dawned on me. I had points I could use for a night, "Hey, I just remembered I have points. We can use them for a room. I don't have enough for two rooms, but I think I have enough for one. We can get a suite. That way, we can sleep in two different rooms."

Kim thought that was the best solution until we could access our bank accounts, so she used our burner phone to look up rewards for the hotel chain where I had points and found a suite. "Do you think they have these flagged too?" she asked.

"I don't know, but I know we are both tired, and I am sure if Cynthia and Brian are looking for us, they are tired too. But we have got to get rid of the rental car. Let's find a big parking lot near the hotel that we can leave the car in and then walk to the hotel."

It took forty-five minutes to get to the hotel, and we noticed a large grocery store parking lot near it, one where we could monitor the rental car from a distance. We parked the car and went to the grocery store to buy food. Kim considered the security cameras and noted that we needed to keep the cameras in mind. After purchasing a few groceries, we walked entirely around the store, using hedges at the back to shield us from the store surveillance. We waited outside the door for a few minutes talking and then walked to two other hotels until we arrived at our hotel, hopefully becoming a misdirect for anyone using store cameras to determine our movements.

When I presented my driver's license to check-in, the hotel desk clerk spent a long time looking at my license and his screen, back and forth, and occasionally at me. I was becoming nervous that someone had flagged our reservation and our attempt to find a hotel using points was the very thing would be our demise. The back and forth went on for a while until I asked if there was a problem.

"No problem, I just have to ask, are you Jack Cash?"

"Yes, that's why my momma told me when I was born."

"The real Jack Cash, in the flesh?"

"The one and only, and why do you ask?

"You don't know me, but you were married to my cousin, my favorite cousin. I came to your wedding because you got married on the beach on the other side of the state. You married my cousin Cybil, or as I called her, Lucy Goosey."

I looked at Kim and said, "Well, I guess we cannot get away anywhere without some former wife coming up."

"Lucy Goosey?" Kim asked Jerry, the desk clerk.

"We called her Lucy Goosey because it was one of the personalities she would mimic. We all had different names for Cybil because, for almost every member of the family, she would have a different personality, a different voice, a different mannerism for that name."

Turning to me, Kim asked, "what name did you give her?"

"Cybil, mostly," I said sheepishly, "because she had a different personality for every mood, I just made up names for every personality she would use for the mood she was in."

"Did she have multiple personality disorder?" Kim asked both of us.

"No," we said in unison, then Jerry completed the answer, "she was a drama queen and used personalities to demonstrate her ability to assume an identity and play the part. It was hilarious most of the time, and then, if you weren't up for the game, it became quite annoying. Anyway, I went to your wedding with Cybil. It was epic. It broke our hearts when she died. I know it did yours too. I am sorry I never called or anything. I kept up with ya'll after the marriage from my mom, Lucy Goosey's Aunt Mary," holding out his hand to shake mine, "I am glad to help you today, though. Is this your wife?"

"No, this is my friend Kim. Jerry, we need a suite, and we don't have enough points to get two separate rooms. We are not sleeping together, so we need something with two separate beds."

"No judgment here, but I respect that, are you still a pastor?"

"Yes, I am. Just came to Florida, staying at a condo trying to get an idea of what is next for me."

"So, I have a suite with a bedroom and a separate living room. The problem is that it has a view of the grocery store parking lot. By the way, I changed the name on your reservation to Jack Goosey. I did that in honor of my cousin. If you need anything, be prepared for the desk clerk to ask for that name."

"Thank you so much, Jerry."

"Oh, Aunt Mary says hello, I have been texting her in between our conversations. She said you are on the run and should lay low until the heat wears off."

"Why did she say we were on the run?"

"I will text and ask her."

"Jerry, do we need to go to another hotel?"

"Hold on, she said someone named Cynthia called telling her that you are a fugitive from justice and if she heard from you, she needed to call Cynthia right away. Don't worry, mom is about as crazy as Lucy Goosey, so you are in good hands. She is not the "I love the government" kind of person, so your secret is safe with her."

Kim whispered, "Do you think they are monitoring her texts too?"

Jerry, overhearing the conversation, said, "Well, that's only a problem if they know who Lucy Goosey is because I told her Lucy Goosey's husband was here. Mom knows you were the only husband Lucy Goosey had, so if they know Cybil was known as Lucy Goosey by her cousin, which I doubt, you should be ok."

"I can't thank you enough, Jerry."

"Oh, and mom said she was going to order take-out for you. I told her that there was a steak house nearby. She said she would pay for it if I would go get it, so what would ya'll like?"

Kim turned away, crying. I only knew because of the sniff and jerk motions when trying to hold it all in.

"What do you want, Kim?"

"I don't know what they have."

Jerry pulled out a menu from a drawer and handed it to us. "We keep menus of local restaurants so people can do what you are doing now, decide on what they want."

"It's been a long time since we had anything to eat, and I am starving," Jerry interrupted Kim, "great; you need to order whatever you want. The secret about mom is that she has more money than people have sense, and she wouldn't be happy if you didn't order whatever you wanted.

Kim ordered the enormous Ribeye on the menu, with baked potato and a side salad. I ordered a Tbone steak, baked potato, and side salad and told Jerry we would drink water.

"Great, I will get this ordered. Ya'll go to your room. It is 521, the top floor, with a beautiful view of the parking lot."

We grabbed our bags of groceries and headed up to the room. It was undoubtedly one of the largest suites, with a small kitchenette with a small stove, refrigerator, and microwave. It even had a dishwasher and all the items needed to cook.

"I'm going to take a quick shower before our steaks come," Kim said, "I guess I will have to wear what I have on afterward." I couldn't tell if she wanted permission to wear something else, or nothing else, but that would not happen. It may have been a simple statement of fact because neither of us left this morning with an overnight stay in mind but going to a theme park for diversion therapy.

I sat on the sofa, thinking through our day. It was a blur, and it was now nine o'clock in the evening. We had a beautiful breakfast and then set out for a day but it went sideways quickly. It didn't even seem plausible all it happened today and then meeting Cybil's cousin. It was just surreal. As Kim went to shower, I thought about Cybil.

CHAPTER FIFTEEN

When I met Monica, we had a first date that was just a friend date, but by the third date, I knew we were officially dating because Monica introduced me to Cybil. Cybil was that friend who vetted all potential suitors for Monica. While Monica's line of work didn't always seem to be the line of work to find a forever love, there were a few men that caught Monica's attention long enough to meet the gauntlet of friend vetting that made Cybil famous. I know because when I met Cybil, she introduced herself as Vanessa Buttersnaps, the famous FBI interrogator who broke the most seasoned terrorists, causing them to "break down in bitter tears and school girl screams" (her words) the next time they met her. When I laughed at the introduction, she met my laughter with a bonafide full course menu of interrogation that made me wonder if waterboarding or bamboo shoots was next. She was outstanding and coached somewhere along the way by Monica, I was sure.

She was Monica's best friend. Most of our dates included a double date with Cybil and some new boyfriend. She never found someone who stayed longer than a few dates, maybe because she could launch into a new identity at any given moment, complete with a change of dialect, language, and mannerisms. It probably turned most guys off, thinking she was certified schizophrenic, but I guess after Monica's death, it was what I needed. Not that I needed crazy, but I needed someone who wasn't afraid to be themselves when I didn't know how to deal with another death. Even though she had various identities she assumed, Cybil always knew who she was and was comfortable being herself around me. I think it was a challenge for her to find new ones. Honestly, there were times after we were married it made loving her even more exciting.

"Has dinner arrived yet?" Kim called out from the bathroom.

"Not yet. Take your time."

"Finished," she said as she walked into the room, without makeup, hair wet, and heavy on beauty, it took me a moment to remember my calling, "Your turn."

I was all too happy to get a quick shower, so I jumped to my feet at said, "I will hurry; dinner should be here soon."

I turned on the shower, anticipating it's refreshing warmth. Once I stepped in and felt the warm water beating down my head, it was as if I was transported back to my wedding with Cybil. The ceremony was on the beach near my condo. Cybil loved the area and wanted a beach wedding. We had prepared for every eventuality, even the possible storm, but not the kind that blew up during the ceremony.

It was epic, just like Jerry described. The wind started blowing everything around, and I mean every chair that did not have a person in it took flight. The rain started, but fortunately, there was no lightning at the beginning because, amid the enormous drops of tropical rain, both warm and soothing, and the wind, terrifying and ominous, Cybil wanted to finish the ceremony. My pastor friend from Arkansas knew storms, at least of the tornado kind, and felt we were about to be caught up in a storm that would take us to Oz.

Regardless of his desire, Cybil told him to finish the ceremony in a British voice that made the fear in him dissipate into laughter. Then, she continued to press him to "lighten up like a yanky and finish the course, else the wenches from Tortuga shan't pay ye the booty." I promise that whoever was near Cybil amid the wind, rain, and pirate talk was hurting from laughing. He continued with the vows and repeating parts, and finally, after a few words of "I now pronounce you, husband and wife, Jack Cash, you may now kiss my lady from Tortuga." With the warm tropical rain, the kiss was long and filled with laughter and joy and all kinds of Cybil.

"Dinner is here, Jack Cash," as Kim knocked loudly, "Hurry up, it's getting cold."

"I am almost done!" it has been a while since I remembered that moment, and honestly, I was glad my shower hid my tears. Since I had barely used soap, I hurriedly finished lathering up and washed my hair as quickly as possible.

After I toweled off and dressed, I hurried into the room. Kim had set the table as if we were eating a romantic meal. When Jerry brought up the food, she asked for a candle, which was not allowed per hotel policy. Jerry found an LED candle that flickered and brought it up, leaving just in time as I entered the room.

"Whoa!!!! Steaks and candles too?" Now, the on-the-run moment seemed to be a beautiful, dangerous date. Too many possible scenarios could arise out of this moment, and after staying with me all day, there was no way I could complain about this or show disdain, but I was genuinely afraid that Kim was a freight train at full throttle and I was the car stuck on the track.

"Are you ok?" Kim wondered.

I guess it was more a deer in the headlight look than a car stuck on the train track. "Yes, just really tired."

"Me too," Kim responded, "but I couldn't pass up a chance to have candlelight dinner with the handsome Jack Cash, in a hotel room suite, on the run from the law and the cartel."

We both laughed, prayed, and started to eat. "This steak is amazing, and the candlelight, the flickering LED candlelight makes it all the better. Thank you, Kim!"

"For what?"

"For staying with me today. You stayed through the craziness, longer than I expected anyone would, and now, steak and a candle."

"Well, for one, the steak is because of your aunt Mary, or Cybil's aunt Mary, and the LED Candle, well, this was the best Jerry could do on short notice. Where would I have gone? The people looking for you have already visited Christy, so it sounds like they are running down every known person we have ever had any relationship with, trying to locate you. Besides, I have waited since eighth grade to be with you. I'll take what I can get!"

That one statement cleared up everything, including the reason Kim showed up in every class I ever had in school, or it seemed that way, and it created a troubling feeling inside of me.

We continued eating, with small talk about the steak and a little about the crazy day until Kim broke the mundane with a startling admission. "I've always wanted to be Jack Cash's wife."

"That's quite a change from the baked potato is overcooked."

"I know, but I wanted you to know that I have always dreamed about being with you. When I was in school, and you fell for Mandy, I was heartbroken. I thought, 'well, it won't last, but it did, at least until the wedding day. I tried to turn my desire for you away after you got married. I didn't realize she died on the wedding day because I didn't want to follow your life, your happy life, when I wanted to be happy in my life too. Anyway, I am so glad to be with you here today. Now I feel stupid. I shouldn't have said anything." Tears started streaming down Kim's cheeks. I stood up and walked around and put my arms around her, and held her.

"Thank you for sharing your heart with me. It wasn't what I was expecting. I mean, I was expecting for you to say, 'Jack Cash, you are an amazing fugitive,' or 'I can't wait to escape with you somewhere.' Or maybe saying, 'if they do a hard search for us, I will go with you to every gas station, residence, warehouse, farmhouse, henhouse, outhouse, and doghouse in Florida until we outrun the law.'"

Kim laughed through her tears.

"Kim, I think you are swell."

"Jack Cash, I think you are swell too."

Then, I held her in my arms while she sat in her chair, and I leaned over her. I held her until my legs, back, and arms started tingling as if they were on fire from the awkward position. Then, I kissed her on her cheek. I knew she wanted me to say something to her in return, which would validate my feelings were the same, but I couldn't commit to anything, especially right now. We were both too vulnerable. We were both grieving, excited because of the events of the day, and trying to make sense of life itself, plus we were in a hotel room and all of the temptations that could come with it.

I walked over to the window overlooking the parking lot. Behind the car, a police cruiser had pulled up, with lights flashing. Within seconds, another cruiser pulled up. An officer had a flashlight, looking into the car, talking to the officer that had arrived. I opened the window to try to listen, but they were too far away.

"We've got trouble. The officers have found the car."

I looked back at Kim, who had been wiping tears from her eyes. I think she expected at least some type of validation of her feelings, and at most, a mutual feeling from me. She stood up and started walking towards me.

She got close enough to see the police cruisers and said, "I will turn out the lights." She pulled her chair over to the window and sat next to me. "Well, running is not going to work. Besides, we would literally be running."

"Let's wait to see if they call in anyone, like Cynthia."

We waited for a long time. Eventually, a vintage Trans Am pulled into the parking lot. It was getting late, but the Trans Am drove slowly past our car and the police cars. It was clear the focus was on our vehicle, not on what looked like Brian's Trans Am. He finally parked a long way from the police cars. Brian got out and put on a hat that looked like it had hair attached to it. Brian was bald. After walking a long distance to get to them, he motioned towards the store's door and then up high. It was clear he was talking about the store and the camera outside the store.

"Why do you think he parked so far away?"

"Maybe he wanted to walk, or he didn't want his car to get dinged from someone else's car door?"

"Then, why the hat with hair attached?"

"Maybe he is ashamed of his baldness, or trying to disguise himself."

"I have no idea."

About then, a knock on the door startled us. I went to the door hesitantly, wondering if Cynthia may be outside the room. Worse, an entire S.W.A.T. team, waiting to bust in and apprehend two fugitives from justice. I was scared to look through the peephole to see who was there when I heard a knock again. After looking back at Kim and the door, I knew I had to answer because they might come in anyway if it was law enforcement.

Knock, Knock, Knock, again, and I finally looked through the peep-hole. It was Jerry.

I opened the door, and Jerry said, "Can I come in for a minute?"

"Yes, what's going on?"

"It's dark in here. Can we turn on a light?"

Kim turned on a light, and Jerry continued, "Well, mom hoped you enjoyed your steaks, plus, a lady by the name of Cynthia just left the hotel. She wanted to know if ya'll have checked in and even said she wanted to see my guest list. I am so glad you are Jack Goosey today, anyway. After a million questions, she seemed satisfied we didn't have you on the guestlist—funny thing about hotels. We share the reservation system with several, and one of the ones in New Port Richey has your name on the reservation list. Who knew there was a Jack Goosey here and a Jack Cash on the reservation list there? Anyway, I think it bought you a little time; ya'll get some sleep. I've got you covered here. Oh, and by the way, the room down the hall is the official room number for Jack Goosey. I put this room on the "maintenance roster" for repair, but don't worry, our maintenance man just had his first grandbaby and is with his family for a few days. You have the room for tonight with no problems."

"Thank you so much, Jerry. What do I owe you?"

"Well, I will tell you what mom said to me earlier. Jerry, she said, Jack Cash treated my niece like a queen, and I never saw her happier than when they got married. That continued until the day she died. Do whatever it takes to take care of him and his friend. So, you don't owe me anything, but I thought I would let you know what you meant to mom and Lucy."

"Thank you so much. I was crazy about Lucy, er... Cybil, Lucy is your name for her."

"Ya'll get some rest," and Jerry left.

"Cybil was one lucky girl," Kim said in what seemed like a dig.

I went back to the window to see what was going on as Kim turned off the light.

"They are still there, but now it looks like Cynthia is there talking to them."

A few minutes later, a wrecker arrived with lights flashing. After the driver talked to the officers standing behind the car, prepared to hook up to my rental, I mused out loud, "I wonder why they are impounding the car?"

"What do you mean?"

"Why didn't they just call the rental car company to retrieve the car, instead of impounding it?"

Kim didn't reply until the wrecker turned to position itself to pull it onto the wrecker bed, and then she spoke up, "Jack, that's not an ordinary wrecker. It is a police wrecker. They use them to take the vehicle back for forensics."

"Forensics," I asked incredulously, "what in the world did Cynthia tell them?"

"Evidently, some crime had occurred. Why is she so adamant about finding you?"

"I have been wondering the same. Why all this, unless something happened that triggered Paddy's death, and all this to find out where I am, I wonder if they think I killed Paddy."

"I don't think they thought that, at least at the beginning. They sent you to a theme park, not to an interrogation."

"Well then, what is going on."

Asking questions in which I have no answer is not productive, and there was nothing I could think of that would explain all of this, nothing at all.

"I think we should go to sleep. It's been a long day, and thinking and talking about everything is just going to keep us up."

Kim walked up behind me as I looked out over the scene in the parking lot. She started rubbing my shoulders and then my back with slow, outstanding, pressured motions that melted my stress and my inhibitions for a moment. I turned to her and said, "That feels incredible but it crosses a boundary that I am not ready to cross. She then kissed me, a long-lingering kiss. I knew there was a point of no return in the stress, mess, and emotion we both were feeling. I also knew I would succumb to the temptation to continue. I was weary and becoming weak, and while it felt so right to kiss, we both had a relationship with God that would not allow anything further as unmarried people. The commitment was most vital for me, and until now, I didn't know if Kim felt the same. I needed us both to be strong because one hint of permission would have been too much.

"I think we should stop kissing and go to separate beds."

"Whew, I am so glad to hear you say that because I thought any kissing any longer would not only get us into trouble, but it would be trouble for both of us."

"Agreed, where are we sleeping?"

"Well," I answered, emphasizing pronouns, "YOU are sleeping in the bedroom. I am sleeping in here, on the pull-out sofa. At least I hope it pulls out."

"Thank you for a lovely day, Jack Cash," and with one last lingering kiss, Kim went to the bedroom, closed the door, and opened it again, "since the bathroom is in the bedroom, I will keep the door unlocked."

"Ok, thank you."

Looking up at the ceiling in a room illuminated by the parking lot lights from the grocery store, I began to arrange the day's events in my mind. I decided a blanket and pillow from the closet were enough to provide me as comfortable sleeping as pulling out a sofa bed.

After arranging my bed covers just so, I sat on the sofa, took off my shirt, shoes, and socks, and lay down. The gentle hum of the air conditioning unit and the occasional door closing in the hallway became the music that put me to sleep. As I slept, the rearranging of my day continued into my dreams.

The dream was strange at first: Cynthia was there, running around the hotel, almost as if she were in a track and field event. Brian stood off to the side timing her laps, calling out to her each time she did another lap. Eventually, Kim started running, the opposite direction, and then what looked like Paddy started putting up hurdles for Kim, with each lap, a taller and taller hurdle. Eventually, instead of Kim falling over a tall hurdle, Paddy fell. He fell so hard it looked like he died, but Kim kept running. Then I woke up for a minute, looking around the room to help me determine where I was, and then I dozed off again.

This time, Cybil was in my dream. She was using different voices and facial gestures at first to get me to laugh. She always did it when my stress level was high, and some of the voices she used were spot-on imitations of famous people. She used different ones and then suddenly started using what sounded like a newspersons voice. She said, "Authorities are on the lookout for Jack Cash and his accomplice, Kim Crane, for the murder of everyone Jack Cash knows, his wives, the mailman, pet groomer, and the guy in the Pollo Hacienda commercial." Then she launched into a British accent, "Scotland Yard is also looking into the yards of everyone Jack Cash knows to see how many yards are in their yards." I woke up again, this time with a lot of confusion about where I was until I was awake enough to determine that Cybil had invaded my dreams.

Before I dozed off, I heard Kim talking. It sounded like she was talking in her sleep, but it was so coherent that either she talked clearly in her sleep or was on the phone with someone. I tried to listen but couldn't understand what she was saying, so I decided to go to the bathroom to see if I could hear to whom she was talking.

As I opened the bedroom door, the talking immediately stopped, and she lay still as if she were asleep. I went into the bathroom long enough to make her believe I needed to go the restroom if she were awake. I just couldn't tell.

I went back to bed and listened as intently as I could to hear any other conversation, but I drifted off to sleep again.

CHAPTER SIXTEEN

Pans rattling in the kitchenette and the smell of weak, hotel coffee woke me from my sleep. It was the fourth day since meeting Kim and I knew I had to maintain a vigilance against her advances. I quickly excused myself and went to the restroom, and took a shower. At least my body would be clean, if not my clothes, and then joined Kim in cooking breakfast.

"Last night, it sounded like you were on the phone, did you call anyone?"

"It must have been me dreaming," she replied, "sometimes I carry on great one-sided conversations."

I looked at my watch. It was 7:43, "I will call Mr. Stein as soon as his office opens, but it won't be for another couple of hours since he is on central time. We need to come up with a transportation plan and find some way to fund our journey," as I walked over to the window, "since our car is gone." Curiously, Brian's Trans Am was still in the parking lot. "The Trans Am is still in the parking lot; they must have stayed in the area."

A few minutes later, I heard the sound of knocking down the hall, so I opened our door just a little. "Mr. Goosey, please open your door," I could hear the demand from some unknown person at the entrance of the room Jerry reserved for us, "please open up, or I will open the door,

I have a federal agent, a US Marshal here, and she needs to talk to you."

Of course, no one opened the door because there was no one there, so they opened the door, and Cynthia went in. "You stay out here. This room may be an active crime scene." The hotel clerk stayed in the hallway, and it was undoubtedly not Jerry.

Just then, a cell phone rang, and the clerk said, "Jerry, the lady with the US Marshal's office is here. Do you know when Mr. Goosey checked in last night, and was he alone?"

I couldn't tell what Jerry said, but it was a long reply. "Ok, they just wanted to know if he was someone they are looking for, a fugitive from justice, can you believe it, here in our hotel. Did you see his identification?" After a few minutes of pause, he continued, "ok, I will let them know. There is no room key in the room."

The clerk told Cynthia, "That was Jerry, the night clerk. He said he checked in last night around nine and keyed into the room about 10 minutes later. He didn't see him leave, so if he left, he left with his room key. Check-out time is 11 a.m., so it is possible he left earlier for breakfast and will return. It's not unusual for guests to take their room keys with them. Some return them, and some don't."

Whatever Cynthia said caused the clerk to reply, "There is no guarantee they will return. I am just telling you our policy and the way things normally happen. They may have left. They used points for the room and can check out using our app, so I am unsure when it will happen. If they don't check out by 11 a.m., they are automatically checked out by the system, unless they request a later checkout."

Cynthia walked out of the room and said, "I am sending my forensic guy to go over the room to see if they were here. His name is Brian, and he will be here any minute. He will check the room for prints or anything that may lead us to where Mr. Goosey is."

The clerk excused himself and returned to the desk as Brian arrived. Cynthia told Brian, "I want you to stay in the room for a little while to see if they return. If they do, hold them. From time to time, look outside and down the hallway to see if you spot them. If you do, grab them. We only have a short time until Phil finds out what we are doing."

It was clear from the comment that Cynthia was not operating with her supervisors' approval, but how much of their investigation centered around any thought that I killed Paddy?

"Ok, I will keep a watch," Brian replied, and then they kissed. At least that is what it sounded like, followed by "I love you."

I whispered to Kim, "I guess they are 'kissing cousins' or a ruse to keep us in the dark about the two of them."

"What do you mean?" she replied.

"I heard them kiss, and then he said that he loved her."

"I think you were dreaming of a kiss," and with that, Kim kissed the back of my neck, and then she heard a long kiss and another exchange of I love you, "That's the weirdest family, or she lied to us."

"She lied, but I don't know what else is going on."

"I cooked us some eggs and a little bit of ham, we have bread and weak coffee. Let's eat and plan."

We sat down, blessed our food and asked God for wisdom for our day, and ate our breakfast.

As we were eating, I noted the obvious, "well, it looks like we will be here for a while until Brian leaves. The only problem is, I never got Jerry's cell number."

About five minutes later, the phone rang in the room. I was reluctant to answer it, thinking it could be someone other than Jerry, but I did anyway.

With a noticeable southern drawl, someone said, "Hello, this is Fred Thompson, with hotel maintenance. I need to come to check out the air conditioning in the room. I am glad I called because there is no one on the guest roster for the room. Can I get your name?"

I froze. I was sure I was about to blow our cover.

"Hello???"

"Who did you say this was?"

"Fred Thompson, I am with" a long pause and then a burst of laughter, "Hotel Maintenance, I need to do a check of your," and then more laughing, "I can't do it! It's Jerry! I was messing with you."

"Jerry, my heart almost completely stopped. Cynthia and what she calls her 'forensic guy,' Brian, are in the other room."

"I know. I got a call from the day manager. It seems they believe Jack Goosey is an alias. Who knew?? And they didn't fall for the reservation across town; they must have checked it out somehow. Anyway, we need to get y'all out of the Hotel and on your way."

"I know, but we don't know how to do that, and we don't have a car."

"I know where you can get a nice vintage Trans Am."

"Yes, and I know where we can get a ticket to jail."

"At least no one can track the Trans Am."

"Right, no one will notice a vintage Trans Am with T-tops, either."

"You're right, Jack Cash, but I can't help you right now. I am with mom at the hospital for a procedure. You have until 11 a.m. to get out. Even though your room is closed for maintenance, they will do a room check after 11, because sometimes rooms don't make it back to the roster. Let me think about this and see what we might do. That Fed chick is waiting for Jack Goosey to show back up and might stay until he checks out. Hey, I've got an idea. Call the front desk, from your cell phone, and tell them you are not going to make it to the hotel and you will mail the key back."

"Are you sure it will work?"

"She is staying because she thinks Jack Goosey is you and that you will return."

"Man, she has great instincts."

"I will call the front desk."

"Ok, I will call you back before you leave. Stay until about 10:45ish; gotta go, the doctor is here, bye."

After he hung up, I called the front desk from my cell phone to 'check out Jack Goosey's room.' When the desk clerk answered, I said, "Hello, this is Jack Goosey."

"Mr. Goosey, we have wondered when you are returning to the hotel." I could hear someone talking to the desk clerk. "Mr. Goosey, I have someone here that wants to speak with you."

At the moment, I wished for Cybil's various voices and knew if I hung up the phone, she would suspect that I was not Jack Goosey.

I answered, "Hallo, dis es Jack Goosaaayy. I not came to leave key, es ok to mail, no?" mixing every dialect I could.

"My name is Cynthia, and I work for the US Marshal service. Can you tell me where you are right now, Mr. Gooosaay?"

In the background, I heard a car alarm going off in the parking lot, and I could hear it faintly in the room. I panicked.

"I mush go now, dank you."

I hung up. Kim looked at me, shaking her head, "you are the worst secret agent, undercover impersonator I have ever heard."

"I know. I couldn't think of anything else to do when the clerk handed the phone to Cynthia. Besides, I heard a car alarm that she may have heard too. She might have figured out we were near here."

I started putting on my shoes, "we've got to go, but I don't know the way out of the Hotel without going past her in the lobby, and don't know where Brian is."

Kim put on her shoes and said, "what's the plan?"

I went to the window and looked out. For a brief second, I caught Brian looking at the hotel and right at me. I wasn't sure if he caught a glimpse of me, but when I stepped away from the window, I kept looking in his direction from the side. "Brian is in the parking lot by his car and he looked this way. I think he may have noticed me."

As I watched his motions, I noted he hurriedly called someone and pointed in our direction. He might not figure out the room number, but he could certainly determine the floor. There were probably twenty rooms on our floor. That would only buy us a few minutes.

I hadn't heard any noise from our adjacent room, so I was reasonably confident no one was in the room. "Kim, we need to get into the next room and hide."

"How are we going to do ?"

About that time, I heard people in the hallway and knocking on doors. It sounded like they were just down the hall, and one voice sounded just like Cynthia. The door had a "Do Not Disturb" sign, which in Cynthia's mind, it was an indication they needed to be disturbed.

They knocked and knocked when finally an argument started with the man in the room and the desk clerk. They were screaming at one another; the man must have been completely nude because Cynthia told him to put on clothes. The fight then turned to Cynthia. The entire floor was peering out of their rooms to see what was going on, everyone but us. Cynthia was not going to let a naked man keep her from searching his room.

Whatever they found included a woman screaming and then crying in the hallway with nothing on but a bedsheet. I know because I peered out and saw her. There was someone in the bathroom, with the door locked. Cynthia was yelling for the person to unlock the door. I guess she thought it could be us hiding in the bathroom, and she was very insistent on getting inside. They were hollering, banging as we walked towards the stairwell at the other end of the hotel. As we were briskly walking, the elevator door opened, and several people, including Brian, ran towards the room Cynthia was searching, screaming, "Cynthia, that is the wrong room."

The man was so angry that he got into a fight with Brian, and we could hear more shouting, profanities, and more inside the room. For some reason, Cynthia still wanted to get into the bathroom to see who was there and so we could hear more shouting, and Brian attempted to persuade Cynthia that it was not the correct room.

We didn't stay to see what was going on. We ran down the stairs opposite the room they were searching for and felt we could quickly make our exit. The woman in the hallway with nothing on but a bedsheet did see us leave, but I couldn't tell if she was too upset to notice us nervously looking around and going. If she made us, we only had a short window of time to get out.

We had to get different clothes but had a limited amount of cash. It was almost time for Mr. Stein's office to open, which may have opened our bank accounts again, but we couldn't be sure. When we left the hotel, Kim noticed a coffee house a few blocks away. We ran as fast as we could towards the coffee house, peering over our shoulders as we ran in fear they were following us.

When we arrived, we ordered a couple of coffees and sat with our eyes towards the hotel. After a few minutes, Cynthia and Brian ran out of the lobby, looking in both directions. Then, they went back in. "They are probably looking at the security cameras outside the hotel to see if they can see which direction we went."

"We need different clothes. I am going to ask if a thrift store is near," Kim went to the counter. I kept a vigilant eye towards the hotel.

She returned, "There is one a few blocks from here. It opens in about 10 minutes, and they have clothes."

"Great, but we need to stay here until they open."

Kim sat down with a sigh, "I was hoping we could stay at the hotel longer."

I wasn't sure what she meant by it and didn't want to ask. Sometimes asking for clarification makes everything else muddy. Right now, I didn't wish for muddy!

While I sipped coffee, Kim came close to me, leaning in, "What is driving this craziness to find you? Cynthia is obsessed with locating you, and it looks like only Cynthia and Brian are tracking us. Let's face it. If it were the US Marshals behind this, they would have sent a team to find us, not Cynthia and her cousin that she likes to kiss on the lips." I spewed coffee out of my mouth, laughing. She continued, "I want to know what you know that they want to know so badly."

If my eyes were closed, I would have sworn I had just heard Cybil speaking. Cybil used a similar phrase often when she wanted to talk: "I want to know what you know so that I know what you are thinking." I was not sure where Cybil got it, but Kim had just echoed that phrase, and now I was a man looking like a deer in the headlight of an oncoming car.

"Whaaaaattttt? You look funny like you just saw a ghost."

"You just said something I have only heard from Cybil. It was weird."

"About the cousin thing?"

"No, wanting to know what I know, that they want to know."

"What do you know that they want to know?"

"I am not exactly sure, but based on their ongoing search for us, it is probably bigger than a few thousand dollars. There was always a rumor Veronica knew where they kept the offshore accounts. Those kinds of banks don't send out statements. At least I never saw any. Some investigators tried to figure it out, including Monica, but no one could ever find a Veronica Gypsy account in any of those banks or account numbers."

"Where off-shore?"

"I don't know, maybe somewhere in the Cayman Islands. At least that was the rumor when she died."

"Yesterday, you mentioned you were going to try to test Cynthia by saying something about a notebook Veronica kept in a different language, like a gypsy language, was that true, or just something to test Cynthia?"

"It was true, but I can't remember where I put the notebooks. Besides,

Monica had Paddy translate them so she could try to figure it out. It was like a journal that she kept. Some with personal things, like a diary, and some related to the life she once lived. There were dozens of handwritten notebooks with that kind of information. So, everything was just a rumor."

"Cynthia thinks the rumors are true, or she has other information. Maybe we should get those notebooks and see if we can see anything different."

"I don't know the language, and they have already translated them. It took months, and Monica's files with the translation were on a computer from years ago."

"We've got to get to those files," Kim insisted.

"My computer crashed," I told Kim, which was true, but the files in question were also on a cloud drive. I kept a digital copy of the journals and the translation.

I did so because she wrote intimate details after hearing about Tamera's murder, praying for me, and meeting me at the souvenir shop.

It was so special to know someone cared enough to journal their prayers and concern for me. After Veronica's murder, I scanned them and kept them. There was one thing that Veronica wrote the I will never forget, 'Today, I met Jack Cash, the same Jack Cash that Paddy and I have prayed for daily, asking God to heal his heart. When I met him, I knew God had brought him my way to be my husband. I fell in love with him before we met, and then, when I saw him, I knew this was God's destiny for me.'

I referred to them often, especially when understanding why someone killed such an incredible woman and how God orchestrated such a first-time meeting.

"There may be something in those files, and maybe we could get someone to look at the hard drive."

"Maybe so, but right now, we just need to get away from here."

We both kept a vigil looking towards the hotel, and it had been long enough for the thrift shop to open, so we determined it was time to leave the coffee shop. Kim got better directions and found out we needed to go behind the coffee shop, over two streets, and down one block. It was like a maze, as there were streets where road work had taken the lanes down to one, with frustrated drivers and construction workers starting their day. We weaved our way through the streets, and across the crosswalks until we reached the thrift store. A woman, with a smile as wide as a truck, and a gap in her smile equally as large, opened the door. "Good morning, welcome to the Hope Thrift Shop. 'Hope' has an address, and you have found it. Would you like to hear my story of hope as you shop?"

"Of course!" I answered.

"Great, what are you looking for and I will steer you that direction."

"We need new clothes."

She took us to the clothes rack and told her story. She spent most of her teens and early 20's on the streets, selling herself to the highest bidder, using and abusing drugs until one day, someone reached out to her and shared hope, a hope that she had never experienced before. It was on that day she met Jesus Christ. God transformed her life immediately. She gave up the street life, founded "Hope Ministries," and started helping other addicts find freedom. We prayed together, and when I asked her name, she said, "my name is Hope, always has been, but I didn't experience the reality of my name until day I met Jesus."

Kim and I were so excited to make this excursion, and regardless of what happened with Cynthia, we met someone who made our day.

"You know, I once was married to a woman who also found freedom from drug addiction. She died a few years ago, but she also knew a similar struggle with drugs. She was a gypsy."

"You don't mean Veronica Gypsy, do you?"

"How did you know Veronica?"

"She was a legend and knew everything about drugs in the state. Everyone knew Veronica. I met her a few months before she left the drug scene, but everyone knew she was as important as the head of the drug cartel. Everyone knew her, and she had control of everything. Her bosses were so mad when she went to the police, it stopped drugs in our area for a long time, and then they went to jail. Some went into hiding. I was so sad when Veronica died."

"She was murdered."

"I know, she made a lot of people mad, and she had all their money too. Did you get all that money?"

"No, I didn't get their money, or her money, whoever's it was."

"I'm sorry, it was the wrong thing to say, sometimes I say the wrong thing to people. It just blurts out, and I can't catch it before it reaches people's ears. What else are you looking for?"

"We need hats, do you have hats?" Kim asked.

"We have a few at the end of this row. We have a dressing room too."

As we looked through the clothes, I thought it would be best to find clothes that would not stand out; not too nice, bright, or anything, so we didn't draw attention to ourselves. "Kim, we should find clothes that say, "blah! I am normal; clothes that cover the body, but don't make any statements."

Then, Kim held up a t-shirt that read, 'In your heart of hearts, you know I am right' on the front. "You mean, like this one?"

"Yes, that would draw too much attention because people would be asking what I am wrong about."

Kim found a blouse and a pair of shorts and then went to the men's section and found a camouflage shirt. "Hey, here is one for you; you will blend in if you are in the woods."

"Are ya'll running from someone?"

"Yes, from some friends who followed us down for vacation and are trying to hijack our time, we told them to do their own thing and to give us space, but they are showing up everywhere we go, we think they hid a tracker in our car." Kim and I laughed, hoping to disguise our fear.

Hope started laughing so loud, "Well, if they come in here, I will sell them some nice stuff they don't need but need to buy so we can continue our mission of setting people free, but I will keep my mouth shut about which way you went after you leave."

"Thank you, can we purchase these clothes and then put them on and wear them out of the store?"

"Sure, if you want to, you are serious about these friends, aren't you?"

"Kind of; we just wanted to wear some nice clothes."

"I tell you what, if you want, I will wash the clothes you leave behind and have them ready for you later today. We have a washer and dryer in the back that we use for donated clothes, and I will have them ready for you because they are nice clothes."

"No," both of us said in unison, "keep them and sell them to someone else."

We paid for our clothes and hats and then changed into our new thrift store outfits, thanked Hope, and left. Kim was wearing a top that was about as blah as you could hope to find anywhere, and I found a beige t-shirt, and shorts, and a hat for the "Bradenton Marauders," a local minor league baseball team.

When we got outside the thrift store, we had no idea where to go next. We just stood talking about our options, mostly walking to nowhere special, when Kim looked around and up. We were standing at the bus stop for the Manatee County Area Transit. "Hey, let's take the bus to another part of the city and then call your attorney."

"Perfect, that's a great idea." As we waited for the construction men to let cars pass, suddenly, a Trans Am turned the corner in our direction. I grabbed Kim, turned her toward the street, and buried my face into hers with a long, wet kiss. She didn't resist at all but instead made sounds as if she enjoyed the moment. Brian was driving, and Cynthia was in the passenger seat talking. She told Brian to go slow because she was sure we were in the area, noting that we had no transportation. Our public display of affection made them too uncomfortable to watch but noticed the bus stop sign over our head.

"They may have gotten on the bus," Brian said to Cynthia.

"Stop! Stop now!" and with that, Brian stopped in a parking spot on the opposite side of the street.

I kept kissing Kim.

"Excuse me, sir! Can you tell me where this bus goes? Sir??? Hey, Mr., get a room!" Brian yelled from his seated position in the car.

I kept kissing Kim, and by this time, she was aware of the situation and kept kissing me, pulled away, and buried her head so they would not be able to see her face.

"Hey, ma'am, now that you have come up for air."

Hope stepped outside the store, possibly noticing Cynthia and us, and spoke up, "Can I help you?"

"Hey, can you tell us where the bus goes, the bus that stops here?"

Hope yelled out, "it goes downtown, to the beach, to the outlet mall, down Manatee, literally all over the city. Do you want to ride the bus? I can get you a brochure with a map.

"Tell her yes," Cynthia said to Brian, "and follow her into the store. We are wasting time."

I whispered to Kim, "Let's talk in hushed tones. Brian is going to walk past us."

I could have touched Brian when he passed me; he was that close. I knew we only had a matter of time before they found us.

The bus rounded the corner, coming in our direction. The construction crew held the bus for a minute while letting the opposite traffic through.

Suddenly, Brian rushed out of the door, looking at the map. "They were here, they have new clothes, and I think they got on the last bus" he yelled to Cynthia, "A bus was here a few minutes ago and could have taken them anywhere in the city."

Finally, the construction crew let the bus through, and it stopped at the bus stop, going the opposite direction as Brian and Cynthia. When we got on the bus, I told the bus driver we had cash, and he told us how much to pay. We paid the fare and scanned the bus for two available seats. There were very few seats where two people could sit together. "Maybe we should sit next to other people until we leave the area," I whispered to Kim.

She went to the back of the bus, conversing with an older woman. She kept her head down all the while.

I sat next to a kid with headphones in his ear, oblivious to the world and me, just one row from the back. I kept my head down as well, leaning over with my hands covering my head as if I didn't want to be bothered.

Cynthia stepped up on the bus and asked the driver if he could call the driver that was at the bus stop earlier, asking if he had a couple that got on the bus at this stop.

The driver refused until Cynthia flashed her badge. She said, "look, I am looking for fugitives wanted for murder, I am a federal agent with the US Marshal service," and then she held up her phone, with a picture of me on it, "I need to find this guy right here, right now. Do you think you can call him or radio him?"

He got on his radio and said, "Bus 24, this is Bus 12. I have a federal agent wanting to talk to you. Can you respond at your next stop?"

"I want to talk to him now," she demanded, "not at his next stop."

"He can't talk while the bus is moving, company policy. He can only talk when his bus is parked. Like mine is right now. You are keeping me from my duties."

After what seemed like forever, finally Bus 24 responded, "Bus 12, this is Bus 24. What do you need, Reed?"

"I have a lady looking for a couple that may have gotten on your bus at the 9th Street West Bus stop # 2. Did you have a couple get on your bus at that stop?"

"Affirmative, they are on the bus now."

"Can they hear this right now?" Cynthia asked our driver.

"Can who hear this right now?"

"The people on the bus, can they hear this right now?"

"I don't know, let me ask, Bus 24, are you on a headset, or can the riders hear?"

"Headset."

"Good, I need to know where his bus is right now, and I need for him to refuse to let anyone off the bus."

Cynthia looked around the bus and asked the driver, "how long until we are at the stop where that bus is?"

"About 10 minutes."

As she contemplated whether to ride the bus or not, I noticed the only available seats were next to me, on the opposite side and right behind Kim. If she stayed, she would pass Kim to sit near me. My heart was racing, as was Kim's, I was sure.

"I will ride the bus," Cynthia called out to Brian, "go-ahead to the bus at the stop at the Desoto Mall. Do not let anyone off the bus."

CHAPTER SEVENTEEN

Why Cynthia wanted to ride the bus was beyond my comprehension, maybe to see if another bus stop yielded answers, or perhaps she just wanted to ride a bus. She made her way to the back of the bus, preparing to sit next to me. The driver hadn't pulled away yet, and called out, "Ma'am, my supervisor wants to talk to you."

Cynthia went to the front and got on the driver's phone. She continued to get louder and louder, insisting a fugitive from justice could be on the bus, but at the same time, insisting local law enforcement not be called. The supervisor won the battle and called local law enforcement to help with the bus search.

Cynthia made her way to the back of the bus again, sitting next to me and calling Brian.

"I just got off the phone with the supervisor. There is a problem. They called local LEOs, I know, we will just have to deal with it when I arrive. If they are on the bus, we can at least try to get them in custody. I know we will have to get my car to put them in it since your TA doesn't have back seats. Call me when you get to the stop."

Cynthia continued to scan the bus as we stopped. A few minutes later, Brian called back.

"Hey," she answered, "Whaattt???? S.W.A.T.??? Why did they call

S.W.A.T, yes, I told them we wanted them for questioning in a murder investigation. I know, we will deal with it when we arrive. I will see if I can take over when I get there. I shouldn't be on this bus."

I thought the same thing. Cynthia now was focused on the direction we were traveling, looked towards me and then at the teenager who by this time was asleep with his mouth gaping open, with a few snores. "Well, someone is sleeping. I hope he doesn't miss his stop."

I looked in his direction and laughed, and then just kept my gaze out of the window.

We neared the bus stop at the Desoto Mall. Police were everywhere, along with S.W.A.T. Cynthia made her way to the front of the bus and told the driver to wait until they had searched the bus.

I saw the tactical team leader discussing something with Cynthia and a lot of screaming between the two. She pulled out her badge and flashed it, and said something that I think she thought would put her in charge. The tactical team leader refused her leadership, and they approached the bus with guns drawn, full S.W.A.T gear on, ready for a full-scale war, surrounding it. The leader instructed his team to breach, and they began pulling individuals off of the bus one by one.

She got back on the bus and said, "Idiots, they are going to kill the people I am trying to apprehend. I would like to know what your supervisor told the police."

The driver shrugged his shoulders and said, "I have no idea. Do I need to wait any longer? I am scared!"

"Wait until they have completed their search on the bus, then I will tell you when you can leave."

Suddenly, the back door on the bus was forced open, and a man jumped off the bus and started running. The S.W.A.T. team followed and quickly deployed their taser, rendering the runner into a heap of a person, jerking like a fish out of water. The focus for Cynthia and the rest of the S.W.A.T. team was on this runner. Cynthia exited the bus and walked up to the S.W.A.T. team leader. "I need to get an identification for this runner."

"He is a known drug dealer in our area and has multiple warrants for his arrest. We just haven't been able to get him. Are you looking for a local?"

"No, the couple I am looking for is from out of town. He is a Caucasian, five-ten, slim build, blue-hazel eyes with a blond female, with cropped hair, five-eight, blue eyes."

Kim kept looking back at me with both a worried look and occasionally winking. I couldn't tell if she was flirting or just nervous.

I needed to call my lawyer but couldn't until Cynthia was out of earshot, and I needed to call Jerry, Cybil's cousin, to see if we could lay low somewhere. Nothing was happening right now, as we waited for the S.W.A.T. team to go through the other bus and then for Cynthia to do the same. It didn't take long, and her conversation with the driver only netted Cynthia a significant amount of frustration.

Finally, she came to our driver and said, "You can go."

The driver closed the door and slowly pulled out into traffic. Kim looked up and over to the left. She looked directly into Cynthia's eyes. It was clear that Cynthia caught a glimpse of Kim as she ran towards the bus screaming. The driver was oblivious to her now and intent on making up for lost time. She ran towards Brian, said something to him, and they both ran for Brian's car, but police cars surrounded his car, keeping him from following right away. I knew we had a short time to get off the bus before they caught up with us.

"I need coffee, and we need to call Mr. Stein and Jerry, but we have got to figure out the best place to get off," I said, scanning the road ahead.

The kid next to me spoke up, "this bus takes you near a great coffee place. It's on the way to my college, or maybe just right after, anyway it's on 58th street. The bus will be there soon. I will show you.

"I thought you were asleep, that sounds great, thank you!"

"No worries, I was awake watching the fed chick do her thing. Sometimes you can see a lot of stuff if no one knows you are watching!"

I put Jerry's number on the phone and called, and someone answered, "This is Brian."

I hung up. Kim looked back at me, "What's wrong?"

"Brian answered Jerry's phone."

Our phone rang. I looked at the kid next to me and said, "Hey, could you do me a favor? My friend pranks us all the time, and if you could answer the phone for me, disguising your voice, that would be awesome."

"Sure," he said as he put his hand out to get the phone, "I am a drama major, so this is perfect."

In a perfect female voice, he answered, "This is Lavender Gooms. How can I help you?"

"Mr. Brian, and what is your last name?" the kid giggles like a school-girl, "That's a cute name! I'll bet you are as cute as your name, and I am glad you called. Who is Kim? I told you, my name is Lavender, and I could... what???" then the kid got a little clever with the caller, "well, how do I know you are Jerry?"

The kid repeated what Jerry said, in the form of a question, "I called Cybil, 'Lucy Goosey,' and Uncle Bill, the missionary to Africa, called her 'Clementine Woollysocks?'" The kid broke character, using his normal voice, "Who names a kid Clementine Woollysocks?"

I motioned for him to hand me the phone and said, "Thanks, I think he has figured us out. We will buy you a coffee at that coffee house to say thanks."

"I am just in time for class, they detained us too long, so I don't have time but thank you anyway."

"Thanks again," I said to the kid and then answered the phone, "Jerry."

"Hey, look, people have been calling mom's cell phone like crazy. She had her minor surgery and is about to be released, but people are anxious to find you, and they have resources too. They are monitoring everyone and everything, probably including me and this call. So, I want to see you, and if you remember the place where you proposed to Lucy, they have a place here too. Go there, and in about 30 minutes, I will come and find you."

"Ok, see you then," I hung up, "Kim, we are meeting Jerry in about 30 minutes."

We had cycled through several bus stops, and the kid said, "excuse me, but this is my stop, and yours too if you want good coffee."

"Yes, and is there an Urgent Care near here?"

"Yes, there is one called something like "DoctorOnCall Urgent Care, right around from the coffee shop."

"That's exactly the one I need."

Kim and I exited the bus, and the kid pointed us to the coffee shop and the urgent care and started running towards the college.

"Why do you need urgent care?"

"That's where we are meeting Jerry."

"Urgent care?"

"Yes, it's where I proposed to Cybil."

"How romantic!"

"It wasn't the plan. I had planned on proposing at a restaurant, on one knee and everything. What I didn't know, and Cybil didn't realize was that she was allergic to something in the meal, and about five minutes after they served our entrée, she broke out in welts and itching, really bad, so the waiter, seeing her, said that she needed to get somewhere to get help. It was a good thing we did because she was starting to feel like her throat was closing up by the time we arrived. They gave her a shot, then another shot, and it reversed the effect of the reaction. I was scared I would lose her, so I got on one knee and proposed to her in the urgent care.

Anyway, when I am on one knee, proposing, the doctor comes in, and he walks right out again. The next thing I knew, I heard a saxophone playing like Kenny G, and Cybil just laid on the bed, thinking about my proposal listening to the sax, and fell asleep. She didn't even answer me. She just fell asleep. The doctor came in playing the sax and saw her sleeping, and then went out of the room. Since she was doing so much better, they just let her sleep. I had to wait 30 minutes before she woke up and said, 'yes,' to my proposal. Anyway, I did it official another time, but technically, That was the first proposal."

The coffee house was packed, so we ordered our coffee to go and left, walking towards the urgent care. About a block away, for some reason, as she sipped her coffee, Kim turned around to see a Trans Am pulling up to the curbside parking at the coffee shop. It was Brian and Cynthia. They got out of the car and went inside. We started moving quickly and turned down a block, out of the line of sight for the coffee shop.

Frustrated, Kim said, "How do they keep finding us?"

"I don't know, but about everywhere we go, they seem to catch up."

"Do you think they have the burner phone number and that is how they are tracking us?"

"They must," I answered, "we need to ditch it."

A college student on a rental bike stopped to take a call. Kim dropped our burner phone into her basket as we walked by her. She was looking around as she talked, oblivious to us walking by her, and turned around to look back, saying to a friend, "I am here, hurry up, I am waiting."

We traveled through an alley so no one could see us. Each time we passed a dumpster, parked car, or an obstacle, we got on the other side of it quickly, using it to shield us from anyone looking down the alley. We darted back and forth, looking back and forward, running from people that meant to do us harm or something. At one point, Kim rolled a dumpster to the middle of the alley and said, "at least this will slow them down if they come down this alley."

We got to the end of the alley when suddenly we caught a glimpse of a Trans Am turning down the same path but a block behind us.

As we neared Urgent Care, we saw Jerry getting out of his car. "Jerry," I called out, "get back in the car, we've go to go."

"Ok, get in the back seat."

We ran to this car, got into the back seat as Jerry and Aunt Mary sat in the front seat.

"Aunt Mary, it is so good to see you, how did your procedure go this morning, oh, by the way, this is my friend Kim."

"Hi Kim! It went as good as expected, Jack Cash, and it is good to see you. We have been worried about you. There are a lot of people after you right now."

"I know, we have a US Marshal and her cousin/ brother/ lover Brian chasing us, and they somehow know where we are everywhere we go."

Kim chimed in, "Hi, Ms. Mary, thank you so much for the steaks last night, they were delicious. Changing the subject, we can't figure out how they are tracking us. We put our cell phones in a truck last night, bought a burner phone, but everywhere we go, they find us."

Jerry spoke up, "where is the burner phone now?"

"We put it in a college student's rental bike basket."

"What are they driving?"

"A Trans Am! A vintage Trans Am."

"There has got to be another way they are tracking you! You have no other cell phone, tablet, smart watch, anything, right?"

Aunt Mary spoke up, "Jerry, I need to get my prescription on the way home. I have to take it at 10."

I looked at my watch and spoke up, "Kim has a smartwatch on, and so do I, is it possible they can track us with those?"

"Maybe that's it," Jerry said, "that's how they are tracking you. I don't know if they know what car you are in or not, but there is a Trans Am at the last light, turning our direction. We need to get rid of your smart-watches, and now, take them off and get ready to get rid of them!"

As we approached another intersection, Jerry zig-zagged through streets. We looked back and saw the Trans Am following our path, several cars away. We don't know if they figured out what car we were in or if they were simply tracking our watches. We didn't even know if that was the means they were using, but it seemed to be the only thing that made any sense. Jerry made a few more turns, pretty much taking us in a circle until he made a left turn and continued down the street. I had no idea where we were, but Jerry tried to get rid of our watches, sending Cynthia and Brian on a wild goose chase.

He turned down another street and pulled into a parking lot with a homeless man pushing a shopping cart filled with stuff. He was talking to himself and not paying attention to anyone.

"Jump out of the car, drop a dollar on the ground and put your smart-watches in the shopping cart. He will pay attention to your money and won't see you put something into the shopping cart."

I jumped out of the car, pulled a five-dollar bill out of my wallet, and dropped it on the ground. "Look, someone dropped money on the ground," I said, pointing to the money, and the man just kept on talking to himself. He looked at me and then around, oblivious to me, talking under his breath. It was evident he had mental problems.

"We need to hurry," Jerry called out, "do it now."

I took the watches and dropped them into the shopping cart. It didn't take the homeless a second to start screaming, "Thief, help, somebody, thief!" he said, pointing to our car. I ran and got in the back seat with Kim. People ran to him as we pulled away, with him pointing to our car.

"You ran, didn't you know that is the international sign of guilt," Jerry piped up. We left out of an adjoining parking lot.

"He probably didn't get any information about us, but the people who ran to him may have. We need to hurry and do what we need to do to get ya'll to a safe place."

"I need to call my attorney. They froze all of my bank accounts."

Aunt Mary spoke up, "well, if the government locked them up, you would not be able to get access without a court order. Here you can use my phone."

"Thank you, they will probably track your phone now, right?"

"They have already called me and asked me if I knew where you were and if I knew how much money you were worth."

"What, how much money I was worth?"

"Yeah, they wanted to know if I knew you were worth at least twenty million dollars in offshore accounts and that you had a bounty on your head."

"You mean to tell me you picked us up knowing this information, putting your lives at risk? For what, ghost money??? Because I wouldn't be buying clothes at a thrift store, riding the bus to who knows where pinching every single penny, if I had twenty million dollars."

"That's what she said. I think her name was Cindy, or Cynthia, anyway, they want to talk to you because the money is illegal drug money."

"I have heard about this ghost money for years. Monica looked into it and found nothing. Veronica did not have any off-shore accounts. They are chasing nothing. Did they say anything about Paddy?"

"Paddy?"

"Veronica's brother, Paddy, someone murdered him. It is where all this started."

"Did someone kill Veronica with heroin?"

"Yes, she should have gone into witness protection, along with her brother, Paddy."

"They didn't mention murder, only that you were a fugitive from justice."

Kim kept looking back for a Trans Am, keeping vigil while we talked. "I think we might finally be free from them."

I took Aunt Mary's phone and called Mr. Stein. Again, Mr. Stein answered, "Hello, this Cass Stein."

"Mr. Stein, this is Mr. Wardlow calling you back. You said to call back today."

"Yes, I am glad you called back. There are a lot of people who want to see you, Mr. Wardlow before you die. Your estate has caused a stir, and I hope your will is up to date because from what I have gathered, you might not live much longer."

"I know it is serious. Before I go, is there any way I can get into my estate and use funds for, say, a plane ticket, a trip to an exotic location, or maybe even buy a steak for a few of my closest friends and me?"

"It would take a court order to get into your estate because of all of the family vultures are circling you right now."

"One question, are the vultures near you right this moment?"

"Not now, but they have big ears and seem to know things people just don't know, and they want to know them really, really bad, so Mr. Wardlow, I suggest you don't do anything until tomorrow. Tomorrow would be a good day to do something with your estate."

"Tomorrow, huh?"

"Tomorrow. While you are waiting for the moment to arrive, we can meet at O'Charley's for lunch, say in about half an hour or so. How about it?"

"O'Charley's sounds great. But which one?"

"Remember when we first met, I had my administrative assistant Julie with me...that specific O'Charley's!"

"Perfect, heading your way, be there in about 30 minutes."

After I ended the call, I looked at Kim and said, "Something huge is happening. Julie wasn't at the office, but Mr. Stein wanted me to call her husband, Charlie, in about 30 minutes. Charlie is a CPA who works for Mr. Stein and consulted with me on Tamera's murder. And Mr. Stein answered the phone, which he never, ever does, so Julie must not be there."

Aunt Mary spoke up and said, "I need to get a prescription filled and then need to go home to rest. I am tired. Do ya'll mind if we go to my house so I can take a nap. Jerry will get y'all something to drink, and ya'll take some time and relax next to the pool."

Jerry pulled into the pharmacy and went inside. "Are you ok? I asked Kim.

"Yes, just tired. This running, hiding, and everything is taking its toll on me, along with the emotional strain. I have a question for you. If everyone is so interested in getting to you, is it possible that Veronica hid the money, maybe under a fictitious name?"

"I have wondered that too. Everyone seems to 'know' something I don't know at all. Monica investigated it, and she was thorough. As far as a fictitious name, I am not sure I would even know where to start with names. Cybil was the one with names."

Aunt Mary laughed, "Did you know Cybil is the one who started the name thing. She wasn't very old when her dad told her to clean up a mess, she informed him her name was no longer 'Cybil' but said to her dad, 'I shall no longer be known as Cybil. For now, everyone may call me 'Felicia Fancybottom.'

He laughed so hard, he almost choked, and that's when he started making up other names, and she followed suit with voices to go with each name. Every family member picked up on the schtick, and, well, it stuck."

"I didn't know where it started. I just knew it was something every family member prided themselves on, their special name for Cybil. What was interesting to me was she never let me call her a special name. I called her 'sweetheart,' but was as far as she would let me go. She told me her dad had given her the name, 'Cybil,' and she reserved it for the only other man in her life, her husband. Not that she didn't occasionally launch into different voices and characters. It sure made married life fun. She was the lift to my wings after Monica died, even though she was grieving too. She focused on me, I guess, as both a diversion and for helping me walk through it. I miss her."

"Well, I wish Jerry would hurry up, I am ready to take a nap, and I'm sure ya'll are ready for relaxing at the pool. I think I have some swimwear for ya'll too."

It was taking Jerry a long time, and it was starting to get too long, and I was starting to get nervous. I finally said, "I will check on him," and left Kim and Aunt Mary in the car. I found Jerry at the back of the store, talking to the pharmacist. He saw me and said, "sorry it has taken me a little while. I got a call right before I got to the counter. We'll talk about it in the car."

After Jerry paid for the prescription, we walked out of the store, with Jerry whispering in hushed tones, "we can't go home. It seems mom's house got raided by people from the government about 10 minutes ago. Our housekeeper texted me to check out the security cameras. I did, and they did a full house sweep. They refused to answer any questions, show any warrant, or show identification. They just said they were with the government. Jack, I think there are people in the government doing things the government does not sanction. They all want to find you and are not leaving any stone unturned. I can't believe they showed up at mom's house. I would have you come to my house, but I am afraid they will be there next. Mom is going to be hot."

When we got in the car, Aunt Mary spoke up, "well, what took you so long? I almost got my full nap in while you were inside."

"Mom, some people raided the house. I think they are still there now."

"Who? My house? What were they doing at my house?"

"They were looking for something, or someone, I guess Jack Cash and Kim."

"Give me my phone. I will call my attorney right now."

"I don't think these were government people, mom. I think they may be with the cartel. I think they think Jack Cash is loaded with money or knows where it is, and they want him something fierce."

"Well, we can't take him home with us. They might come back. I don't want them to catch Jack Cash or hurt anyone."

"I guess they are calling every former wife's family looking for me."

"Who is the next wife?" Kim asked.

"That would be Callie!"

CHAPTER EIGHTEEN

When I was in high school, we went on a short-term medical missions trip to Ecuador. For over a week, we treated hundreds of Ecuadorians in a medical clinic with doctors, a dentists, and optometrists free of charge.

Mandy and I worked in the triage area, taking blood pressures, temps, and such. On the first day, a missionary teen named Callie worked with us. She was beautiful, with the biggest smile and brightest eyes you would find on anyone.

Mandy and Callie hit it off immediately, developing a solid friendship, so much so that one day Callie made a big deal about the cute shoes that Mandy was wearing. So, Mandy wanting to bless her friend, took off her shoes to give them to Callie. She put them beside Callie's feet, and immediately, we all could see how long Callie's feet were, with someone saying, "you have the longest feet in the world, longer than anyone I know." Callie wasn't embarrassed. After all, she already knew she had abnormally long feet, just sad because she liked Mandy's shoes.

Mandy was intent on finding shoes that would fit Callie when we returned from our trip. She found some Callie's size and shipped them to her.

About a month before our graduation, Mandy got a thank you package from Callie, in it was a small leather purse from Cotacachi,

Ecuador. She treasured it and her friend, even inviting Callie to our wedding. Her family was on furlough, raising missions support for their continued work in Ecuador, and during that time, they would send Callie off to college in the U.S.A..

After Mandy died, I lost touch with Callie. In fact, I didn't think about her until after Cybil was killed. That is until one day, in my church office, the phone rang. "Is this Pastor Jack Cash?"

"Yes, who is calling?"

"I don't know if you remember me or not, but this is Callie, from Ecuador!" There was a long pause, and for some reason, when she said that, we cried. Both of us. I can't explain why, and we even talked about it. It was like a long-lost friend had called, a close long-lost friend. Every time I remembered the call, it transported me back to the day Mandy tried to give away her shoes. That memory led to the day I married Mandy. It led to the moment Mandy died and the embrace Callie gave me when I showed up at the reception with no bride. I felt it all, great heartbreak and then poignant joy the moment she called me. Her entire family was involved in missions work in some of the most remote parts of South America.

Kim interrupted my thought train, "You zoned out, what about Callie's family?"

"I don't think they would be able to find any of her family." I knew if the Cartel intended to find them, they would need a guide and a lot of mosquito repellent. I wasn't even sure where they were at the moment.

"Why not?"

"They serve as missionaries in Ecuador, deep in the Amazon, one of the most remote areas. They do not have cell towers there."

This time, Kim sounded more anxious than any other time, "what are we going to do? We are almost out of money. We have no place to stay. We have no transportation. We have nothing."

Aunt Mary spoke up, "ya'll have each other, and you need to stick together regardless of the problem. Jack Cash, I heard you preach about Jesus being asleep on a boat on the Sea of Galilee. A storm arose, and the disciples knew it was bad. They woke Jesus and complained he was unconcerned that they were about to perish. Things were grim, but you said, and I will never forget it: "If Jesus is on your boat, in your court, on your side, in your heart, you have nothing to fear. Nothing. He is the one who tells winds and waves to shut up and be still, and he is the one who tells our heart to do the same. You just have to trust him while the storm is raging."

"That is a good message, and I needed to hear it," Kim replied.

"Well, we have got to figure out how you and Jack Cash are going to get around and go on the offensive. I think instead of running away, you need to face everything. Go back to your condo, fight for your life back, find out who is after you, and go after them. It's time to turn it around."

"I think going on the offensive is a good idea, but I feel like we are handicapped."

"Nonsense! I will let you use one of my cars. I will give you one of my credit cards and add you to it, I will give you some cash, and you can head back and fight. Fight as you have never fought before and take down those who mean to do you harm."

"Thank you, Aunt Mary. I don't know what to say."

"You just said it and you are welcome, so I will call my credit card company and add you to my card now, at least one of them. While you're at it, find out who killed Lavender Gooms."

"Who is Lavender Gooms?"

"Haven't you been paying attention? That's what I called Cybil since she started the name thing. I thought it would be hard for her to come up with a voice for 'Lavender,' but she did. It was a soft velvety voice."

I just smiled. A soft velvety voice came out many times when she called my name. Just hearing 'Jack Cash' in that sultry voice was enough to light my fire.

All the while we were talking, Aunt Mary was pulling out her credit cards, deciding which one to let us use. She finally decided and called the company to put us on the card. "Hello, I am calling to add someone to my credit card." She rattled off the numbers to the customer service rep and then a few verification points, name, address, date of birth, and last five of her social security number. "What do you mean it is locked? I didn't lock it. By whose authority was this locked?"

It sounded like the cartel, or the government was going after everyone who had anything to do with me. But I didn't know why it was so intense and why now.

"I want to talk to your supervisor, yes, I will wait," then Aunt Mary turned and looked at me, "Well, I guess I am a part of your world now. They have locked this credit card." Aunt Mary turned her attention back to the phone, "Are you a supervisor? Why has my credit card been locked? What do you mean the government did this? I demand to see the paperwork they sent you and whoever signed the paperwork. Do you have any paperwork? Do you mean you locked my card because someone called you and told you they were with the government? I don't care who they talked to, well, then let me talk to them. I don't care if they are busy." When Aunt Mary responded to the supervisor's answer, her voice was louder than the previous response. "Ok, I'll wait!"

She turned to me, "They are getting the supervisors supervisor. Someone very high in the company got a call from someone in the government. They locked my card because of suspicious activity, utilizing some type of anti-terrorism or anti-drug law, but they did this without due process. I am going to own this credit card company."

The representative hung up the phone.

To say Aunt Mary was hot was the understatement of the day. She was wealthy, able to command others to do what she wanted, and now, at least with the credit card company, that had changed. She then called her banker, Samantha. "Hello, Samantha, this is Mary, please say that again, by who's authority? How can they do that? How can you do that? Do you know my account balance? Do you know how quickly I can pull it out of my account and find another bank? WHAT, whose signature is on the document? I will call you back!" Aunt Mary ended the call and turned to me, "Jack Cash, it is dawning on me that you are a valuable asset and a lot of people are after you, some high up in the government. They have locked down my credit card, at least one of them, and have instituted an order to seize my bank account. It's time for you to fight, and you are not just fighting for yourself now but for me too."

"What are you going to do, Aunt Mary?"

"Well, I am going to call my attorney, no, I will see my attorney, and I will sue whoever signed the warrant to seize my accounts, but first, I will get you a car to take you back to where you were staying. You need to get your stuff and then start going after the people who are after you. I would suggest you go to Cayman and investigate any money your wife may have had there."

"I have less than $200 left in cash. Someone has locked down my accounts too."

"I will give you cash. I will have to get it from my safe at home and get you a car you can use. Do you have a passport?"

"Yes, it's at my condo."

I looked at Kim, "Do you have a passport?"

"Yes, but I don't know if I brought it in my travel pack. I usually keep it with me, but I can't remember if I did this time."

"Ya'll need to get your passports and go to Cayman."

"Will the US government have our passports flagged?

"Likely, I do have some connections, but first, we've got to get you what you need to go, but you have to trust me. We need to find a place for you to lay low while I get cash for you and a car."

Jerry spoke up and said, "And you will need a couple of burner phones. I will get them while mom is at the attorney's office. So, you will need to lay low for at least a couple of hours."

She called a family friend who built houses, "Hey, Jeff, this is Mary. Do you have any staged houses for sale? Where? Ok, I need it for, I don't know, a day or so, maybe less. Yes, they are homeless but only for a day or so." She laughed out loud, "I will make sure they don't show up with their shopping cart, wearing raggedy clothes. Are all the utilities on? Great, what is the address? I will drop them off there. Is there a code to get in? ok, [writing furiously], and I will send a crew over to clean it afterward. Thanks, Jeff, oh, do you still have a house in Grand Cayman? Is anyone staying there right now? The homeless people may need it for a few days, yea, put it on my tab! Thanks Jeff, we are heading there now. Bye."

Aunt Mary turned to look at me, "I loaned Jeff his startup capital and have owned a part of his construction business for years. He only builds the nicest houses. Anyway, he has a house on 17th Avenue he just finished, staged it for sale, so it has almost everything you would need except food. All utilities are on too."

"Thank you!"

"Yes, thank you," Kim echoed.

"No problem. I am a part of this because of 'Lavender Gooms' and Jack Cash, so, if I am a part of anything, it's all in for me."

Jerry noted, "Once we drop you off, we will bring you a car and cash! I recommend a restaurant near there, they serve seafood, but swordfish is their specialty."

Kim squealed! "I had swordfish with Jack Cash a few days ago. It was incredible."

Ten minutes later, we were pulling into the drive of a beautiful, post-modern three-story house with fresh landscaping. After inputting the codes Jeff had given Aunt Mary, Jerry led us inside. The inside boasted stark white and grays, with furniture professionally chosen to accent each room's clean lines and aesthetics. I had only seen such beauty in magazines or online, never in person and never to stay in such a place. Once inside, Jerry said, "We have got to go, but I will be back later with phones, cash, and a car. Y'all just relax."

The builder had placed a terrace overlooking the Gulf on the second floor, complete with beautiful furniture. Kim and I walked throughout with our mouths wide open, unable to comprehend the beauty of the place without saying, "Wow, look at that, come look in here, you won't believe this room," over and over again. I opened the door to the outside, and we both sat down and sighed a heavy sigh.

We had no way of contacting Jerry, so we waited. An hour turned into two hours, and we were getting hungry, so we decided to find something to eat near the house. After walking a couple of blocks, a man was getting something out of his car, so I walked to him and said, "we are new to the area, is there a place to eat near here."

"Yes, there is a good place about 4 miles away."

"Is there anything closer where we can walk? We want to walk there."

"Not really, it is a couple of miles away for anything food-wise, anything worth eating, at least, it would be best to drive."

"Ok, thanks."

I looked at Kim and said, "We might need to go back to the house and wait for Jerry to come back."

When we got near the house, there was a large SUV in the driveway. Because of our day, we didn't know if it was the car Jerry had for us or if someone else was at the house, so we waited around the corner. A few minutes later, someone stepped out onto the terrace, the one we had been on a short time prior. At first, it looked like Jerry. Then after a few seconds, another person stepped out with what looked like a sub-machine gun in his hand. "Um, that's not Jerry, and I don't think it was someone he sent for us."

"Yes, we need to leave!"

"How are we going to get anywhere, we can't walk, there's no place to hide?" Full panic was about to set in for both of us when suddenly a man in a pickup truck pulled up next to us, "Are you Jack Cash and Kim? Jerry sent me to pick you up. There has been a problem."

"Who are you, and where is Jerry?"

"I am Jeff, the owner of the construction company. I built the house where you were supposed to stay. I went there to let you know that Jerry wouldn't arrive until later."

The longer we stood outside of his truck, the more vulnerable we were. I knew we needed to figure something out soon because the men at the house would be looking in the area soon. "How do I know you are Jeff, the owner of the company?"

He turned and pulled out his driver's license and then a business card. It was the one Aunt Mary called. We were not in a trusting mood yet, but we knew we needed to do something quickly. I could see that SUV in the driveway was now turning in our direction. I didn't think they could see us and replied to Jeff, "there are people coming this way."

"Get in! Hurry!" So we opened the door, only to find Jerry hidden from view. He got up enough to let us in and told us to "duck down" until the SUV passed us. We did, and when they did, Jeff pretended to be looking at the paperwork. When they got near, they slowed down, creeping slowly by his truck. When they were next to Jeff's truck, they stopped and looked at Jeff. He looked back at them, nodded hello, and looked back down. The people inside keep a vigil out for a couple of walkers. A few hundred feet ahead, a couple was walking away from them, so they sped up to get a better glimpse of the couple.

"They took off to check on a couple ahead of us. I will turn into the driveway ahead of us. I know the people who live there and will go to their door to see if they are home. I will talk to them for a minute until we can leave without arousing any suspicion.

Jeff pulled into the driveway and went to the door. Jerry whispered, "the people looking for you have gone full force, Jack Cash! They are everywhere, using all kinds of government people and surveillance, they are going all out with all of this, and they never left mom's house. So, mom drove home, and Jeff picked me up before I got there. When we got to the house, we saw the SUV, so we figured they had found you at the house or you were walking to find food."

"Why are you whispering?"

"Because it seems they can hear everything. They know everything, mom said you need to go on the offensive. It will be hard without a car and some cash," Jerry looked around for the signs of the SUV, "they are active right now, and it makes me wonder what is going on, mom thinks that you may have something on someone high up in government, or Veronica did, because they are obsessed with getting to you."

Jeff walked back to the truck after ringing the doorbell for a few minutes, "no one was home."

"Jerry, I don't have anything, but Veronica must have had something. I think I need to go to Grand Cayman to check things out in person but don't know how I am going to get there."

"What, you need to go to Grand Cayman today? I can get you there," Jeff chimed in.

"How?"

"You have two options. I have a friend who has a yacht who can get you there in about five or six days, depending on weather, or I can you there by air."

"My passport is at my condo if they haven't raided my condo like everywhere else."

"I don't know if I have mine," Kim interjected, "I have to go back to my condo to see if it is in my luggage."

"I have a friend in government in Grand Cayman that might be able to get you in the country, but there is no guarantee that we can get you in without your passport. But once you go in, it will flag your entrance. So, if anyone in the government is looking for you, you will have a short time to get in before they detain you, and they may already have flagged your passport. Can I ask what you need in Grand Cayman?"

"I need to check on a bank account there."

"Well, unfortunately, you will need a passport for the bank. I don't know anyone at any bank there that will let you access any accounts without a passport. The first thing is to get back to your condo to get your passport. I can fly you there. I have a King Air , and can get you there pretty quick. Where do you need to go?"

"Vero Beach."

Jerry insisted, "Is it possible to go now? Mom will pay for the trip. She already told me to do whatever it takes to take care of Jack Cash."

"I will make a few phone calls, one to my wife, to let her know where we are going."

As we sat in his truck, Jeff called his wife using the Bluetooth connection, so we heard everything, "Hey honey, I have to make a trip."

"Hey George, have you seen Jeff? He is needed back at home."

"No, George hasn't seen Jeff. Does he need to find him?"

"Yes, that would be good. Please let Jeff know he is needed at home right away. I have his garage door opener so the garage door will be up and he can pull right in. Do you understand, George? I don't want you to mix up anything that I just told you."

"Ok, I will let Jeff know. Hopefully, I will see him soon. Bye."

"George, tell him to hurry! I need him back here, bye."

After Jeff disconnected the call, he turned around and looked at me. "Jack Cash, what in the world is going on, and who is looking for you?"

"So, I take it your wife was sending you some code?"

"Yes, she asked if George had seen Jeff. George is my friend from college. He is blind, so the answer is 'no, he hasn't seen Jeff.' The last time I forgot to put down the garage door, some people walking down the beach just walked into our house. They were a little drunk and just wanted see the inside. Anyway, we had set the alarm, so the police came, but it became a long-standing joke that if you leave the garage door up, people will come in, so someone came in, and they are there now."

"Do you need to go home?"

"No, I will send the police to do a welfare check on my wife, and then we will go to the airport and take my plane to Vero Beach. No one will know where we are going, and I will file my flight plan after we arrive in Vero Beach."

We headed south to Venice Municipal Airport. On the way to the airport, Jeff called 911 and asked for a welfare check. We went straight for the hanger for his plane, a Beechcraft Air King. "We have to hurry and get this bird in the air," Jeff said as he began his pre-flight inspection, walking around the plane. He went through the paces to ensure a safe flight and then pulled the aircraft out of the hanger. As he was opening the plane door, his cell phone rang. "This is Jeff."

"Ok, no, don't tell them where my hanger is, tell them I will be there in a minute."

He looked around at us and said, "We've got to go, there are people at the office wanting to know where my hanger is and where I am, get on the plane." He quickly closed the hanger door, got on the plane, and began the interior pre-flight check. He called out, "left engine [looking around for anyone near the plane], starting up, rpm, up, right engine, [looking around for anyone near the right engine], starting up, rpm up, all systems go."

He then radioed airport control for permission to take off. As we left the hanger, a black SUV was pulling around the corner of the hanger. It wasn't clear if they knew Jeff's plane was from that particular hanger. It only looked like they were going to check it out. Clearance to take off was swift, and Jeff positioned the aircraft for maximum thrust. Fortunately, we could see the black SUV at the beginning for take-off, and as we reached minimum speed for take-off, Jeff announced, "rotating" and radioing to control that the flight plan was pending.

He looked back and said, "we will have a bumpy flight part of the way to Vero Beach and some thunderheads to go around, but the flight will be around 30 minutes."

Kim and I settled back, both watching outside as we flew over swamps and small towns to Vero Beach. Jeff got word that the people at his house found out about his aircraft and sent people to the airport, looking for him. His wife was fine but shaken. Jeff called Jerry to the front, explaining he needed to turn the plane around as quickly as possible and if he were staying in Vero Beach, he would need to find another way back to Bradenton. He needed to let us know we were on our own after landing if he was waiting on the plane. Jerry decided to go back with Jeff and came to us and explained we would need to find an alternate route to Grand Cayman as Jerry was concerned about his wife.

He also said we would need to find a way to get a cell phone after landing. His bank account was frozen, along with his mom's, so he couldn't help us.

"We are on approach to Vero Beach," Jerry called out. It wasn't too long till we had pulled around near the General Aviation office, and Jerry shut off the engines so we could disembark. As he was opening the door, I said, "I don't know how to thank you for doing this for us. I wish I could explain what is going on, but I can't, and I am sorry we pulled you into our drama."

"I am sorry I can't fly you to Grand Cayman. My wife is beside herself, and since I committed to you, I wanted to keep it, but now I must get back."

"Please apologize to your wife, and once this is all over, we will repay you for your kindness."

"No payment needed, be safe!" Jeff said as he stepped off the plane to help us navigate the steps.

When we left the plane, we had no idea what to do or where to go and were a few miles away from our condos. I knew the office number for our condo and knew they could get a message to Ilean. Hopefully, she would get someone to pick us up, so we went to the office to make a call. There was a gentleman finishing paperwork at a desk. "Is there a phone I can use to make a local call," not looking up, he pointed to the phone on an adjoining desk, "thanks."

I called the front desk at the condo. "Charlene, don't say anything, I am about to tell you my name, and I don't need you to say anything but 'I understand.' Do you understand?"

"Yes, I understand. Did I get it right?" Charlene said, amused at my introduction.

"This is Jack Cash, and I need help."

Suddenly her slight amusement went to full-blown anxiety, "Do you know what has happened around here."

"What has happened?"

"Some people found Paddy. Someone killed him. Since then, it's like the world has turned upside down. There have been FBI, US Marshal, and agencies with all letters of the alphabet coming and going, more than I can count. People looking for you, some with and some without badges or government identification. They have ransacked your condo. I mean, there is not one thing left in its original place. There are a lot of people wanting to find you."

"Are you alone right now?"

"Yes."

"I need to get to my condo, but I don't have a car, they took it in Bradenton."

"Well, I still have a few hours on my shift, but I can send Ilean's nephew. He is working on a problem at one of the condos. He told me he was near completing the work when I last talked to him."

"Does he work at the restaurant and the condo?"

"No, that is Josh. Josiah, her other nephew, is the one who works here. Is it ok if I send him to get you?"

"Yes, but no one can know where we are or what he is doing, no one."

"Ok, wait, he is calling through, hold a second."

I looked at Kim and said, "Ilean's nephew might be able to pick us up."

"He is done and is willing to come to pick you up. He will be at the office in a minute, and you can tell him where to go."

"Sir," I said to the gentleman filing paperwork, "what is the name of this airport and the address?" As he was about to rattle off the name and address, I held up a finger to indicate to wait. Charlene handed the phone to Josiah, "Josiah, I need you to pick us up. The address is 3400 Cherokee Drive."

"Isn't that the airport?"

"Yes, we are in the FBO office to the left when you pull into the airport complex, and Josiah, do not tell anyone you are coming to pick us up."

"Ok, but who are you?"

"I will tell you when you arrive!"

"Ok, if Charlene says it's ok, I will head your way."

I heard Charlene tell him it was safe.

"Ok, I am on my way."

CHAPTER NINETEEN

We were so fearful, we didn't trust even staying in the office, so we went outside. After about twenty minutes, a blue Ford Focus pulled into the parking lot, and turning a few times to figure out where to go, Josiah pulled up near the office where we were standing. He was so focused on locating us he didn't look in our direction. As he was about to open the door, I called out, "Hey, are you, Josiah?"

"Yes, are you the person I am supposed to pick up?"

"Yes, there are two of us."

"Where do you need to go?"

I looked at Kim, "Where do we need to go?"

"We need to go to your condo and my condo."

"Let's go to yours first and see what condition it is in," I said to Kim.

Kim told Josiah her address, and we were on the way. Josiah asked my name.

"You have to keep my name to yourself, do not tell anyone. My name is Jack Cash."

Josiah almost ran off the road excitedly, "Are you kidding me? You are like, like a legend around here. I think I have heard your name more from my family than my own. They all love you, and up until now, I wondered if you were imaginary."

"I can assure you I am real, and it is nice to meet you."

We drove for a few minutes and pulled up to Kim's condo. On the outside, everything looked normal. We slowly walked to the door, very suspicious of anything or anyone around. As Kim put the key into the lock, I kept watching for anyone monitoring her condo. We walked inside, and the living room was clean, nothing out of place. "Well, so far, it looks like I left it." When we walked into the bedroom, however, someone had turned the room upside down.

"What kind of party did you have in here," I jokingly said.

"This is NOT the way I left it," Kim insisted. She opened the closet, and most of her hanging clothes were on the floor. They had moved all of her shoes, and her shoulder bag had its contents strewn on the bed. She moved several items in the closet, then on the bed, and then went back to the closet, thinking out loud, "I remember putting my passport in... think, think Kim, I put it in my overnight bag."

There was a compartment inside her overnight bag that held her insurance card, some credit cards she rarely used, and her passport. She pulled a smaller bag out of the larger bag, "voila' my passport."

"That's strange that they didn't pull those out."

She held up the bag, "it's hidden. I didn't find it after I bought it until a few trips into using it. I thought it was a nice place to keep stuff I didn't want to leave at home but didn't want to keep up with on a trip. I guess it worked." She pulled out her passport and a debit card, "hey, if they haven't shut down all of my accounts, I have an account tied to a family trust. I have access to it, and it is not in my name but the trust. This card is from a trust."

I sat her down on the edge of the bed and looked into her eyes, "Kim, I can't expect you to continue running with me. You have endured enough, and I think using trust money to continue to support this is not a good idea."

"It's my choice to do this. If you don't want me anymore, I will cut my losses and go home. But, if you do want me, if you want me," as Kim wrapped her arms around me, whispering in my ear, "if you really want me, then you have me. I am yours!"

Tears started streaming down my face as I was hoping she would not take me up on my offer to leave because I was falling for Kim, falling in the worst way. As we held each other, Josiah cleared his throat. "I hate to break up your moment, but my aunt Ilean wants to see you right away."

"I don't think it would be a good idea to go to her house."

"She doesn't either. She gave me an address to meet her."

Kim looked at us and said, "I think I need to get a bag together," and started grabbing makeup, clothes, halfway folding them, putting them in a shoulder bag.

"Can we run by my condo? I need clothes too."

"No, Aunt Ilean said to come to the address before you go there. She thinks someone is watching her house and your condo."

We got in Josiah's car and started heading towards the address she had given Josiah. We traveled away from the beach towards some residential area. "Aunt Ilean owns several condos and bought a house in a subdivision to renovate. We are going to the house."

When we arrived, there were no cars outside, the garage door was down, and then, Josiah's phone rang, "No one followed us. There is no one coming down the street. Ok," then the garage door went up, revealing another car and we drove in, and the garage door closed. Josiah looked over at me, "Just a precaution."

The house was clearly undergoing renovation, with end of project construction debris, everywhere, some still with appliances, and some empty. We walked into what was to be a great room with a view of the backyard, along with five lawn chairs, where we found Aunt Ilean sitting. She stood up and gave me a huge hug and said she was so sorry to hear about our trouble.

"Aunt Ilean, I have no idea what everyone is looking for and why all of the sudden Paddy was murdered. Veronica has been dead for years."

"My name is Ilean," she said as she walked over to Kim.

"Hello, my name is Kim, and I have heard so much about you, thank you for helping us today."

"Jack Cash didn't tell you the I lean thing did he?"

"Yes," Kim said laughing, "he did! I don't suppose I can use the restroom, can I?"

"Yes that is fine. The bathrooms are ready."

When Kim left, Ilean leaned in and whispered, "Jack, how well do you know Kim?"

"I knew her in high school, and she showed up at the beach a few days ago, and we have pretty much spent the last few days running from the cartel, US Marshals, and more."

"Be very careful, there are a lot of people looking for you, and they will send people that will get very close to you, because they have an agenda. Jack, you always think the best of people, but some people will use it to their benefit. Maybe that's what Kim is doing. I am worried Kim might not be who she said she is."

"Thanks for your concern, we have been running so much, I haven't had time or technology to figure out much about her."

"There are things you don't know, things that happened right before Veronica died, and things I have learned lately. Recently, someone that Veronica testified against was able to get out of prison. He was supposed to be in for forty years, but some 'technicality' allowed a judge to set him free. We believe the judge had been groomed for years by the cartel because it was almost like the judge said, 'the prosecutor combed his hair the wrong direction, so I will change the sentence to time served.' He let Juan Carlos go."

I remembered the name. He was the prominent leader that Veronica had gotten close to, so close, it was almost a romance, except Juan Carlos had a different girl under his arm any time anyone saw him.

Ilean continued, "The only consistent woman in his Juan Carolo's life was Veronica, and she knew everything. The sense of betrayal he felt towards Veronica was profound, and he said he would get revenge if possible. Veronica had spent a lot of time creating a document filled with the names of people, some in the government, like people in congress, the senate, the FBI, the US Marshal service, big name people that were the higher-up people, completely in league with the cartel."

"They turned a blind eye to the dealings of the cartel in exchange for money or safety. The cartel's influence was vast, and the web of people caught in it was just as significant. That's not all, there are even people in government who have amassed wealth in excess of a hundred million dollars on a yearly salary of $175,000. Some gained their wealth through influence peddling, illegal activities and more.

Because of Juan Carlos' ties with them, Veronica was able to assemble a dossier that contains names, dates, interactions, accounts, verifiable criminal acts, money laundering, you name it.

Right before Veronica was murdered, she came across additional information that included more names, video's and etc. that would implicate hundreds. If the dossier were to find its way to an honest federal prosecutor, it would destroy the wealth and careers of many. Jack, she changed some of the offshore accounts she was responsible for to a different name."

"Wait, she had a dossier and money? Where is it?"

"That's why people are hot and heavy after you, people in the government and people in the cartel. They have vast resources to track your movements. They think you have it, and it can bring a whole other wave of convictions if taken before a grand jury, and that's not all. They know about some money. She turned over some of the accounts but not all. It was a part of the racketeering conviction. Those accounts were what nailed the prosecution's case for conviction, and they were worth tens of millions of dollars. The government did not seize all the accounts, and the cartel found that out. Veronica changed the names the accounts to Paddy's name. Paddy's name was really Paddy Čigonai. It is Latvian for 'gypsies', but instead of using the Latvian name, he changed it to 'Gypsy' when he moved to the United States. So did Veronica when she turned 18. Anyway, everyone used 'G.y.p.s.y' to spell their last name, but no one used the Cignoai spelling, so it went under the radar for years. Until a few days ago!"

"Wait, you mean her last name was originally Cigonai? I was married to her and didn't know that . What else did I not know?"

Kim returned, and Ilean motioned for us to sit in the chairs, "Juan Carlos knew most of these things but didn't know her last name. Suddenly, some people in Juan Carlos' organization got antsy about the dossier. Someone is running for a higher office, but I don't know who it is because I don't have the dossier; anyway, they believe that you have it, Jack Cash, you have the dossier, and you have the accounts that Veronica changed to Paddy's name."

"If they were in Paddy's name, why are they after me?"

"Because, Jack Cash, they were in Paddy's name, but you are the beneficiary to those accounts, they are P.O.D. accounts."

"P.O.D.?"

"Payable On Death. If the primary dies, the second person then receives the proceeds from the account."

"Ok, my mind is blown. Why didn't I know this information?"

"To protect you in case something like the last few days happened. Someone found out Paddy's real name and found out he had the accounts, and they pressed him for information about the dossier. He must have refused to tell them the information. Jack, they tortured Paddy. It was especially gruesome, and the people I know in the coroner's office said they had never seen anything like it. They tortured him so badly, he died. The people I know said it was likely he died before he gave up the information. Your life is in more jeopardy than you know."

"But, I don't have the dossier, and never have heard about the POD accounts, or any of this."

"I know, and I only know about the list because we had been discipling Veronica. Veronica was confiding a lot of things to me. So much so that I kept a diary of our interactions. When she became a Christian, she broke free from her past. She cut ties and took names, literally. We walked her and Paddy through so much. There was a total transformation from their past as a drug addict and a part of a drug-running cartel. There had to be, but it was a messy time of discipleship, God did work in their hearts. When she met you, she had left that old life so she made us promise never to tell you the whole story unless your life depended on it."

Kim finally spoke up, "Any idea where the dossier is?"

"No, but think of the dossier and the accounts as a two-headed poisonous snake. One head can destroy a lot of lives, futures, political ambitions. You name it. The other head can set someone up for a life of luxury they could never imagine. Poisonous for those it touches."

"Why didn't the government seize those accounts too?"

"Veronica did not go into witness protection, so the government either knew about the account and looked the other way so she wouldn't have to worry about finances, or they had no clue, and she secreted the money before taking the case to the authorities."

"Ok, but how did anyone know about the accounts in Paddy's name?"

"I am not sure, but it was someone in the U.S. Marshal's office who started digging again, when they released Juan Carlos for time served. I am not sure, but it sounds to me like there is some connection from Juan Carlos to someone there."

"Was the person's name, 'Cynthia'?"

"I am not sure, but I can tell you that the person that came to see me is tied up with someone who drives an old car with T-tops, you know, the one like on Smoky and the Bandit?"

"Yes, a vintage Trans-Am."

The pieces started coming together, "Aunt Ilean, how did you find out about all of this?"

"As I said, I knew about the dossier before Veronica died, but I didn't know about the money, for sure, until the woman showed up and started questioning me. Shee wanted to find you, but I didn't tell her anything. Later, Phil Townsend with the U.S. Marshal's office called to ask me some questions, but I didn't know who I could trust."

"Why did Phil call you?"

"I think he called because he worked on Veronica's case and knew me from then. He wanted to find out anything else about Juan Carlos to get him for additional crimes. He felt that justice had not been served yet, but I only knew what Veronica told me, which is not admissible in court. He did tell me that a female US Marshal agent tried to find you in Orlando but was unable to locate you."

"Oh, Cynthia found us but either the real Cynthia was late, or the Cynthia who found us is one of the people working for the cartel, and the US Marshal service."

"Oh, dear, if someone is working for the US Marshal Service and the cartel, well, that's going to change what I was going to suggest."

"What was that?"

"Well, I was going to suggest you call Phil, but if Cynthia is with the cartel, he could be too."

"I don't think we can trust anyone in government now, and any movement by us will likely involve someone watching us. If we try to get a rental car, buy an airplane ticket, whatever, someone will likely know."

"You need to go to the Cayman's, Jack. I think that the answers you are looking for are there."

"Yeah, besides, I can't get to my passport. It's at my condo, and I am sure someone is watching."

"The good thing is that I own the condo and it probably needs a maintenance filter check and filter change in the A/C or something," then Ilean yelled, "Josiah, come here." When Josiah came into the room, she asked, "can you take care of the problem in Jack's condo?"

"What problem?"

"Well, I think there is a need to have the A/C checked out, and he might even need some clothes, passport some other stuff, but no one needs to know about it. Jack, can you give Josiah a list?"

"Sure, it's straightforward. I have a backpack with my passport, computer and a couple of gift cards. A small carry-on bag with a few clothes, grab it. Oh, and my toiletry bag in the bathroom. I think that's all I need."

"You got it," Josiah said as he left.

He was gone about ten minutes and came back. "Jack, the guy who flew you here, called the desk at the airport, he is looking for you, and he wants to talk to you."

"I didn't leave any information about who I was calling. How did the guy find me?"

"Call the desk at the airport back. Here is the number," Josiah said, holding up his phone.

"I don't have a phone. We got rid of all of our phones because someone even tracked our burner phone. At least that is what we thought, a friend tried to help, but their bank accounts ended up being frozen."

"Call them back on mine."

I dialed the phone, and a female answered the phone. "Hello, this is the Vero Beach Airport, can I help you," the voice sounded very similar to Cynthia's, so, I just hung up. "It sounded like Cynthia, the one who is chasing us from the US Marshal office, I hung up."

Kim spoke up, "How do they keep finding us?"

"I don't know unless they have people who tracked the flight, from Bradenton, to here and then at the airport. Maybe they found out who we called, but it would be ridiculous if they had that capability."

Josiah looked at Kim and said, "were you on the phone earlier, in the bathroom, I heard you talking in there."

"No, I was talking to myself. Were you eavesdropping?

"No, I needed to use the restroom, and before I tried the door, I heard your voice, so I went to the restroom upstairs."

Ilean looked at me with a great deal of worry on her face. I had seen that look before, right when she called me to come to her house to tell me Veronica was missing. We had been followed by someone constantly, and it seemed every time we were about to break free from tracking, they still found us. Was it possible Kim had a cell phone? Maybe she kept her phone instead of putting it in the truck at the convenience store? All of these possibilities were too much for me to figure out right now!

"We need a burner phone too, Josiah, can you get us a burner phone?"

"Yes, I think a small Mexican grocery store has phones. I will stop there. They also have some killer tacos. Are you guys hungry?"

"Yes, please, thank you so much, Josiah!"

Ilean spoke up, "let's try to come up with a plan, Jack. You need to get out front on this, and we need to get you to the Cayman's as soon as we can. We can charter a plane, but that may be too expensive at least until Jack gets his money."

"Who's to say they are not at the bank right now, waiting on me to show up?"

"The man in the car from Smoky and the Bandit asked what bank Veronica put the money in, so I don't think they know. I don't think they know Paddy's last name, and I don't think they know it is a POD, so time is critical."

"This is all too much." I turned away from everyone, and that was it. I completely fell to pieces. With all the running, fear, and reminders of Veronica, all of it hit at one time, not to mention, I was fresh off of the funeral for Marie, my wife, who died just a few weeks ago. Then it hit me that the coroner's report from Marie's murder was due any day, and my phone was long gone, probably still in a pickup truck. So here I am, forgetting my wife. I'm completely broke and running for my life.

I just broke. I was broke. I started crying with hot tears and a pressure filled, overwhelming weight on my life. Kim and Ilean had both stepped up to hug me. Neither said a word, they just held me, and I sobbed. Kim started crying, and then, Ilean said, "look, guys, if you don't stop your crying, I lean to cry too."

I started laughing, crying, and then something in between. Then Kim started laughing, crying, and holding me tight. I forgot everything we had just discussed.

Suddenly, I felt really weak like someone had just drained every ounce of energy from me. "I need to sit down."

Kim and Ilean both let go, and I sat down. Immediately, I was thirsty like I had just walked a thousand miles across the desert with no water. My mouth was dry, my strength was gone, and I was so thirsty I couldn't think of anything but water, "I need water, and I need water now." Ilean recognized I was in distress and ran for a bottle of water in her car. On her way in, she said, the bottle was half-full, but the sink in the bathroom works, so we can fill it as much as needed. I drank as fast as I could, then Ilean ran to the faucet and refilled. I drank another bottle as fast as I could, then Kim also got thirsty. Ilean filled the bottle, and Kim drank furiously, and then Ilean said, "could you guys move closer to the faucet because I am getting thirsty quenching your thirst."

I got my chair and started towards the bathroom. "I was kidding, I can do this," and Ilean went back and refilled. We both drank several bottles of water, and within a few minutes, we both started feeling better. As quickly as I felt weakness, I felt strength. "I think I was dehydrated."

"No doubt, keep drinking, but slower now, you too, Kim."

Ilean's phone rang, "Hello? Yes, go in the condo maintenance truck. Take a tool pouch in with you, hold on, Jack, Kim, do you want food now or wait until Josiah goes to Jack's condo?"

Kim shrugged her shoulders, "don't matter to me."

Ilean looked at me, I shrugged my shoulders, "me either."

Ilean continued, "get Jack's stuff and then stop and get food, ok, bye." Looking at us, Ilean said, "Josiah is at the condo. He should be able to get the stuff in about 15 minutes, and then he will head this way. He will call to find out what to pick up for dinner."

"Tacos sounded good."

"Well, he already picked up a phone somewhere. He can go back; it's not far from here. You know, I just had a thought. What if we could book a cruise to Grand Cayman for you? It would only take a day to get there as opposed to several by Yacht. I know someone who works for the office of a cruise line in Miami. I could call and see if you can show up with a suitcase."

"Let's call using the burner phone Josiah is getting, just in case someone is listening in to your conversations."

"That's a good point. Going on a cruise line would be faster than a yacht or sailing but slower than a flight; the problem with the flight is that it may instantly flag your passport. A cruise may do the same; I'm not sure."

"A cruise would be nice. At least we wouldn't be looking over our shoulders for Cynthia or someone chasing us," Kim said.

A cruise sounded like the best plan until Kim spoke because the sleeping arrangements would be hard to manage. I had no access to money, so any help Ilean could give would probably be limited, and I was sure it would not include enough for two rooms. I liked Kim and was falling for her, but not enough to jeopardize my integrity, plus, just the same room would create an issue with appearances. I had already stepped over the line in Bradenton, but at least it was a separate suite. I felt a knot in my gut as I thought about it.

Ilean knew me well and spoke up, "I probably can't get two rooms, but there may be a family suite available, where you could have separate sleeping arrangements."

"That would be good. Let's see what is available before we decide."

Kim put her arm around me and said, "Of course, if we got married, we wouldn't have to worry about what people thought, right?"

My face suddenly went flush. I was just a few weeks away from Marie's death, and Kim was just a few weeks away from her husband's death. Now, Kim is talking about marriage!

"But, you haven't met my kids yet, and they have to approve before marriage."

"You have kids? How many?"

"Dozens, every wife wanted at least one!"

If someone ever had the shock of their life written on their face or the 'deer in the headlight look,' Kim had her moment, or at least it seemed that way.

The moment lasted an eternity with Kim uncertain about my surprising disclosure and Ilean about to bust her gut laughing.

Ilean couldn't contain it any longer and laughed as loud and long as I started laughing, and eventually Kim.

"You got me, you really got me. Touché, Jack Cash, touché."

At least I stepped away from the marriage question for a minute, but it didn't settle the issue of sleeping arrangements, and I didn't want to get married so I could sleep in the same bed. Marriage is a sacred thing not moved by momentary pleasure or convenience.

Ilean's phone rang, "Hello? Great," looking at us, "it's Josiah, he wants to know what you want to eat."

"Tacos," we said in unison.

"Tacos, did you get everything? Did you see anyone? What did they say? Do you think you were able to, ok, keep a close eye for anyone following you, ok, see you soon, bye! Well, it sounds like someone was watching your condo, Jack, because they asked him where the occupant had gone. Josiah asked if they checked the beach, and then they wanted to know what he was doing. He told them he was changing the filter for the A/C. They went back to their car but kept watching. He was sure they didn't follow, but when he stops for tacos, he will double around the block before coming here to ensure they are not following him."

"He got everything, right?"

"Yes, he found the things you said, but because of the questions from the guy at the condo, he couldn't come out with everything. He fit all he could in his tool bag. He got a change of clothes and your passport. The toiletry bag was too big to fit, so he grabbed a couple of items he felt you would need the most and left."

"We have got to get this thing done, whatever it takes because it needs to be over!" I looked at Kim and continued, "Kim, I like you, but putting you through more of this running is not going to be good. I am afraid that this could get me killed, and I don't want you to die too."

"Well, thank you for thinking of my safety, but I think I am safer with you than leaving this adventure unless you are trying to dump me."

"I am not trying to dump you, I just don't want to put your life in danger any longer."

"I think she is right," Ilean offered, "someone is willing to kill to get information, and she would be vulnerable if she went back to her condo, I am afraid that being together is safer."

Within a few minutes, Josiah arrived with our food. What thirst had done earlier, hunger had now taken over. We devoured our dinner. It was starting to get late, and we had been through a lot in the last few days, but the house we were in had no beds at all.

"I am getting tired. Can we sleep here?"

"Not on your life, Jack Cash!!! I have a condo down the beach you can stay in tonight, but let's call about the cruise." Ilean pulled up the number on her phone as I fumbled around with the burner phone Josiah had picked up for me. "Let's go to the condo," so we loaded up and headed to it.

After turning it on and going through the paces for the SIM card, the phone activated cell service, "It's ready, what is the number?"

She rattled off the number, and I gave her the phone. "Chelsea, this is Ilean. How are you doing? I know it is late, but I have a couple," looking at me shaking her head, "that wants to book a cruise at the last minute. Is that even possible? It has to be a cruise that stops in Grand Cayman, yeah Georgetown, tomorrow, what time, ok, I will call then, can you text me the number, thank you so much. How are your mom and dad, great, tell them I said hello. Ok, bye."

"Well, she said if we call tomorrow morning after 7, she will check to see if there are any cancellations for the next couple of cruises. They have one sailing tomorrow. You would be in Grand Cayman the day after but, she was sure it was sold out a long time ago. That doesn't mean there has not been a cancelation."

"So, we need to call back tomorrow morning, after 7?"

"Yes, let's gather everything up and. It's getting dark. We can go to the condo under cover of darkness."

About fifteen minutes later, we were pulling up to the condo. "You can stay here the night, until tomorrow but you need to be out by noon, hopefully, we can get you on a cruise. But, it takes a little over two hours to get there, so, if there is a room, you will have to leave first thing tomorrow."

"No problem, thank you so much. I hate to say it, but my bank account is locked up, or it was, and I am afraid to recheck it until we have all this settled, just in case they are tracking activity on the account."

"Say no more. I will take care of the costs of the cruise and everything. You can pay me back when you get all this done."

"Thank you!" I knew my tab with about everyone was reaching the point I couldn't repay, and now, thousands of dollars more to pay for a last-minute cruise for two. It was going to cause me to have to tap into my retirement.

As she opened up the condo, it was an all-in-one-room bedroom complete with a small loveseat, kitchenette, small dining table with four chairs, and an easy chair. The bed was a full-sized bed. "I'm sorry, but this is the only condo I have available and the smallest one too."

"It's very much appreciated, we will rest well," I said but I would not rest well, regardless of where I ended up sleeping. And with Kim in the same room in chasing Jack Cash mode, that would not happen. I had to dislike her in my mind and heart to guard myself, but not in my attitude. I had to focus on that and hope the sleeping arrangements would be better if the cruise worked out.

"Thank you so much, Ilean. I think this will work. We will just have to snuggle closer." Kim said, winking at me.

I knew I was in trouble no matter what. Just being in the same room was going to pose a problem. It was becoming obvious Kim thought this was a race to the finish line, full throttle to marriage. I was thinking reverse, full bore. The kind of fast reverse that runs into everything because most people can't drive quickly in reverse, and tonight, I was afraid she was going to move faster forward than I could drive in reverse.

"Well, goodnight, I am going to come early to help you make the arrangements, let's plan on 6:30."

"Goodnight, Ilean, thank you again."

"Yes, thank you."

CHAPTER TWENTY

When the door closed, Kim started going through her clothes and pulled out a very silky negligée, held it up, and turning toward the bathroom, "perfect, nightgown, I'm going to take a shower. Do you want to join me?"

I stood there wondering if she was playing some kind of joke or if I found the place of the reverse where I was going to back up so fast that a wreck was coming. My face did not betray the way I felt.

"Jack Cash, are you blushing? Are you going to join me for the shower or not?"

"Um, no, I am going to sleep outside."

"You don't have to take a shower with me if you don't want but I do have some candy for you later."

"That's ok, I will sleep in the beach chairs. I don't think I am strong enough to handle this temptation, you, you, temptress, you!"

I opened the door, and I could see someone shining their flashlight around. I closed the door quickly.

"That was quick. I don't think I want you to take a shower with me, anyway. I'm not in the mood anymore."

"Good, because that's one thing I don't need."

"What?"

"I don't need someone I care about trying to seduce me. I am not sure

I am strong enough."

"Don't worry about it, Jack Cash. You are too uptight. I was just kidding. I am not interested in you taking a shower with me."

"Ok, then I have a question for you."

Kim ran with breakneck speed to me, and got as close as she could, looking at me eye to eye. She got so close that every time I moved my lips, they would touch her lips, "What is your question, Jack Cash?"

"If I would have said yes, I would love to take a shower with you, what would have happened?"

"I guess we won't know until the next time I ask, and you answer that you want to take a shower with me."

"Fair enough. Take your shower, alone! Take it alone!"

Each time my lips moved, hers touched mine, then when she said something in reply, it became a short kiss, and then she pulled me in an embrace, a really tight embrace. "If you said you wanted to take a shower with me," running her hands up and down my back, and in the most seductive voice yet, "Do you know what I would say?"

I cleared my throat, but my voice cracked, "No, what would you say."

"I would say, come on Jack Cash. Your wife wants you really, really bad, and she is ready to clean you up," she said, bursting out laughing, "I'm going to take a shower, and I am locking the door."

Kim's seduction was over the top and almost too much for me to resist. I knew if I gave in, I would regret it. She would also consider it a guarantee we were going to marry. I was in trouble and needed a diversion to think of things other than sex with Kim.

So, I thought about a long prayer walk, but then, she shut the door and started the shower. I was relieved and I sat down contemplating everything. It dawned on me I may not even be able to get into the account if it is a POD account without a death certificate, so a trip to Grand Cayman would be a waste of time and money. I texted Ilean, "do u think Paddy's death cert. is ready, I may need it in Grand Cayman." A few seconds later, she texted back, "I know the coroner, I'll text him." It took about ten minutes when she texted back, "call when u can."

I called Ilean, "Were you able to contact the coroner?"

"Yes, that's what I wanted to talk to you about."

"They need someone to claim the body and decide which funeral home to send the body to, there is no one else."

"My bank accounts are locked up; I can't do anything right now."

"The coroner said there is an investigation to determine who killed him, but they know how he died. So, they are ready to release the body, and with it, the death certificates, but need someone who will be responsible."

"I will do it but will have to have them hold the body until I can work out finances."

"Call the coroner, and Smith & Singleton Funeral Home is a good choice. They have handled a bunch of people I know. They are outstanding and affordable. They will work with you."

"I will. Text me the coroner's number, please."

"I will send it right away. I am not sure how long it will take, but the coroner will know how to get a copy. Let me know what he says because it may determine what we do tomorrow."

"I will call back."

I dialed the number. It rang a few times and then went to voice-mail. I left a message and felt it was probably a cell phone, so I texted, "Hello, I am Jack Cash, and someone murdered my friend Paddy Gypsy a few days ago. I need to get his body to a funeral home and a death certificate. Can I get the information about these two things?"

Immediately the phone rang, "Hello, is this Jack Cash?"

"Yes, thank you for getting back so quickly."

"The answer to your first question is what funeral home do you want to use?"

"Smith & Singleton!"

"Ok, I will call them. I have completed the autopsy and filed the death certificate. You should be able to get a copy of it soon, I doubt it will be available tomorrow, but it is possible. Mr. Cash, I am sorry for your loss. How well did you know him?"

"He was my brother-in-law, but his sister, my wife, was murdered years ago."

"Yes, I remember that case. How much have you been in touch with Mr. Gypsy?"

"He called several times a month, or I called him, more so around birthdays, holidays, times like that."

"Have you heard from him recently?"

"Yes, several times before, well, before this past week."

"What did he tell you?"

"He just said that my life was in danger and called multiple times to tell me."

"What was the nature of the danger?"

"Something to do with Veronica's death and what happened before she died."

"What happened before she died?"

"Several years before I met her, she worked high up in the cartel, so high she knew where they buried bodies. She knew the location of every financial account and knew many people in the government involved in it. Anyway, God changed her life, and when He did, she decided to turn in those in the cartel. The government offered her a new identity and more in a witness protection program after she testified against the cartel members. She did but refused the witness protection and lived a normal life. I met her a year or so later, and we married. Someone murdered her, but the investigation never uncovered her killer."

"Jack Cash, it is possible whoever killed your wife killed her brother. Juan Carlos' release from prison had to come with scores to settle. Your life is in danger, and you need to be protected."

"I know, but I can't do anything until I get a death certificate for Paddy. I need it as soon as possible."

"Call my office tomorrow morning, after 8, and I will try to have one by then. It's been filed but has to go through a couple of processes."

Boom, Boom, Boom, Boom, all of a sudden, someone was pounding on the door. "What is the sound, Mr. Cash?"

"Someone is at the door."

"Don't answer it. Your life is in danger, do not answer your door, hang up with me and call 911.

BOOM, BOOM, BOOM, BOOM, the pounding was louder, and by this time, Kim finished her shower and was towel drying her hair when she opened the door.

BOOM, BOOM, BOOM, BOOM, I hung up and called 911. I told

dispatch someone was pounding on an adjoining door, and the people were scared. When they asked my name, I told them, Earnest P. Tutwiler, even disguising my voice as an older man. When they asked me to see what he wanted, I told them I was afraid for my life. That alone sent most of the shift officers to the location. When they arrived, they confronted the mystery person. I couldn't make out what they were saying, but he was furious. They knocked on our door, I looked at Kim, and she shook her head "no," and we just stayed quiet until they left.

"We need to get some sleep, tomorrow is going to be a long day. I realized we would need Paddy's death certificate, and it may not be ready yet. I will call the coroner's office tomorrow and see if they can help me out."

"Okaaayyyyy, but where will you sleep?"

"I will sleep on this tiny love seat, and I love to sleep, so maybe this love seat will be kind and allow such a thing."

Kim looked at me and the love seat and then at me again. "Enjoy! I hope you sleep well."

"You too," I said as I started moving things around to make things more comfortable, "you too."

After lights out, it didn't take long for my mind to fire up, running through every eventuality, every possible problem to plan for a day that held no promises, maybe few answers, and a lot of danger.

The last thing I remembered was sighing a long sigh, looking at my watch, frustrated it was 1:30 a.m. and I was still awake, then falling asleep. The dreams were epic. I dreamed Cybil was using a deep sultry voice telling me I needed to check the basement. The stairs to the basement were like funhouse stairs shifting and moving different ways with each step. I had to steady myself by holding tight to the railing while I descended. Each step, though, brought back a memory: Cybil on our wedding day. Callie, when she called me out of the blue, the next step was when we met after the call.

Callie may have had long feet, but her eyes were a beautiful hue of aqua blue, the blue you see in the Caribbean waters that call for you to go deeper. Callie was that type of person, the one that you always wanted to experience life with, not afraid to jump in with both feet. She did that with everything. She dedicated her life to reaching people who had never heard the gospel in the jungles of Ecuador and used every possible means to make it happen. She served in some dangerous places, from predatory creatures to local populations, some of whom had killed missionaries before. She hosted teams constantly to bring medicine, Christmas presents, education materials, or simply pitching in to help build a house or a church in the middle of the Amazon, all with the hope of reaching another person with the love of Jesus. It was her passion.

She visited the church I was pastoring after Cybil died and shared her passion with the people. They responded in ways I had never experienced before at that church. They rallied to give to her outreach tens of thousands of dollars. No one had ever received such an extravagant offering. She thought our church would only give her a few hundred dollars and other churches would follow suit, but the people gave over and above what was needed. Looking back, it may have been their matchmaking ways, trying to create something between Callie and me. If they were, it worked. Callie was blown away and attributed their generosity to my leadership. Our leadership team offered to host her and me for lunch after the service, most likely ensuring that the matchmaking worked. We went to a Mexican restaurant, and just a few minutes into our conversation, we found two important things. First, our waitress was not from Mexico but Ecuador. The chances of it happening are only something God knows and God engineered. Second, Barbara, one of our team members, spoke up and asked Callie if she was married. "No, never married."

"Are you opposed to marriage?"

"No, just finding someone with the same passion that I have is hard. Plus, I have to know God is in it for me even to date someone."

Never mincing words, Barbara said, "We know a guy who loves God and would make an excellent husband."

I felt like crawling under the table but knew Barbara would continue down this trail if I didn't stop it right away.

"So, what is everyone going to order?"

An uncomfortable silence fell on the table. Finally, Callie spoke up, "I think if there were anyone on the planet that would meet the criteria for marriage; a husband I could love and adore, someone, filled with a heart of adventure. Someone who loves Jesus, it would probably be the rarest find, one destined by God," then Callie turned to me and winked. If there were any questions about her intentions on this trip, that one statement cleared everything up for me. From Mandy to Callie, most of my wives chased me first instead of me pursuing them.

"Well, that settles it. I think they should get married right away. We can get the church ready this weekend and have a wedding on Saturday," Barbara offered.

"Slow your roll, Barbara. We haven't even dated. Today is the first time I have seen Callie in years. She serves overseas, and I pastor this church. There are a lot of things that have to happen before it is even on the table." It was as if slipped out of my mouth without me even thinking about the words and how Callie might interpret my words, "Besides, she has other places to go while she is in the states."

"Callie, where do you have to be next weekend," Barbara questioned, "Because if you don't have a place to stay until you leave, you can stay with us."

"I have been staying in a mission's house a church in Nashville offered me, I planned to come here, determine how much more I needed to raise to support my project, and then head back to Nashville. My team in Ecuador is not expecting me for three more weeks. Since I raised all the support needed for my project, I will likely head back early unless something comes up between now and then."

All heads turned in my direction, as if their eyes were drills, drilling through my brain, beating it up, and taking names. I turned to look at the menu and remarked, "The tacos here are quite lovely."

Everyone laughed and laughed. The one next to me punched my shoulders and ordered their food. Callie excused herself to the restroom.

Barbara leaned over and whispered in my ear, "Well, Pastor, you didn't ask for my opinion or anything, but you need to take a vacation, starting right after this meal, and you need to take it with Callie. We will take care of the church while you are with her, just take some time and see if this is from the Lord. I will take care of everything, but if you are even close to being interested in Callie, I mean even to date, this is your time, and we aim to make sure you have the time to figure it out."

She leaned away and whispered to her husband, and he nodded in agreement, and then, scanning the rest of the leadership team, each nodded in agreement in succession. It was as if they had discussed this before, evidently, after the massive offering, something was up, and now they were in full-blown matchmaking mode.

Honestly, it was what I needed. I had several local women who tried to pursue me, but none had the passion for serving the Lord and would have struggled with the glasshouse lifestyle of a pastor's wife. I had resigned myself to being single for a long time. I was too tired to even think about it, and besides, I didn't want to lose another wife.

When Callie returned, we all ate and made a little bit of small talk. I decided to take the team up on their offer for a vacation. I had nothing to keep that from happening but by pouring my life into my work. I wrote, "Yes, but I want to see if I can take her somewhere" on one of my business cards and handed it to Barbara under the table. She almost choked on her burrito. She nodded in agreement and giggled, elbowing her husband. I guess he got the message and then, the mood around the table changed drastically. It was as if I envisioned everyone chatting, and suddenly a song started playing on the overhead speaker, with everyone breaking out in song, singing at the top of their lungs, standing up, dancing, drunk on the news Jack Cash was going to ask Missionary Callie out on a date. That was the mood for the moment.

I didn't want to ask Callie out on a date in front of everyone, but it didn't take long for people to get the hint they needed to leave. Everyone started looking at their watches, nudging one another, when finally Barbara spoke up, "Well, we have to go. If you want to stay here for a day or so, we have a lovely 'mother-in-law' house where you can stay. My mother-in-law died before we bought the house, so we have had people stay there from time to time."

Callie looked down for a second, as if she had just gotten terrible news, and said, "Thank you, but I may need to get back to Nashville."

"Well, Pastor Jack Cash can get our number to you if you change your mind. It was lovely meeting you. We will be praying for you."

"Thank you!"

With that, everyone left Callie and me at the table. I moved closer to Callie. After an awkward silence, we both spoke at the same time. She began with, "Well, it's a long way," as if she were leaving, and I started with, "Would you like to go on a trip with me?"

"Wait, what??? What did you say?"

"I asked if you would like to go on a trip with me. I haven't taken a vacation in a while. The leadership team offered me one, and staying around here and dating in our area is not advisable, so how about a trip somewhere? We can leave today."

"I don't know what to say. I can't afford."

"I will pay for everything. I will get us separate rooms everywhere we go. We can date somewhere else without people interfering. If you are up for some beach time, I know a place."

"Anywhere with you would be a great place."

"So, then, it's a date?"

"Yes, it's a date."

I grabbed my phone and called Ilean to see if two condos were available. It was off-season, so it was easy to get two places, side by side. After hanging up the phone, "Well, are you packed and ready to go?"

"Yes, I brought a couple of changes of clothes but can get other things if needed."

"Let me see if there are seats available for a flight today or tomorrow."

I pulled up my travel app and started looking. There was nothing available Sunday, but Monday morning offered seats for two, side by side. Looking at Callie, I said, "Well, today is out of the question, unless we drive but tomorrow morning, there is an early morning flight."

Tears began streaming down Callie's face.

"Did I say something wrong?"

Callie shook her head, "no," but the tears continued.

"Are you ok?"

She shook her head, "yes," with even more tears but now with a smile a mile wide piercing through the tears, "I couldn't be better."

I called Ilean, then Barbara, to set up our condo and a place for Callie that night. Barbara was ecstatic and wanted to "prep" Callie on all things 'Jack Cash.' I was sure that was what the plan was, but when I told her we were going for some beach time, Barbara insisted on taking Callie to buy clothes in preparation for the trip.

"Well, it looks like our date starts tomorrow because Barbara wants you to come to her house now, and she wants to take you shopping. She and her husband are wealthy, so don't worry about the cost. They will pay for everything, and the mother-in-law quarters they have are better than any place I have ever stayed. I stayed there when I first moved to town."

Callie leaned in close to me, with tears streaming down her face, and said, "I can't believe this is happening. I really can't. I can't believe this is happening. I get to go on a date with Jack Cash!"

I heard it again, "Jack Cash!"

It was one of those kinds of dreams you simply want to stay in forever, too surreal to call a dream and too wonderful to leave, but an exact recall of an event.

The next time, it was louder, "Jack Cash!"

It was evident Kim was afraid of something. I woke up to Kim standing over me, trying to wake me up. It was the fifth day since meeting Kim on this beach and it seemed the nights were getting shorter.

"Someone is trying to open the door."

It sounded more like tapping than trying to get inside.

"What time is it?" I whispered.

"It's 5:45."

I looked through the peephole and couldn't see anyone, but the sun was about to rise. Then it was a scratching at the door, but I couldn't see anyone near the door. "I think we have a small visitor."

The scratching gave way to a tapping sound, but there was no way I could see anything. I looked through the blinds, still, nothing to see.

"I am going to open the door."

Kim took a pan from the kitchenette and handed it to me. Slowly I opened the door, think I would find some type of animal or a bird. It was Josiah lying in front of our door, beaten and bloody. He was alive but in severe pain. "Josiah, we are going to pull you inside."

He motioned for us to wait while attempting to get into a crawling position but realized his left arm was broken.

"Kim, take his right arm, I will try to get him by the torso. Let's pull him into the condo."

He waved us off, "I think I have a broken rib or two. Please don't pull or grab me in any way. I will see if I can move inside. Jack Cash, they know you are in the area. The guy that was watching your condo knew you were around. He found me last night after we dropped you off and tried to get information from me. He doesn't know you are here, in this condo."

"Is he the one that beat you up?"

"Yes, there may have been two, at least it felt like two, anyway, they beat on me until they got tired, and then someone called, and they left. I waited for a while and crawled here. You are in danger. You need to leave as soon as you can. Take my car, and head to the port, and call the number Aunt Ilean gave you for the cruise line. Go, now!"

"I have to get a death certificate before I go or the trip will be a waste."

"Jack, we've got to go! They may have followed Josiah."

"I am in a lot of pain, but I waited a long time before coming this way even moving around different condos, waiting, and then moving on. I think the only way they can find you is if they are watching from the beach."

I looked around the beach, and only a few older adults were out this early, one walking a dog, another looking for shells that had washed up during high tide, and a couple walking hand in hand talking, no doubt waiting for the sunrise. In the distance, I could see a yacht anchored, with no noticeable movement on it. "I don't see anyone who looks concerning unless there is someone on the yacht is watching."

Josiah looked towards the sea and said, "I didn't think they may be using someone out there to track my movement. You need to go. I will call for an ambulance." He pulled out his keys and said, "You know the car, right? It is the blue civic, license number ending with 81Q. You need to go now."

I took his keys while Kim grabbed our luggage, pulling it to the door. "Can we at least get you inside," Kim offered, "before we leave?"

"No, just go! It hurts to move in any way."

We stepped over him and ran to his car. We heard him call 911 to tell them where he was, and just before we were far enough, we heard him say, "Aunt Ilean," but that was all.

We threw our suitcases in the car, jumped in the car, and left. As we were leaving, a police car passed, then an ambulance passed us. We pulled over to pray for Josiah. Then we left the area.

"We've got to find a place to lay low. It will be a few hours before the coroner's office opens."

"Do you think we can trust him? Do you think we can trust anyone?" The fear in Kim's words indicated that finally, this was taking a huge emotional toll on her. Tears started flowing down her face, "Jack Cash, I am not sure what to do next. I am afraid! They beat Josiah severely just to find you."

"I don't know who we can trust, but we have to get the death certificate, regardless. I can't get into an account if I am not officially on the account, so we have to start there."

"They won't open for several hours."

"I have the coroner's cell number," pulling up his number, "I am calling him now."

The call went to voice mail, "Hello, this is Jack Cash. I was wondering if we could get the death certificate early. You were right. We are in danger and need to go as soon as we can."

About five minutes later, he called back. "Sorry, I was unable to answer your call. I was finishing up a DOA and had to load the body. I was able to get a copy of Paddy's official certificate and have it with me now. Where do you want me to meet you?"

Kim put the call on mute, "Can we trust that someone is not with him, or is he not involved in this too?" Her paranoia any other time would be just , but now it had become heightened awareness.

"What else can we do?"

"Jack Cash, are you there?"

Kim unmuted the phone, "Yes, we are here. Where are you?"

"I am on the north side of Vero. I can be downtown in about ten minutes."

"Perfect, let's meet in front of the police station?"

We hung up. "Kim, we can be there in about 10 minutes too, but we need to get to a place where we can see if he is alone."

"I don't know anything about the downtown area. I don't even know where the police station is, so I can't help."

"Pull up a map of the area on your phone. See if there is a multistory building near the police station or a park, something that can conceal us as we look."

As Kim was pulling up the map, an unknown number called my phone. Since we had just had this phone for a few hours, it was not a call we wanted to answer, "that's not good. Someone has our number."

"All I see is one-way streets, and the street view is showing the police station, and government buildings are the tallest but only a few stories."

"We will drive by then and circle the block until we see him, but before we do, let's find a place to pull over."

"There is a neighborhood market." so we pulled into the parking lot between two cars at the edge of the parking area.

A few minutes later, the coroner called, "Jack Cash, I am in the parking lot at the Police station in Vero Beach."

"I am a few minutes away, do you have the death certificate?"

"Yes, but hurry. I just got a call to go to the hospital, someone severely beat a young man, and they are consulting with me about gathering some forensics."

Kim looked at me and mouthed, "Josiah."

"Did he die?"

"Not yet, but they are not sure he will make it. He was only able to say a few things before he became unconscious. Anyway, I need to head there as soon as possible.

"We are on our way, about 7 minutes out."

Our need to get the death certificate was greater, so I pulled out of the parking lot and headed toward the police station. Once we arrived in the area, Kim charted a course to circle the block several times to see if anyone was following or in any parking lot nearby who could be watching. After about three times, he called again, "Are you close? I need to go!"

"We are pulling in now," next to a van with the "Medical Examiner" logo on it. He stepped around the van with the paper in hand. I pulled up to him and held my hand out, "I am Jack Cash."

Immediately we were surrounded by police officers. "Hands, let us see your hands!" Kim and I both held our hands up. "We need for you to put your hands outside the car."

We both complied with a lot of shouting from various officers, each one saying something different. Finally, someone said, "reach out and open your door from the outside, first the driver, and keep your hands outside your vehicle." I reached outside the vehicle and opened the door. "Now, step outside with your hands where we can see them." I slowly did as they instructed, knowing for some reason they were on edge about us. "Now, I need for you to step out of your car, hands behind your head. Now turn around, now, walk backward toward my voice." I took about three steps, hesitantly, so I wouldn't fall, and then he commanded, "Stop!" as someone handcuffed me.

"Am I under arrest?"

"You are being detained while we complete our investigation."

Then they focused on Kim, and finally, they handcuffed her and took her to the police station. They led me inside as well, but to another room. When I questioned what this was about, the officer simply said, "we will ask you some questions in a minute." They gathered all the items in my pocket to verify my identity and left the room.

After a few minutes, a detective arrived and introduced himself. "Are you Jack Cash?"

"Yes, sir!"

"Do you know why we are detaining you?"

"No, sir!"

"Because you are in a car belonging to a young man who someone severely assaulted, did you steal the car?"

"No, he gave us permission to use it."

"When did you last see him?"

"At our condo."

"What condition was he in?"

"Someone had severely beat him."

"Who is he to you?"

"He is a friend who was helping us."

"Records from the 911 call indicated he was the one who called. Why didn't you call?"

"Because he wanted us to take his car and leave."

"Oh really, so, a man shows up at your condo, severely beaten, and instead of calling 911 and getting help, he offers you his car so you can leave the area, and calls 911 himself, is that your story?"

"Yes, sir, it's the truth."

"Did you beat him?"

"No, sir, he arrived at our condo that way."

"Well, doesn't it sound a little suspicious that you left him almost dead, took his car, and we found you riding around?"

"Is there a supervisor I can talk to?"

"No, I am the one you will talk to."

"We didn't hurt Josiah we found him hurt. I am sure this is about Juan Carlos," suddenly, the detective jumped to his feet and left the room.

Within a minute, the captain over the detectives and the Police Chief was in the room. "Are you Jack Cash?"

"Yes, do I need to get a lawyer?"

"No, we talked to Josiah. He told us about Juan Carlos and Paddy, and he told us that he permitted you to drive his car, even after his assault. Sir, we can offer you protection, but only if you stay in the police station. We don't have the manpower to have an officer escort you where you need to go."

"Thank you. I don't need any help. What I do need is to get Paddy's death certificate and leave. The coroner was meeting me in the parking lot when you arrested me."

"He left something for you, but he had to leave."

"Am I free to go and is Kim free to go?"

"Who?"

"Kim, the woman who was with me."

"The only person in holding right now is a woman who goes by Penny. You are free to go."

I left the room, picked up the packet from the coroner, and found my way to the parking lot, hoping to see Kim. I circled back to the front desk and asked about the woman who they brought in with me. The desk sergeant called back, and again, no one was in the back at the moment.

I walked back out to the car, and Kim was standing next to it with two coffees, a sack, and a massive smile on her face. "I found a coffee shop that had donuts. Just around from the police station, donuts and coffee near a police station. I call that product placement at its finest."

"It's so good to see your face. After all of this, I was afraid they would lock us up for being on the run."

"I know me too. Here, drink some coffee and have a donut."

Kim watched me as I took my first sip, "Well, what do you think?"

"I think it is one part pecan, one part coffee, and one part awesome."

"I thought you would like pecan coffee, now try a donut."

I reached into the bag and found a cinnamon powdered donut filled with some type of cream filling. One bite, and my taste buds were lit up, "Wow, this is amazing."

"Yea, the place had these donuts, and they call them "Amish Crack," because an Amish family started selling these on their front porch, and then it became a thing. Anyway, the place around the corner is Amish, or at least, I think it is."

"These are amazing. You should have gotten a dozen."

"Well, we might need our money for food later, and these were not free."

"We need to get on the road," I said as I opened the manila envelope left by the coroner. Paddy's death certificate was inside, along with a post-it note on it. The message read, Do not trust anyone. The cartel is everywhere. "We need to go now and I need to call Ilean, she is paying for our trip, and we need to get on a ship as soon as possible."

Once settled into her seat, Kim pulled up navigation to the cruise port outside of Miami. It was about a two-and-a-half-hour trip. Then she pulled up Ilean's number. No one answered, but we left a voice mail.

Kim reclined her seat, sighed, and closed her eyes. It looked like part of my trip would be me alone with my thoughts. I spent a good bit of time hoping Ilean would call to know if we were on the cruise. Honestly, I was kind of excited about going on a cruise, even if it was something else. I had only been on one other, with Callie.

CHAPTER TWENTY-ONE

hen Barbara offered to take Callie shopping, she did it right. She bought Callie clothes, new luggage, and so much more, treating her like royalty. While they were shopping, I went home to pack. While there, Paddy called me and told me he had a lead on who killed Veronica. It was not unusual because he regularly had possible murder suspects and made it his mission to find Veronica's killer. "Paddy, I am coming to Vero tomorrow with a friend. Maybe we can have coffee."

"Who is your friend?"

"Her name is Callie, and I have known her for a long time."

"Is she your girlfriend?"

"More like a friend, who is a girl, but we will see where it goes. We are staying in a couple of Ilean's condos. I will call you when we get into town."

"No, I will not interfere with your date. Just come by and buy a cheap t-shirt, and we can say hi."

"I will bring her by. See you soon."

The following day, Barbara picked me up with Callie smiling as big as I could imagine. "Well, kids, you have a great adventure awaiting you. I have booked you a five-day cruise for the week, and I called Ilean to let her know. I figured that was where you were going. I got you separate rooms and expect you both to be on good and godly behavior on this trip."

"Thank you so much, Barbara. You can't just take a thing. You have to takea thing, strap dynamite on it, and blow it up to awesome."

"Hahahahaha! You are welcome."

"Yes, thank you, Barbara and thank you for the clothes and everything. I have never been treated so well."

When we arrived at the airport, we said goodbye to Barbara and thanked her again, and then we went through flight paces and waited for our flight. The urge to pull out my computer and do a few things never crossed my mind. I just wanted to talk to Callie. We talked constantly in the airport, on the flight and when we arrived at the cruise port. I learned from Callie that she had very very few men interested in dating a missionary. She felt her calling had somehow disqualified her from that kind of happiness and there would be no one who even approached her about dating. No one did until the day before. She even remarked that when God finally opened the door for a date, it was epic. When she said that, the door opened for tears, it was her first actual date since college. I had to admit; it was the most epic first date I had been on as well.

We only went to our rooms when we had to change for a meal and to sleep. We spent as many moments together as one could, even though we were staying in separate rooms. By the end of the cruise, I wanted to ask Callie to marry me and felt that she was the one. On the last night, when I finally went to bed, I paused for prayer, asking God if it would be possible to marry someday someone I could spend the rest of my life with, and I would go to Ecuador if that was what it took for Him to say yes to my prayer. While I didn't hear an audible voice, I did experience a peace I couldn't describe.

Since we both woke up extremely early, as we did every day on this cruise, we got together on the "watch the sunrise" deck. By the look on her face, it was evident Callie had spent the night in great turmoil. My peace was as profound as her war. She declared first her calling to Ecuador was more important than her happiness and that she felt that she had breached the wall between the two. Knowing the peace I felt, I knew that I had to speak into her apprehension as I listened to her. I found a point of no return in life, a kind of defining moment that determines whether you proceed with reckless abandon or simply revert to the comfortable place of ordinary. Unfortunately, 'normal' place loses its normalcy once you have experienced love at this level. I knew Callie was at such a place, but I couldn't be the one speaking to her heart. It had to be God, for He is the one who called her, and only He could change her assignment.

"Let's find some coffee and talk," I insisted. As we walked to the coffee bar, I felt like Callie was about to break emotionally, and she did through bitter tears. I took her into my arms as she wept. I figured that the raging war inside her would make her pull away and distance herself from me to protect her heart, but she didn't. Rather than pull away, she came closer, holding me in such a way that with a little more force, I would have been the one pulling away with the need to breathe.

"Jack Cash, I have a huge problem, and it kept me up all night long. I have not slept at all. I wrestled, I wrestled with my own heart, I wrestled with God, and for a time, I wrestled with you. Honestly, I started wishing I had never agreed to this date. It was dangerous if I was going to stay single for the rest of my life. It was the kind of temptation that was too good but not completely wrong. I knew it would likely lead to this but didn't care. Now I do care, and I don't know what to do about it. Does anything I just said make sense?"

"Complete and total sense!"

"I wondered because I haven't slept, been up all night, and all I wanted to do was be with you. That's all I wanted, I wanted," as she started sobbing in my arms. She was beginning to draw a lot of side looks and whispers, but I didn't care.

"Is it my turn to talk?"

"Yes!" she sobbed.

"Well, I wasn't up all night, but I did pray because I knew we were likely at the point of no return. Callie, I told the Lord that I really liked you, as if He didn't know, and that I would be willing to go to Ecuador if He brought us together. I just wanted His will, but I shared with God my desire. I told God I wanted to be with you."

That statement set off a sobbing rant, most of which I couldn't understand, but she kept trying to communicate with me. Finally, I said, "Callie, I can't understand a word you are saying. Maybe we need to wait until later to talk about this."

"No," she said through blubbering and blowing her nose, "We need to talk now. I told the Lord I would be willing to give up Ecuador," and then the waterworks really kicked in and her voice took a higher pitch as she continued, "I told him, I really like you, and that if He wanted me to drop this relationship to continue my calling, "bljekjgh enaldkje tlelay," or at least is how the end of it sounded. Still, Callie didn't comprehend that I didn't know that form of tear language, but whatever she said calmed her heart almost immediately.

I waited for a minute and said, "ok, I hate to ask, but isn't there a language in Ecuador that is different than Spanish?"

"Yes," she said, alternating blowing her nose and wiping her tears away, "there are several. I know Quechua most; why?"

"Because, in the end, you said, 'if He wanted me to drop this relationship and continue my calling, and then you broke out the Quechua on me, and I didn't understand."

"Hahahahahaah, you are funny, it wasn't Quechua, it was estrogen." We both laughed, and she continued, "Jack Cash, I think you are an incredible man of God, and you have proven over and over this week. I told the Lord during the night that I couldn't continue our relationship because it would interfere with my calling, and then, what you just said took me by surprise. I thought I had to choose between you or my calling. I even prayed that I would be willing to leave Ecuador if God's will was bringing me to you. And then, you said the same thing."

"You said all that with three words?"

She laughed, "Yes, estrogen is a complicated language."

"So, where do we go from here?"

"First, I need to go to find more tissue. I will be back."

"Let's watch the sunrise together." She left and was gone for a while, almost missing the sunrise. When she arrived back, I had positioned our chairs to face the dawn. Our last morning at sea would end in about five hours, but the sunrise we experienced the final morning was beyond beautiful. It was a new day dawning, in the quiet beauty of creation, and a relationship that a few hours ago was on the verge of ending before it began.

Callie stood up and asked if she could join me on my chair. It was barely large enough for two, so I moved over and invited her to sit and watch the sunrise with me. She put her head on my open arm, and I held her as we watched the moment the sun rose over the ocean, and then she fell asleep. I didn't entirely know how she felt about us, but at least for this moment, I would just let it happen. If it was God's will for us, He had to work on her heart. For me, though, I finished my part. If I had a ring, I would have been on my knee proposing right then.

CHAPTER TWENTY-TWO

"I need to find a place to stop," Kim said, waking from her nap. I had never walked down memory lane so much in such a short amount of time, remembering past loves, as I was possibly starting another, but now it was time to focus on the things at hand.

We took the next exit and chose between two stores when suddenly Kim saw a Trans Am. "Jack Cash, there is Brian, drive! Drive!"

I just kept driving. Kim watched but didn't see Brian, only a car like his. "Where does this road take us?"

Looking at the navigation on the phone, she noted that it would take us way out of the way if we continued.

"Are you sure it was Brian's car?"

"It was the same color, same style, I didn't see Brian or Cynthia."

"Maybe it wasn't his car," I said, trying to reassure myself, hoping we were not on a fool's errand.

"What do you want to do, we still don't have a room on the cruise."

That jarred me back to reality. I need to call Ilean again. When Kim pulled up the number, the phone went to voice mail immediately. "Hey, Ilean, it's Jack Cash, can you call when you can."

"What if she already took care of the cruise?" Kim wondered.

"Pull up the number we called yesterday, and let's see if her friend answers, what was her name again?"

"Chelsea, I think."

The phone rang, and Chelsea answered. "Hello, this is Jack Cash, Ilean's friend. I was wondering if we were booked for the cruise today?"

"I haven't talked to her since yesterday, but maybe she booked with someone else, Jack Cash, right, and is there someone traveling with you?"

"Yes, Kim Crane."

"Let me look, please bear with me, my system is running slow, yes, here it is Jack Cash and Kim Crane. I have you booked for one room."

"We need two rooms."

"There was only one room available."

Kim shook her head, affirming to accept it. "Ok, when do I have to arrive?"

"You must be at the port in Miami between 12 noon and 2 p.m. today. If you are late, you will not be able to board. Since you are a last-minute, high-profile passenger, you will need to get your travel documents at customer relations. Show your passport, and they will check you in."

"How do we pay?" I asked, wondering if Ilean had paid for our trip.

"Pay for what? No need to worry, you have a zero balance, and you have money on your account for excursions or drinks."

"Thank you, Chelsea, we are on our way there now."

"Don't forget, 2 p.m. is the final minute you can board. If you arrive after 2, you will not be allowed to board. If you don't have any other questions, have a fantastic time on your cruise.

"No other questions, thank you."

After we disconnected the call, Kim wondered, "What does high profile mean?"

"Maybe it is like a frequent flyer benefit, I don't know. Do you want to call Chelsea back?"

"No, let's get there as soon as possible."

"If we double back and get on the turnpike where we exited, it will have us there around 2:20 p.m. If we continue on this road, it will have us at the port at 1:40 with twenty minutes to spare."

"We will stay on this road."

We both were getting hungry, but any stop would jeopardize our boarding time, so we determined to stay focused on our arrival. There would be plenty of food on the cruise.

Eventually, we arrived at the port and took the exit. The parking lot was huge and full. We had arrived a few minutes earlier than our navigation said, but we hurried anyway. On the way, Kim said, "Jack, Jack Cash," with a very nervous tone," there is a car like Brian's over there," pointing towards a distant row of vehicles.

"It can't be, there is no way Brian or Cynthia could be on this cruise, no way, absolutely no way," my mind was racing, thinking of the fact that somehow they found us, we had to maintain some type of vigilance because this was the only way to Grand Cayman.

We immediately went to customer relations. "Hello, my name is Jack Cash, we have a last-minute booking. We don't have a confirmation email or a way to print anything."

"No problem, Mr. Cash, could I please see your passport, and is this young lady traveling with you?"

"Yes!"

"May I have your passport as well?"

After a few minutes, he called a supervisor, mentioned some code whispered words, affirmatives, and then did a few more taps of the keyboard, it was clear something was going on that required focus. I raised my eyebrows at Kim, suspecting this trip would be this way. Kim kept a watchful eye out for any sign of Cynthia or Brian.

"Sir, we have a problem with the booking of your room assignment. We don't know if it was coded wrong, or why you were assigned this," then his phone rang, picking up the phone while typing furiously, "yes, do you...yes, I know...I will explain it, ok....yes, no, right here....we have to board them in a few minutes, ok, I will let them know what is going on."

"I take it there is a problem."

"Yes, someone booked your cruise at the very last minute. We typically don't book rooms the same day a person is to travel, but for high profiler's, we make an exception."

"What is a 'high profiler?'"

"It is someone famous, who often cruises, with more points than they know what to do with, or who requires extra attention."

"So, what's the problem?"

"Well, we explained the room assignment to whoever booked the cruise. We only have one room available. We couldn't upgrade to another room because there were no other rooms available. The room they booked for you is a room type for a single traveler. The bed is full size, so for a couple, it is very small, but as was explained at booking, there are no other options. I reached out to my customer relations coordinator, and they verified with the booking agent that someone was alerted to this issue. I am sorry, but it is the only room available. I guess you will have to sleep especially close."

"Oh, we are not married!"

"No judgment here!"

Kim smiled, almost ready to laugh, "well, does the room have a balcony?"

"No, it does have a portal."

"That's the only room you have?" I knew such rooms were probably as cramped as they could be and sleeping on the floor would make for a long night.

"Yes, sir, I am sorry."

I looked at Kim, and she said with extreme giddiness, "We will make it work, we could get married on the ship, you do have a chaplain on the ship, right?"

"Yes, we do. Would you like for me to alert the chaplain you would like to discuss our wedding options?"

"No," I said emphatically and then looking at Kim, "We can't afford to get married today."

"How much is the cheapest wedding package?"

If ever I felt put into an uncomfortable situation, it was now, and Kim was full bore to find out what it would take to get married. She had only been married once. I had been married seven times and wasn't ready to make it number eight. I also knew I didn't want to sleep on the floor, and appearances would seem we were doing things we shouldn't do as followers of Jesus. Plus, I didn't know her motive in marrying me. Was she in love, was she in love with adventure, because I was sure that when this time of crazy was over, life would return to dull. Plus she was likely on the rebound after her husband's death, or I was about to become wealthy? That wealth part was so uncertain. I wasn't even sure that this just wasn't a wild goose chase.

I thought I would throw off things for a second, "The wedding can't be public. It has to be private.."

"I will check on prices and have the chaplain call on you when you board. It will be a few hours as your room will not be ready until after 5. You can enjoy walking around the ship until then, and he will likely leave you a message in your room. The most basic wedding package includes a bottle of champagne."

"We don't drink."

"No worries, flowers, a photographer, and the cost of the chaplain's services, the package is $2,500 plus a $498 license fee."

"We will wait on the wedding. No need to alert the chaplain," I replied.

"If you change your mind, you can call the chaplain, and he will set up what you need. Here you go, you are all set to board, you have five minutes to present yourself at the gangplank," he said, taking our luggage, "Our porters will have them to your room by 5 p.m."

We hurried off to board. Once onboard, we were alerted to a safety drill we were required to participate in and a sail away party as we began our journey. I looked at Kim and whispered, "We need to find a vantage point to watch the fun and to see if we see Cynthia or Brian. We will probably need to be in separate areas, so we don't attract too much attention."

We made our way to the lowest point of the ship that we were allowed to go to before sailing, separated so we could keep a keen eye out for Cynthia or Brian in different areas. We didn't see them at all during either the muster drill or the sail away party. I motioned for Kim to come to me, rubbing my belly indicating I was hungry. She gave me a thumbs-up as well. She walked up to me and whispered, "I found us a minister who will do our wedding."

"Oh, yea, I found us a restaurant where we can get something to eat."

"You're no fun. We can get married before we eat, I mean right now."

"It's not legal. We don't have a license to marry in hand, and you won't like me anyway. All my wives die."

"This one won't, I mean not now anyway, um, well, I know I will die but not like any of the others have."

She was flustered, so my redirect away from a quick marriage worked, at least for a minute. "Let's find a place to eat."

As I turned to walk away, Kim put her hands on my shoulders and began massaging them. I can't describe the soothing effect it had on me immediately. She worked her hands on my shoulders and then down each arm, and I froze. The momentary pleasure took my ability to move away from me as she worked her way down my back, then wrapped her arms around me and held me. It was like I were a bug in a web, and the spider now was wrapping its web around me, preparing to change my destiny, wrapping me tightly in someone's life. A much older couple walked by us and said, "Are you on your honeymoon? You both are so cute."

"I'm working on him," Kim said as they walked out of earshot.

I turned to Kim and briefly glanced at a woman with sunglasses and pantsuit, motioning to another person. It was Cynthia and Brian. She motioned for Brian to go up and look and she would take the lower level. "They are here, let's go now."

We knew our room number, but the announcement that rooms were ready would not come for a few hours. We intended to spend our time eating, getting familiar with the ship, and having fun. Instead, we would need to spend our time playing cat and mouse with a rogue US Marshal and her cousin/boyfriend.

Kim looked at a map of the ship and the different options for duck and cover until our room was ready. She found an eatery near a theater that might offer us a blanket of darkness until we could make it to our room. We made our way to the eatery, moving through a mass of people, most of which were stopping and taking pictures. Our cruise was not one of pleasure but necessity, and stopping for a minute may give up our position.

Once arriving at the "All American Eatery and Pub," we sat in the booth farthest from the door. It offered a view of the entrance, an escape from another door if needed, and an incredible view of the city as we sailed away. As Kim sat down, she put her hand on mine and said, "I am serious about the marriage. I am in love with you, have always been, and don't want to lose you again to another woman."

"Another woman?" Her statement struck me as entirely odd, "Which woman?"

"Mandy," she replied quickly, "Mandy, when you and Mandy started dating. When her cancer returned, I was sure it wouldn't be long until you were available. So after she died on your wedding day, I thought, Jack Cash will be available, but then you went to Florida and met Tamera, and you were gone."

The waiter asked us for our order, and we quickly said, "Two cheeseburgers, two orders of spicy fries, and two orders of ice cream after the meal, and two iced teas."

"So, you were keeping up with me?" my suspicions were now realized.

"Maaaay beeeee," she slowly drawled, running her hands up and down over me, "who wouldn't want all this, for a husband?"

I was flattered and creeped out. I wondered, was the moment we met again by chance, some God-ordained moment where destinies crossed, or were there a great deal of planning that made that meeting possible? Was that moment a combination?

Squeezing my hand, Kim said, "Don't worry, I will not pester you any more about marriage, until tonight when we go to bed." I knew it would present a problem for me and Kim, mainly me, it seemed. That was one of my greatest fears right now.

It wasn't long before our meal arrived. We quickly ate, but talked very little. I couldn't decide if I had hurt Kim's feelings or if she were planning her next barrage of 'will you marry me now' moments. We had to maintain a particular vigilance for Cynthia and Brian. I had to keep a watch for Kim's desire to turn this fugitive moment into a wedding.

After the ice cream arrived, we ate and quickly found the theater. It was about ten minutes before the movie began, with just three other couples in the theater. It was clear that no one was there for the movie but to enjoy the cover of darkness before their room was ready. After the movie started, Kim started kissing my cheek, taking my arm, and putting it around her shoulder. "If we are going to fit in, we have to fit in, Jack Cash," she whispered as the movie started and then began to try a full-on kissing session with me. I kissed for a minute, and before I felt it was going to be too much, and pulled away. "Let's watch the movie."

I was not interested in the movie at all, and Kim knew it. But she would not stop touching me, kissing my cheek, and making a play for my full attention. It took all that I had not to give in and added to that, every so often, the door to the theater opened, and a couple arrived or looked in to see a minute of the movie and leave.

I tried to keep an eye out for the door, maintaining a readiness if Cynthia or Brian walked in and settled into a comfortable, non-kissing position. Kim leaned against me and slowed the public display of affection.

The movie still had about thirty minutes to the end when the door opened and Cynthia and Brian walked in. When I saw them, I started kissing Kim, much to her surprise. She moaned affirmation to me as I kissed her passionately. My purpose was to throw off Cynthia and Brian but noticed that they did not come to the theater looking for us as much as desiring to spend time together under cover of darkness.

I stopped kissing Kim and whispered, "Cynthia and Brian walked in, a few rows behind us, and I don't think they are cousins. Don't look, but they are in full make-out mode."

"I think we should do the same, so we don't stand out in a room where others are doing the same thing," Kim offered with a wink, and then leaned in, kissing with more passion than before, running her hands through my hair, rubbing my arms and working her way down my chest. I grabbed her hands, knowing her intentions. I pulled away from her kisses, and kissed her hand, and said, "Be very careful because I can go from loving to angry in a minute. I am serious about going too far, and if you press it, this will be miserable for both of us."

With a cute pouty lip, she said, "I just want to show my love to Jack Cash."

Finally, the movie was ending, and the lights were about to come up. Cynthia and Brian were not leaving but were otherwise engaged in heavy kissing, so we turned our faces to the screen and left. When we walked outside, the brightness of the sun caught us off guard, and we strained to see. An announcement that cabins were ready for occupancy rang out over the loudspeaker, and we made our way quickly to our room. For me, it was to find a safe place to stay out of view. For Kim, something entirely different. Once we arrived at our room, Kim walked in and turned to me, "It's a perfect size room."

There was barely enough room to turn around. The bed was scarcely large enough for one person, not two, and there was nowhere to sit other than the bed. Kim sat on the bed and patted it, "sit here," and then pulled me down to sit, "Look, I know I came on strong earlier. I am saving myself for our wedding night and had hoped tonight would be the night. I am willing to wait; tomorrow would be a great day to get married too!"

"Tomorrow, we will be on Grand Cayman, focused on banking, not a wedding, or marriage," I said matter-of-factly, "and we will probably need to stay in our room until we arrive tomorrow, staying out of sight."

Kim sighed and then perked up with a smile, "we do have a room to ourselves and I get to be in this close quarters with the man of my dreams, who knows what can happen."

I felt the 'coming on strong' vibe Kim was exuding, and she didn't mind any overstep she could get away with, even if it meant compromise.

"Let's see what is on TV," I said as I slowly went through the few channels, the cruise ship offered, "it's clear people don't get on a cruise to watch tv, because there is nothing to watch." Finally, I found a movie and began watching it, ignoring Kim's glaring eyes Kim. Finally, she laid down on the bed and curled up with a pillow, and fell asleep, and I was glad. She came on so strong. I almost gave in to her advances but never wanted to give that away to her at all. As the movie played, the ship started to encounter seas that were a little rougher, making it feel as if we were in a storm.

We were in a room with a portal, but I couldn't tell. Kim just slept for the entirety of the movie. I leaned against the wall and fell asleep a few times, every so often waking up, looking at Kim, and falling back asleep. The final time I woke, Kim was not on the bed. I was almost sure she was in the bathroom, but she was there for a long time.

"Are you in the bathroom?" nothing but silence. "Kim, are you in the bathroom?" then I got up and slowly opened the bathroom door, "Kim, are you in here?" The light was on, but Kim was not inside.

I waited for over an hour, watched the television, looked at the door, and then got angry. I had no idea where Kim had gone and didn't want to venture out searching for her. We were too vulnerable for her to be out of the cabin, and I had no idea if she had encountered Cynthia or Brian or why she was gone so long. Finally, the door opened, and Kim walked in, closed the door quickly, and looked through the peephole.

"Where were you?"

"Shhhhhh…"

"What are you looking at?"

"Shhhhhhh.Cynthia and Brian were on the upper deck, and I think they saw me."

"What were you doing on the upper deck?"

"Shhhhhh."

Whispering as loudly and angrily as possible, "What were you doing out of the room?"

"I had to get some fresh air, and you were asleep! You are no fun at all."

"Kim, do you realize some of the people closest to me are dead, beat up, or suffering in some way because of me. This trip is not a fun cruise. It is a means to get me to Grand Cayman, and I don't know what I will find when I get there. Someone may be waiting for me there, and after I do my banking business may want to kill me if there is even any banking business to do."

"Shhhhh."

"I don't want to shhh."

Kim turned and whispered, "they are outside our room looking at the door," and then they knocked.

Kim tiptoed to the bed and sat down As the knocking turned to banging, someone stepped out of their room and said something to Cynthia and Brian, but we couldn't make out what they said.

Cynthia said, "I am a US Marshal, and I need to talk to the people in this room." Whoever they were talking to called the deck and asked for help. When the steward arrived, we heard an argument begin with the steward eventually telling Cynthia we were no longer in US waters and she had no jurisdiction here. She needed to leave the room and enjoy the rest of her cruise. She argued for about 15 minutes, and then another cruise ship employee arrived, then another. Eventually, we heard one of them offer to call her superior to verify her story. She refused to give them their name or number, which made her actions seem as rogue as they were in the last few days, and eventually, she left.

I was seething. Did Cynthia and Brian know for sure we were on the cruise, and did Kim give away our room?

"What in the world were you thinking, Kim?"

"I was thinking, the ship is rocking, and I am going to get sick, I need some fresh air, and I went to get some. It was starting to get dark. Of course, I watched the sunset over the ocean without Jack Cash because he didn't want anything to do with me, and then I walked around to check things out. That's what I was thinking. I thought I made a huge mistake even coming on this cruise. I should have gathered my things from my condo and gone home. I should have gone home. I am miserable." She began to sob, "all I ever wanted was to be your wife, all my life."

I shook my head in disbelief about everything she just said, "Do you want me to fly you home from Grand Cayman, see if you can stay there after the ship leaves and not return with me on the cruise?"

"I don't know. I just don't know," as she sat on the bed, grabbing a pillow and curling up in a fetal position with her back to me.

I was so angry. Angry about everything now. There were so many moving parts to this, and now one, the one I was closest to, made choices that exposed us to those seeking to capture us, "I am sorry you feel that way. I gave you the option of leaving, but you refused."

She waited a moment, and in a hushed tone, said, "I thought we were hitting it off and we had something, something that could be more than friends or fugitives running from the law together. I thought we could be lovers, husband, and wife, together forever."

"Kim, we are running for our lives. The last thing I am thinking about is marriage right now. I am thinking about keeping me and you safe, keeping us away from those who seek to kill us, not to see if we are compatible for marriage. I am sorry you feel I am resisting you. I am focused on other things right now. I think you are fantastic, but I am not ready to enter into the level of relationship you want right now. I just can't.

"Do you think there is a chance for us?"

"I don't know, but can we focus on staying alive and free right now?"

"Yes, I am sorry for wandering around the ship. Cynthia and Brian were not in the hallway when I came in the door. I don't think they know for sure what room we are in."

"We can't take a chance by going out right now. We will need to order room service and stay in here the rest of the night."

Kim put her arms around me and said, "I won't leave again. Will you forgive me?" and then kissed me.

"Yes," I said, trying to pull away, "but you need to give me space because this coming on strong is about to take me down."

"Ok, I will let up, but I won't give up."

"Let's order room service." We looked over the menu and ordered room service. By this time, it was a little past seven o'clock, and the room service would take about 45 minutes before arriving. We settled in to watch another movie. The phone rang, room service was on its way. When he arrived, Kim almost answered the door without looking, but I quickly shouted, "close the door, verify it is room service." As soon as she opened the door, she closed it, looked through the peephole, and saw a uniformed gentleman pushing a cart of food, "it's room service," she said as she opened it again.

As I spoke to the attendant, he turned his head away and only answered with yes or no, nothing more. I couldn't see his face well, and he quickly left after delivering our food. As he was walking out, Kim noticed he had a ring on his finger. It looked like the one she saw on Brian a few days prior, when we saw him for the first time. When the door closed, Kim spoke up and said, "I think that was Brian."

"I think it was too, he turned his head away when I spoke to him."

"Do you think they will be back?"

"No, they are probably waiting for me to go to Grand Cayman, and after I do banking business, then do what they are going to do."

"Should we eat the food?"

"Good question, maybe we shouldn't."

About ten minutes later, someone knocked on the door. I slowly crept to the door and looked out. It was a female with a cart of room service food. "Who is it?"

"Room service, we have your cheeseburger with olives."

"Look at the food. It just came, is it a cheeseburger with olives?"

Kim looked, "no, it has onion too."

It was clear that the first meal was not legitimately from the right people and was pretty careless. "Can you tell if Cynthia is the one delivering it?"

"No, I can't tell, she is keeping her head down."

I yelled through the door, "we changed our mind. We don't want it."

That delivery person was agitated, pacing back and forth, so I called room service again, "Hello, this is Jack Cash, and I ordered room service, and two different people have arrived with orders and both of them were wrong."

"Mr. Cash, room service just left with your order. The person at your door is in the wrong room. Could you please give the phone to them?"

"No, I am afraid to open the door. The people outside the room are very agitated. I think we need security."

"Hold, please."

Kim kept an eye out of the peephole watching the person outside. After about thirty seconds, she ran towards the rear of the boat as if being chased. A few seconds later, security officers ran in that direction. As she kept a watchful eye, room service arrived again.

This time, the room service attendant showed us an employee identification badge when Kim looked out. She opened the door, and the person over room service told us that they had two carts that were missing food and the people who took them were the ones at our door. They asked us for their names.

The employee thanked us and left with the other two carts of food.

"Well, I guess we can eat this one safely. I am glad you ordered olives on your cheeseburger. That one distinction helped us know the truth. Were they trying to poison us?"

"No, probably verify it was our room. Which they were able to do. I will call and tell them I would like a different room." I called, and the ship was at maximum capacity. There were no rooms available, which I already knew. They assured me they would keep an eye out for anyone in our hallway.

We ate and, after finishing, wheeled our cart outside. Kim wondered, "do you think a midnight stroll on deck would be ok if it is clear, it should be a beautiful night."

"That sounds great, let's wear darker clothes not to stand out too much."

"It's a few hours before midnight. Do you want to walk around and see the other places on the ship?" It was clear Kim wanted more of the cruise experience. I felt terrible that she was in this predicament, almost as if taken against her will and thrust into impossible scenarios. She has handled them well, and a walk around the ship would be about as dangerous as staying in our room at this point, especially since Cynthia and Brian knew our room location.

"I think that would be lovely. Let me find some clothes and change, and we can go."

It was as if we had just arrived on the ship, as everything was so clean and bright. Happy hour was in full swing as music pumped from about every level, one with teens dancing, another with older people. Kim was like a kid in a theme park, running on to see what was ahead, wide-eyed and filled with excitement. I walked a little slower and kept a watchful eye. We didn't want to find Cynthia or Brian and expose our intentions the following day. As I thought about it, I was sure they already suspected I would discover Paddy's account, but still, I couldn't allow them to know everything. I found a drink cart that had coffee and hot chocolate and some apple cider I had never heard of. I looked for her, but Kim was out of sight.

"I think I would like two apple ciders," even though I wasn't sure if I would find her before the apple cider turned cold. I think she was disappointed I wouldn't go along with her romantic scheme, but I couldn't. I couldn't because I love God and because I really liked Kim. Anything but what was right would diminish our relationship. Once you enter those waters, there is no turning back.

I walked with my two apple ciders, and I remembered the sunrise with Callie because it was the morning I proposed to her.

CHAPTER TWENTY-THREE

My mind began to wander into my memories of Callie again. The sunrise over the ocean was mesmerizing, especially when the clouds and sun combined in a beautiful tapestry. My heart was the same. I didn't have a ring but felt as if there ever was a moment that called me to propose, it was at this moment. I kissed her on her forehead and got out of the chair. She rose as if I were signaling a time to leave. I didn't say anything to her to change; instead, I took her hand and knelt on one knee. "Callie, I can't offer you a lot, but I promise to cherish you and love you and love God with you if you marry me. Callie, will you marry me?"

At first, the look of surprise on Callie's face was mixed with laughter. She wanted to laugh and was doing everything she could to keep from laughing, almost like a pent-up sneeze. It finally broke through. She laughed, and laughed and laughed, out loud. The people around thought her laughter was her way of saying no to my proposal. I felt it was something entirely different. It was a joy pent up, bursting forth with laughter. It was the kind of joy you experience when the very thing you pray for and long for finally arrives, wrapped in the best wrapping because it is full of meaning, but you still can't believe it is true.

She laughed, I laughed, and soon people around us, trying to act as if they were not paying attention, started laughing. Finally, she said, "Jack

Cash, you would make me the happiest woman in the world if I say yes, so, I say..." and then the laughter turned to tears of joy but tears of yes... "I ....say....yes... Canda munani"

"Ok, translate."

"I said, 'yes' Jack Cash, I will marry you." Everyone around started applauding, with a generous mix of awe, and so cute, "and 'canda munani' means "I love you."

"Canda Muani" I said in reply, emphasizing the "a" in both.

Callie burst out in laughter, "You just said the lion farted in the jungle."

I laughed so hard until she confessed, "I am just kidding, you did good, and I love you so much."

Our whirlwind romance, including time at Ileans and the general longing that went back years and years, brought me to a happy place once again. I will never forget the day, our wedding day, which was as fast as our courtship. Just three months after the proposal, Callie and I were married. We had a joyous year of marriage, and in the end, joy and the most challenging thing ever.

I had never had children. Some of my wives wanted kids, and some were not for or against, but Callie was different. She wanted kids and lots of them. I knew Callie would make a remarkable mom, and I was excited to have kids of my own too. By this time, she was in her early forties, so I knew that we were both pressing the clock for her to become pregnant and successfully deliver a baby. About a year after our wedding, Callie suddenly started early morning sickness and a general feeling of nausea all the time. She couldn't keep anything down and struggled to maintain her balance. After about a week, she decided to go to the doctor. The doctor ran her through a battery of tests, and nothing was conclusive. He noted her symptoms could be the onset of something severe, and while he was preparing to order an MRI, his nurse said, "I may be out of place, but when was the last time you had a period?"

"I missed the last one."

The doctor looked at his nurse and said, "How did you know?"

"She glows like an expectant mom."

He ordered a fast response pregnancy test and a blood test. The rapid response was positive, and after sending off the blood test, it was positive as well. We were going to have a baby. We both were so excited, and Callie had a glow that was immeasurable. At about four months into the pregnancy, Callie decided to go shopping for baby furniture. At lunchtime, she called me at my office and said, "How about lunch and a trip to the furniture store to find baby furniture?"

"Sure, let's meet at the Mexican restaurant near the furniture store on 5th street."

I finished my work and headed to the restaurant. On the way, several police cars blasted past me, then a fire truck and then an ambulance. It looked as if there was a wreck that would cause me to be late. I called Callie to let her know, and she didn't answer. I felt an overwhelming heaviness fall on me. The traffic completely stopped, so I pulled off into a parking lot. When I did, I noticed a car upside down in the road, a fireman dousing the car, and working with someone trapped. After a few minutes, moving in and out of the vehicle, one fireman shook his head 'no' to the EMT. I knew the person likely died in the accident. People had gathered in the parking lot with me, asking questions, some offering suggestions as to what happened. Then my phone rang, a picture of Callie popped up, indicating it was my wife calling. "Hey, sweetheart!"

"Is this Jack Cash?" a male voice asked.

"I am with the police department. Mr. Cash, your wife, has been involved in an accident. Where are you now?"

"I am in a parking lot near an accident now. I had just crossed the light at 3rd street, in the parking lot of the nail salon and Chinese takeout."

"What are you wearing?"

"I looked at my shirt and pants and started to describe what I was wearing as if time was standing still. I felt I needed to tell the officer the color of the buttons on my shirt; and the color of my shoelaces. I was numb, and by the time I finished describing my clothing, I looked up to see an officer standing in front of me.

"Are you Jack Cash?"

"Yes."

"How do you know Callie Cash?"

"She is my wife. She is pregnant with our baby. We were going to meet at the Mexican restaurant and then go baby shopping. We have been married for a year, and we are excited." I thought sharing the story would somehow change what he was about to tell me. The sense of foreboding was unreal, and I just kept talking, sharing meaningless details when he interrupted.

"Mr. Cash, I regret to inform you that your wife died in a rollover accident. I am so sorry for your loss. Is there anyone we can call for you, a pastor or chaplain we can call on your behalf?"

"No, I am a pastor, are they taking her to the hospital to check her out?"

"No, Mr. Cash. She died. She likely died on impact."

I broke, "What happened?" and began weeping.

"We will do a complete investigation. The coroner is on his way and will talk to you afterward to find out what funeral home you would like to choose."

"Can I see her?"

"I don't recommend it Pastor, it would be best for you to remember her from any other time, but now we have to extricate her from the car. It will likely take a while."

As we talked, I turned to look at the car, and by this time, a white sheet was covering the side of the most intact vehicle. A helicopter circled the accident as if he were going to land. "Is a medical helicopter?"

"No, Mr. Cash, it is to help us with our investigation."

"I don't understand."

"We think your wife was pushed off the road by another car. Witnesses said someone was driving next to her. They described a PIT maneuver and, in the push, pushed her into a rollover."

"Who did that?"

"We don't know yet, but I can assure you we will do all we can to find out!"

I was numb, and even though I had just received the worst news, I still expected Callie to call from the restaurant, wanting to know why I was late. I went from numbness to gut punch, tears, and hyperventilating. Then, a torrent of tears, more than I had ever experienced.

CHAPTER TWENTY-FOUR

"I found us a place a great place to go, out of the mix of people, it is on the upper deck," Kim broke through my remembering, "Are you ok?"

"Where did you go?"

"I was so excited. I just started wandering around. What's in the cup?"

"Oh, it is apple cider. It may be a little cool."

She took her cup and took a sip, Mmmmmm. It's perfect. Come on. I will show you the way up to the place I found."

When we climbed the stairs, the vista was beautiful. The moon was just starting to rise over the ocean, more prominent than I had ever seen. There was only one chair available, but I knew it didn't matter. Kim was sitting with me regardless.

At first, we sat up and drank our cider, taking sips and watching the moon rise. Then, we alternated looking at the decks below, watching some dance, and just general people watching and leaned back for an evening of being together. The DJ from the deck below started a slow song called "Waiting for a girl like you," Kim began singing along. "Do you want to dance?"

I was not a dancer, and my steps would be halting, but it was a beautiful night, and the stars were shining, so we stood and started a slow dance, alternating kissing and gentle movements to the song. Kim was never more beautiful than tonight, and I was about as tired and needing a break from the craziness, that I welcomed this moment and Kim with open arms. As we danced, she whispered in my ear, "you are the most handsome man I have ever met, and Jack Cash, I have to admit, I have always loved you. I loved you in high school. I loved you all my life. My love never stopped! It never stopped and now, I am more in love with you than ever before."

The moment was too good, and everything seemed to be so perfect. I almost gave in to Kim's advances. If she were in full press mode before, it was nothing like now, and I feared it would take me to a place I didn't need to go, I was so vulnerable and the temptation was so strong.

"Let's go back to the room," Kim suggested.

"Before we go, can we find a place for dessert?"

"Great idea!"

I didn't want dessert. I wanted diversion. I knew Kim intended to make love, and I was not going to, even if it meant I found a lounge chair on a deck for the night, at least until security found me.

We found a dessert shop and ordered a banana split and split the dessert. Kim intended to feed me the dessert, so I did the same for her, with each bite an even more intense look in her eye. It didn't take long, mainly because Kim was feeding me the largest spoonful possible, wanting to get to the room.

On the way back, Kim did everything she could to touch me and contact some part of my body. Any time she tried to touch my waist, I pulled her hands away. I called her 'handsy' for a bit, telling her I didn't want that kind of attention. It was as if she didn't hear a word I said.

We made it to the room, and Kim excused herself for a minute to the bathroom and quickly emerged in lingerie that decidedly left very little to the imagination. I turned my head away because the last thing I wanted to do was partake of that fruit. I went to the bathroom after she exited and took a change of clothes with me. I intended to go to a deck to find a chair and sleep there until I knew Kim was asleep. I took as long as I possibly could, and every so often, Kim spoke up and said, "Jack Cash, your cruise mate is ready for you."

I stepped out of the bathroom, and Kim was on the bed in the most seductive pose she could find.

"I need to go upstairs for a while."

"What for," she wondered, "you have everything you need, right here!" She tapped the bed and said, "why not let me love your frustration away."

"That's why I was going upstairs, to get some sleep. I am exhausted."

"Ok, Jack Cash, what is the deal. I have made moves on you that would have turned any man with low testosterone into complete babbling idiots, and you have not given me the time of day. I want you, and I want you bad. I am yours, and you act like I am not even here."

"Oh, you are here, alright, and your come-ons are making my life difficult. I would love to make love to you, and if I don't do something to change my thinking, I will fall into that web right away, and I won't be able to get out. I care too much about my walk with God to compromise it, and honestly, I am surprised you are going full-on with these moves. I have to find another place to sleep," and then left the room. I made it to the stairwell, then to an upper deck, and stepped outside. Suddenly I was met with a drenching downpour and people started running inside laughing because they too were drenched. What followed the rain was loud thunder and lightning, so the captain ordered everyone to their cabin. So, back I went.

"Well, that didn't take long," Kim said as I walked into the room. "I am still waiting for you." She was dripping with seduction. I was dripping with the rain I had just experienced. I wondered why I put myself into this situation in the first place. There was enough room to walk around the bed, so I took a pillow and laid on the floor. Kim peeked over the edge of the bed, looking down, "is that where you are going to sleep?"

"I think so!"

"Well, then, so am I," and then proceeded to lay next to me.

"Ok, this is not going to work. You will have to put clothes on, nothing slinky, nothing see-through, nothing sensual or erotic. You have to get some clothes on now, or I will have to leave the room. I can't do this. I can't sleep with you. If you want any future at all, any possible future, you have to respect my feelings and my calling. I will not compromise it."

"Jack, we are already sleeping in the same room. Don't you think we have compromised?"

"God knows what I have done, what we have done and what we

didn't do! It is important to me to wait until marriage to have sex with someone. It is my personal conviction, and it has served me well. I have been able to offer my girlfriend a stress-free dating experience, where we can get to know one another in every way but sexually. There is no pressure that way. There is no compromise that way. There is nothing but building a friendship based on respect. Then, when we are married, we are ready to take it to that level. You can't imagine how wonderful sex is until you save it for the woman you have committed your life to in marriage. It is amazing! You may not understand what I am talking about, but it is the most important thing to me. I know I may have to deal with sleeping in the same room with you later, but I will not sleep next to you dressed like we are about to have sex."

"Very well, if 's the way you want it."

"It is!"

Kim went to the bathroom and changed into clothes. She started slinging clothes, banging on the wall, acting very agitated, but I ignored her. I did the right thing and wasn't worried about how angry she was or how it would affect our relationship.

She stepped out of the bathroom fully clothed and shoes on as well, "Are you happy? I have clothes and shoes on too?"

"Yes, but you didn't have to put on shoes. If you feel better wearing them, fine."

She plopped on the bed, rolled over with her back to me, and sighed deeply. I sat on the floor with my back to the wall and said, "Goodnight, Kim, thank you!"

"Ummmph!" she grunted and didn't move. I settled in for as much rest as I could get. We were due to arrive at 9 a.m. on Grand Cayman, and the bank we were to go to was not very clear. Since there were over one hundred banks on Grand Cayman, finding the exact one would take a while. My mind was running through all the scenarios, and even if we went to a bank every five minutes, it would take longer than our 9 a.m.- 5 p.m. time frame could accomplish.

Now, it was six days since I met Kim. I woke up at 6:17 a.m. with pain in my neck and back from sleeping against the wall. The soreness caused me to moan as I stood up. Kim was gone, so I just shrugged it off. She was probably still mad at me, but at this point, I didn't care. I took a quick shower, and the heat on my sore neck muscles was therapeutic, in fact, almost too nice. I stayed in the shower a long time, letting the heat relax my neck and thinking through the day. Finally, I turned it off and opened the curtain, and standing there was Kim with a cup of coffee. I quickly pulled the curtain across my body and screamed, "ARRGGGH-HHHH GET OUT!!!" She laughed as she said, "You're welcome, and thank you for the show," she put the coffee next to the sink and closed the door.

I quickly got dressed and was about as mad as I could be. I stepped out into the room ready to lay into Kim for walking in on me, but she was gone again. I sat on the bed, writing down every bank that sounded similar to Veronica's that Ilean remembered. There were ten, and knowing the banking would be discrete in their business dealings, I knew that each place was going to take time. There was no way to know which one was first.

The door opened, and Kim walked in, "Hey, big guy, you ready for breakfast, or do you want to stay here and gawk at my fully clothed body?"

"I'm glad you are not taking it personal. Although staying here and looking at your fully clothed body sounds appealing, I am hungry."

"Well, special birthmark guy, time to find a great place to eat, I have finished recon and have a place scoped out. I found a beautiful woman there too if you want to have breakfast with her because you certainly don't want to have breakfast with me. You have hurt me, and I am done."

"Kim, I asked you to put on clothes because you were tempting me. I respect you more than to take advantage of you. I care about you, but I care about my relationship with God more. I am sorry if I hurt your feelings, and if you don't want to be with me, that's your choice. It's not something I want, but I understand. Thank you for going with me until now. I will find my breakfast and will not frustrate you anymore. Thank you again!"

I walked out of the room, and away from her, found a deck plan for restaurants and decided to go to a crepe and coffee place. When I sat down, I ordered breakfast and watched a thunderhead in the distance. Another storm, more uncertainty, and now loneliness. The time I felt so alone, it felt so much like standing there watching Callie's car being turned right side up after her accident. I felt so vulnerable, lonely, and furious. Angry with whoever ran her off the road and angry with God. I lost my wife, my baby, and a part of me. Right now, I sensed the same feeling as tears streamed down my face. I turned toward the horizon again. The beauty of the sunrise creating an ominous glow felt like what I would experience later today: a storm with terrifying beauty.

"There you are, if you think you can shake me, after all we have been through, you are dreaming big guy."

"Kim, look, I know I hurt your feelings."

"Jack Cash, I am a big girl, and I can take it. You want to maintain your integrity, yada, yada, yada, I get it. I just thought, hey, here is this sexy guy, we are on a cruise and then in a singing voice, "it's the right time of the night for making love. But, hey, it's your loss. You had me right where you could do anything, like the burger place, have it your way."

"Enough, Kim. If you are going to keep it up, we will have to part ways. It's clear that you are angry, hurt, and want to take it out on me, and I get it! You wanted to sleep with me. It is not personal, it's a God thing, and I won't apologize for it at all. You were a pastor's wife, right? I would think you would have welcomed chastity."

"Jack Cash, I have wanted to be your wife my entire life. Your wife, your lover, your best friend, your everything, and when I had the chance, I took it. I took it and slammed it upside the wall with enough force to move the world, and you didn't blink. Most guys would have paid good money for what I offered you for free."

"Stop, Kim, stop. Do you know that a few weeks ago, I buried my last wife? I buried her, and I went to Vero to grieve, cry, and figure things out. I got thrust into a fugitive, penniless lifestyle with a woman who can't get enough of all this; and then find myself on a cruise with said woman, in a room the size of a car trunk, chose clothes are more transparent than cling wrap, and about as tight."

"I'm glad you noticed."

"Noticed?!?! Noticed???? Of course, I noticed, and you might want to get the mole on your back checked out."

"Jack Cash, you were looking!"

"I was just kidding. I turned my head away. You may or may not have a mole."

"Well, I didn't see any moles on you in the shower. I am sorry, but it was a sight to behold."

"That's great, just great, I will make sure the door is locked next time."

"Oh, it was locked, but I had this needle and put it in the hole, and it opened up."

"You picked the lock?"

"Yes, I had your coffee, and you clearly needed it, and you need it now."

The waiter cleared his throat behind me. I turned around, "How long have you been there?"

"Long enough to wonder if she has a mole. Here are your crepes and coffee. They are severely underrated, you will see. Ma'am, would you like to order something?"

"Yes, get me what he is having because I am about to eat half of his right now," and with that, Kim took the fork from my hand and started eating. I glared at her as she made moaning sounds, licking her lips and telling me how wonderful my crepes were; fortunately, I was not hungry anyway, but the coffee was so needed, "so, Jack Cash, what's the plan today?"

"I have a few bank names to try. There are about ten that sound similar to what Ilean told me. I'm not sure where to start, but probably with the first one we find on the island. Hopefully, they are all fairly close. Another thing I thought about was the banks in Grand Cayman deal with international people, most of whom want discretion. I don't think they will be in a hurry, so if we have to hit all ten, I am not sure we have enough time."

As we talked, the waiter brought Kim's order. "What can I do to help?"

"Stand outside and keep watch for Cynthia or Brian. They are bent on following us, and I am not sure what they are up to, maybe a hostage situation, rob me after I do the banking. I'm not sure, but you will need to get security in the bank involved if they come. Tell them there is a threat."

"I can do that. Jack, do you have any idea how much money we are talking about?"

"No, I have absolutely no idea, and until this week, I had no idea about an account or anything. I hadn't spent much time thinking about the amount, but I did think it was probably at least $25,000. I don't know why that amount stuck in my mind, but it is the amount."

"That's a whole lotta stuff for only $25,000."

"I know, I'm not even sure there is anything at all."

We ate and went back to our room. I wasn't overthinking about Cynthia or Brian as I was sure they either tried to do something with our food or at least verified we were in the room, so we hadn't seen anything from them.

CHAPTER TWENTY-FIVE

When we got back, the room had been gone through. Clothes were all over the bed, including a couple of pretty skimpy nightgowns, which by this time didn't surprise me. We both figured they were looking for something that would indicate where we were going. I had put the list in my pocket, so there was nothing they could find.

I called to complain, and the room steward was going to check with the cleaning personnel and report back later today, after the island excursion. We were about to dock, so I knew we would need to be vigilant on our travel. We gathered passports and a small backpack for documents, bottles of water and left. I thought about waiting a half hour before leaving but felt Cynthia and Brian could find positions to surveil us without us knowing, so we opted to be among the first off of the boat.

Most cruisers were doing some type of paid excursion, drinking rum, snorkeling, or stingray encounters. One lonely guy had a small van willing to take us on a special tour of the Island, anywhere we wanted to go. When I asked him how much, he said, for you, I make it special two hours for $25 each. It was perfect because we had no idea the location of the banks. I asked him if he took cash. I had $60 left, which left us only $10 for food and water. He agreed and took us to the first bank on the list. It had closed.

The next was a branch bank for a bank in the UK, but they had no account for Paddy, Veronica, or me. There were four banks within a close walking distance, so our van driver waited at the last of the four until we finished. Kim stood watch, and I went in each one. They were surprisingly efficient and speedy until the final one of the four. When we walked to the last one, I told her that if something came up with Brian or Cynthia, we would make a mad dash to the van so he could take us to the ship or the next bank. It was the most professionally slow service I had ever experienced. All of the banking was out of eyesight; even the computers were in another room.

I walked up to a desk where a gentleman was pulling a sandwich out of a drawer, ready to eat lunch, and I told him I needed to see if there was an account for Paddy, Veronica, or me. With frustration, he put his sandwich back into his desk, took my passport and Paddy's death certificate, and went to the back while I waited at his desk. A few minutes later, one of the other bank officers received a call, looked at me, and quickly returned to the back. After a few minutes, another one walked quickly to the back, glancing in my direction, and then another until there was only one person left in the front. Their phone rang, and they whispered into the handset, hung up, and then went to the back.

I waited what seemed like forever, wondering if we would make our next bank or if I was going to be tied up here for a while. A couple of women walked out of the backroom, looking in my direction, speaking in hushed tones. I felt like a caged animal at a zoo. Finally, the bank president walked up to me, sweating profusely, "Mr. Jack, I am Eduardo Espinoza, the president of this branch. We have branches in the UK and Europe and are well-positioned in those other branches, but honestly, we don't have enough to pay you today. We will have to order the cash to pay you."

"Pay me? I don't understand. I am just verifying the account is active."

"Yes, Sir, you have to understanding, we are not positioned to honor your request."

"Is there an account?"

"There was an account!"

"What happened to it?"

"You showed up. The account is no more."

"I don't understand."

"You see, Mr. Jack Cash, the account is a POD account, which means when you produce a death certificate, we must pay you everything in the account. We simply are not positioned for that today."

"When can you be positioned for it?"

"Well, if you want cash, it will take about two weeks. If you want to transfer to your bank, it will take 5-7 business days."

"Why so long?"

"Because it is 159," he said very quietly.

"159 dollars?"

"No!"

"159,000?"

"No Sir, 159.3. Here I wrote the exact amount down."

The note read, "159,342,198.12"

"I don't understand, Mr. Espinoza, is this 159 million???"

"Actually, it is $159,342,198.12."

"Are you sure?" I sat there dumbfounded. And mouthed it a few times, "159.3."

"Yes, Sir, I am more than sure and it belonged to the deceased, the terms of the account indicate it is payable on death, so now it is yours. If you would like, I can open an account in your name, transfer the funds to it, but if you need money today, I can send you with four today and twenty tomorrow, and by the middle of next week, the remaining.

"If you set up a new account, what is best to shield your funds, and to do that you must establish an LLC that is, in turn, owned by an asset protection trust. Trusts and LLC's can be established on the island of Nevis if you currently do not have one set up."

"How long is that process?"

"Generally, it can be done in a day or so, wait a minute, I need to check on something."

Kim ran into the branch. "Cynthia and Brian just went into the third bank. They are about 10 minutes per bank, so you need to hurry. Does this bank have the account?"

"Yes, I am working it out now! Did they see you?"

Kim whispered, "No, I was hiding, how much?"

"Enough to kill people over. I will know better in a few minutes."

"Oh, my," and then she went back to her hidden post.

Mr. Espinoza walked back to the desk. "Do you know Veronica Gypsy?"

"Yes, she was my wife. Someone murdered her a few years ago."

"I am sorry for your loss. It seems the account was a trust account with a POD provision. Veronica had it changed years ago. You are the beneficiary of the trust assets, and you are the POD recipient. In other words, you are a trustee for the trust. We can establish an account under the same LLC and trust because your name is on both documents."

"I don't understand, I just found out about the account this week, and I haven't signed any documents regarding this arrangement."

"Here is the signed LLC and signed trust documentation. Is this your signature?"

I looked at both documents, and they were my signatures. How did I sign those documents without knowing? "When were they signed?"

"It looks like October 17, 2013."

That date was when we signed the papers for our house, and the same day Veronica had me sign papers for a trust for Paddy. She led me to believe it was only for him. She never told me anything about my connection to the trust. "How do we deal with the POD provision in the trust?"

"The POD provision was for the account. The trust names you as the beneficiary of the trust assets on death, and you are now the trustee. We don't have to file additional paperwork, except to establish a new account."

"Is it a checking account?"

"It is a savings account with a debit card and a credit card attached to the account, restricted to the amount you set, so if they are lost or stolen, the one attempting to use it can only access a certain dollar amount. If you require more funds to buy a car or house, the bank will wire the funds. It will take me about an hour to set up the account and activate the debit card. The credit card will come from a third party in about seven business days. Did you fly to the island?"

"No, we took an excursion from our cruise ship."

"When do you have to return?"

"I believe we need to be on the boat by 4:30, ship sails at 5."

"Great, you have plenty of time. I suggest touring our beautiful island. I know someone who can take you around and show you places no one knows about but locals, plus a wonderful place for lunch. Don't worry about the cost. It is on me."

Kim ran into the bank, "They are on their way here."

I looked at Mr. Espinoza, "Would it be possible to leave through another exit, rather than the front, there are people who wish to know our banking business, and I would prefer they not know anything."

"Certainly, discretion is our business. Follow me."

He moved like a gazelle chased by his prey, and we followed as fast. By the time they walked through the door, we were out of their line of sight. We stopped near an exit, he turned to us and said, "Let's wait here for your ride to arrive."

A camera monitored Cynthia and Brian's movement, and we could see them talking to the same banker we spoke to first. They sat down as he began to talk to them. Mr. Espinoza was arranging transportation for lunch and motioned us to come with him.

"The couple following us just sat down with the banker at the desk on the left."

"That is Jorge. She is my brother." I looked at Kim and shrugged my shoulders, and mouthed, "I thought she was a man."

"No, I think it's a pronoun thing."

"Are they asking about me?"

"If they are, they wouldn't have any way to find out about you because we offer complete privacy to all our accounts."

Jorge walked up to Mr. Espinoza and said, "They asked if a Jack Cash had an account here. They asked while I was setting up an account for him."

"What did you tell them?"

"I told them that we can not divulge other deposit accounts at our bank to anyone."

"Excellent, Jorge!"

"As you can see, we hold this information to ourselves. Your ride will arrive any minute. The driver will come to the back door. It is my administrative assistant, she will drive you around. She will also bring you back here."

After a minute or so, the door opened, and a beautiful woman entered, whispering, "Are you Jack Cash?"

"Yes, I am, and this is my friend Kim."

Immediately Kim, overcome with jealousy, put her arm around me, "He is kidding you. I am much more than his friend," and then kissed me on the cheek.

"Why????" I shrugged my shoulders, shaking my head no.

"I am here to take you to lunch, to show you a good time for a few hours."

I wasn't sure what she meant because idioms in the US are different than other nations, but Kim wasn't as aware of it as I.

"So, what kind of good time are you going to show Jack Cash?"

"Well, first we have lunch, then I show you other things. I sorry, my English is not good like Mr. Espinoza."

"What is your name?"

"My name is Chastity."

"What a wonderful name," I said, elbowing Kim.

"Yes, it is lovely."

"I take you to a very nice place to eat. Very important people eat there, and their lobster risotto is the best."

When we arrived, the restaurant was filled with people and over-looked a beautiful lagoon. Chastity walked up to the maître d', told them who sent us, and then the maître d' proceeded to take us to a room down a long hallway. There was a separate dining room with a lot of people as well. As we sat down, Chastity said, "Order what you want; everything is delicious."

Kim said, "I want what Chastity recommended." I ordered the Chilean Sea Bass.

"I need excusing for a minute."

Kim leaned over after Chastity left and said, "She is quite the beauty, right. What kind of good time will she show you, because they sure are treating you well. How much money is it?

"It is not enough to quit pastoring, but enough to live well."

When Chastity returned, our first course arrived, "I have great news. Your account is established. Mr. Espinoza said we could come there for the documents after lunch, and then I could show you a good time.

Kim raised her eyebrows and looked at me jealously.

"That sounds wonderful."

Chastity said, "There are many famous people who come here. Sometimes we see famous actors and actresses. Once Angelina was here with Brad, I got to meet them. Also, we have had politicians through here. Your president had a villa on the Island at one time. I think he sold it but came to this restaurant often. Over there is a guy who was famous in the US. Once he was in prison, but he is out now. He is a celebrity on the island. His name is Juan Carlos."

Instinctively, I turned to look briefly and turned back to Chastity and Kim.

Kim picked up my apprehension immediately. "Chastity, do you know Mr. Carlos?"

"Yes, I know him, I can introduce him to you. He knows my boss very well."

Every panic button in my body said run. I couldn't concentrate. I was likely a few feet away from the one responsible for Veronica and Paddy's death, maybe others. The last thing I wanted was to be in the same building as Juan Carlos and add to the body count. He was evidently on a mission to find the money. Money that suddenly was now mine.

I fumbled around with my napkin, dropped my fork on the floor, and when I bent down to pick it up, Kim also went down to 'help' me, "What do you want to do?"

"Keep a watchful eye for any movement in our direction. I am about as scared as I can be," I whispered to Kim.

We both sat up, and Chastity said, "You are a cute couple. Would you like to meet Mr. Carlos?"

"No," we said in unison. I hoped there was enough noise in the restaurant he did not hear her ask about meeting him and that he could not hear any reference to my name either.

"Chastity, would it be possible to refer to me as Pastor Warren from here on out? We want to maintain our discretion with everyone on the island."

"Certainly, Pastor Warren. Are you a pastor?"

"Yes!"

Kim interrupted, "Yes, he is a pastor, and he is not open to good times. I tried to show him a good time, and he just acted like I was nothing to him! Nothing, and it was going to be a VERY good time."

"Don't mind her, Chastity. She has good time issues."

"Well, I am not sure you have what I have for good times," Chastity matter-of-factly replied to Kim. If I had a picture of Kim's face at the moment, it would be worth more money than I had in my newly established account.

I leaned over to her and said, "I think your idea of good times and her idea of good times are completely different. But if not, I can understand why you have that look on your face. It's kind of cute. I have to admit." Kim kicked me under the table.

Our order arrived, and we began to eat. Without notice, Juan Carlos walked by our table and stopped, "Chastity, it is so nice to see you again. I am stopping by to see your brother soon. Is everything well?"

"Yes, we are well."

"Who are your friends?"

"This is Pastor Warren and his wife, Kim."

"A pastor, like a priest kind of pastor, or that is your name?"

"A pastor of a church."

"You look very familiar to me. Where are you from?"

"I am from Missouri, but I was born in Arkansas. Maybe you know me from there?"

"No, I don't think so. But, it's a big world, and I meet a lot of people," and then he leaned over and kissed Chastity on the cheek. "Good to see you, querida amiga. You should show Pastor and his wife a good time while they are here, no?"

"I will," she replied, "I will show them a very good time."

I ate a few bites and stopped eating. "This food is delicious, but I am not really in the mood for eating right now."

"Is everything ok? I show you a good time, but you need your strength."

"Yes, Pastor Warren, you need your strength for the good time you are about to have with Chastity." While Chastity didn't get the dig, I certainly did. I knew I couldn't arouse any suspicion from Chastity about my knowledge of Juan Carlos or the account I was establishing, likely from his cartel.

"Chastity, that gentleman that just left, used a phrase I am not familiar with, what does it mean?"

"It is querida amiga or dear friend. We used to be very close. He used to call me that often, then he found a woman from the US and entrusted everything to her. Juan never loved her like a man loves a woman, like romantically, but trusted her with everything. Anyway, she betrayed him and took his money, while he was on trial, he called me often and called me dear friend, like today. I do some business for him, but not often."

By this time, the panic button was sounding on every front. I had no idea what Chastity knew about me or Veronica's relationship with me. All I knew, I had just likely met my wife's killer and was sitting at a dining table with one of his assistants—the person who was taking the place Veronica once held. Plus, I was now completely unsure about Mr. Espinoza's understanding of who I was or the history of the funds currently assigned to me. I wasn't sure if Kim understood everything that was happening at our table, either. I wanted to run but didn't know where.

I took a few more bites, contemplating what I needed to do when Kim spoke up, "Are you feeling ok? You are sweating like crazy."

"Yeah, I think I need some fresh air. Would you ladies mind if I step outside for a minute? I am finished eating."

"No, you can go. We will join you soon."

I stepped outside just in time to see a heated discussion with Juan Carlos and another man, where Juan made his fingers look like a gun and put it to the man's head. I hid behind a van and watched the exchange. The other man looked as if he were pleading for his life, but I must have missed the context of the conversation because then Juan looked to see if anyone was looking and then pulled a gun from his back holster and handed it to the man. The man said a few more things and then got into a car and continued to speak to Juan as he drove away. I may have witnessed a contract to kill but had no idea if I or someone I knew was the target. Almost immediately, an SUV pulled up, and Juan got into the back seat, screaming an order to the driver, "Ir al otro lado de la isla, rápido!" The SUV left in a flash, and another car behind it followed as quickly.

About ten minutes later, Kim ran outside, "There's a shooting at the bank; Chastity is talking on the phone with someone now."

Chastity ran out of the restaurant, shouting on her phone and crying, saying, "We have to go. Someone is at the bank shooting at people."

"Do I need to drive?" I asked because of her emotional state, but she stopped talking on the phone for a second and said, "no, you don't know the way to where we are going," and then continued on her call, attempting to find out who was injured.

Kim got into the passenger side, and I got into the back seat. Chastity started driving the opposite way from the bank when we started moving. "Where are you going? We are going the wrong way. The bank is the other direction."

"It's not safe there. The person who shot people at the bank went outside, and they didn't know where he went. My boss was the one shot, and they are trying to keep him alive now. They told me to stay away for a while. We need to go to a safe place."

"Where is safe?"

"I know a guy who has a yacht. We can stay on his yacht until things settle down. It's on the other side of the island."

Chastity kept her conversation going with the person on the other line, at the same time, kept us informed. I had to wonder if that hit was from the man I saw with Juan Carlos and if it had anything to do with me.

"Mr. Espinoza is critical, and for some reason, he was very concerned that you had your documents, Mr. Cash. He's such a caring man to think of others as he is trying to stay alive. One of the assistant managers will bring us your documents."

"We have to get back to the ship in a few hours, as we are on a cruise, and we can't miss the departure," I said, hoping we would make it back to the ship so we could stay alive.

"I will get you there in time, and the assistant manager will be able to get the documents to us soon because he was not in the bank when everything happened. The people there need to talk to the policia. Where we are going is very safe. Many people have guns to protect us.

Kim sat in the front seat next to Chastity and turned around with a furrowed look and mouthed, "Who is her friend?" I shrugged my shoulders and kept a watchful eye on our location.

We arrived at a small marina quickly. Chastity was correct. There were men with automatic guns everywhere. As she pulled up to one, she talked to him in Spanish. He nodded to her and a man on the other side of the car. He was looking at Kim and me. They motioned for us to proceed. Surrounded by all of these guns made me feel more vulnerable than ever, and

I must have looked that way because Chastity spoke up, "Mr. Cash, you shouldn't worry. These are nice people. Well, they are nice people to me and will be nice to you and Ms. Kim. They are like family to me. We should have your documents soon, and we can relax until then. If the captain is on board, we can go out into the ocean and enjoy swimming together."

We pulled up to the largest yacht, as Chastity indicated we had arrived. When we exited the car, I noted many eyes were watching us, and when we got on the boat, many of them followed us but looking out to see if someone was following. The main deck was full of people, primarily women surrounding someone on the main deck, and a few men surrounded by a few other women. "Welcome to Santa Maria," the voice among the women exclaimed, "I have never had a pastor on the Santa Maria before, so we should have some type of ceremony, yes?"

The women, all scantily dressed, moved away, revealing the owner of the voice, Juan Carlos. He was sitting with a cocktail in one hand and his other arm around one of the women. Sweat was soaking my body, and Juan said, "Pastor, you should jump in the water when we get out to sea. Then you can cool off. You look very hot. Would you like something to drink? Manuel can make anything but water. He doesn't know how to make water, Manuel, get the Pastor something to drink."

The man walked over to me and asked me what we wanted to drink. Kim and I both asked for a cola on the rocks, and he hurried away to provide us what we needed. Chastity stepped away sometime while Juan addressed me but reappeared with a swimsuit that left little to the imagination and brought one for Kim.

"You can change in the bathroom down the steps on the left. Pastor

Warren, you can change into a swimsuit after Ms. Kim. Here it is," she handed me a costly swimsuit with the tag still on it.

The tag said $450. When Chastity saw the label, she motioned for me to hand it back, and abruptly tore it off, and handed the swim shorts back to me. Kim changed very quickly, and within minutes, I was on my way to the bathroom. While I was changing, I prayed. I prayed like I hadn't prayed in a long time. I was afraid for my life, more like terrified. I wondered if Juan was toying with me before killing me or if Chastity knew who I was. I played out all the scenarios in my head, and then wondered that if she were to tell Juan who I really was, what would happen. It was clear! The only one I could trust was God, so, my prayer focused on that. On the way up the steps, I decided to become proactive. Juan expected a pastor to be a pastor on his boat, and I would take every opportunity to talk to him in a way he would allow. If he were going to kill me, it would have to be while I was obedient to my calling.

When I stepped onto the main deck, the music was loud, and people were just as loud and filled with alcohol. Manuel had my cola ready. I took it and began drinking. I was so thirsty I almost finished it in one giant swallow. He turned to see my empty glass and took it to refill it. Juan yelled, "Pastor, sit by me. I want to talk with you."

I hesitantly walked over to him. "Pastor, you are a man of God, no?"

"I am."

"I know you are, and I offer any one of these beautiful women to you to help you feel good. They show you a good time, and I look the other way. I want you to be happy on my boat, to bless my boat with your presence. You have already done so, so here is Gabriella. Gabriella, come take Pastor downstairs and convince him to have a good time."

I quickly started shaking my head no, and Juan spoke up, "Pastor when you are on my boat, you have a good time. What they say? It is non-negotiable. You will offend me if you refuse my offer, and I don't like to be offended."

Gabriella took my hand and pulled me up from my seat, and said, "Let's go have a good time," while Kim looked on in despair. Juan read her immediately, "Wait, Gabriella, I think pastor's friend wants to join them for a good time, go have fun with Gabriella, three of you together, and then, come back upstairs."

Gabriella took her by the hand and said, "Let's have a good time," Kim and I went with Gabriella downstairs. She led us to a large suite with a bed and we all sat down. "I am here to fulfill your every desire. What would you like?"

My eyes met Kim's, and then we looked at Gabriella and began asking questions. We found out that Gabriella was 14 but looked older. She was bought from her parents by one of Juan's men. She had become a sex slave, as were most of the "women" on the boat were under 18. Juan tried to make them look older not to arouse suspicion, but it was clear he was trafficking women along with his other enterprises.

"Gabriella, I am a pastor, and there is no way I will have sex with you. I am not trying to offend Juan, and you can tell him what you want, but I will not. You are too precious, and I love God too much."

"You are the first person ever to turn down Juan's offer," she started crying. Kim sat next to her and put her arm around Gabriella. Gabriella melted into Kim's arms, sobbing. We shared the gospel with her, and she readily accepted it. We knew Juan held her against her will, and she feared for her life if she left.

After we prayed, I said to her, "You have shown me a good time. You can tell Juan you did," she laughed. "He will ask if we had sex, what should I say?"

"Tell him this Pastor is a true man of God, and he refused to have sex but prayed for me and for you. If it offends him, it does, but I can't violate my calling with God."

"Believe me, he will NOT violate his calling with God, with anyone," Kim interjected.

Gabriella stood, and began her slow walk upstairs, and turned to me and said, "He might kill me if I tell him I was unable to seduce you."

"Then tell him I was good in bed."

When we were on the main deck, Juan was talking to several men with guns. He was animated as they were looking towards the road leading up to the marina. A minute later, a car turned towards the marina. The men ran towards the car with guns drawn, and it looked like something was wrong. The car occupant was screaming at the men who were there, and one called Juan's phone. "Let her through."

It was the assistant manager of the bank, coming with the documents for me. "Pastor, you have someone here to see you, how do people know you are on my boat?"

Chastity spoke up, "I told them we would be here. Pastor has some documents to sign so he can get money for the rest of his cruise. It's ok Juan, she will be gone quickly," she walked over and kissed him with a passionate kiss. After her kiss, she said, "Pastor, let's go out to the car and get your money. You need it to buy Kim something nice."

I was unsure what Chastity knew now, especially after she continued the scenario, until we got to the car, out of the hearing of anyone associated with Juan. "Pastor, you need to sign these papers and get your card. Mr. Espinoza had already completed your documents and procured cash for you before he was shot. It was crucial to him that you had your account, your card, and your anonymity. His business card is in the bag. It is the kind with a flash drive built into it. It is significant for you, no? They shot my boss, but he wanted to give this to you. That's why they shot him. They didn't know Paddy's real name or who the money was going to go to." She cleared up whether she knew who I was quickly.

I signed the papers as Kim looked on. I wasn't sure if she saw the total amount until we were on our way back to the yacht. "Did you even have a clue about the amount coming to you?" Kim whispered.

"No, and for our safety, you have to keep your mouth shut, especially right now and today, really forever."

"Chastity, how long until we can leave?"

"Well, something is going on causing Juan Carlos to be very agitated. I think the policia is asking many questions about the shooting at my bank, and they are on their way here. If we leave, we have to do it so Juan doesn't get suspicious, but we can't wait until the policia interrogates him. It could get bloody."

Suddenly, the yacht started up, and Juan started screaming, "Hurry up, Chastity, we need to go."

Chastity looked at me and said, "We need to get back to the yacht now." We started running. Kim stepped in a hole and fell. When Juan saw her on the ground, slowing getting up, he made Gabriella get our clothes for us and get off the yacht. Then they sped out of the marina. Within seconds, the police were pulling into the marina. As they did, the men who were standing guard all went into hiding.

The first officer to exit his car ran to Chastity, "Where is Juan Carlos?" she pointed at the yacht motoring out to sea. He screamed words in Spanish I did not know.

Gabriella walked up with our clothes and handed them to us. "Juan made me leave, said I was not worth anything to him after I told him I was unable to seduce you, when I told him you were a man of God and seducing you when you were faithful to God would have brought God's anger on him, he decided I should live, but not live with him, so he made me leave. He told me there was something about you made him feel like he knew you, but for some reason, he was afraid of you."

The officer looked at Chastity and said a few words in Spanish. He knew her but was saying things I did not understand. She bowed her head and started weeping.

I knew it was bad, and asked, "Did Mr. Espinoza die?"

"Yes, he did not make it. We need to go back to the bank. I have to answer some questions and secure the property. You need to get back to your ship."

"Thank you so much, Chastity! You risked your life for us!"

"You are welcome. It was Mr. Espinoza's last wish to me."

"Can I come with you? I have nowhere to go," Gabriella asked.

"You can, but then you will need to find a place to stay, after Mr. Cash leaves, you will be on your own."

This time, I rode up front with Chastity, while Kim and Gabriella rode in the back. It was a short ride to the bank, but Kim asked Gabriella many questions about her life. She was from Honduras, and the cartel bought her for twenty dollars as a sex slave from her parents. They were from the Mosquito coast, a very impoverished area, but one teeming with members of several cartels. It was one of Juan Carlos's bases of operations.

CHAPTER TWENTY-SIX

When my last wife, Marie was alive, she partnered with an organization that rescues women in the sex trade. After a hit-and-run driver killed Callie, I went into depression. I had lost six wives, and losing Callie almost broke me. Ilean called me when Callie died and begged me to come to recuperate at her condo. At first, I refused and felt that the beach was just a bad reminder of every marriage. I know there was no divorce and I loved every wife with reckless abandon, but in my darkest moments, I took their deaths personally, to the point of feeling a deep sense of failure. I vocalized that to Ilean a few times, and she encouraged me to fly down and see a counselor near the condo. I was in a state of denial and told her I was ok.

Two weeks after Callie's funeral, I was a wreck of a man. I didn't get out of bed except go to the bathroom and eat, what little I ate. I just slept, hour after hour, day after day. I called Barbara and told her I was sick and scheduling someone to speak Sunday. That happened for several weeks. She knew me better and was at my house with an army of men and women, cleaning, mowing, and working around the outside of my house in the evening. At first, I didn't know anyone was around, sleeping so soundly, but then, she knocked on the door. When I opened the door, in my pajamas, my hair unkempt from sleeping for five days and unshaven, I looked a mess. Barbara said as much. She came into my house with her crew, and they started working on the inside. Dishes were piled so high in the sink, and trash was everywhere, just what the team came to help with, but I was so depressed I didn't notice how dirty my house had become. "Pastor, you are depressed, and you need help, and you need help now."

"No, I am not depressed, just too tired to do much. I think I may be coming down with some type of virus."

"It is not a virus. You are depressed."

"That's what Ilean said, and even offered to host me in a condo and set up counseling with someone."

"You need to go now. I will get you on a flight just as soon as you can pack."

"I can't go back there. It holds too many memories every time I go back. It reminds me of my failure every.single.time." I started crying. The crying turned into wailing, so strong everyone that was in my house was weeping too. I hadn't realized how deeply my pain had affected my congregation. They were grieving too, and after seeing their response to my depression and grief, I realized that I needed help and needed to help them through their pain too.

That moment, surrounded by hurting people who cared about me despite their grief, was just what I needed to encourage me to find healing. I agreed to go, and Barbara made a few calls. Before long, I was showering and packing. The flight was at 6:12 a.m. the next morning, which bothered me because I was so 'tired' I didn't think I could get up early enough to be at the airport in time. It was no problem because, at 3:15 a.m., a couple from the church arrived to wake me, feed me, and take me to the airport. The level of care my church showed me was impressive.

We arrived in time for the flight, and before I knew it, I was on my way to the place I didn't ever want to see again.

I secured a rental car and went to Ilean's to get the condo information. She knew I was coming and prepared everything. When I knocked on the door, she opened up and invited me to go to her kitchen table to talk to a friend. It was a counselor she knew. I felt hijacked and unprepared for the meeting. It was not on my terms, so I didn't even say hi to him. He calmly spent the next hour getting to know me, asking me about my ministry, my favorite restaurant in the area, and more. By the time we finished 'getting to know one another,' I felt comfortable sharing with him but was very tired. "That's enough for today. You probably need to get to your condo." It was time for lunch, and I was starving. I didn't want to eat alone, and I didn't want anyone around. It was crazy how I felt. I went to a local café and sat down. The owner knew me and walked over and welcomed me back. As I ate my lunch, I noticed a woman eating and reading something on her tablet. She had her hair pulled tight into a ponytail, wearing a light pink top and white shorts and noticeably tanned from spending her time in the sun. After lunch, I went back to my condo, thinking I would take a short nap.

I had been up since 3:15 a.m. and was extremely tired, but decided to go to an unoccupied cabana near my condo, relax as a cool wind blew off the water. I had a book to read but really didn't feel like reading, or even peopling right then. I pulled up a chair, positioned it just so, put a towel on it, and sat down to rest. I fell asleep, not noticing the wind starting to get stronger, and a storm off the coast heading my way. It was then that Marie came to me and said, "Sir, you need to get up and find shelter. The storm is almost here." It took a while to rouse me, and she was getting worried because I was not waking up very quickly. She shook me, moved me, and even opened my right eye and said, "We've got to go. The storm is almost here."

Waves were crashing on the sand, eroding it quickly, the rain was falling in buckets, and the thunder and lightning were fierce. I finally woke enough to realize that the storm was bearing down furiously. I stood up and the rain was blowing sideways, soaking both of us. "My condo is right here," she said as she took me by the hand and pulled me to her door, opened it as quickly as she could, and pulled me inside. The wind was howling by this time, and unsecured chairs and cabanas were rolling down the beach, and I realized that if this mystery woman hadn't had compassion, I would have been in the middle of the storm. "My name is Marie," she said as she walked into the bathroom to retrieve towels. "Here, use this to dry off. What is your name?"

"Jack Cash, and thank you. You saved my life."

"Don't mention it, but I think you would have awakened when the cabana blew away."

"Yeah, with me in it. Where did the storm come from?"

"I know, right? It happened so fast. I saw you at the café earlier, you looked so sad, and when you came to the cabana next to my condo, I thought you were a stalker, following me. I saw you looking at me at the café."

"I am sorry, it wasn't my intention to gawk."

"You didn't, but I did notice you looking my way. After you showed up at the cabana, I called the owner, and she told me your story."

"So, you really thought I was trying to make a move on you?"

"Well, maybe, and now, you are in my condo, so who made the move??"

"Thank you again!" I kept an eye out for the storm to diminish, mainly because I didn't want to be around people, especially a potential relationship, like she was doing right then.

"You are welcome. Would you like something to drink? I think the storm may be hitting us for another half hour or so."

"Water would be nice."

"Here you go," she said, handing me a bottle of water, "have a seat on the couch."

I sat down, and she carried the conversation the entire time. She never asked a 'yes' or 'no' question but questions that required longer answers than I wanted to give. It was almost like she was trying both to help me express my pain, and getting me comfortable with her company, at the same time. It worked. We talked for four hours while storm cells came and went. Finally, she said, "You know, the storms have been gone a while, and it is safe to go out, and," I interrupted, "You are probably ready to get rid of me."

"No, actually, I was going to see if you would like to join me for dinner. I am famished."

"If you had asked me four hours ago, I would have said no way, but now, I don't think I would enjoy anything more than going to dinner with you."

I learned Marie was the kind of person who could draw out the most profound things in you and calmly talk you into a better place. It was just what I needed. While I went to the counselor a few times, Marie served as the kind of friend who helped draw out the poison I had let infect my heart. At the same time, Marie was in the area on a mission. After a couple of days, she asked me if I had ever gone to a strip club. It was a strange question, one that came out of nowhere, and I immediately answered, "no," and then, "why did you ask that random question."

She divulged that she had not been inside a strip club but positioned herself at the back exit waiting for girls to come out to smoke or leave and then offered to buy them a meal, take them home, or something.

Unbeknownst to me at the time, she rescued underaged girls caught in the sex slave industry, and there were many. When she felt comfortable enough with me, feeling that I would not secure the services of someone in the sex industry, she told me that sometimes ministers were caught in stings. She had rescued over a hundred girls, some were as young as 13.

Gabriella's story reminded me of Marie's work.

As Kim talked to Gabriella, I knew the lifestyle she had come to know because Marie shared with me over a year ago.

We arrived at the bank, and Chastity went to an officer standing guard outside the bank while investigators were coming and going. He motioned for her to go inside, and she disappeared inside the bank. I looked around at a crowd of people outside the crime scene tape. Cynthia and Brian were there, so I hid behind the doorpost in the car so they wouldn't be able to identify me. "Kim, keep your head down. I see Cynthia and Brian. They are at my 10 o'clock." Kim asked Gabriella to change seats so she could keep a low profile from "our friends who won't leave us alone."

While Chastity was inside the bank, I pulled out the cash, which was about $10,000, a couple of debit cards, and random "paperwork," which was nothing more than brochures for the Island. The "business card" Mr. Espinoza had placed in the bag contained everything I needed, the trust and all banking information.

"Gabriella, when we finish here, we have to get on a ship that brought us here. We are sorry, but you cannot go with us. Do you have a passport?"

"No, when Juan Carlos bought me, and he took me anywhere, he would tell people I was his daughter."

I knew she couldn't get on a flight without a passport and couldn't get one without some documents. Transporting her home would require a different way of thinking.

Cynthia and Brian separated, with one to our left and one circling to our right. I whispered, "they are separating and moving in different directions, have they seen us?"

As Gabriella noticed who we were talking about, she spoke up, "I know them. They were on Juan Carlos' boat for about 20 minutes today. They were looking for him, but he was having lunch." Gabriella was starting to piece together what was happening and who we were, "Are you 'Jack Cash' because if you are, the people who walked around us were talking about you, and you were going to a bank to get money."

"Did Juan Carlos know who we were?"

"I don't think so."

"Do they work for work for Juan Carlos?"

"I don't know, I saw them for the first time today. But, Juan Carlos knew them right away, and they acted like they had known each other for a while."

"That clears things up, they are rogue."

Kim nodded her head in agreement.

"Gabriella, I am going to give you some money. Is there a way you can go back to your family?"

"They will turn me in for more money, and I will die. My father and mother are very poor."

"How much money do your mom and dad make every week?"

"My dad makes about five dollars a week, he sold me for a month's wages or twenty US dollars."

"Is there somewhere else you can go?

"I have an Aunt in LaCeiba. She works at a resort and has a house near the resort."

"Can you go to her house?"

"I don't have a way or any money."

"I will give you money, and we will see if we can find a way there."

The police captain walked Chastity out to the car, talking as they approached. He kept his eye on me the entire walk, causing me to feel he was trying to memorize my facial features. When she got to the car, she opened the door and introduced me as "Pastor Warren," but it somehow felt off. I don't know if he knew better or if she told him something in the bank.

He introduced himself and said, "Enjoy my country, but be very careful, Pastor, you might not know who you can trust and who you cannot trust."

I thanked him for his advice as Chastity sat in the driver's seat. He bent over and kissed Chastity and said he loved her, then he looked up at someone and nodded. I was afraid to turn around to see who he acknowledged. He nodded to the area where Cynthia had moved.

Chastity said, "Let's get you back to the ship."

"That would be good because we are running out of time. Chastity, is there a way to get Gabriella back to Honduras?"

"I know a guy who makes runs to Honduras weekly. I can see if he has room on his airplane?"

"Is he with the cartel? I want her out of the sex industry."

"He is, he runs for their operation. I know someone else with a plane who may be able to fly there."

"Can you call him and find out if he can, and how much it will cost to fly her to LaCeiba?"

"Yes, I will call Oswaldo now." She looked up the number in her phone and pressed send to dial while she pulled out of the bank parking lot. I couldn't see Brian or Cynthia at all and couldn't tell who the Police captain was signaling. After the man answered, Chastity asked a few questions, most of which I couldn't understand. "He told her that he can fly her there, but it will cost $3,000. It will take about four hours to fly if the weather is good."

I turned to Gabriella, "Do you feel comfortable going back to Honduras? I don't know what I can do for you on Grand Cayman."

"Yes, my aunt will take care of me."

"I am going to give you money for the flight, and the rest, I need for you to give to your aunt to help her keep you." I looked at Chastity and said, "I was thinking about giving her my cash. Do you trust the man you called not to steal it?"

"Yes, I trust him. He owes me anyway, I help him out sometimes, and he owes me this."

I pulled out the debit cards and bank docs and gave Gabriella the envelope with some cash. She looked inside and started crying. "Why are you doing this?"

"I want you to live your life as a normal teenager, not as some object for a drug dealer."

"Thank you."

"I will take care of her, Jack Cash, and will tell Oswaldo to treat her very well, and I will also tell his wife to go with him. That way, he doesn't try anything with Gabriella. She is my brother-in-law's sister. They are very nice and don't do bad stuff like that, but having a woman on the plane will be good."

We arrived back at the ship and said goodbye to Chastity and Gabriella. I had to admit, I cried when we left them. Mostly because my heart went out to Gabriella and knew some of the struggles she would face; even though she was going to a safe place. Marie took many girls in after rescuing them, but because they had no way to make any money, they would resort to the only thing they knew. There were many heartaches that Marie would share with me.

The last rescue Marie was a part of happened about forty-five minutes from our house, outside a strip club. She loaded up an SUV with food, water, clothes and waited for girls to come outside the strip club after they finished their work.

Most came outside and cried, vomited, or did drugs outside the view of their handlers. Marie knew this and waited for one to come out and approach them with an offer to leave the life. Some would take water, food, clothes, and every so often, after building rapport with them, one left with her.

Most of them were 12-14 years of age, and even though they were at a strip club, they didn't strip, mainly because the girls looked so young if undercover officers were in the club, the officers would immediately raid it, so they worked in VIP rooms so those men could use and abuse them. Some were runaways from very dysfunctional or drug homes, and others were from other countries, no doubt promised a wonderful life in America but then sold as slaves.

On the fateful day, Marie and another rescuer, Kristine, had positioned themselves outside the strip club waiting for Tina, a 12-year-old girl they met the day before. After about thirty minutes, Tina came out.

She was vomiting violently and crying. Marie and Kristine slowly exited the SUV, aware that helping Tina was dangerous. Kristine lived long enough to tell the story, but a woman stepped around the corner when they approached Tina.

Tina pleaded with her to leave them alone and not hurt her friends, but the woman said something to Marie and shot her. She died instantly. Tina ran towards a convenience store parking lot nearby, and Kristine ran to save Marie's life. The woman walked up to Kristine, preparing to shoot her point-blank, but the gun didn't fire. Sirens started, and the woman started running. Kristine stood to run for a first aid kit, thinking Marie was still alive. But then, the woman turned and shot Kristine. She was alive long enough to give the police a description of the woman and why they were there, but then she died. The police never found Tina.

So, Gabriella's plight was dear to my heart. I knew similar stories, and my last wife gave her life to help these young women.

CHAPTER TWENTY-SEVEN

We hugged for a long time, I prayed for her, and then we headed back to the ship. Most of the other passengers were just starting to make their way back, so, the rush to get on board had not yet started and we were able to do so quickly. I went directly to the room and placed the "documents" in the in-room safe, keeping the card with me, and then asked Kim, "Are you ready for dinner?"

"Yes, but I want to shower first, do you want to join me?"

"No, but I will leave the room if you ask me again."

"I was kidding, don't get all holy again."

I was so mad because of antics like this. Now, I was rooming with Kim for the remainder of the cruise. I liked her but still wasn't going to compromise my walk with Christ.

She stepped into the shower, and I decided to leave the room until she was completely dressed, just in case, but when I looked through the peephole, there were two people at our door.

They were too close to determine who they were, so I decided to stay in the room until they were out of the way. Kim's shower took about five minutes. Then she yelled out, "I forgot to bring my clothes into the bathroom with me, would you please turn around while I get them, I don't want to upset you again."

I looked out, and the couple was still standing there, so I just stayed at the door, with my back to the bathroom door. Kim stepped out of the door and rubbed my shoulders, "Would you turn around and tell me what you think about what I am wearing?"

"That depends. What are you wearing?"

"Do you trust me?"

"Not at all!!!"

Kim grabbed and turned me around. She was wearing the biggest smile and a lovely sundress and sandals. "I just need to do my make-up and hair, and I will be ready to go. I can do it in the room while you shower."

"You look very nice. Thank you for dressing up, and um, dressing," I said, laughing.

My shower was a little longer. Once the warm water hit my head, I fell apart. The stress from the day was too much, and I slowly started to decompress from it all. There was so much to process. The memory of Marie hit me again in the shower. I was wrecked.

Marie's murder was still an ongoing investigation. Because she rescued girls, authorities believed someone with the strip club was directly responsible. What they didn't understand was the female aspect of it. All the people in the strip club were men, and the only other women were underaged. If there was anything good that came of it, a vast sex trade network ended on that day. There were 40 girls at three different strip clubs associated with the same organization that were able to be rescued. They arrested hundreds of men in the process, including workers, patrons, and owners. The road to healing would be a long one for those girls. I would likely have to answer more questions from the investigators when I returned home. So if there was a consolation, it was that Marie's death saved more girls in one moment than she had since she started her work.

Knocking on the door, Kim said, "Jack Cash, your dinner date is waiting!"

I was jarred back to reality, "Almost done."

I hadn't even used soap yet, so I quickly washed, rinsed, and dried off. I was in such a hurry for my shower, I had forgotten my clothes. I yelled out, "Ok, now my turn to get my clothes, please turn away while I come and get them." I didn't hear anything, "Kim, are you out there?"

I heard nothing, so I carefully opened the door, peeked around the corner to see if she were playing around, but she was not in the room. I quickly got dressed, spritz cologne on me, gathered my passport, the business card with the flash drive, and placed it, along with the debit cards, into my wallet. I had no idea where Kim had gone, so I went to the observation lounge, found a little bit of a hidden place, and sat down.

The final people were arriving from the excursion day, and we were about to set sail again. I kept an eye out for Kim but also for Cynthia and Brian. I also had a good view of the hallway heading to our room so I could watch out for everyone. I waited for about fifteen minutes, then went exploring. I stepped into a duty-free shop and found a wonderful necklace to give to Kim. She had endured an amazing amount of disruption to her world, not by her choice. "Would you like a gift bag for this?" the attendant wondered.

"Yes, and I would like to use my debit card, is it ok?"

"You can, but the cruise line already has an onboard account for you. You can simply use your cruise card for the purchase."

"Someone else paid for my cruise, so I will need to use my card or change the payee on the original card."

"Hmmm, let me check, can I see your cruise card?" I handed him my cruise card. "The issuer of the account has flagged your account. I will need to see your identification." He looked at his screen and then my passport. "Your name is on this cruise card, but not on the account the cruise card is attached to, I am sorry, but the cruise card is no longer valid. The card company for the person that paid for your cruise has locked your account."

"Locked the cruise card or the credit card account?"

"Well, the credit or debit card this cruise card is attached to is now locked."

"Can I attach my debit card to the account? I wanted to do that originally."

"Let me see what I can do." He picked up a phone and called someone, "I am having a problem with my screen on server 17A, can you pull up this code, it is code '4e5d,' ok, see you soon. Sir, I am having a problem with my screen. If you can wait just a minute, we should be able to get this completed."

"What is the problem?"

"I am not sure. I have never seen this screen or code before. Probably a problem with the merchant services company."

A few minutes later, I was surrounded by security, "Sir, put your hands on the counter."

"What's the problem?"

"Sir, put your hands on the counter. You are under arrest."

"WHAT??? For WHAT????"

"For suspicion of murder and fraudulent use of a bank card, put your right hand behind your back," click went on the handcuff, "now your left hand," another click, and then I was being escorted to the brig.

"Who was murdered?"

"Sir, I don't know. The account holder has died, someone flagged your name and the account after, and it just now populated to our server."

"The Captain will come and talk to you with more information. We have alerted the authorities in Florida that you are on the ship. At the next port, we will release you to them."

The brig was a small room with a cot and a toilet. The cruise ship officers took my handcuffs off and closed the door. "Can I at least let my travel companion know where I am, and can I get dinner?" No answer.

I sat down on the bare cot and wondered who was dead, or was it a ruse by Cynthia? I started patting myself down. I left my debit card in the duty-free shop. With the sudden turmoil of security, I forgot to get it back. I had no idea what happened to Kim. I started looking around for a way to escape. I know it was crazy to think, but after running from so many, I had the desire to run now too. About thirty minutes later, the Captain knocked. "Come in, I guess."

"Yes, sir, I just wanted to make sure you were not using the latrine. Are you Jack Cash?"

"Yes, why am I being held?"

"I have as much information as I could get. It seems you were with the bank president on Grand Cayman just a short time before his murder. You talked with someone named, "Paddy, in Florida, just before his murder? You were with a woman named Ilean? She paid for this cruise for you just before her murder. You have been married seven times, and they are all dead. Murder surrounds you. They posted an 'armed and dangerous' alert with this bulletin." He handed me the bulletin.

"Wait, Ilean? Ilean? Ilean's dead?

"Yes, she was murdered, that is why I am holding you here."

It was if someone had punched me in the stomach with such force that all I could do was double up, and wail. Eventually, I just buried my head in the pillow wishing for some type of relief from the pain. I was spent, and at every turn, death followed me like a curse.

I am not sure how long I cried, but long enough for the Captain to leave, return with a chaplain, and then leave again. The chaplain just sat there, trying to console me, but I couldn't handle much more death, murder and a chase. A pastor is equipped to help people walk through all kinds of tragedies, but when it comes to the pastor, he needs someone to help him. It was becoming a full-time job.

Eventually, I calmed down, and the Captain returned and asked, "Is there anything I can do for you?"

"When was Ilean murdered?"

"Let's see, it was yesterday morning, at about 10:30 a.m."

"We were on our way to the ship from Vero Beach. It is a two-hour drive, and we stopped at places that should have a record I was there."

"Sir, I am not the judge or jury. I am a ship's Captain. When I get a bulletin like this, I am obligated to take action. So, that's why you are in the brig. We are looking for the person who was rooming with you. When we find her, I will have to detain her as well. I am sorry, I am just doing my job. I suggest getting an outstanding lawyer when you get back to the states."

There was a knock on the door, "Captain, you are urgently needed on the bridge."

"I will be back later to let you know the arrangements."

I just sat there. Ilean had been a friend since Mandy's death and my first trip to Vero. She took me in, and even this week, was instrumental in informing me of this account. I laid down and cried so more, but then I got angry. Angrier than before with Paddy because the people I loved were systematically dying. I didn't know what to do then, but I was beginning to realize if I didn't do something now, the murders would continue. I was also afraid for Kim.

Someone knocked on the door. It was a steward to find out what I wanted for dinner. "I get dinner in the brig?"

"Yes, sir. We cannot refuse food or water to anyone."

"Anything?"

"As long as it is on the ship?"

"Thank you! I want a loaded chicken sandwich, with fries, catsup, a large glass of iced tea with the pink sweetener."

"Excellent sir, I will have it down promptly."

"Do you know if they found my roommate?"

"No, sir! This is the only brig available, so I would guess if she were not in here, she has not been found."

"Ok, thank you."

He left, and within minutes, there was another knock on the door. "Hello, Mr. Cash?" came a voice on the other side of the door.

"Yes," I yelled through the door.

"I just wanted to tell you we have located your roommate. She is in another secure room. She is safe."

I looked at the tiny bed in the room and was thankful we were not in the same room. Kim is too much when it comes to sleeping in the same room. Most importantly, she was safe.

As I sat on the bed, I thought again about Marie. Her life's work was saving girls, but really, she rescued me. Our time together after meeting at Vero was as often as she was not doing her ministry work. I don't think she slept much, and neither did I. Before we were romantically involved, I knew I needed healing, and she helped walk me to that place. I never felt like she was using any kind of therapy with me, and maybe it was just her presence, questions, and perspective that helped me, but it certainly changed my life. After two months of interaction, both at Vero and over the phone, I was in love with her when I returned home. I often flew down for three or four days at a time to spend time with her. It started slowly for a day or so, and then, it grew to extraordinary. We were inseparable. Some said it was because of the short time we were together, but I don't think it was that at all. I was madly in love with her, and although boundaries were in place and never breached, we were passionate about one another.

When I decided to ask her to marry me, Ilean talked to a friend who owned a house on the Indian River. They let us use their cabana and their kitchen. I hired a chef to prepare the meal and some local artists to play while we ate. It was epic. The food was delicious, and the musicians were terrific. I had planned every detail but forgot to account for a sudden pop-up storm in the evening. The evening was beautiful, and when I arrived to propose, I got on one knee. When I did, Marie started crying.

"Marie, I met you in the storm of my life, literally and figuratively, and the last thing I wanted was a wife. You rescued me from those storms and loved me. You loved me through my pain. You were patient with me in my grief and helped me find healing. Through all of that, I learned to love again, hope, and give my heart to someone. If somehow, this moment comes and goes without you, I would still say that I have never been happier. You are my love and my life, and the only thing that would make me happier than now is if you were my wife. I love you with all my heart, Marie. Will you marry me?"

"Jack Cash, I have never met anyone like you, but my dream husband was everything you are and until a few months ago, that dream was as elusive as ever. Then, in the storm, I saw you, and instantly I wanted to know you, be with you, be your wife, and love you forever. I love you too, and the answer is yes, YES!!! I will marry you."

The wind suddenly picked up, and a thunderclap announced we had moments to find shelter. We ran into the house, not missing that it was a storm that brought us together in the first place. Our wedding and life together was anything but a storm. It was as close to perfect as it could be. Marie was brilliant, warm, sassy, and intuitive. She was probably the most intelligent person I knew, with education, wisdom, and a healthy dose of street smarts. Marie could read people better than anyone I have ever known, including Monica, and read me like a book. Any time I was happy, she knew it; if discouraged, she figured it out; and frisky, well that was easy. We were married for a little over two and a half years when someone killed her. Just two months ago, we started planning a trip to Europe for a working vacation. She was going to a meeting of professionals combatting the trafficking of women in the sex slave industry in Europe. It was her passion and life's work, and it cost her life.

I will never forget the morning that I got the news. I was reading in my study when the doorbell rang. I looked through the side pane and noticed a police car in the driveway. I opened the door and said, "Hello." Next to the officer was a law enforcement chaplain. Both had grim looks on their faces. They asked if I was Jack Cash and how I knew Marie. "She is my wife." I started shaking my head no because I knew a chaplain is a part of the team providing death notifications. "No, NO, not Marie." I fell on my knees, burying my face on the floor, sobbing. The chaplain and officer pulled me up, led me to our couch, and sat me down.

"Mr. Cash, someone murdered your wife behind a strip club. An unknown female shot her." At the moment, it was as if time slowed down so much that every minute felt like an hour, and every word poured out of people's mouths slowly as if at half speed. "Our investigative team is attempting to apprehend the suspect, and I can assure you we will do everything in our power to find her. Meanwhile, the coroner will call you later today with information about Marie. They will likely do an autopsy to help them in the investigation. Is there anyone we can call for you? Maybe a pastor."

Trying to catch my breath, "No, I will need to call some people in a minute."

My first call was to Barbara, and then Ilean. They were my closest friends. I couldn't believe that Ilean was dead.

As I sat in the brig reminded of this most recent death notification, my memory was shaken by a knock on the brig door.

"Hello, sir, I have your dinner," an officer wheeled in a cart of food. It was more than just the food I ordered, but snacks and additional drinks.

"This is more than I ordered."

"Yes, sir, the Captain called you a VIP, and said we needed to take care of you on the ship. He will be here in a few minutes."

"Thank you," I said as I opened the hot food container, the steam and aroma indicated it was in the container only a short time before its trip to me since it was so hot. "This smells incredible."

"Yes sir, enjoy."

I pulled up the cart to the bed and started eating, and another knock on the door, this time the Captain. "Mr. Cash, I am releasing you. I am sorry I had to detain you."

"I don't understand. Why did you detain me, and now why are you releasing me?"

"It seems the US Marshal's office did not issue the bulletin, but instead, one of their agents on our ship did without agency approval."

"Cynthia?" I asked, hoping there was not another rogue agent on board.

"Yes, we are looking for her now. Their office indicated we were to detain her at once when we located her. That is what we are focused on now. Do you know her?"

"Yes, I am familiar with her."

"Sir, you can finish your meal here, go to your room, or you can go to any of the restaurants you wish. I am truly sorry for this."

"Where is Kim?"

"I am releasing her as well. The bulletin called for both detentions. Is there somewhere she can meet you?"

"Yes, have her come to the room."

Instead of going directly to the room, I headed back to the duty-free shop to retrieve my debit card. When I arrived, I asked for my debit card. They verified my identification and went to their secure area, and retrieved it. "Did you use it for the purchase I wanted?"

"No, sir, we kept your card for safekeeping. Would you like to purchase something?"

"Yes, I found a necklace. I would like to purchase the necklace I found earlier. I also need to get a cruise card attached to my debit card. Is it possible?"

"I will need to change your card, I will see what I can do."

As I waited, I looked around the duty-free shop a little longer. I found a beautiful blouse for Kim, guessed her size, and brought it to the counter. "You are set. I have attached your debit card to your cruise account and deactivated the original one attached to the cruise."

"Wonderful, please add this blouse." As he was completing the sale, I heard someone familiar, it was Kim, and she was on a cell phone with someone. I couldn't make out exactly what she was saying and wondered how she could use a cell phone on the ocean.

" That will be \$3,151, sir."

"Are the diamonds real?"

"Yes, and they are guaranteed to be what the tag indicates, or we will refund your purchase. Do you still want it?"

"Yes, can you wrap it?"

"I will see what I can do!"

The diamonds were the highest quality one could expect on a cruise, and I didn't want to wait to buy something at home, so I purchased it, and looking at the cashier, "Quick question, can you make a cell phone call from the ship?"

"Yes, but this far out, there are no cell towers. Instead, people use the Wi-Fi function on their phones to make calls. As long as there is Wi-Fi and our link to the satellite is working, you can call. I will be back in a moment."

"Thank you!" At least that answered the cell phone question.

He returned with a gift bag and tissue, placed the necklace case in the tissue, and wrapped, taped, and put it in the bag. He did the same to the blouse. And he then puffed the tissue out to make it look like a dozen tissue points. It was clear he wanted it to impress. He finished it and completed the sale. I was very proud of my purchase and saw Kim walking towards the room.

I followed her without seeing me as she made her way through the mass of people coming and going on the deck. People were moving around a lot, as they were going to shows, dinner, and the deck for a party. As she was about to enter the room, she turned towards me, saw me, and abruptly ended her call. She was startled. "I thought you were waiting in the room."

"No, after I finished my shower, I decided to go for a walk. I got arrested, thrown in cruise jail, and posted bail. How about you?"

"Wow, it sounds like you had an interesting evening. I was thrown in jail too, but it was bigger than our room," looking down, Kim asked, "What's in the bag?"

"A get out of jail gift bag, didn't you get one?"

"Ummm no, they let me go, and said I could meet you back here."

"Well, here I am. Wanna get something to eat?"

"Not really. I had dinner earlier."

"How about dessert?" I said, hoping I could give her my gift over a meal.

"I don't know, I am pretty tired. I am not up to doing much."

"We can get dessert and come back to the room if you want, I mean unless you want to go to the room for some alone time."

She stood there with the most disappointed look on her face.

"What's wrong?"

"Well," she said as she started to cry, "I have been chased, put in jail, ignored, and every advance I have made at you has been turned down, I mean completely ignored. I don't think you like me."

"Kim, I like you. I like you a lot, and you have put up with a lot. How can I make it up to you?"

"I don't know," she said between sniffles, "I don't know."

"Well, let me start by dinner, dessert, or at least let's go out on the deck and enjoy the evening."

"I need to step inside first."

Kim opened the door at the same time Cynthia and Brian were opening the safe. "HELP" Kim screamed, "WE ARE BEING ROBBED," her screaming brought several to our door.

"Are you ok?" a man asked, "I am a police officer from Georgia."

"These people have broken into our safe."

Cynthia and Brian both started fighting their way out of the room. They got past Kim, and I held Brian as long as I could. People were running to get help, the officer was trying to apprehend Brian as well, but Cynthia got past Kim and started choking the officer that came to our aid. He let go of Brian to ward off Cynthia, but her training matched his, and Brian was too much for me to hold alone. Brian was able to get away after punching my ribs, and then Brian and Cynthia started on the officer. He was on the floor quickly. There was screaming and shouting and others who were trying to figure out what was happening. They darted out of the room, and within seconds security from the cruise ship had arrived. "They went that way," I shouted as I motioned the opposite direction from where they came, "Cynthia and Brian are their names."

There were doctors and nurses, all enjoying the cruise, who came to our aid. The officer suffered bruised ribs, and I did as well. Kim had a few fists to the stomach but seemed to be alright.

A few minutes later, the Captain arrived. "Folks, I am so sorry this happened. We have been trying to locate this couple for a while. We will ramp our search for them. Did they get anything?"

I stood up and looked at the safe. It looked as if everything was still inside. I pulled the documents out and said, "I think we caught them as they were opening the door to the safe, so I think it's all still there."

"We are going to place security outside your room, and if you are going anywhere, we will have plainclothes security shadow you. We will do everything we can to maintain your safety. Again, I am sorry."

After the medical people cleared us, I looked at Kim and said, "How about a banana split?"

"How about a steak? I wasn't hungry before, but now I am, and I am angry."

"At me?"

"No, I am mad at those nutjobs and I will not stay in the room while they are free. We are going to go to dinner, and dessert and who knows, but I know this, I am not staying locked in my room while they are free. Not today, not today!!!"

"Let's go," I secured the safe with a different passcode, grabbed the gift bag, and left for dinner.

We found a restaurant called "Gerald's Steak and Ribs," and as people were leaving, a lady grabbed Kim and said, "You haven't had amazing till you have had Gerald's Steak and Ribs with his 'amazing' barbeque sauce." Kim giggled, which let me know she was all kinds of excited about this place.

I don't know why we didn't see this place before. There are so many restaurants on board, but tonight, this restaurant fits so well. The décor was chic with light browns and wall paintings from the south, some depicting cotton and people chopping cotton, and a picture showing children in front of shacks from what looked like the '30s. Kim spotted on our way to the table, with kids so hungry you could see their ribs, but the looks on their faces were pure delight. She noted, "Sometimes you can have nothing, and yet have everything."

I stopped cold. The picture was incredible. Kim said something word for word, opposite of something Marie often said. She said, "sometimes you have everything, but have nothing," primarily to girls who, even though they were slaves, relished the attention, clothes, jewelry, and money given for their obedience. Some realized the danger and degradation the lifestyle presented and wanted out. They either ran or were beaten until they died or obeyed. Marie rescued some.

"Are you coming, or are you going to stare at the picture?"

"I am coming, what did you say just now?"

"Are you coming, or are you going to stare at the picture?"

"No, before ."

"I said, 'sometimes you have everything, but have nothing,' why?"

"Because it is so close to something she would say."

"Who would say?"

"Marie, my late wife."

"Hmmm, I am sorry if I brought up a memory. Let's sit before the rest of the ship comes in."

"No, it's ok, just hit me and the picture is haunting."

We sat down the looked at the menu. "Baby-back ribs, and salad, that's what I am getting, how about you?"

"Hmmm, I think I will get a plate of country-style ribs. It sounds delicious."

The waitress came to the table, and with as much southern flare as one could speak, she said, "Howdy ya'll, thank you for coming to Gerald's, once you come, you will leave so full your belly will need a cart to get it through the door."

"Is it your motto?"

"What's a motto?"

"I don't know. What's a motto with you?"

"Stop it, Jack Cash, and order."

We ordered, and the waitress said that Gerald would be by our table soon. She hurried off and eventually made her way back with two iced teas and two glasses of water with ice. As Gerald walked up to the table, he introduced himself, asked my name, and said he started grilling steaks for family and friends, and it took off. Eventually, he earned a place on a cruise ship to see the world and cook fantastic food. He shook my hand and said, "Mr. Cash, it is a pleasure to serve you. I hope you enjoy our food and tell others about our place."

I shook his hand, thanking him for his hospitality, and then he left for the grill. Kim leaned forward and said, "I like it already."

I leaned over and took the gift bag out. "Kim, I went to Vero Beach to grieve, to find solace and rest. My soul needed it, and the pain was intense. It was there I met an amazing woman. I want to thank you for traveling the world with me, through peril and storms, through rogue agents and cartel killers. I got this as a way to say, 'thank you,' thank you for being a friend and not killing me when others are trying to, or at least it seems that way. I want you to have this as a token of my appreciation."

She sat there, with unblinking eyes, staring at me.

"Well, say something."

"You haven't gotten on one knee yet, I am waiting for you to get on one knee, and the answer is yes, but you have to get on one knee."

I handed her the bag and said, "That's not in the bag today. Today, it's 'thank you.'"

"So, you are saying it is the bag for another day."

"I am saying 'thank you, and here is something to show you how much I appreciate it."

"You are welcome, but if you want to get on a knee, and ask me, oh, ask me, anything! Anything you can ask, but I hope this doesn't have one of those floppy sun hats in it, I already have one."

She opened the bag and removed the top tissue, and pulled out the blouse. "It's beautiful, I will put it on now," and she pulled it over her head and adjusted it.

"Ok, I will see how we can remove the tags when the waitress arrives. It brings out the beauty of your eyes, that's for sure. Your eyes carry a gold shimmer, and this enhances the gold very nicely."

She put her hand in pulled out the box, began unwrapping it, and then pulling out the chain. Her eyes widened as the light in the restaurant hit the necklace. I could see the shimmer on her face and the wall behind her. I stood up, walked to her side of the table, and took the necklace, putting it in front of her, her tears hitting my hand, and then put it around her neck and fastened it. I then leaned down and kissed her wet face. "Thank you! You are amazing, and I love you."

The tears flowed freely, for it was the first time I said those words to her, and it slipped out so naturally I hadn't considered the full ramifications of those words in this setting, but Kim was ready. "Jack Cash, you are amazing, and I couldn't think of anyone else I would want to run from the law and cartel with than you. Thank you so much, and if you got this on the ship, you had to pay a lot of money for it. Thank you, it's beautiful."

"With the blouse highlighting the shimmering gold in your eyes and the diamonds highlighting the glow and beauty of your face, I feel so awkward. I feel like the awkward kid who has just asked the most beautiful girl to the dance. Your beauty is stunning and I am completely out of my league."

"Are you kidding me?!? I have wanted to date you, marry you, and be with you all my life. I feel like the awkward girl who every other girl would die to be in her place, and every time I got up the nerve to make it a point to notice me, you found someone else. But here I am, in this place, and I don't think it could get any better unless you have a ring somewhere. Even if you don't, I love you! I love Jack Cash, always have, and nothing will stand in my way now."

It was like a sweet reply sprinkled with a weird, stalkerish vibe.

"And Jack Cash, your night is going to be even more amazing."

"I hope it means we are going to watch a show, a movie, or watch the stars."

"We'll see," she said with a wink and puckered lips.

CHAPTER TWENTY-EIGHT

s I sat there, it dawned on me I had probably come on too strong and I had likely unleashed a caged animal. I actively wondered if there was another room on the ship I could stay in for the night because the temptation I had been able to overcome might be too much tonight. Vigilance and something that could wear us both completely out might help my problem, so I got to wondering what we could do that would cause us to collapse with exhaustion when we made our way back to the room.

The food arrived, and we devoured it. Kim talked non-stop, giddy like a kid who just found out they were on their way to Disney. She wasn't asking questions, which was good because I didn't think she would pause long enough to hear a reply.

After dinner, I suggested we walk around the ship. I forgot about security shadowing us, but it was pretty clear who they were, which didn't bother me since it would hopefully keep Kim from anything crazy. The evening breeze was incredible, and the chairs on the upper deck were available, so I suggested we go up and enjoy the evening. It was happy hour. Some were happier than others by the laughter and expressions of everyone. We found out later our shadows were married but we didn't know when we found two chairs, they found one to share and promptly started kissing. If they were maintaining a cover, they were pulling it off.

Kim pulled her chair near me, but it wasn't close enough for her, so she sat in my chair and snuggled up to me. The air was moist, of course, but a little cooler than we first thought. A murmur started on the deck and then went quickly to a fevered pitch, "shooting stars." The night sky was clear, and the seas were somewhat calm, and every minute or so, chatter because of shooting star sightings.

About ten minutes later, the party started on a lower deck. The music was loud for those in the area, but where we were, it was tolerable. "Sailing" by Christopher Cross started playing, and everyone started singing along.

Kim stood up and pulled me up to dance, along with other cruisers. The slow dance continued as the DJ got the romance playlist, "I'd really love to see you tonight," by England Dan & John Ford Colley; then "I honestly love you," by Olivia Newton-John.

As I held her, I whispered, "I love you," turning with a slight shuffle of a dance." As I turned to see our shadows and they were dancing as well, but oblivious to us. We moved right and left, doing our best to stay away from bumping other dancers but caught up in the moment. It was an incredible feeling, and I didn't want it to end.

Another ship was about to pass on the starboard side. Right in the middle of it, the Captain blew the horn twice. It changed the moment, so we sat down and huddled close. The DJ took the horn blast as a signal to ramp up the party, and the slow dance gave way to an all-out party dance. We decided to walk around the ship.

We walked by an ice cream shop, and got a couple of hot fudge sundaes, and ate as we walked. I looked back, and our shadows were gone. It bothered me only because they were to shadow us and provide security, but they were getting frisky on the deck and may have decided to go to their room. Regardless, there were plenty of people around, so I wasn't as concerned.

"Operation Rising Star, Operation Rising Star," the Captain announced over the cruise ship speakers.

"Someone has died. That's what the Captain announces when someone dies."

"Oh wow, that is so sad. I am drained and want to go back to the room."

I was exhausted too, so I agreed. I felt I would have to deal with Kim somehow but hoped she was too tired to care. We had a long day.

When we went to our room, two members of security were waiting for us. "We need for you to go into your cabin and stay."

"What is the problem?"

"Someone murdered your security detail. We found the wife alive, and she described the suspects right before she died. We are looking for the couple now. Your life is in danger. I am very sorry."

Until now, I wasn't worried, but now they had stepped up to murder. Kim must have felt the same way. "Jack Cash, I am scared."

"Ma'am, we are going to post someone outside your room constantly. Your security is our priority. The Captain is about to order everyone to their rooms."

As soon as he said it, two other security officers walked into our room, one of them whispered something to the first officer. After hearing the news, he noted, "Well, the Captain will order everyone to their rooms now, for sure."

He looked at me and said, "we have found the couple we were protecting you from, Cynthia and Brian. Someone murdered our prime suspects."

"Are you saying that Cynthia and Brian are dead?"

"Yes, they just found them, and the one's protecting you too."

"I am not relieved at all, even though we have been running from Cynthia for days...now I am scared because clearly others are trying to get to us."

Kim spoke up, "I AM relieved, because at least we won't have to look over our shoulders for them anymore!"

"That's true, but at least we knew who they were, we don't know who killed them, because they are likely also chasing us," looking at each security officer I asked, "Who is going to stay outside our room tonight?"

They looked at one another, and then one of them said, "That's the problem. You are the one who everyone is after, so we will post two outside and someone inside your room. That's three of our security detail. We already are down two and have two active investigations for four murders, so we are significantly challenged. We have trained every crew member for these situations, so they will not be your typical security officers. They might be wait staff in the restaurant, DJs for the night experiences, or someone who cleans your room. We have highly trained everyone, so you can rest assured no matter who it is, they are highly trained to do the work you need."

"So, who are the ones taking care of us tonight, and you are posting someone in the room???? There is barely enough room for us to turn around. Where will they sleep?"

"They will not sleep but will maintain vigilance, along with the two outside. Every two hours, there will be a shift in personnel. The first one inside the room is going to be, hey Chip, who is inside first?"

"Oh, it would be Heather, voluptuous Heather."

Kim protested, "WHATTT???? You are sending voluptuous Heather! What does that even mean? And why a female?"

Chip spoke up, "I am truly sorry. I didn't mean to use her name from the show. She is part of a trio comedy act, and her stage name is "Voluptuous Heather!" It's part of her act. We call her that all the time. I think her real name is Ginger, or Mary Ann, something like that."

"I DON'T CARE!!! I DON'T WANT VOLUPTUOUS HEATHER IN OUR ROOM," Kim adamantly protested.

"Ma'am, the Captain has ordered her to the room. She is probably the best person for in-room security. She is Israeli, and at one time was in Mossad, there is no one more skilled than Heather in security. She took down one of our security officers in a training exercise. He was also in the military. She will protect you like no other; besides, she is gorgeous."

"Can we opt out of the security?"

I looked at Kim, "Why do you want to opt-out? They are sending her to protect us, and it sounds like she is competent, and there have already been multiple murders around us. I think we should let them do their job."

She huffed and turned her face away from me.

"Sir, she will be here when she changes out of her stage costume." As he was talking, a woman started down our corridor. She fit the name, "Voluptuous," and she had not changed out of her costume, so when

Kim saw her, she immediately when to the bathroom, slamming the door.

Chip said, "Heather, this is Jack Cash, he and his…"

"Friend, she is my friend Kim."

"Girlfriend," Kim shouted from the bathroom, "I.AM.HIS.GIRL-FRIEND AND…WE KISSED!!!! AND…AND HE GOT ME A NECKLACE."

"Ok, Jack Cash and his girlfriend, Kim, are the people you will be protecting. You are staying in their room. Two other crew members are on their way. They will stay outside."

Heather spoke up, "You didn't tell me I was staying in the room with the most handsome man on the cruise ship," immediately, Kim flew out of the bathroom with toilet paper stuck to her waist, unrolling it into the room from her clothes as we walked. She was apoplectic! I think at that moment, if anyone had said anything else, Kim would have exploded right there. I don't mean with anger. I mean, a literal explosion with spontaneous combustion and C4 blowing body parts to the USA and Cayman Islands. I had not seen this side of her at all.

"Look, Jack Cash and I are a thing, and don't you think you can come in here and get all sensual, throw off all kinds of sexual stuff. He's not that kind of pastor, oh, and he is a pastor. He is a man of God and I am a pastor's wife so, don't think you can come in here and make him compromise. I already tried, and he won't."

Heather looked at her with a deer in the headlight look and said, "Umm, I am here to make sure you are safe, and I am not your judge. And I am not trying to steal him. So you are a pastor's wife, he is a pastor, and you are not married, and you are staying in a room with one bed?"

I looked at Kim, "Please stop talking! Look, Heather, thank you for staying in our room. We really appreciate it. My wife died a few weeks ago, and Kim's husband died recently as well. We are on this cruise because, well, it's a long story, I need to stop talking and just say thank you for staying with us."

The other security officers raised their eyebrows, shook their heads as if in disbelief, and left.

"Is there a way you can change?"

"Kim, let it go."

"No, they sent me here right after my routine ended. The captain said it was urgent, so here I am. I am sorry, but this is what I am wearing tonight."

Kim looked at me and said, "well, I hope you are happy. This night is NOT ending like I hoped it would."

With her statement, I was thankful Heather showed up. There was no telling what Kim had in mind for the night.

Kim sat on the bed in a huff, and Heather walked over to the chair in the room, moved some clothes, and sat down. Immediately, Heather texted someone and spoke up. "I just texted my boss. He said someone would be here in a few hours to take my place. You two can go about your routine. Act like I am not even here."

I started laughing so hard. I almost didn't make it to the bathroom. When I closed the door, I heard Kim beginning to argue with Heather. It was like hushed shouting, and when I finished, I walked out of the bathroom and said, "Kim, knock it off, leave Heather alone. What were you saying anyway?"

"Mr. Cash, I can assure you my purpose for being in your room is only to ensure your safety. It is not for any other purpose, and I have been ordered here by the Captain. He is the one in charge of everyone, and I cannot violate his order, regardless of anyone's problem with me."

"Thank you for coming to ensure our safety. How long have you been working for the cruise line?"

Heather and I started a long conversation while Kim pouted. Heather told me of her days in Israel and her work and how she finally got weary of everything. As a cross-agency liaison, she did detail in the US, took a cruise, and fell in love with cruising. Heather also had a knack for comedy and used her wit and her body to make people laugh. She told me that she finds the most jealous-looking wife in the audience and spends the time using her husband or boyfriend as a prop for her comedy. Then, two others join her for a comedy trio. She has been doing this for a year and loves every minute of it. She said, "it's not as exciting as working for the government, but every once and a while, I get to use my skills like tonight."

Kim didn't say much and eventually changed into very modest pj's and got in bed. Heather and I continued to talk, and Kim asked when

Heather was leaving. She told her she was about to be relieved, at least that was what she thought.

Heather said, "you can go to sleep, Mr. Cash, I will stay up until I am relieved."

"Heather, you can call me Jack or Jack Cash. That's what everyone else does, but I am not very sleepy."

"So, you are a pastor, like a protestant pastor?"

"Yes, Kim was married to a protestant pastor. Both of our spouses died recently."

"I am sorry for your loss. I like talking to you. I feel safe with you."

"Safe?? You are the professional. I feel safe with you."

"No, you don't understand. I have always had to have my guard up because of my job and because of my body. I don't think I have ever talked to a man as long as we talked without reference to my body. Or wondering what kind of motive the man had, or the worrying about him making a move on me."

We talked for hours while Kim slept. By the time I realized it, it was 3 a.m., and Heather's relief had not arrived. I looked through the peephole, and the two guards were still there.

"I told my boss I was good to stay the night so they won't send anyone until morning. I am enjoying talking to you. It's like I am talking to my best friend."

"I am enjoying it too!"

Kim started stirring and sat up in bed, "You are still here?"

"Yes, still here!"

Kim got out of bed and began looking for something in her luggage.

"Is there anything I can help you find?"

"No," she said as she quickly hid whatever she was looking for and went to the bathroom.

When the door closed, Heather whispered, "I am not sure she can use that here."

"Use what?"

"A cell phone, unless she is using the WIFI calling, there is no cell reception.

"What do you mean?"

"She took a cell phone to the bathroom."

"Hmmmm." I wondered who she was calling, or texting, or whatever. Of course, she could be playing some mindless game on her cell phone too.

Heather was very observant and spoke up, "Why are people after you?'

"One of my wives worked for a leader in a cartel, she turned against him, and he went to prison."

"The wife that just died?"

"No, four wives ago."

"How many wives have you had?"

"With the last one, seven."

"Seven wives? Are you divorced?"

"No, they all died."

"You have had seven wives and all died?"

"Yes," and then I proceeded to tell her briefly about each wife.

"If the wife died that was responsible for getting the cartel leader arrested, why are they after you?"

"It's a long story."

Kim had been in the bathroom for over 15 minutes, and I wondered if she was ok, so I called out, "Kim, are you ok?"

"Yes, I am fine. Leave me alone."

"She has a problem with me. But I will tell you, Jack Cash, there is something about her that I am not sure about," Heather whispered.

"What do you mean?"

"Well, it is not unusual for a woman to be jealous, but there is something that is not sitting well with me, it's not that, at least 's not all."

I thought about that for a minute but didn't know what to do with it, especially at 3 a.m.

"Keep an eye on her!"

"I will!"

"I know I have already said it, but I enjoy talking to you. Can I stay longer?

"Sure, I would like that."

The door to the bathroom swung open with force, "When are you going to leave?" Kim demanded.

"She is not going to leave. She is staying the rest of the night."

"She can't, she is not supposed to...she needs to leave!"

"Kim, what's wrong, you are not...?"

"Don't say it, I wanted last night to be us. No one else, especially not this," Kim made hand gestures like her silhouette, "this this vixen, no, what did they call her?"

"Heather?"

"No, voluptuous, That's what they called her and now you have stayed up all night talking to each other. I am not losing you again."

"When did you lose me? We have just been talking, that is all."

She shook her head "no" as she started crying. I reached out to hold her, but she pulled away and laid on the bed. Heather looked at me, raised her eyebrows, and shrugged, then mouthed, "I am going to get someone else to stay here."

I reluctantly shook my head "yes."

She texted someone, and about 15 minutes later, a soft knock on the door. Heather opened it to Joseph. He was a part of Heather's comedy act and was initially assigned to take over for Heather. He walked in, introduced himself, and then sat on the chair. I said goodbye to Heather and laid down next to Kim. She knew Joseph came in to cover for Heather and then turned over and went to sleep. I laid next to her and went to sleep.

I woke up at 8:31. It had been seven days since I met Kim, but when I woke up, she was gone, and no one was in the room. When I got up, I looked, and two people were standing at the door. I opened the door groggily and asked where Kim had gone. They told me she had gone to get fresh air about 30 minutes before. They told me the Captain lifted the cabin order, and we were about to dock at "Seven Point Cay," the private island owned by the cruise line. They wanted to know if I wanted to go ashore so they could prep a security detail. I told them I wasn't sure, and that I would decide after my shower.

I started the water running and heard the door open. "I've got coffee," Kim said in sing-song fashion, "hurry before it gets cold."

"I will hurry!" I jumped in the shower and took a 3-minute shower, and toweled off.

"Can I come in and help you dry off?"

"Absolutely not! I can take care of it myself. I will be out in a minute."

I quickly dressed and walked out to a hot cup of coffee and Kim, with a flowery swimsuit and a white cotton wrap, and her large hat.

"You look nice and ready for a beach."

"Yes, it is the last full day on the cruise, and I want to enjoy it on the beach. You are not ready for the water, though."

"I wasn't sure I was going to get off the ship."

"I am, and I want you to come with me."

"Let's get breakfast first. I am starving, and I will decide what I want to do. You know, we have to have security with us, right?"

"I know, and that's ok as long as it is not Ms. Hot and Bothering."

I laughed as I opened the door. "Let's go eat."

We found a place for a quick bite, most everyone going to the island had already left the ship. I told our security detail that we were going to the island, so they arranged to have a "couple" follow us. Kim waited at the restaurant while I went back to change into swim attire, our security detail following. While I was in the room changing, our security detail changed. When I stepped into the corridor, our "beach" security detail, Chip and Heather, were ready to go with us. They were dressed in swim attire and prepared to enjoy the beach while watching us.

"Hello, so, you are our beach security?"

"Yes, where is Kim?"

"She is waiting at the restaurant."

"The Captain put us on the detail because we are the highest trained but I know Kim will not like it. There is nothing I can do. We will shadow you from a distance, though. No one but you will know we are there, and unless you tell Kim, she won't know we are shadowing you."

"Then, I won't tell her."

"Jack, I overheard her talking to someone on her cell phone while I was eating breakfast. She talked about me and said something that made me wonder how long she has pursued you."

"What do you mean?"

"Well, she said, 'I am not losing him again, I lost him to the librarian, the drug addict, the police chick, and then I couldn't make out what she said.'

"She said librarian, drug addict?"

"That's what it sounded like."

I stood there dumbfounded. How could Kim lose me to those wives when the last time I saw her was in high school?

"Oh, and she did say something about marrying you before someone else got your attention, like a hat blowing across the beach. I think she was referring to me. She was pretty agitated when I came to the room last night."

"Yes, she was," my voice trailing off and my mind was going full speed ahead. Tamera's hat flew across the beach when we first met, but how did Kim know? "Could you tell who she was talking to?"

"No, but she said, 'I love you too, I will see you later."

Suddenly, I didn't want to go to the beach. I wanted to know what Kim was talking about on the phone call but didn't know how to bring it up.

"Heather, can I ask a favor?"

"Sure, what can I do?"

"I want to talk to you on the beach. When Kim goes to the water, can Chip go too, and then, would you come to me and start talking?"

Chip said, "I don't understand. What's going on?"

"I don't know, but I am afraid I am in danger from several different people. I need to find out what Kim is up to."

"When she goes to the water, I will talk to her, find out how long she has known you, that kind of thing and see if she tells me anything."

"When Chip starts talking to her, I will come over to you and talk."

"Perfect, thank you both for helping me."

"See you on the beach!"

I left the room to find Kim. She didn't see me coming and was talking to someone on her cell phone. When she turned to me, she abruptly disconnected the call. "Hey, I wondered what happened to you."

"Who was on the phone? I didn't think we had cell service here."

"I was talking to my sister, telling her about the cruise."

"Awesome, are you ready?

"Yes, it's beach time!"

The sand on the beach was as fine of sand as you can find and white as snow, and the water was a crystal-clear turquoise that made you want to move to the island. There was a DJ playing music and a definite beach vibe going on. After we scored a couple of colas from the bartender and two chairs, we sat down and enjoyed the beautiful morning. I hadn't slept much but was afraid to sleep on the beach, knowing the sunscreen would not completely shield me from the sun. Kim rubbed some sunscreen on her arms and neck and then asked me to apply it to her back. I did, and she returned the favor, and we sat back.

"Jack, I am sorry I acted like a crazy woman last night. I was tired. Heather was a very nice woman. She is over there with the other security guy. They are a cute couple."

I looked over, and Heather and Chip held hands laid back in their beach chairs next to one another. I couldn't tell if they were acting like a couple or were together. It didn't matter. I just needed help from them.

Kim and I talked for a while, and I kept looking for a chance to bring up what she said during the night about losing me to other women, but I couldn't find a way.

"I'm going to go for a swim. Want to join me?"

"Maybe in a minute."

"Ok, come and join me when you are ready."

She went out into the water, and Chip went to the water too. They were wading around, looking down, and talking. Every so often, one would go into the water and pull out a shell. She enjoyed her shell gathering, and I could tell she and Chip were talking a lot.

Walking over to me, Heather asked, "well, is your plan working?"

"I am not sure. We will know soon. Was there anything else you could tell about Kim's conversation on the phone?"

"Not really. I told you everything I heard."

"I caught her using her cell phone after I finished with you and Chip. She told me she was talking to her sister."

"Is her sister on the cruise?"

"No, at least, not that I know of, why?"

"I don't know. There was someone I mistook for Kim this morning. If it was not her sister, she could pass for her sister."

"I met her sister and her husband for breakfast a few days ago. They told me they had come to check on Kim. They do resemble, but her sister has brown hair and is a little taller than Kim."

"Hmmm, I'm not sure."

While we talked, it was clear Chip and Kim were talking about us, mainly Kim. Kim was animated and frustrated. She was agitated, and Chip was carrying on, laughing and talking.

"Heather, could you point out the person you saw earlier?"

"I only saw her once, and I don't see her on the beach."

Kim had enough of our talking and started towards us. Chip shrugged his shoulders to us as she was very animated coming our way.

"What are you and Heather talking about?"

"Heather was telling me about her and Chip." I looked at Chip and said, "I don't think I can marry you and Heather on the island. I don't have credentials to do it here."

"That's too bad," Chip said, playing along, "I guess we will have to elope if we can't get Jack Cash to marry us."

The look on Kim's face changed immediately. Just like , Heather was no longer a threat. Heather spoke up, "I need to go to the restroom. I will be back," kissed Chip and started walking away.

"Do you mind if I come too?" Kim asked.

"Not at all."

After they left, Chip sat in the chair next to me. "Jack, Kim said something to me when you were talking to Heather. She commented losing you on the beach again to a librarian. I asked her how long Kim had known you, and she was so agitated she just started talking. She was on the beach with you when you met the librarian. Kim said you didn't know it was her because you were paying attention to the 'cute book lady' (her words), and by the time she was ready to start a conversation with you, you were asking the 'cute book lady' out on a date. When we were picking up shells, she mentioned losing you to the seashell drug addict. I laughed when she said it, but she said, 'yea, I had followed him in my car to one of those seashell t-shirt places and pulled up and was about to go in when all of a sudden, the seashell gypsy lady had thrown her arms around Jack and was so happy. Kim pulled away from the store very upset. Anyway, she has been around you a while and often."

"You got all that while you were in the water with her?"

"Yeah, she was pretty upset seeing you talking to Heather, she is very jealous and it sounds like she has been after you for a long time."

Now the words of her brother-in-law were going over and over in my mind. He said that he finally got a chance to meet Jack Cash after hearing my name all these years. "Maybe Heather can get more out of her, she is excellent at getting information from people without knowing they are interrogated."

They were gone for a long time and eventually made their way to us with food. We were all getting hungry, so this was perfect timing. As we sat down to eat, Heather spoke up, "Jack, Kim tells me you have been married seven times."

"Seven???" Chip shouted, "Seven marriages?"

"Yes, seven, and seven funerals." He went somber.

"That's the reason I went to Florida, someone murdered my last wife a few weeks ago."

"So, that's why the Captain is so adamant about your protection."

"Yes, that and probably a few other murders."

While Chip and I talked about my wives, and my ministry, Kim and Heather went to find an umbrella as shade. They were gone about fifteen minutes and had two giant umbrellas to shade us.

After Chip and I set them up, Kim laid back and said, "I am going to take a nap."

I wanted to do the same thing, but I also wanted to find out what Heather knew. I went down to the water and acted like I was looking for shells, Chip came down, and eventually Heather came too. We were far enough away, and with the waves hitting the shore, the noise drowned out our conversation.

"Jack, you are in danger. Kim has made her life work stalking you."

"Danger like 'you are going to die' danger?"

"I'm not sure about that, but I can tell you she knew about every first meeting you had with your previous wives, I mean, like she was there. She has a fascination with you and tried to work out "meeting Jack Cash in different places." Each time you met your previous wives, she was there, ready to meet you again and chase you until she married you, but each time, they stepped in the way. that's why she went so crazy last night. She felt like her one time was slipping away."

"I don't know what to say," slosh, slosh, slosh were the sounds of Kim wading out quickly to us.

"What are you doing?"

"Shell hunting, and looking for unusual sea life and talking about life."

"Can I play too?"

"Sure, but the one with the best shell wins."

"What's the prize?" Kim asked, "can I determine what the prize is if I win?"

"Sure," Heather answered.

"Wait a minute. I need to have a say in this because Kim will want to marry me or sleep with me as the prize, and I don't want her to win that kind of prize."

"Well, then," Kim said, "you better get to finding the best shell there is, shouldn't you."

Right then, I wanted to leave, to back to the ship. I wanted to go back to my life. Someone had hijacked it a long time ago as I was learning, and now I was living on this crazy train with Ms. Chasing Jack Cash Crazy Lady.

After a few minutes, I found the most incredible shell and pulled it out of the water. "I win."

"No, we are going to two o'clock," Kim said, "That was the challenge!"

"That's an hour from now."

Heather pulled one up better than mine, "Looky what I found, better than Jack Cash. I win!"

"Two o'clock people, two o'clock."

Chip dived in the water and kicked with a splash, came up and down again. He pulled an enormous shell out of the water so far, "I found the best shell ever."

"Chip wins," Heather called out.

"Two o'clock people, two, not one and some change,"

Kim's focus on getting the best shell was so intense. She dove in, kicked up water, surfaced, and repeated the action. She did it again, swam a little, dove again, emerged with a giant shell, "I win, game over! Game over, I win."

Time went so fast.

"Wait a minute, we have to take it to the judges and besides, it's not two yet. We still have ten minutes," I said, worried about what her plans were.

"Who are the judges?"

"I don't know," Kim said.

Heather said, "Hey, there is a woman in the distance that looks like Kim."

Sure enough, there was a woman in the distance that looked like Kim's sister.

"She looks like your sister, Kim."

Kim didn't look. "I don't think she looks like my sister. There's no way you can see her from here."

"No problem, let's at least see if she will judge our contest."

Now, Kim didn't want to play. She went from 'I will win and get my way to 'I don't want to play anymore.' "No, I think Chip won. His shell looks better than mine. You win, Chip. What do you want to win?"

"Wait a minute. It is not for you to decide and wait for it. It's not two o'clock yet."

"What about mine?" I dove in and brought up a Conch shell. It was beaten up and had holes in it, but I pulled it up, holding the worse side towards me.

Kim started moving towards the shore. "Where are you going?" I called out.

"I'm going to the bathroom," she shouted. Before she rounded the corner out of our line of sight, she looked back one more time.

"I'm going to listen," Heather said as she started towards the restroom, "I think I saw Kim's head motion to woman to go there."

I asked Chip, "I am going to sit down. Want to join me?"

"Yea, want something to drink first? I am going to get something to drink."

"Yes, how about some kind of soda, whatever they have."

"I will be back," Chip said as he headed to get our drinks.

CHAPTER TWENTY-NINE

few minutes later, Heather rounded the corner and joined Chip at the bar. She was very animated and upset. They talked for a few minutes and then said something to the bartender. He handed them a phone. Heather called someone, constantly moving as she was waiting for someone to answer. No one did.

When she saw Kim, she hung the phone up and started towards me. I didn't see the other woman leave the restroom or the area. When they got near me, Heather said, "We've had something come up at the ship. We have to go back and see the Captain. We've enjoyed our time together."

"Who will keep an eye on us?"

"We can't. We can't now. You need to go back to your room. Stay there. Just go and stay there."

About then, Kim came close enough to hear them, "What's going on?"

"I don't know, they have to go back to the ship, somethings going on, and they want us to back to the room."

Kim started rubbing her hands together like she had won the shell game, "Good, now I can claim my prize."

I shook my head and started gathering our things. I felt so vulnerable. I started walking back quickly, and Kim tried to keep up and finally said, "Are we racing too?"

"I am sorry! I just got a little focused about getting back to the room."

"Who's the one anxious to go to the room, whatcha' have in mind?"

I knew better than to answer the question because Ms. Hot Trot would make life unbearable.

"Hey, big guy, whatcha' have in mind, want to have some fun?"

I ignored Kim. "If you won't answer me, I have ways to make you talk."

"I have a headache."

"I have just the cure."

I couldn't win.

When we arrived back at the room, neither key worked. We found a room attendant and told them our problem. She left us with our key cards to determine why our key did not work. We waited for a long time and finally decided to get something to drink. At least it kept me from worrying about what Kim had in mind.

We sat down to order a drink, but there was a lot of activity down a corridor leading to rooms. People were talking, pointing, and someone walked towards us, so I got up and walked to them,

"What's going on?"

"I think someone died or was murdered, in the hallway, outside a room, tall guy." About then, several crew members ran by us towards the body. Then, a minute later, Heather ran by us. She was crying as she was running, running in the same direction. A few seconds later, I could hear someone wailing, a guttural cry I had experienced at the news of a loved one's death. I knew the sound and thought I knew the person. It sounded like Heather.

I looked around at Kim, and she was looking outside as if nothing had happened. She had no expression at all as if it was just another day in paradise. I walked to get a better idea of the dead person, but too many people were in the hallway. I knew we were about to experience an order to shelter in our cabin again, which would not help me at all because we couldn't even get in ours.

I turned to Kim and shrugged my shoulders, and she still had no expression. She didn't act as if she cared about what was going on. Chip ran by us and started shouting for people to get out of the way. I thought it was Chip in the hallway, but it was not. "Kim, someone was murdered."

She took a drink and sounding like a psychopath, "Well, I guess it is going to take longer to get back to the room."

"Did you hear me, someone was…" someone walked by and said, "Who is the Captain when someone murders the Captain?"

I looked at Kim, and she said, "Whaattt?" in a sarcastic tone, shrugging her shoulders like she didn't care about anything.

"It was the captain, someone murdered the captain."

"Do you want to go grab something to eat since we can't go to the room?"

I saw a side of Kim that seemed to have changed overnight. It started with Heather and had gone from bad to worse.

"Sure, but first, let me see if anyone needs prayer."

"Whatever, I'm going to walk around and see if there is a restaurant we should try."

I was so disappointed. If there is ever a time when a pastor's wife and a pastor should step up, it is in these kinds of moments. I determined to go anyway. I got as far as I could and called out to everyone. "If anyone wants to talk or needs prayer, I am a pastor. I will be in the commons area for a while."

Heather called out, "Thank you, Jack Cash. Folks, we need you to go, and if you need someone to talk to, please take him up on his offer. Jack, I will come to see you soon, do not leave the commons area until I come."

I wondered if Heather needed prayer or if she wanted to share about the conversation she overheard between Kim and the mystery woman, so I waited. But, Kim left.

About fifteen minutes later, people started dispersing, and they wheeled a gurney past me. After they loaded the Captain's body on the gurney, Heather came to my area. "We need to talk, but not here." She took me by the hand and led me down a corridor, then swiped her key card and opened the door to an entirely different area. Music was playing, and people were in rooms with doors open, playing cards or board games. This area was where the employees let their hair down like a family. All were unaware of the captain's murder.

Heather swiped open a door for the surveillance area for the ship, a room filled with monitors watching every portion of the common spaces on the ship. The room was abuzz with activity, as they knew of the Captain's murder and were scouring the surveillance footage to determine who killed him.

"There have been a lot of developments since we were on the beach. When I listened in on the conversation between Kim and the mystery woman, Kim blew up and screamed, "Why are you messing up my plans? I have the man I have always wanted, and I know it is just a matter of time before he asks me to marry him.""

Evidently the woman mentioned something about your wealth, because Kim said, "I don't care if he is worth two hundred millions dollars, I have always wanted him.

Heather continued, "The screaming at one another continued until it almost came to blows. Finally, Kim asked the woman, 'Exactly what did you do to the captain?' and the woman said someone, and I couldn't make out the name 'cornered him and slit his throat.' That's when I came running to the bar and made a call to the ship. No one answered, and I knew something was terribly wrong. I am not sure how much Kim has been involved in the decisions the last couple of days because we have had more murders on this ship in three days than we have had in ten years, maybe twenty, total. There was one thing I heard you need to know. Kim insisted she had it all taken care of and her lifelong dream of spending the rest of her life with you would be in jeopardy if a connection was made with the murders of six of your wives and Kim."

"Six of my wives?" I asked incredulously, "how can it be six? My first wife died of cancer, my second wife, at the hands of a crazed father."

"All I heard was six, Jack, it sounds like Kim and the person she was talking to in the restroom were in a long-term plan to get you married to Kim, and no one, including a wife, or even a woman on a cruise, like me, would stand in her way. I am not sure I would be alive if Chip and I had not acted like we were a couple."

"You are not a couple?"

"No, it was to throw her off and find information she would have kept from me if she thought I was after her man."

"Heather, we have the footage from the corridor," the security technician said, "but I can't make out the face."

"He is skilled," she noted, as the camera panned to the next camera. "He knew exactly where the cameras were and planned his attack around them. Go both directions to the end of the corridor and see if someone who looks like him leaves the area." The technician moved to different camera's but the person never exited the area, at least not right away. "I can't locate him."

"Were there any key cards used in the area right after the murder?" Heather asked.

"The Captain's card was missing, and it swiped into a room two doors down from the murder. It was a large suite, and we have people on our way down there now."

A radio squawked, with someone saying, "We have made entry, the sliding door to the outside is open, and the room is empty. They must have left via the balcony. Whoever did it had a plan and some skill. It looks like there was a rope or something tied to the bed frame."

"Someone planned this and came prepared. We need to find the mystery woman, the man who killed the Captain and find Kim. Where did you last see her?" Heather asked.

"She was waiting in the common area with me, on the deck near the murder scene. She acted strange when I told her someone killed the Captain. She wanted to find something to eat and left for food."

Heather looked at the technician, "Look at the common area for Jack Cash, about fifteen or twenty minutes ago and see if you can see where Kim went."

He started scouring the footage and finally found her leaving the commons area. "I found her, she leaves here," panning to the next camera, "And goes here, the third deck, goes here, and meets up with a woman."

"That looks like her sister!" I shouted.

"They exchange words, and then, they go to the next deck, now they are meeting up with a man."

Heather noted, "It looks just like the one who murdered the Captain."

The technician continued, "They talk and leave to go to a room. They run in and out of this room, and then they go to the embarkation deck. It looks like they left the ship."

Heather radioed for security to go to the island, "There are three people, one male, two females on the island, wanted for questioning in multiple murders on board. They should be considered armed and dangerous." She radioed their description and clothing and turned to the technician, "We've got to find them before they make it to the marina."

"Why the marina?" I asked.

"Well, for one, there are a lot of places to hide. They could steal a boat used for excursions, flee until we have sailed away, and then return to the island to pay for passage with a boat that comes to the marina for fuel or mechanical problems. The opportunity the marina offers to them is too good to pass up."

The radio squawked again, "Any idea where they could have gone?"

"They headed east, or left off of the boat, towards the marina."

"10-4."

"Arrange transport for three. We are going to the marina once we are off the ship."

"10-4, arranging now."

Heather looked at me and said, "I hate to get you involved in the island search, but if they split up, you know them, right?"

"I think the man is Kim's brother-in-law, he told me he was into derivatives, whatever that means, but yes, I know him."

"Good, then you are going with me, and we are taking Chip and one other for your security, let's go." She grabbed my arm and started pulling me, first trotting and then on long hallways, running as fast as she could. I did my best to catch up when she had to swipe to get to a different corridor. Finally, we made it on deck and started running for land. There was what looked like a dune buggy ready to take us to the marina, and within seconds Chip and another security officer were joining us.

"Go, go, go to the marina."

We were going so fast up a hill, and it almost tossed me out. I buckled in and held on as tight as I could.

The radio squawked again, "We have eyes on them. They are boarding a yacht called Santa Maria."

"That's Juan Carlos' boat, we left it yesterday."

"Who is Juan Carlos?"

"He is the leader of a drug cartel! If he is here, there is bigger trouble. He is heavily armed."

Heather radioed, "Stand down and take cover. We will proceed with a plan when we arrive."

The radio squawked again, and this time with the sound of automatic rifles blasting, "We are under fire, we are taking cover."

Heather looked at Chip and said, "We have to ditch the pastor, he is too valuable to take into live fire, and we don't have the firepower to overtake them."

Suddenly, live rounds were whizzing past our heads, and the driver of the dune buggy turned as quickly as he could. They shot him in a barrage of bullets. He died immediately. Heather pushed him out of the dune buggy and floored it away from the live rounds. The other security officer with us took a bullet to his shoulder, which pretty much incapacitated him. A bullet grazed Chip's arm. He ripped his shirt into a strip and tied his arm where he was bleeding. He took the remainder of the shirt, made a ball, and told me to hold it on the officer's wound. I did as he yelled in pain.

"We are going back to the ship," Heather radioed security at the marina, "fall back to the ship."

She called again, asking for some type of response but got nothing. She said their radio must have suffered damage or they were dead.

"What about the murders, aren't we going after the people who murdered the captain."

"Well, if we are dead, there is no way to apprehend them, and our first priority is the security of the ship. They are briefing the second mate for protocols, but we have to leave the island. If the people with guns enter the ship, we have an even bigger problem."

I couldn't imagine men with automatic weapons on board, and neither could Heather. She radioed the ship, "Send out the distress call immediately. Anyone in the area that can help us is needed immediately. Tell them pirates have overwhelmed the ship's security on land. They are armed and have killed several security officers."

"10-4, first-mate initiated distress protocol, you have three minutes to get back to ship."

"We've got company, more dune buggies!" Heather was driving as fast and furious as possible. I looked back, and there looked like an additional dune buggy's heading towards us in the distance.

"Mayday! Mayday! The alpha team is down. Hostiles are actively pursuing us, brace for hostile action."

The ship sounded a long blast and then several shorter blasts. They were preparing to pull away from shore. Then the ship sounded seven short horn blasts.

I looked back, and the dune buggies were closing in, but we were almost there. Heather drove the buggy as far up the ramp as would not impede the launch, and we ran. The ship was beginning to move, and the gangway was lifting. We jumped on it and ran towards the ship. The other dune buggies were very close and started shooting at us. Bullets whizzed past us, most striking the ship. The First Mate ordered everyone shelter in place and no one on balconies. Of course, some people wanted to know why and were on their balconies until they saw the men shooting at us. Then they retreated to their cabins. Ship security started shooting at the men onshore. At least that provided enough cover for us to make it inside. The ship continued pulling away from shore quickly.

Heather took me to the command center of the ship. They had just sworn in the Chief Mate as Captain. He shared that the US Coast Guard had a vessel within hours of us and headed our direction. They also requested naval air support since we were in active engagement with hostiles. Within ten minutes, two F/A 18 Hornets flashed past the ship. They made a sweep east to west and then turned for a north to south route. On the second sweep, they radioed the Coast Guard for the info concerning the pirate boat. Once we told them the name, they laid down 20mm cannon fire in the water to turn the vessel away. They turned back to the island.

Heather spoke up, "Captain, this is Jack Cash, the object of many people's affection."

"I am not sure I would say nice to meet you under the circumstances, but we will do everything we can to bring you and the 4,238 passengers to safety. That is our priority. I have instructed my crew to begin debriefing you immediately. Heather, I would like for you to accompany Mr. Cash to the conference room. Others will join soon. I will stay on deck until the danger has passed, which is likely when the Coast Guard arrives, and then join you for the debrief."

"Come this way," Heather said. She was quiet the rest of the way, and I didn't know what to say either. She lost several friends, and I had the person I thought was just a friend betray me, and from the way it sounded had been instrumental in the murders of some of my wives, and now, the fact she was somehow with Juan Carlos hit me the hardest.

When we arrived, there were already people in place, some with laptops, one with a camera connected to a computer, and the rest just quiet and somber. I felt this would be more of an interrogation than a debrief.

Heather motioned for me to sit in the seat opposite the camera, and someone placed a bottle of water next to me. "Thank you!" but no one said a word.

After a few minutes of complete silence except for a few whispers between a few, ensuring everything was like it should be, I decided to say something. "Everyone, I know you suffered a great loss when we left port in Florida. There have been murders, and some of your friends have been among those killed. I am truly sorry for your loss, and I can assure you if I had known the danger that I put anyone in, I would have never set foot on this ship. No one was supposed to know I was on the cruise. Someone booked the cruise for us at the very last minute to keep Kim and me under the radar. What I didn't know..."

"Mr. Cash, please stop talking. We will debrief you in a moment. Until then, please do not say anything," Heather said matter-of-factly.

"I was saying all to say, 'I am truly sorry for your loss.'"

The radio squawked that another Coast Guard cutter was near and the new First Mate would take over the helm while the Captain was in the debriefing.

Within minutes, the Captain assumed his chair and called for the debriefing to begin, "In conducting this debriefing, the entirety of which will be video recorded, and will be turned over to the law enforcement when we arrive back the United States. They will likely take you, Mr. Cash, in for questioning."

From there, everything felt like a tribunal, "Sir, state your full name, address and social security number, the full name of the person you traveled with, her address, if you know it, and social security number."

I gave them my information but noted, "I only know Kim's first and last name, Kim Crane. We knew each other from school, and I met her again on Vero Beach a few days ago."

"How long have you known her?"

"In High School and most recently about a week and a few days."

"What do you do for a living?"

"I am a pastor."

"Are you telling us a pastor met a woman on a beach a few days ago, and you booked a cruise at the last minute with her?"

"Yes."

"So, while you are away from your congregation, you decide to bring a murderer onboard a cruise ship so you can have a good time."

"We didn't take a cruise for fun. We did it to go to Grand Cayman."

"You slept in the same bed, right?"

"Yes, we slept... S.L.E.P.T. That was all. I refused to have sex with her."

"You expect us to believe you slept in a bed as wide as a large recliner and did not have sex?"

"Look, the reason we went to Grand Cayman was to bypass a rogue US Marshal and her friend, Cynthia, and Brian. They tracked our every move, and we couldn't risk buying an airline ticket and getting flagged. So, we opted for a cruise."

"Wasn't there two people named "Cynthia and Brian" who were among those murdered?" the Captain asked Heather.

"Yes, sir, someone murdered them, and she was a US marshal, and he used to be.

"Why Grand Cayman?"

"Because there was a POD trust there. I had to get there to change it over to my name and establish a trust myself. The trust had a substantial amount of money in it, and I had to claim it as quickly as I could."

"What interest did Kim have in the trust."

"None, she came because she was a friend. I now know she had other motives.

"How much money was in the trust?"

"Is that pertinent?"

"Yes, it is."

"Will this information go beyond these walls?"

"Only to law enforcement."

"It was over 150. I don't remember the exact amount."

"Over $150,000? And you don't remember the exact amount."

"No, over $150,000,000, but I don't remember the exact amount." The atmosphere in the room became awkward. Some cleared their throats, most raised their eyebrows, but everyone moved in their chairs as if they had suddenly become uncomfortable.

"I would think someone coming into that kind of money would know to the penny how much they had."

"If I had not been lied to, shot at, surrounded by murderers, and worried I was about to be stolen from or killed, yes, maybe I would have had time to think about the money. Honestly, I haven't had a moment's rest to even think about anything but survival."

Heather, who had spent the most time with us, was probably the most surprised of anyone, "That explains a lot, Jack. Kim murdered your previous wives so she could get to all your money."

"Well, until a few days ago, I had no idea I was worth that kind of money. I don't think Kim knew either."

"Why did she murder your previous wives."

"I don't know. You will have to ask Kim. Even this news is so surprising that I can hardly process it."

"Where were you when during the previous Captain's murder?"

"When was he killed?"

"Earlier today after people left the boat."

Heather spoke up, "He was with Chip and me. We were his security shadows. Were you aware of the threat Jack Cash has had on his life or aware of the actions of the previous Captain? He determined Jack and Kim were in danger. What he didn't know was that Kim was a part of the threat. The murderer was sleeping with the target."

"No, I wasn't aware. Can I borrow a laptop to look at the Captain's logbook and security logs for a minute?"

While he looked, I spoke up, "I want to clarify, all we did was sleep. S.L.E.E.P."

Nervous laughs filtered through the room.

The Captain found entry after entry detailing the security threat I posed. At first, the danger was the same as they encountered when a famous person was on board. It changed with actual murders, then significant security measures were put into place. "Well, it looks like threats have surrounded Jack Cash, and the Captain verified his whereabouts during each murder. The Captain could not verify Kim's, though. So, it looks like Jack may have S.L.E.P.T with Kim. The Captain was watching Kim before his murder."

There was a knock on the door, "Sir, the bridge needs you immediately." Then an announcement, "Assemble at Muster Stations." Everyone but Heather darted out of the room. There was some type of emergency, but she stayed behind since I wasn't formally released yet.

"What's going on?"

"It could be anything. I will get further information soon."

Suddenly chatter on the radio was broadcast ship-wide because someone commandeered the intercom. Crew-related codes were broadcast, with only those familiar with specific ship coding understanding any of it. It sounded like radar detected something ahead that could pose a security threat to the ship, but nothing was on the horizon.

"Did I understand the radio transmission to say that there is something in the water the coast guard detected?"

"Yes, it sounds like some underwater vehicle, like a submarine or a slow-moving unmanned drone."

"Could it be a torpedo?"

"Hahaha, well, it is a very slow-moving one if it is. A torpedo's design is to hit with excessive force to detonate the warhead. This object is too slow."

"This is unreal."

"What, the unknown vehicle?"

"No, all this...nothing makes sense. I was saying my life is unreal."

Heather stood up and walked behind me. She put her hands on my shoulders and started squeezing. It was so startling I couldn't protest but instead enjoyed the short massage. "Now, maybe that will help with the craziness of the day."

The sun was getting low, and the conference room had the best view of the setting sun. I turned and stared at the beauty of the rays of the sun shooting through thunderheads in the distance. The hues of this sunset were epic. It was about as good of an ending to the day as I could have hoped for, but the one thing that hit me was the fact I was going to be alone. Alone!! Alone for dinner and alone for the evening. At least this was the last night on the ship.

"Do you have plans for the evening?"

"Not now, the girl I was s.l.e.e.p.i.n.g with has gone so I will be all alone."

"I am not sure if Captain will order everyone to cabins tonight or not. There is still some work to do on the investigations, and there are several investigations, but if we have time for a dinner break, I will call your room."

"By the way, my key card did not work for my room. I gave it to someone to check out. They left but never came back. Of course, I left the area outside the room a long time ago. There is no telling where the person or my key card ended up."

"I will find out!" Heather called the room steward to see if they could find the keycard.

I spoke up, "I think I gave it to 'Stanley!'"

Heather told the steward, but the steward said there was no one named Stanley on the ship's employee roster.

"I thought that was what the name tag said, but at least the key did not work."

"We need to go to the room now."

We started to the room, and Heather called for additional security to meet us on deck, down the corridor from the room. When we got on deck, two other security officers were waiting for us. We walked to the room, and the door was slightly open, allowing a crack of light through. The officers drew their service weapons, and Heather slowly opened the door. The man who took my key was standing at the safe, trying to remove it from the wall. Immediately the person started swinging a crowbar, and the security officers were able to subdue him immediately.

"Leave me alone," he screamed, "You can't detain me, you have no jurisdiction. I am from Malta, and I am a citizen of Malta. You can't hold me."

Heather ordered the security team to take the perpetrator to the brig. As they took him away, he screamed, "they will find you too and kill you, they will kill you Jack Cash, they will kill everyone. EVERYONE you care about!!!"

Heather walked over to the safe and looked at the intruder's work to pry it out of the wall. It had breached another layer of the wall, so there was no way the safe was secure. "Take your documents out of the safe. We need to find another place for your papers. Would you like to retrieve them?"

"No, there are no papers there. I have secured them in another place."

"You mean people have been trying to find these documents in your safe, and they are not there?"

"Yep, they are safe but not in the safe."

"Ok, but is there anything in the safe."

"Yes, a letter to whoever opened the safe."

"What did the letter say?"

"It said, "Answer the riddle, and you will find the papers that show you the way to the gold mine, but don't give up, for this you will see, the sea, the beach, the lady has the key.""

"What does that mean?"

"It means the papers they seek are not in the safe."

"That's cunning, but were you trying to send people on a wild goose chase?"

"Of course, it means absolutely nothing."

"Well, I know that the letter is in the safe, and anyone finding it will find nothing, but it doesn't make you any safer. I recommend you stay somewhere other than your room on your final night at sea. It is clear that there are people still trying to get to you and the documents."

"Where would that be?"

"I will find a bed for you. There is only one more night until we arrive back in port, but it is my responsibility to get you there safely."

Heather called to find an empty room. Because of the murders, every occupant near each room near the murders was relocated to vacant crew rooms. There were no other rooms available. "You can s.l.e.e.p in my room," she said, winking at me.

"I can't do that, why not let me sleep in a chair on a deck."

"Because security is best in a room, and that would not be possible, and because there is no other room, we will post security in my room. It is nice and a little bigger than the one you were in."

"Do I need to bring my luggage?"

"Yes, you will not need to go back to your room."

I started gathering my things. I lifted the bed, pulled a grocery bag out with the "documents," tucked them in a backpack I brought, and put it over my shoulder.

"You are a sly man, Jack Cash."

CHAPTER THIRTY

We made our way to Heather's room, and when we arrived, it was clear her room was larger than the one we had, with two twin beds across from one another.

"Two beds?"

"Yes, don't get excited. The other bed is for the second person of my comedy trio, "Bobbi Jean."

"What part does Bobbi Jean play?"

"Well, I play voluptuous Heather, not my real name. I am mean and hard to get along with, and Bobbi Jean, not her real name, is the sweetest, most affectionate woman you would ever meet. But she is ugly, and from the hills, they call her Hillbilly Bobbi Jean. The premise of the comedy act is that three of us are stranded on a deserted island."

"Three? Who is the third?"

"It is a man named...."As Heather pulled something out of her nightstand.

And then I blacked out. When I woke up, Heather was standing over me with a taser in her hand. She had tased and tied me up. "Where are the real documents? I looked in your backpack, and there were only brochures of excursions, where are the real documents?"

I realized that the taser had unwanted consequences. I had urinated all over myself. I looked down and was all wet. "Can I change clothes?"

"Tell me what I want to know, and I will change your clothes."

I was tired, and it had been a long day. I decided if I were to be tied up, I would sleep. So, I closed my eyes. A few minutes later, I was asleep, but not to Heather's liking.

"Wakey, wakey, wakey, you are not going to sleep until I find the documents," she said as she straddled my body, slapping me awake.

"You will not find the documents on the ship. They are not here."

At that point, in walked in "Bobbi Jean," Heather's roommate. "What's going on here? Do I need to leave? You should have told me you had a friend tied up in here. Let me know these things before I come."

"No, don't leave. I need you to help me."

"Is he drunk?"

"No, I tased him."

"Who is he?"

"He's the guy everyone keeps getting killed over!"

"Did he try something with you?"

"No, he's got 150,000,000 dollars and a dossier of criminals worth even more."

"He has that much money on the ship?"

"No, he has documents for the money. It's the dossier we want."

"Do you want to kill him?"

"Not until we have the dossier."

I had no idea where the dossier was. If I knew and turned it over, someone would kill me. The only way to stay alive is to keep quiet about something I had no clue about.

There was a knock on the door.

"Who is it?"

"It's the Captain. Where is Jack Cash?"

I started to yell, but by this time, I didn't know who I could trust.

"He's in here!"

"Can I come in?"

Heather opened the door, and the Captain walked in. He looked at me, tied up in the bed, and said, "At least change his clothes."

"I was about to when you knocked."

"Has he told you anything?"

"No, the only thing he told me was that the safe had a letter with a riddle in it, he said the documents were not inside."

"He was right, and we tore the room apart and couldn't find anything. There was nothing there. The Coast Guard wants to take him back to the US. Jack Cash has murder surrounding him everywhere. They want to question him, so we have to do everything we can to find the documents as soon as possible. We maybe have one hour. I can stall that long."

"But he knows what we are trying to do. He will tell the authorities."

"Well, then you will have to take care of that, won't you?" Then, he left the room.

Heather looked at Bobbi Jean and said, "Well, we have to get information from him as soon as possible. I know a way to get him to talk. Help me take his clothes off."

"What are you doing?"

"Don't worry, Jack Cash, we are changing your wet clothes for dry ones."

As they started, it was clear that Bobbi Jean was bothered by everything going on and turned her head when they took my shorts and underwear off. Heather barked, "get a washcloth and wet it, I am going to wash him quickly."

Bobbi Jean went to the bathroom and brought back a wet washcloth, still with her head turned.

"Help me wash him, oh, and get a towel to dry him with."

Bobbi Jean quickly retrieved a towel, and while Heather was washing me from the waist down, Bobbi Jean kept her head turned away.

"Dry him off!"

Bobbi Jean draped the towel over my waist and moved it around hesitantly, staying clear of my groin.

Heather put the towel over my groin. "Now we are going to get information out of Jack Cash, either through force or compromise."

"What do you mean?" Bobi Jean asked.

"Well, he was very adamant about letting us know he did not have sex with the woman in his room. He is a man of God. So, we will try to make him compromise his walk with God, or he can tell us where the dossier is."

Heather started taking her clothes off. Bobbi Jean protested, "Are you really going to try to seduce him? That is wrong, and God will punish you for it. I won't be a part of it. Technically, it is rape. I have gone along with you for a few minutes, but I am..." Within seconds, Bobbi Jean was on the floor squirming around, Heather had tased her too.

"Well, I hated to do it, but she left me no choice. Now, I am going to...."

There was another knock on the door. "Who is it?" Heather called out, exasperated.

"I am with the US Coast Guard. I am here for Jack Cash."

Immediately, Heather put a pillow over my face and put all of her weight on it. "He's not here." Fortunately, I was able to turn my head enough to breathe, but the officer persisted.

"Ma'am, I need to secure Jack Cash immediately."

"He's not here, sailor, can't you hear?"

About this time, Bobbi Jean was starting to cry. The officer knocked again, "Ma'am, open the door."

Heather took the pillow off me and then moved towards the door. When she opened it, the officer walked into the room, noticing me tied up on the bed and Bobbi Jean on the floor crying. He said, "Is this Jack Cash?"

"I am Jack Cash, and she is...." Then, she tased the officer. He was on the floor next to Bobbi Jean. Heather opened the door and looked out to see if anyone else was coming.

"We are going to a secure place in the engine room. Only a few people, other than the people who work there, know about it. If you make any sound, I will tase you again, do you understand?"

Then she pulled me up, and the towel fell to the floor. "I am going to wrap the towel around your waist, but make one sound, and the towel comes off, and you are charged with exposing yourself, do you understand?"

"Yes, Heather, why are you doing this, why??????"

"Just keep your mouth shut, or I will yell rape quicker than Potiphar's wife."

At least she knew something about the Bible. She took the hand restraints off and told me to hold up my towel. She had the taser on my bare back, walked me down the corridor to a set of stairs. They were stairs that employees used, and no one was coming or going when we descended to the lower part of the ship. We took so many turns, I lost my way and knew I would have no clue where to go if I ran. I am sure that was Heather's intent.

We came across two men noting pressures in the steam system and passed by them. "Going to have some fun?" one called out. The other one laughed and said, "Do ya'll need any help?"

Heather looked back and said, "Yes, watch out for anyone coming this way and keep our secret."

"It will cost you," he replied.

"I will pay. Just give us privacy."

I could hear them talking about what they thought would happen, but I was afraid Heather would carry out her intentions if I said anything.

We made a few more turns, and hidden away was a small room with a bed.

"Do you know what this room is for" Heather asked and answered, "it is for secret staff rendezvous, no one comes here unless they are trying to stay away from others. This is going to be our little room of torture, love, or whatever you make it. Jack Cash, it's going to be a long night, or a quick night, with a happy ending, your choice."

"Heather, there are two things I know, number one, it is going to be a long night, and two, there is absolutely no scenario where I will have a happy ending. So, the secret to my staying alive is to keep my secret inside."

"Oh, a rhymer, huh, well, I am about to make you compromise everything, plus, I am going to make a video of it and send it to people in your church. I will ruin your life, and if you run, I will yell rape, and since you don't have clothes, who are they going to believe?"

Heather started taking off her top, revealing a bra, so I turned my head away. "You can turn your head away now, but soon, there will be no way you can turn your head. I will turn you on. You will be begging me to keep going and not stop."

"Heather, do you think you can get away with this? The Captain may be in on it, but now you have assaulted an officer with the Coast Guard. I am pretty sure they won't take that very kindly."

"Well, by the time they find you, naked in this room, I will be long gone with the dossier and your money. LONG.GONE. Juan Carlos is just a few miles away, and when I radio him, he will be here right away."

I was starting to wonder if everyone in the world was on Juan Carlos' payroll. "The Coast Guard will not let him anywhere near this cruise ship."

"I've got connections. You just worry about what you are going to tell your congregation when they see the video."

Heather started fumbling around with her camera to get the video in the right spot for her purposes when I grabbed the taser and stuck it to her back, and pulled the trigger. She fell to the floor immediately flopping like a fish out of water.

I knew I had only a few minutes to get out, so I took out in the only direction I could remember, all while trying to keep the towel wrapped around me. I rounded a corner, and suddenly nothing looked familiar. I ran back to an intersection of pipes and gauges and went in another direction. Still, nothing looked familiar. My towel fell, and as I was picking it up, I heard Heather's voice calling out to the guys we passed earlier. I heard them running to her. When they passed me down another corridor, it helped me to know which direction to run. I waited holding the towel around my waist, ran as fast as I could away from Heather. I ran down the same corridor where the men were. I ran and rounded a corner and came face to face with Bobbi Jean and a different officer with the Coast Guard.

"That's him," she said, "he's the one Heather had tied up."

"Sir, where are your clothes?"

"They are in Heather's room, she took me hostage."

Bobbi Jean spoke up, "They are aware of what is going on" She turned to the officer, "I will lead you to the room where Jack Cash can get his belongings."

When we arrived, the Coast Guard medics were attending to the officer who initially came to the room. Two other officers were guarding the door. They let us in, and I went into the bathroom to put on clean clothes. I was relieved and scared even more. I didn't know who to trust at all.

When I opened the door to walk back into the room, Bobbi Jean was waiting for me and grabbed me, hugged me, and told me she was so sorry things had happened the way they did. She claimed she didn't know what was going on and was sorry for how Heather treated me. I didn't say anything to her.

An officer with the Coast Guard spoke up, "Sir, we understand you are under extreme danger, and we are ready to take you aboard the Coast Guard ship. There you will be assessed and returned to port ahead of the cruise ship. We have alerted law enforcement, and they are ready for your return. Please gather your belongings."

I gathered my things and followed the officer. Within a couple of minutes, we were joined by three more officers, two in front and two behind me. All had their hands on their sidearms, and I felt both protected and like a prisoner. We made our way to the deck so they could transfer me to the Coast Guard ship. Thousands of people were on their balconies, on deck, everywhere, watching me get on the ship.

Once on the ship, they led me to the Coast Guard Captain. He had already ordered his crew to prep for my arrival. "Sir, we have arranged for you to rest in a bunk until we arrive in port. Once we arrive, we will transfer you to the local FBI team, who will be debriefing you and offering you protection. We do not have cruise ship accommodations but promise to do our best to keep you comfortable. We should arrive at the port in six hours. My crew will take you to your bunk and will show you the mess deck, where you can eat if you wish. If you need anything, please do not hesitate to ask. Unless, of course, it is a pool, jacuzzi, spa, show, casino, theatre, virtually anything you would find a cruise ship. We do not have those here."

The crew laughed, only when I laughed. The officers introduced themselves, and told me they would be my security while on deck. I asked them why I needed protection onboard a Coast Guard ship, and they said, "because it is what the Captain ordered, so that is what we will do."

Due to the nature of the threats around me, they determined I should not go to an open deck, so I stayed below deck for six hours until port. I had dinner with my two security officers as well as their friends. After I sat down, the Captain arrived and ate with us. The ship had a chef prepare a gourmet pizza to rival anything I had eaten on the cruise. The officers shared their story of joining the Coast Guard during the meal and then launched into stories of life at sea. They likely embellished most, maybe to impress the preacher onboard or to see how they could outdo the tale from the other. Finally, one asked me, "No one told us not to ask questions, but why are you on the ship, and why are people trying to kill you?"

"I am not sure they want to kill me. I think they just want what I have."

"What do you have?"

I knew better than to divulge everything. "It's just a lot of stuff dealing with drug cartels, government coverups, and crazy women."

That final word started a frenzy of "crazy women" stories, which diverted their attention from me. After about an hour of talking, they offered to lead me to my bunk. Since we were still a few hours from the port, they told me I might want to rest because the FBI would meet us immediately. I laid down on the bunk and fell asleep immediately.

CHAPTER THIRTY-ONE

"Sir, please wake up. We are arriving in port. We need you to prepare for disembarking. If you need a shower, you should do it now." It had been eight days since meeting Kim. She was gone.

I opened my backpack and took out clothes to change into and showered quickly. I felt a few sudden movements of the ship and a whistle through the intercom, so I hurried to get dressed. The main officer was waiting on me to finish and then led me to my bunk to gather my items. When we were topside, four officers led me off the ship to an SUV waiting for me. Three FBI agents identified themselves, showed me their badges, and opened the back door to the SUV. A female agent rode next to me and introduced herself and the others, and said, "We are taking you to the regional FBI office for a debrief, and then we will transfer you to wherever you need to go."

On our way to the regional office, one agent received a phone call, redirecting us to a safe house. Looking at the driver, he said, "We need to go to 201, there is a threat at the office," and then turning to me, "Sir, we are going to do our debrief at a safe house. There is an unusual increase in traffic around the office. It is out of the ordinary, so, out of an abundance of caution, we are taking you elsewhere."

"Could I suggest something?"

"What is it, sir?"

"Can we do something that only we know? Something not on the radar of others?"

"Why?"

"The tighter the network is, the less likely the people on the outside would know. We could go to a different place for the debrief, one we know about, somewhere safer than a safe house."

"Where would that be?"

"I don't know, but book the highest-priced place you can find in Miami for one night, somewhere that has a parking garage or valet."

"Our office would not approve it because we have a safe house, and it would be too expensive."

"I will pay for it. It needs to stay off the radar. And no one will be able to track it by your card."

"I don't know," Special Agent Davis added, "there is nothing wrong with the safe house."

"Tell you what, send an SUV to the safe house, give it about 30 minutes, and if the safe house is safe, then we can go there."

"Ok," she said as she made a call, "send Agent Gomez to 201. Have him call me when he arrives," then addressing us, she said, "he is 10 minutes away from 201, so we should know something soon."

The driver turned into a coffee shop drive-through and said, "coffee or whatever you want to drink is on the feds, so decide what you want to order quickly."

Everyone decided, and he placed our order. As we were pulling away, a phone rang. It was the in-field tech support noting the power grid for 201 was down for several hours. When pressed, the tech said that the power company did not know why. The agent said, "Well, the security system has a battery back up, and the generator will kick in. There were camera's but tech support could not access them. The WIFI for the property provides camera support, but it was down too. There was no way to determine what was going on at the property. A minute or so later, Gomez arrived and called the agent in the car. He couldn't open the garage door, and they talked through a couple of reasons why it was odd and what to check. While he checked on the generator, he rounded the corner and found the generator cabling cut in two.

Suddenly, someone opened fire on his SUV and the house. They showered it with what sounded like an automatic weapon, as he stayed in the back. It lasted a good minute, and then the car drove off as quickly.

Gomez and the agent were talking furiously to each other, and because he had gone to check on the generator, this action spared his life. While they were talking, ascertaining the situation, the driver had pulled over and phoned in the hit on the safe house so a tactical team could arrive and assist Gomez. Now, they were all ramped up as they talked to someone different within their department, someone who could help give reasons for the security breach.

I sipped my coffee calmly. This kind of thing had become routine for my life, so I knew anything on any type of schedule was dangerous.

"How can you be so calm, and how did you know something like this was going to happen?" the agent wondered.

"I hate to say it, but this has become my normal. This is why I said we needed to shake things up a little. They have people everywhere, and I'm not even sure one of you was not in on the conspiracy too."

"We are all sworn FBI agents. We are not part of anything like this."

"Yeah, I can tell you about a sworn US Marshal who went rogue too."

"The driver looked at agent in the front seat and said, "Make a reservation at the hotel downtown, the tall one. Do not call it in. We will call it in when we finish our debrief."

"How about I make the reservation and pay for it?"

"Suit yourself," Tyler said, handing me his phone, "the digits for the hotel are in it now. Just hit send."

I pulled out my debit card and made the call, reserving a room. I asked for the nicest room that had immediate access. The hotel had a room for $1,249 per night, a suite that had direct access. I ordered room service snacks and reserved the room. Davis overheard the rep repeat the cost and said, "that's too expensive. Ask for the governmental rate. I will show my credentials when we arrive."

"Is there a governmental rate?"

"Yes, the cost is $822 for this room, but you will need to show identification on arrival, and it has to be official government business."

I assured the rep of the validity of the business and secured the room. Davis said, "It is still a lot of money."

"I know, but we need to do this quickly, and I need to leave. I have to figure out my life."

We arrived and checked into the room. The room was on the hotel's top floor and was as luxurious as one would expect for $1,249 per night. The Atlantic ocean view was the most remarkable feature, one I would enjoy for a short time only. Being on the top floor didn't offer much for an emergency exit, but it also had a dedicated key for the elevator to get there. There were only three rooms on the floor, and the only access was by the key card.

We sat down, and Davis started the debrief. I figured this was nothing more than an interrogation about my whereabouts, contacts, and more, stemming back a few days and then to Veronica and her dealings with the cartel. They knew I had come into a lot of money from Paddy, but I didn't tell them it was money likely attached to the cartel. They didn't make the connection but probably already knew. When I mentioned Monica and that she worked for the FBI, an agent suddenly became agitated, teary-eyed, and excused herself. An agent looked at her, then the driver shrugged his shoulders and shook his head as if it was something he had seen before. They continued to ask questions, asking the same question differently, creating a negative, backward, and confusing question to try to confuse and fluster me. On every question, I clarified what they were asking and answered what I knew.

The female agent that left in tears, returned to the room, this time with a tissue, and sat down. "I am sorry, Monica went through the academy with me, and at one time, we were close. I knew she married someone, but we were not as close then, and besides, she didn't invite me to the wedding. But I can tell you when she died, even though it had been a while since we talked, it hit me like a ton of bricks. I had to see my counselor about it. He called it vicarious grieving, grieving over someone you don't know or don't know well. I can tell you that it was real."

"Mr. Cash, your profile says you have been married seven times. Six of them died at the hands of someone else. Can you explain?" An agent wondered.

"No, and if you can explain it, please let me know. On the cruise ship, Heather said she overheard Kim talking to her sister, saying she had killed six of my wives."

"Ok, who is Heather, Kim, and is it Heather's sister or Kim's sister?" the agent asked.

"Heather is known as Voluptuous Heather on the ship," everyone laughed, "she was a part of my security shadow. Kim was someone I knew from high school who somehow found me on Vero Beach and was with me on the cruise. We slept in the same room but didn't have sex. I think she has been stalking me for all of my life. Kim's sister somehow made it on the cruise ship, and they went on a murder spree to eliminate anyone attaching them to the cartel, ran by Juan Carlos, and they wanted the documents I had."

"I don't think I want to write all this down. It sounds like we just went crazy, writing crap down," one agent said.

"I think I am going crazy after living through it all."

The female agent spoke up, "What documents were they wanting?"

"They were the trust papers I had completed on Grand Cayman, transferring another trust to my trust. I am not sure why the papers are so important, and some people think I had some kind of dossier with me. Besides, I think Juan Carolos wanted the entire trust."

"How much are we talking about?" Davis asked.

At this point, I knew divulging this information was what put me in jeopardy repeatedly, and I didn't feel comfortable telling anyone. "Enough to kill for."

"How much exactly?"

I just sat there smiling.

"Sir, if we are going to help you, then we need to know how much and where the documents are now."

"First, I have heard that repeatedly, and when I trusted people with the information, they wanted the documents. They wanted dossiers I didn't have and virtually everything else, including my life. Second, I don't know which one of you is with the cartel or of those who seek to harm me, but I am not willing to find out. I don't want your help. I want this nightmare to end right now. I want to go back to Vero Beach, gather my stuff, and head home. I have been away too long, and I haven't talked to anyone back home, and they are probably wondering what happened to Jack Cash."

"Sir, we are here to help. No one is with the cartel. We are all FBI

Special Agents, and we want to ensure your safety. How much are we talking about?"

"North of 150, just a little north."

The agent spoke up, "I don't understand, north of 150, is that code?"

The female agent answered, "No, he is saying north of $150,000. Am I right, Mr. Cash?"

"Yes, north of $150,000."

"Wait, I don't understand, why all the murders for $150,000, it doesn't make sense," she wondered.

"It doesn't make sense at all," I offered.

"Well, I think we have all we need for now. Where will you go from here?" the driver asked.

"Well, I am going back to Vero Beach for a day or so longer, and then, home."

"Where can we take you?"

I told them I had a car at the cruise port, and they prepared to take me to the port. When I told them the small amount, it seemed they were ready to get rid of me. I imagine if they knew how far north 150 was, they would treat me like royalty.

"Hey guys, if it is alright, I want to stay in the room here until tomor-row. That way, maybe the interest in Jack Cash will die down. The only thing I ask is, would you please do not divulge my whereabouts."

"No problem! We will keep your location discrete, even in our reports," one promised, "that wraps up our work. Good luck in the future, Jack Cash."

"Thank you all."

They left, and I about fell on the floor in exhaustion. I was hungry, so I ordered room service. I thought I would buy a car for Josiah instead of picking up his car. The chances of someone monitoring his car were pretty high. I also needed a replacement phone for the one I ditched near Bradenton. I called the local cell phone store just about three blocks away and told them my phone was lost. Someone had turned it in, but I asked for a newer phone. They told me they would have it ready in about an hour, which gave me time to eat and walk to the store.

After room service arrived, I ate as if I hadn't eaten in days. I didn't realize how much stress had kept me from eating a full meal. After I finished, I found the cell phone store and picked up my phone. Before leaving, they downloaded all my data I had backed up before Kim and I put it in the truck.

Once I had the phone, I called the desk at the condo and asked for Josiah. He was not in, but they readily gave me his cell phone number when I told them I was Jack Cash. He was home, recuperating from his beating. He was elated that I was ok. He said that there were people lingering near my condo and I should wait before coming back.

"Thanks for letting me know," I said, "Quick question, if you had the car of your dreams, what would that car be?"

"Oh no, you didn't mess up my car, did you?"

"Not at all, but curious."

"Well, my Civic had a lot of miles and was kind of old, but it was mine. If I got another car, I would probably go with a Civic again."

"What color?"

"Blue, but the newer color of blue they have out now."

"Ok, I am staying where I am for a least another day. I will call you tomorrow."

"Sounds good, and don't worry about getting back with my car right away. My girlfriend is bringing me whatever I need. It's kind of nice, and she is making it a mission in life."

"Awesome, thanks. I will bring back your car tomorrow, though."

After we got off the phone, I searched for a Honda dealership near downtown. I called the closest one and found a salesperson willing to sell me a new blue Honda Civic with everything you could want on one over the phone. He had one in the showroom that was so nice, the owner of the dealership was eyeing it for personal use. He planned for me to arrive around 11 a.m. the next day to pick up the car. We made our deal, and I hung up.

Now, I had to retrieve the documents. I had my debit card with me, but all of the banking information and the trust were on a business card with an embedded jump drive, which Mr. Espinoza had made for me. The "documents" in the bag were only brochures for Grand Cayman tourist excursions. Everyone kept looking for papers, actual papers, which drew attention to the bag. I couldn't risk having the jump drive in the bag, especially with everyone trying to get "the papers." The jump drive was password protected with some type of bank encryption. The bank was responsible for billions of dollars in off-shore accounts, so I was sure they had sufficient security. The password was my social security number, followed by my birthdate.

It was getting late in the afternoon, but I had to get to a computer to pull the information off the flash drive. To keep from exposing my data on a public computer, I found a store near my hotel to buy a laptop. I had to be very discrete in every way to keep people from knowing where I was or the amount of money I had.

I also had to change my appearance so I purchased a hat and sunglasses from a Hotel Botique that would hopefully change my look and then walked four blocks to the computer store. On my way, there seemed to be a lot of activity heading towards my hotel. A police car flew past me, then a few more police cars. Within a minute or two, an ambulance and then fire truck after fire truck headed in the direction of my hotel. I wasn't sure if they were going there, so I proceeded with my purchase. When I finished, I walked outside, and first responders and many police officers surrounded the hotel. I found a bench at a bus stop to sit and watched from a distance. More police cars sped that direction, and people were starting to assemble at the corner near the bus stop, looking and talking, all wondering what was happening. Finally, someone walking from the direction of the hotel started talking to the group, explaining what was going on. I walked over to hear what he was saying, "and then they rushed the room and shot the room up. I don't think anyone was in the room, but they just went in shooting. Security for the hotel ran up the back stairs, and they shot one of them. I am not sure he is going to make it."

I leaned into one of the men near the group that heard the initial report and whispered, "What did he say?"

"He said a group of people went up to, like the top floor of that hotel and shot up a room, like a drive-by shooting but in a high rise hotel. They were leaving after shooting up the room and shot a security guard. I think the people got away."

"Ok, thanks." I knew I had to run. My room was compromised. I had to get some cash and find a hotel that would not check my identification. I rounded the corner, and by now, police were swarming the area, but I noticed a car at an intersection with tinted windows, tinted so dark I couldn't see anyone inside. Since I had sunglasses on, I looked in their direction without them knowing I was doing so. They drove slowly down the street, so slow that the cars behind them were honking for them to move faster. They slowly went by me while I walked in the other direction. Soon, though, they tried to do a u-turn in the middle of the busy city street. Fortunately for me, their action caused a bottleneck in the traffic with a lot of people honking. When they did, I walked faster and then rounded a corner to find a coffee house. I ducked inside immediately.

I ordered an iced coffee and sat down, keeping an eye out for the car that passed me earlier. I wasn't paying attention to the people inside the coffee shop or the few who were coming in until one woman who looked very familiar walked through the door. I kept my head down, not knowing if the car was associated with her or not. My trust in people was deficient. She got her drink and sat down at a table next to me. Now my focus was on the window outside and this beautiful woman seated next to me. She quickly pulled out a small tablet from her purse and started reading. I could tell it was a Bible reading app, one I had on my phone. She started reading and didn't seem to pay attention to anyone in the coffee house. I kept looking around, and it must have caused her to wonder what I was doing, especially since I wasn't reading or talking to someone. She looked directly at me and said, "Do you like what you see?"

"Excuse me?" She looked familiar, but in my running and lack of sleep, I could not place her face.

"Do you like, what you....hey, I know you!"

I got extremely nervous, afraid that she was a part of the group looking for me, so I said, "No, you have me mistaken for someone else."

"No, I know you, you are probably still very mad at me."

I looked closer, and I realized who it was, "Bobbi Jean, is that you?"

"Yes, and I am so sorry for what happened to you. I am a Christian, and I know you are a pastor, and I was so upset about the way Heather treated you. You didn't deserve it, and honestly, people shouldn't treat people like that. The ship laid me off because one-third of our trio was going to jail. I hope you can find it in your heart to forgive me."

"Well, Heather tased you too. I figured you had joined the cadre of the tased people. It's a special gang where a crazy woman strips people down to nothing and tases for kicks or whatever else."

"Yeah, after you left the room, I didn't think I would ever see you again. I really wanted to..." and Bobbi Jean started crying. "I mean, I really wan...." And her crying turned to uncontrollable sobbing, then the rest of the coffee house was watching.

I leaned over and hugged her, and she melted into my shoulder, washing my shirt with her tears and snot. This scene of meltdowns was happening way too often. It seemed to last forever, and I didn't want any attention right now, so I said, "I forgive you, Bobbi Jean."

She laughed through her tears, "Bobbi Jean is my stage name. She dug around in her purse and pulled out some false teeth that were about as ugly as you can imagine, and put them in, "they are part of the act, 'Hi, I'm Bobbi Jean," she said with an obvious slur of speech and southern drawl, "I am supposed to be sweet but ugly to look at, Heather was the one with, with...you know, and I am dowdy. My real name is Amanda."

"Well, you certainly clean up nice when you don't have your teeth in."

She laughed so hard she snorted her drink.

"And, you are a snorter too."

"So, do you live here in Miami?"

"Oh, no, I don't." I certainly didn't want to tell her I just got off the Coast Guard ship, checked into a hotel, left my room right before it got shot up, and now I am on the run from people in a black car with tinted windows.

"That's good because this city is nice but not a good place for Christians."

"Do you live here, Amanda?"

"No, I pretty much have lived on the ship for the last 18 months, and until now, it was home. Now I have to find a place to live until I find a new job. Maybe I can find a third person for our comedy act, but I'm not sure I want to do it anymore, are you interested? A pastor, voluptuous whoever, and ugly Bobbi jean would make for great comedy."

"No, not interested in it!"

"That's too bad. I would have liked to get to know you."

It dawned on me that very moment that I meet women in the weirdest ways and she was sending me a signal. Mainly, my signal was to leave and find a safer place than this coffee shop offered.

I looked up and saw a couple of guys with sunglasses stand in front of the coffee shop. Immediately I felt in danger.

"I am serious, Jack Cash."

I was unsure what she said from here on because the men outside talked about coming inside, and one kept his hand on his side. Either he had significant pain on his hip, or he was holding his hand on his gun, ready to present it when needed. I looked around the coffee shop for an exit and then stood quickly, grabbed my things, and said, "I've got to go."

Amanda looked at me and then looked at the guys at the front and knew I was in some kind of danger.

I quickly walked to the counter. "Is there an exit I can go to other than the front door? My life is in danger."

"The back service entrance opens up to an alley," the barista said, motioning to the back, "Follow me."

I walked as fast as I could behind him, when he opened the door he asked if I needed to call the police and I told him he should.

I was walking as fast as I could when a voice said, "You sure can move quickly. Who were those guys?" Amanda had followed me.

"I don't know. They are following me. It would be best for you to find somewhere to go. It is not safe to be with me."

"I know a place you can go that is safe. No one will know you are there either."

"Amanda, I have trusted a ton of people over the last week, people who turned on me, shot at me, tased me, tried to molest me, you name it, so, my trust level right now is below zero. I can't...."

Bang, Bang, Bang, the coffee house was under siege. I was right to think the guys on the outside were coming inside. Amanda spoke up, "I am scared. Can I go with you?"

Against my better judgment, I knew that letting Amanda tag along might be the worst thing ever, but I had no idea how to navigate through the city.

"Where is this safe place?"

Panting as we were running, she said, "The cruise company put me up in a hotel for two weeks until they decide what they are doing. They also have to do investigations on board because of the murders and cleaning up the ship too."

"What hotel?"

"It's right around the corner."

The hotel was a vintage hotel from years gone by, with an lingering musty smell, like a room shut up for years smells. It would be off of the radar since my name would not be on the room.

Amanda led me to the elevator, pressed the button, and we waited. The sirens that were blasting past us were deafening, likely heading to the coffee house. The desk clerk asked what was going on, and Amanda said, "gunshots were coming from the coffee house."

"My boyfriend is a barista there, was anyone hurt?"

"We don't know," Amanda said to her and then walked over and started calming the clerk, "Can we pray for you? My friend is a pastor."

The clerk started crying, shaking her head; yes, "Please, I am terrified."

I prayed for her and then told her it would be best to call security to keep an eye out for anyone in the area who could pose a risk to the hotel. She told me they didn't have day security, only a maintenance guy who served in the role, but he was off that day.

She fumbled around for her cell phone and pulled it out, hands shaking, "I'm going to call him." She pressed the buttons and pressed 'send' and waited. Eventually, it went to voice mail, and she left a garbled message through many tears, words only a kindred heart could understand.

We needed to be out of view, but the need to console her outweighed any other need. Sirens continued to scream past the hotel, and then I noticed a S.W.A.T. truck heading that way. "I think it would be best to lock down your hotel."

"What, why?"

"S.W.A.T. just passed the hotel. They only get involved in an active scene. You need to do it now."

She ran to the back to retrieve keys, and when she did, there was a lot of activity out front. "Amanda, get on the elevator!"

"Find a place to hide." I yelled to the desk clerk. The door to the elevator opened, and as we stepped on, I started pressing the buttons to close as quickly as I could. The desk clerk got on just as the doors were closing.

"I am too scared to hide alone. What is going on?"

"People are trying to find me. They have been chasing me for days and have been behind me every step of the way. We need to get to a room and hide." I pressed the button for every floor.

"I have the master key to every room, but without checking the daily log, I am not sure which rooms are occupied and which are not."

"Do you know your occupancy rate this morning?"

"Yes, I ran the report. It was 45% as of 8 a.m."

"Are there any open floors without occupants?"

"No, every floor has some, the least occupied, as of now is the top floor."

"Do you have a service elevator not open to the public?"

"Well, yes, but it can be opened by anyone, no special key needed."

"Can you lock it?"

"Yes, if I do, only the fire department or law enforcement can use it until I unlock it."

"Let's get to it, lock it and find a room."

On every floor, the door opened until we made our way to the top floor. I pressed every button on the elevator going down. The clerk made her way to lock the service elevator in the housekeeping room and then ran to room 421 and opened it. The room had a balcony, making it easy to scan the street below and see around the entrance. The entrance itself had a canopy so we couldn't see anyone at the door.

A heavy police presence surrounded the coffee house. The S.W.A.T. team was acting as if they were searching adjoining buildings.

They brought in tracking dogs as they were loading the injured into ambulances.

It was clear the coffee house was no longer the epicenter of the search for suspects, and the car I saw earlier was parked on the street near the coffee house.

I looked at the clerk and said, "What is your name?"

"Melissa."

"Melissa, is there a back entrance…and is it unlocked?"

"During the day, it is."

"Let's go to a room that overlooks that entrance, is there one?"

"Yes, if the room across the hall is unoccupied, it will probably give us a good view."

We hurried to the room. Someone occupied the room, but he was in the bathroom. Melissa knocked and opened the door. "Sorry, this is Melissa from the front desk. We are on lockdown; please remain in your room."

"Ok, thanks for letting me know."

She shut the door and said, "let's try the next room." She knocked, unlocked the door finding an unoccupied room. I put the computer down, ran to the patio door to the balcony, opened it quietly, and peered out, first to the left, then slowly scanning to the right. The men I saw earlier were in the alley scanning to the left and right, hidden behind rolling dumpsters. They saw me and started running towards the hotel. I stepped back into the room.

"They saw me. We need to leave. I am going to put this computer in the closet under the additional pillows. Is there a way to get downstairs without someone knowing, like a secret passageway."

"No, but we can use the service elevator and go to the basement. The basement has a passageway to the next building over. Both used to be owned by the same company. You can get out of the building by going up the far stairwell. It opens up to a different alley."

I looked at Amanda and said, "Thank you for coming with me. I am afraid I will continue to get you into trouble. My life lately has been one scary scene after another. I can't stay at this hotel now. They have found me."

"I understand. I had hoped it would work out too. You are a really neat guy, but you are right. People want you bad, and I am afraid I will spend my life in fear or die if I come with you. I will pray for your safety."

In a short time, I was with Amanda, I saw a dedicated ministry-minded woman, more so than with Kim, whose husband was a pastor.

Come to think of it, I never really knew if what she told me was true or not. Maybe just another lie or embellishment to manipulate me.

"Thank you, Melissa, could you show me the way?"

"Yes, it's this way." When we made it to the end of the hallway, the elevator opened midway, and out stepped the three men I saw in the alley.

One of them shouted, "Agárrenlo y mata a las mujeres!"

Amanda yelled, "They are going to kill us," so we ran to the service elevator and locked the door going into the room.

Melissa was pushing the button repeatedly, yelling at the elevator to hurry. The men outside were trying to bust through the door. The man in the hallway the men were in stepped out and yelled, "Hey, what are you doing?" and they shot at him, he slammed his door.

The door finally opened, and we got in. Melissa held the basement button as it closed, just as the men broke through the door. We could hear screaming and banging on the door. Finally, they were able to open the outer door of the elevator, but the elevator had already descended to the second floor. I knew they would be coming our way as soon as they could. The public elevator did not go to the basement, only the service one did, so they had to wait for the elevator to get to the basement or run down five floors.

When we arrived in the basement, Melissa ran towards the passageway door. There was a padlock on the door as she tried to open it. Melissa got her key and opened the lock. We went through, and she closed the door, locking it. Melissa stopped, breathless, bent over, and held on to her knees. "The passage leads that way and into another alley." She could barely talk, trying to breathe. Amanda was winded but not so much so.

It was probably a few hundred feet to the exterior. Running to it, I told Amanda she was free to go, and Melissa wanted to go to the coffee house to see about her boyfriend. She would be safe there surrounded by police.

When we climbed the steps from the basement level to the alley, I told them to look around to see if the men were near. I walked into it and turned toward the street for the entrance to the hotel. In the distance, I could see the many police cars and the S.W.A.T. team had converged on the hotel. They eventually brought the men out in cuffs.

I ran back and told Melissa and Amanda, and they both started crying. For them, the chase was off. For me, it didn't seem to be true. I needed to get to the computer I left in the room and said it out loud.

"I will get it and bring it downstairs," Melissa offered, "but I may get tied up with people. My shift ends in an hour."

It would get dark soon, and I could not retrieve the contents on the flash drive so far. I also needed to find a place to stay.

Amanda must have thought the same thing. "Where will you stay tonight, Jack Cash?"

"I don't know. I am afraid to go back to my hotel. I can't get a room and use my name."

"Would you like to stay with me in my room?"

"I probably shouldn't, and you don't want a hunted man like me staying with you."

"I think the people who were looking for you are gone. You can stay with me and then leave tomorrow morning. I know the drill too, you only S.L.E.E.P. in the same room,that is all. No sex. I like that, it's what I like about you. You are devoted to God and are very adamant about living right, even if circumstances put you in awkward situations. I don't think there is anyone on the planet who would do the same."

I thought about it and knew I had to get my computer. I also knew I had to get off the street. I could pick up the car for Josiah tomorrow and head back to Vero. Maybe Amanda's suggestion would be best.

Melissa spoke up, "Wow, a guy who will treat a woman like a queen and not want something out of her, so rare. Can you talk to my boyfriend, sir? He needs to hear how a man should treat a woman!"

Every car that drove past us on the road seemed suspicious to me, and probably because I was paying close attention to the driver and occupants of each, they seemed to pay attention to me.

There is a slight difference between paranoia and heightened aware-ness, and I was slipping over the cliff to paranoia.

"Amanda, I will take you up on your offer. Melissa, is there a place we can get something to eat, a nice place near here?"

"Yes, about three blocks down and one over, there is a very nice

Italian restaurant, or across the street, a Cuban restaurant. I love that place."

"Amanda and Melissa, would you be open to allowing me to take you to dinner at the Cuban restaurant?"

"Yes," they said in unison, with Melissa adding, "I have one more hour on my shift. I need to get back, and I need to check on my boyfriend."

"If he is free, he can join us."

CHAPTER THIRTY-TWO

Both ladies were now chattering non-stop as we walked towards the entrance to the hotel. I don't know if the offer to take them to dinner was what opened their chatterbox or if they were experiencing post-chase joy, but they were laughing and talking non-stop. With this kind of emotional break, tears would likely follow at some point, but right now, the tears were nowhere near us.

Police were talking to everyone coming and going. Amanda told them she had a room in the hotel, and they asked her to show a room key. She presented hers and then took me by the arm and said, "And this is my boyfriend. He is staying with me." Melissa told the officers she was the clerk on duty and ran for safety when the men started their chase.

At first, the police thought the men were choosing random places to either hide or find someone. They weren't sure of the "someone" and hadn't gotten far in the investigation. They asked for Amanda and my identification, and I handed them my passport and driver's license. The officer wrote it down, looked at me and my license, and looked at it again. "What room are you staying in, sir?"

Thankfully, I saw the room number on Amanda's key card sleeve and said, "321, with my girlfriend."

He radioed in our names, addresses, and then the last four numbers of our social security numbers. Mine was flagged immediately. There was some code they gave him to cause him to become agitated. "Sir, I need for you to put your hands over your head and cup them together. Turn around and put them behind your back."

I did, and he handcuffed me.

Then he called in Amanda's and said, "Because you are together, I need for you to put your hands over your head, cup them together and turn around, put them behind your back."

"Are we under arrest?"

"No, sir, you are being detained until I call this in."

He called someone on his cell phone to get information about the code given on the radio. I spoke up, "Officer, I am afraid for my life because you called it in over your radio. I have people trying to find me and kill me."

He put his index finger up as if to have me wait and continued his conversation on the phone. I could tell he was getting a lot of information and trying to process it and decide what to do with me. His eyes got bigger as the conversation continued, and then the person on the phone told him to contact the police chief. He hung up and said, "I have to make a call, but I think I am to transport both of you to a safe place."

I looked at Amanda and said, "Well, I guess the Cuban restaurant is out."

"Hello, this is Corporal Andy Collings, I have Jack Cash with me, he and his girlfriend! Yes sir, that's what I was told, yes sir! Is it going to happen now, do I need, yes sir, my squad car," he laughed, yes, Bomber is with me! [more laughter] I understand, yes sir. I will, thank you, sir." He hung up.

"Well, it looks like the Chief wants you to be safe in our fair city, so far, that's not been the case. He has ordered me to stand watch, along with two other officers, for tonight. I have my K-9 partner "Bomber" with me, so I have to take him for a walk. I will bring him in with me when we return. The chief wants someone to take you to get dinner. You mentioned a Cuban restaurant, and I have an officer on the way who will take you there. They will stay with you while you eat and bring you back to the hotel afterward. The chief will have someone from the US Marshal service come to talk to you about protection. They will arrive later this evening."

"I am not interested in a U.S. Marshal coming, the last one I had turned against me. But I need to retrieve my computer, is it ok for me to go upstairs?"

"Me too," Amanda chimed in.

"Yes, but stay in your room until I return."

We went up to the room where my computer was stashed, retrieved it, and then put it in Amanda's room.

Her room was simple, with a Bible open on the bed, a journal notebook next to it, and soft worship music playing in the background. Since we had just arrived, I knew she didn't do this for my benefit.

There was a knock on the door, and a male and female officer were standing outside. When I opened the door, "We are ready to take you to dinner."

Amanda took her purse and was ready to leave. We followed the officers to their car. There was no longer any police presence on the street. Melissa ran out to the car and told us her boyfriend was safe and they would get something to eat elsewhere and said, "Goodbye."

One officer spoke up, "So, you want Cuban food?"

"Well, it would be a change of pace, and I am up for good food, so where is the best place for Cuban in Miami?"

"I have friends who own a place not far from here. We have to have you back soon. Would it be ok if we went there?"

"Sure," I said, but my trust level, even with law enforcement, was not as good as I needed.

We arrived and chatted for a few minutes, ordered our drinks and meal. The officer whispered, "Is it true someone shot at you getting on a ship?"

"Yes."

"They found you with nothing but a towel on?"

"Yes."

"You slept with a woman named Kim, S.L.E.P.T?" and then she laughed.

"Wait a minute, how do you know I S.L.E.P.T. with Kim?"

"Because that was in our briefing. You are like a legend in the department now. A pastor running from the cartel, shot at on a cruise ship, running around a ship with a towel and nothing else. The pastor who S.L.E.E.P.S with women," she laughed so hard she almost fell out of her seat.

"I think it is sexy, he is faithful to God," Amanda said with indignation towards the officer, "he refuses to compromise even when put in compromising situations."

"No one cares. He could do what he wanted, have sex, and no one would be the wiser. He doesn't have to do act like he is good."

"Yes, he does. He has to answer to God and has to be able to live a life where he doesn't compromise, so he has integrity with the people he leads. I think it is incredible."

The other officer spoke up, "I think it is amazing, especially in situations where women throw themselves at you. It takes a lot of conviction and strength. I commend you, if you even needed me to say it."

The female officer said, "If you had women throw themselves at you, your wife would throw you off a bridge and then drive her SUV below and run over you until you were a greasy spot on the pavement," looking at me, she said, "His wife is my sister."

We all laughed.

I spoke up, "Guys, I am a pastor, a man of God, and I am not perfect. On my best day, when I do everything right, I need Jesus. On my worst day, when I blow it, I need Jesus, every day, I need Jesus. So don't think I am perfect. I just want to do everything I can to please God and do His will for my life. That includes remaining pure while single. I gave each wife a gift and want to continue it for my next wife."

"That is incredible," Amanda said, "are you taking applications?"

"Well, my last wife died a few weeks ago, so, right now I am not thinking about a future wife."

"I didn't mean to make fun of you," the officer said.

"No worries, it does sound funny, though."

Our food arrived, and we pretty much ate silently, except for a few interruptions entering our food critiques. All were exceptional, as the food was delicious.

The check came, and Collings said, "The chief said to pay for the meal. The city of Miami is paying."

"Thank you," Amanda and I both answered.

We loaded into the SUV and headed back to the Hotel. Once we arrived, Collings received a call from the US Marshal. He was ten minutes away. I asked Collings to stay outside our room and explained my former handler, "Cynthia," to him. They told me their job was to keep us safe throughout the night.

We exited the SUV about the time a man in a suit arrived with a briefcase. He walked up and asked if I was Jack Cash. The officer got out of the SUV and asked for his credentials. He presented his badge and identification. He was a Deputy in the Witness Security Division. "Yes, this is Jack Cash and his girlfriend, Amanda."

"Are you staying here?"

"Yes!"

"Can I accompany you to your room?"

"Yes."

He inquired, "Is the room secure?"

"Collings is sweeping for bombs with K9 officer "Bomber.""

"Other than bombs, what about covert listening devices?"

"No, we don't have the capability."

"I will," he said, "once 'Bomber' has completed the bomb sweep."

Bomber and Collings swept the room, and it was clean. The Deputy then took his briefcase and went to the room. He was gone about 15 minutes and returned with several covert listening devices, likely placed after going to the restaurant. "I found these," he said, holding them up for our inspection, and then he proceeded to get a cup of water and place the listening devices in the water, "They can't listen in the room now. Let's go."

Once we arrived, he described the threat package his agency forecasted for me. He told me the cartel was a vast organization and had people in various levels of government on their payroll. I was at the top of their list because I had the money from the cartel and information that could bring down the highest in government.

"So, where is this information about who is who in the Cartel? I haven't seen anything about any list."

"Well, you might have it and don't know it. The thought is someone murdered Paddy Gypsy because of the list and the money. It is thought he had the list in his things he left for you, that list is the reason you are being hunted."

As I sat there, I thought through my running. At each turn, everyone was interested in getting to me before I went to Grand Cayman, even more so after. Maybe the information was on the flash drive I had been carrying with me. I didn't want to say anything to him because he could also be with the cartel, and I didn't want to pull out the flash drive to see at the moment either. I even wondered if the covert listening devices were just a gimmick to give me enough peace to divulge the whereabouts of the list. If he were trying to extract the list, then anyone associated with it would be in danger, and even if I didn't tell him while he was in the room, it would be dangerous to discuss it or access it when he was gone. I didn't even know Amanda enough to trust her, and now, everyone was beginning to look suspicious. Suddenly, something swept over me, a desire to flee, to run as fast and as far as I could away. Here I was, with all the money I could ever need for my life and more people than I know wanting it or wanted me dead.

"Mr. Cash, did you hear what I said?"

I was completely unfocused on the room. The deputy repeated himself, "I said if I could I would put you in witness protection with a full staff of security to keep you alive and safe. The information you have is so vital to our national security the need to protect you is a priority for the U.S. Marshal service."

"Do I get to decide or is it an arbitrary 'we are going to put you in a prison of our choosing' statement that I cannot weigh in on?"

"Oh no, it's not prison. It's protection. You will have agents around you constantly, and they will be out of sight. They will monitor anyone trying to get near you and will provide security for you, is all. You will not have to stay home, or locked up, or anything. You can be a pastor, and they will attend your church and blend in with the rest of the congregation, but they will provide you and your church a safe environment to live your life."

"This sounds nice, but it also sounds like it comes with a price, what is the price?"

"We need the list. The list is what the FBI and the US Marshal service want. Turn over the list, and security for the rest of your life is available at no cost to you."

Now, the impending feeling of doom had arrived in my room, settled in my heart, and anxiety was ramping up my desire to run somewhere. Anywhere, to get away from the constant threat I seemed to be experiencing.

"I will see what I can do to find it."

"I need for you to look now."

"I need for you to leave, now. I will look when I am ready."

He stood up and began throwing things in his briefcase, noticeably upset with me. "I can't offer you any protection if you do not surrender the list."

"I don't have the list, so I will get protection for myself."

He left the room, slamming the door in the process.

"He's upset," Amanda said.

"Well, he is upset with me over something I don't have control over."

"Do you know where the list is, or could be?"

"No," I replied, not knowing Amanda's intention either. I thought it would be a good idea to test Amanda to see if she was truly working with someone outside to gain access to the list. I knew it had to be something that would not endanger someone else either, something I could monitor.

I also had to see if the deputy listened to us through a covert listening device he supposedly debugged earlier. He was a little too dramatic in finding the covert listening devices earlier, so maybe it was an attempt to gain trust through the dramatic moment.

"Amanda, I have the documents everyone is looking for in my bag, don't say a word. I also need to get online to set up my computer to send the document to someone."

"Sure, the passcode is "rooms4miamiTim." I pulled my new computer out of the case and began the process of setting it up. It took about 20 minutes to go through the paces of setting up and then downloading the latest operating system update, and finally, I was ready to open my email program. In that moment, wondered if maybe Paddy had sent the files everyone was looking for by email. No one came running in when I said it, and I changed my mind about setting my email up using an unsecured

WIFI. If there were something from Paddy before his death, it would be available for any snooping device that could worm itself into my computer. I shut it down immediately after the download.

"Well, I will wait till later to log on."

"Great, hey, I think I am going to get something from the snack machine. Do you want something?"

"No."

As she walked out of the room, I watched her direction through the door peephole, then gathered my things and followed her. If she genuinely were going to find a snack machine, I wouldn't have to worry, but I needed to be ready for my exit if she contacted someone.

She turned down a hallway towards a snack machine near the ice machine. As I got closer, I heard a conversation she was having with someone on her cell phone. It was one-sided.

"Yes, he is in the room. I met him on the ship, yes, I know, but he is a pastor, no, no, I don't think he will try anything like that, the US Marshal Service, they wanted him because he has some kind of list, they didn't arrest him, no, but...look, Teresa, I will tell you if you don't...if you don't stop interrupting me...He is like really nice, handsome...I mean really handsome...(she giggled), and I think he is wealthy. Jack...Jack Cash... yes...look I have to go...he will wonder where I am...and what I...I know...I will be careful. Goodbye, Teresa... I love you too."

I quickly ducked into a small open area next to the elevator, different from the room. I heard something drop in the snack machine and then saw Amanda heading back to the room. Her conversation sounded like women chit-chatting about a possible boyfriend, not about a dossier. I had abruptly left with my things, and I was sure she would wonder where I was, so I went down to the lounge and opened my computer to type. I was typing away when she came down looking for me.

"There you are...I thought...I just got to know Jack Cash, and he left. I was hoping you were still here."

"I am here, just wanting to get online outside of the unsecured WIFI in the room."

Amanda walked over and began massaging my shoulders. "You seem to have a lot of anxiety now...how can I help?"

"That's nice... it helps... thank you. Why don't you sit down? We need to talk. Amanda, the danger surrounding me has gotten worse, and I don't think I can trust the Deputy. Anyway, I wanted to tell you that I am going to get another room. The last thing I want to do is put you in harm's way, and it is clear there are people intent on hurting me, so I think it would be safe to get another room."

My security detail from the police department arrived and Collings asked, "What room are you going to get?"

"I was telling Amanda I was getting another room so she would be safe."

"We can't let you do it. We need to discuss something with you two, but not here and not in Amanda's room."

They pulled us into the exercise room, and Collings said, "There is talk on the street that the cartel has narrowed your location to a ten-block radius around the coffee shop. Even if we wanted to get you out of the hotel tonight, there is not enough activity on the street to pull it off. So, you are stuck in the hotel. We are also stationing undercover officers and detectives in the rooms surrounding Amanda's room. They will monitor all activity off of the elevator, the hallway, the stairwell, virtually every-where, and in every way someone could get to your room. Because of the chatter, we need you to go to the room now. It is not safe in the lounge, and as of two hours ago, the chatter from the street was that they had no idea if you were in the ten-block radius. They probably have people watching for you, homeless people, people in hotels. You name it. So, we need for you to get to your room and stay there the rest of the night."

Amanda helped me gather my things and then took me by the hand as she carried half of the load while I held the other half.

Her hand in mine felt so lovely, warm, gentle, and very calming. When we opened the door to the room, Amanda said, "Well, I am going to get ready for bed. I will be a few minutes," she gathered her bedclothes and disappeared into the bathroom.

When she did, I heard noise from the hallway. I looked through the peephole to see an older Hispanic woman pushing a cleaning cart. I thought having someone clean this time of day was out of the ordinary, and her actions were strange. At every door, she moved something towards the door and then back. On her cart was some type of monitor and it stayed dark until she aimed it towards the door. The other odd thing was our security outside the room was non-existent, so I called Collings cell phone, "Hey, this is Jack Cash, first, there is no one outside our room, and second, there is a Hispanic cleaning woman aiming something at every door, like a long microphone or something."

He explained to me that her job was to determine if there was a heat signature in the room, indicating if people were inside. This action was the first step in moving undercover into the rooms.

"That's pretty elaborate!"

"Yes, but necessary. The cartel's reach into our city is bigger than we thought. We found out twice today."

"I just got a text. The rooms are clear. We are sending the teams into the rooms. They will monitor everything for the rest of the night. Tomorrow, we will move you."

We said our goodnights. I turned to see Amanda standing with a short, black silky nightgown on, smiling at me, "I apologize if this is too revealing, but honestly, I wasn't expecting a man in my room tonight, or I would have brought something different."

"How different?"

"Depends on the man."

"Well, that's more than I have, my clothes are still at the other hotel, so I am wearing what I will sleep in."

"S.L.E.E.P.?" Amanda asked, laughing.

"Yes!"

She pulled back the covers and said, "Well, goodnight, it's past midnight, and I am too tired to talk any longer."

"Good night. I am exhausted too."

I went to sleep immediately when I put my head on the pillow. Amanda slept under all the covers, and I slept on top, covering myself with a sheet and a bedspread from the closet. During the night, I dreamed about Marie, pointing to the beach, shaking her head no, then Tamera, walking up behind Marie, pointing to a ship, shaking her finger, no. Veronica came from behind me and lightly kissed my neck, whispering my name. She whispered it three times, and then I woke up to Amanda shaking me.

The room was completely dark, except for a bit of light from the hall coming from under the doorway. "I heard something, like a bang."

I sat up, and then, "BANG, BANG, BANG... BANG."

I screamed at Amanda to get on the floor, crawl to the bathroom, the farthest from the sound. She did quickly, and then, another BANG...there was shouting in the hallway, and lots of shuffling of feet, doors opening and slamming shut and then the sound of a lot more people. Then, someone started pounding on our door. "Sir, open your door."

I ran to the peephole, and it was Collings, so I opened the door. He came into our room and closed the door. Out of breath, he said, "they came in from the roof... the roof, dropping down from a helicopter, military style! No one saw them coming, and when they entered the hallway, we knew something was going on because no one entered any entrance, but then suddenly, men in black opened fire on us in the hallway. We don't know how many got away. There is a basement corridor leading out of the building. Anyway, most got away, but your location has been compromised. We need to get you out of here. We are waiting for the US Marshal to take you to a safe house."

"No, I won't go with him! Wait, what time is it?"

"It's 4:47 a.m., and I suggest we wait on him. He has a place and will keep you protected." It hit me. It had been nine days since all this started with Kim. She was gone, and now I am doing my best to make sense out of it all.

"I don't trust him, so, I refuse his protection. I want you to take me somewhere."

Amanda spoke up, "I don't think it is a good idea, Jack, they are after you with all they have and the US Marshal will keep you protected."

"The police department had an army here, and they couldn't keep the people from finding out where I was staying. One US Marshal can't do any better."

"Sir, I am not confident I can keep you any safer than the US Marshal."

"No problem, I will get UBER to take me where I need to go."

Collings alternated between a frustrated look and resolve, looking at Amanda, then me, then the door. "Where do you want to go?"

"To a car dealership to pick up a car, then, I will head back to Vero Beach and my condo."

"Let me talk to the chief. We want to bring down this criminal enterprise too, and they may be waiting on you at the dealership if your name is attached to anything, when did you set this up?"

"Yesterday, and I used my name."

"Let me see what the chief wants to do but go ahead and get dressed."

I laughed, "Well, I am wearing the only clothes I have to wear, but I will take a shower."

I stepped into the bathroom and turned on the shower. I felt like I was in a vortex of a storm that had no end, with one wave of trouble after another. But now, I had to do something to stop it and get my life back. The steam began to fill the room, and I knew I needed to hurry. The warm water on my shoulders was just the therapy I needed. The stress had built up, and as I started sorting through everything, a wave of weeping came over me, then a lot of anger. Maybe it was because I had relaxed enough to encounter the pain of grief, or perhaps it was a cascading of events hit me at one time, but the gut punch was real.

Amanda knocked on the door and then opened it a bit, "Are you ok?"

"I'm ok," but I was not.

"Is there anything I can do?"

"I will be out in a second."

She shut the door. I turned off the water, stepped out, and removed some fog from the mirror. My eyes were bloodshot, tears were streaming, and an overwhelmed feeling gripped me to the bone. Staring back at me was a man who looked like he had aged ten years in 10 minutes.

I stepped into the room, and immediately, Amanda embraced me with the biggest and most perfectly timed hug I could have dreamed of, and I cried. Collings went into the hallway, and Amanda just held me, silent as she could be.

I don't know how long we held the embrace, but the feeling of trust and love captivated me. I was as vulnerable as anyone could be and knew there was nothing I could do if she were a part of the cartel, and at that point, I didn't care. I knew I had to trust someone, or I would go crazy. I turned to kiss her cheek, and she turned to me. Our eyes and lips met. Her kiss was gentle but sensual, caring but much more. I knew this moment was too much for me, but I didn't care. I needed someone more than I had ever needed someone. Amanda was not just at the right place and time. She was what I needed.

We kissed for the longest time until Collings came back into the room. We stopped, and I looked at Amanda and said, "That was really nice."

"Yes, it was very nice."

"Ahem, I would say get a room, but you have one," Collings interrupted, as we backed from our embrace. "I know you want to go to the dealership, but the Captain wants to set up a massive sting at the dealership, involving as many officers as we can. But, it will be perilous for you. Is this something you want to do?"

"Exactly what are you going to do?"

"Well, if you agree, you will keep the original appointment. You will go and purchase the car. All around you will be officers. Some will be in new cars, some will overlook the dealership from sniper positions, some will walk around like new car buyers, and some will look like salespeople. We will have you surrounded. We need to start cleaning up this massive enterprise."

"It sounds like a great plan, but if you are right, they will not stay detained too long. Someone will get them released immediately."

"Hopefully, it will be long enough for you to find out where the dossier is and has what we think it is, then we will be able to elevate it to our county prosecutor and then to the feds, but not until we have indicted them locally."

"I agree to do this, but I want you to keep Amanda safe."

Amanda spoke up, "wouldn't it make more sense to have a couple buying the car rather than an individual. In other words, I want to be by Jack Cash's side and don't want to leave it."

"It is risky, and if Jack Cash agrees, you assume all the risks for your safety."

"There is a woman who was with me during most of my running, and she was on the ship, she is bat crazy about me, so much so that from the way it sounds, she claimed credit for murdering some of my previous wives. I think she was a part of the cartel. So, Amanda, if she is anywhere near, you could be in danger too."

"I remember hearing about her, and the fight she had with her sister, or at least that is who people believed she was, anyway, I am not afraid and I can't think of anywhere I would rather be; other than with Jack Cash."

Collings said, "Ok, Amanda and Jack will buy a car. You both understand the risks, and we will get our team ready. Excuse me while I make the arrangements."

CHAPTER THIRTY-THREE

When Collings left the room, Amanda turned to me and kissed me, wrapping her arms around me, then leaning back, said, "Whatcha doing after buying a car?"

"I am taking it to the young man who loaned me a car for the cruise. He got severely beat by people in the cartel. It's the least I can do. What about you?"

"I have no plans and am waiting to hear back from H.R. at the cruise line about my future. I can get that information over the phone, so I can go anywhere and find out later."

I knew she was hinting about going with me, and at this point, I didn't have an idea what I was going to do after I bought the car. Suddenly it dawned on me I was not prepared to buy the car. I needed the routing number and account number from the trust to complete the transaction. I could use the debit card they gave me, but I was sure they would flag a purchase for over $30,000. I kissed Amanda on the cheek, walked over to the computer, pulled it out, and started it.

"Are you setting up your email?"

"No, I need to get some information for the car purchase. I just remembered, I don't have everything I need."

As the computer was booting, Amanda walked up behind me and started massaging my shoulders again. "You are severely stressed. I can work on your shoulders and your back to help you de-stress a little. You would need to take off your shirt. Would you like that?"

"Ummm, yes, it would be nice, but it is too much for me. I am tired, weak, hungry, and probably just a little compromise away from something I would regret. If I removed my shirt and you started, I don't know if I would be able to stop it. Thank you, but I think it would be best if I leave my shirt on, and if you want to massage my shoulders, that would be ok."

I knew better but didn't want to discourage Amanda completely. She worked my shoulders with precision, all the while asking about my life and ministry. It was challenging to focus on the task at hand, unveiling my life to someone I didn't even know twenty-four hours ago, but it was profoundly de-stressing.

I began telling her about Mandy, and then the computer was ready. I reached into my wallet, retrieved the business card with the built-in flash drive, pulled it out, and inserted it into the computer. Immediately, fifteen file folders populated on the screen, and some type of program began downloading. The program seemed to be a direct portal to the bank, and as one aspect of the program loaded, a progress bar appeared at the bottom of the screen. Each time it reached an increment of 10%, terms of service agreement populated, or something of that nature. At 50%, it began the direct connection to my account but required internet access. As I was reading the information, I realized I would have to get online at some point, but if I did, it would expose my information to any snooping device in the area. "I need to get online but can't use the hotel WIFI."

Amanda suggested I get a strong VPN. She told me they use VPN's on the cruise ship because they have over 4,000 new passengers every sailing, some of which may have snooping devices that can steal information. She suggested a name brand one that cost a few dollars, but security was the best of the other providers.

I was impressed at her knowledge in this area, connected my cell phone to my computer for access through my hotspot, downloaded the VPN, and prepared for the remaining program's download. Within a few minutes of opening the VPN, the computer continued to establish a direct connection to my account, and then, out of the blue, a message appeared, "Warning, the files contained in this trust are highly sensitive. Proceed with caution and only provide them to trusted entities. Proceed?"

I pressed, "yes," then a video appeared.

It was the bank president with a personal greeting to me, "Jack Cash, the files in this trust document are also available through the bank portal. There are additional files Paddy had in his trust, highly sensitive files, they were likely responsible for his murder. I include them for you to use in whatever way you choose. I have not personally opened these files due to my responsibility to my clients."

"Be very careful who you trust with them. They are being down-loaded to your computer as I am talking. They will remain on the bank portal for 30 days, encrypted, and then will disappear. Mr. Cash, I can't emphasize the extreme danger these files pose to you. Godspeed to you, pastor."

Amanda heard everything. I didn't expect anything like this to happen, or I would have waited until no one was around. Now, I was as vulnerable as I could be because now, I had the dossier everyone wanted.

"Are you going to look at the files?"

"If I do, it will put both of us in a position that could cost us dearly."

"I think you are already there, and the only way to stop this is to reveal this information to the world."

"But how?" I wondered. They had infiltrated the US Marshal service, and likely every agency I would contact may have operatives inside. "I've got an idea. Could we kiss when we hear Collings come back into the room?

"We can kiss anytime you want!"

"I found out years ago a public display of affection causes people around to be uncomfortable, and they leave away rather than view it. Maybe it will cause him to turn around and leave."

"That sounds like fun. Maybe he will come in, leave, and come in again for hours!"

Amanda was beginning to sound like Kim.

"It's just to get him to leave while I look at the files. Amanda, I did not know opening these files would divulge this information. I needed the routing number and bank account for the car purchase. Now I am scared you may be with the cartel too and I have just opened myself up to die."

She looked at me dumbfounded and then laughed. The kind of evil laugh someone laughs to sound insidious, but then, the door started to open, someone was coming into the room. Amanda turned me around and kissed me with the most passionate kiss I think I had ever experienced. At least it seemed that way. As we kissed, she moved her hands on my back with the embrace and a few moans thrown in for effect. The door quickly closed, and she pulled away.

"You were right. It does make people uncomfortable. Hopefully, he will come back soon! It was fun."

"Yeah, it was like a roller coaster at a theme park fun."

"Oh, and Jack Cash, let me tell you if I were with the cartel, I would have tied you up and tortured you for the information. I would have made you beg for relief, help, the military, 911 and your momma, all rolled up into one moment. I would have tied you up in bed, and I would have stripped you down to nothing and made you compromise everything, your walk with God, your integrity, your everything. I would have done it until you gave me the information. I would have made passionate love to you, even if you protested so I could extract whatever information you had, but I did not, and do you know why? Because I am NOT with the cartel, I am NOT with the cruise line anymore because I AM with Jack Cash. So, take that."

"Come up for air, girl. If what you are saying is true, you are probably the only person on the planet who knows as much as you know and is in as much trouble as me. Welcome to what happens when someone meets Jack Cash."

I clicked on the first file, and it contained a spreadsheet, unlike anything I had seen before. It listed names, associations with those names, and salient verifiable criminal acts. Each one had hyperlinks which took me on a deeper dive into the criminal enterprise.

I saw names I was familiar with, such as Cynthia, Brian, Kim, and other names I did not know personally, such as prosecuting attorneys, mayors, police officers, senators, representatives, and even the Vice President. I sat there amazed at what I was seeing, and every click took me deeper into the associations and activity of the cartel.

Amanda was looking over my shoulder at the information when someone was ready to come into the room. She quickly moved the computer to the side and sat in my lap facing me, kissing me passionately again. The door opened wider, and Collings and his Captain walked in, "Ok, guys, you can get a room later. We need to go over some things."

"Can you give us five minutes?"

"Yes, but the door is opening in five minutes, and you better be clothed."

They closed the door, and I took the computer, prepared to eject the flash drive but then saw Kim's name. When I clicked on Kim's name, a hyperlink with "Bare Dancer Strip Club, Marie Cash" populated. It had a picture of Marie taken from the strip club security camera, the same place where Kim murdered her. It also had a time stamp for the times Marie was at the strip club attempting to rescue girls. It was clear Kim was involved in Marie's death. Someone sent an advance payment to her for $10,000 transferred one month before Marie's death. I started shaking and sobbing.

Amanda put her arm around me and held me tight. "Are you ok?"

Through bitter tears, I said, "I shared a room with my wife's murderer. I bought her meals, I took her on dates..." and then couldn't control it any longer. I grabbed a trash can and vomited.

The door opened, and Collings and the Police Chief were at the door. "Are you ok?"

"Yes," Amanda replied, "he's just not feeling well."

"Are you going to be ok to do this today?"

I shook my head. "Yes," with my head turned away, "let me clean up."

"Ok, we will give you a minute," and closed the door.

"It's ok not to be ok right now. How can I help you?"

"I need to close this computer out and pack it up."

She rubbed my neck as I did, knowing I had just received a gut punch.

I stepped into the bathroom and rinsed my mouth, and walked back into the room just as Collings and the Chief were walking in, "Are you feeling better?"

"Yes, let's get this going."

They laid out the operation. Our part was simple, arrive in a car provided by their office, meet with the salesman and conduct the transaction. They wanted me to take a test drive to keep suspicion down but had a pre-planned route for it. Once it was completed, we were to stand outside for a few minutes talking about the car and walking around the car while opening the trunk, hood, etc. Following "kicking the tires," we were to go inside and complete the purchase. It was an easy car buying experience with about seventy undercover officers rallied around the car lot.

"Now, we need for you to gather your things to go to breakfast. Then, we are going to get you a car. Until then, we will have you wait in this room until we are ready to eat. We have surrounded your room with three dozen officers, mostly undercover, but a whole host of uniformed officers too."

We still had a few hours before the car buying experience would begin, so they left us alone until closer to the time to eat breakfast.

"What are you going to do until they come back?"

"First, I have to find the routing and account numbers for the transfer. Then, I am going to call a Sheriff Boyd, a friend from back home. Hopefully, he can help us find someone we can trust."

After opening the computer, I was able to locate the routing and account numbers for the transaction. I also quickly searched the dossier for names of the local law enforcement, including the Sheriff, the highest-ranking constitutional officer in the county. I then searched the files to see if there was a cross-referenced name. Fortunately, there was no match, but the chief deputy's name was in the file. I called my friend back home. When he answered, he shared his condolences agin over Marie's death again, even though he was at the visitation and funeral. I told him what had happened so far and I had information that implicated individuals from local law enforcement to the Vice President. I also shared my concern about a vast conspiracy to kill me over the information.

"Jack, it sounds so unbelievable. Have you seen the proof?"

"I don't know enough about what I have seen, but I know there is enough concern about the information that people are willing to kill for it. My problem is that I don't know who I can trust."

"Let me make a couple of phone calls to people I know you can trust."

Within ten minutes, there was a knock on the door, and then it opened. "Hello, Jack, I just got a call from a mutual friend. Sheriff Boyd and I have been good friends for about 15 years, we were at each other's weddings, and he just called and said you had some information for me."

My cell phone rang, and it was Sheriff Boyd. I anticipated that he was going to tell me he had reached out to Collings. I answered, "Jack Cash."

"Hey Jack, Danny here, look, I called a friend, but he is no longer in the department there. He moved to Albuquerque, New Mexico. I will keep trying. Sorry I couldn't help."

"No problem, Tim, thanks for preaching for me Sunday. I am not sure when I can come back."

Danny knew there was a problem. "I understand, Jack. I will keep trying to see what I can figure out. Talk to you soon."

When the call ended, I felt sick again. "I think I am going to vomit again."

"I've got a weak stomach. I will step out for a minute."

When the door closed, Amanda quickly handed me the trash can.

I took the trash can and put it down, grabbed Amanda, pulled her close, and whispered in her ear, "My friend didn't call him. He is lying. There has to be a listening device in the room, and must be listening in on my call too."

"What are you going to do?"

"We have about an hour before we go to breakfast. We have to plan our escape, but quietly, kiss me like you mean it."

Amanda started kissing me as hungrily as she could about the time Collings opened the door. He closed it as soon as he saw what was going on. "It worked. He didn't watch for 10 seconds," Amanda said with glee, "should we continue to kiss?"

"Only if the plan is to do something other than escape."

"Hmmmmm, I much rather like the alternative, but since I want to live, we might need to plan the getaway. How about if I turn on the television, to drown out our voices?"

"Perfect!"

She turned on the television to a sports channel.

"Ok, we will change the plan up a bit. I don't need a test drive because it's not my car. I will make all the financial arrangements before the test drive. Then, when we get in the car, I will ask if we can take it around the block for a test drive. We will get in and take off. The dealer is right off the interstate, so we can hit the interstate and head north, get off some-where, and hit Highway 1 into Vero. Once there, I can find a ride for you to get back and make arrangements to go home, or you can wait at the dealership while I take a test drive."

"I want to go with you. I really would like to go with you."

"You have the most beautiful brown eyes!" I didn't know why I blurted it out and then acknowledged it, "I don't know why I said that out of the blue."

"Thank you for noticing. I am glad you like them. They are original."

I laughed as we held one another. When the door opened, we started kissing again.

"Ok, kids, you need to knock it off. We need to go to breakfast. Our team is in place, and we can talk about the information you want to share with me at breakfast, Jack."

We pulled back, and I began gathering my things. I had the financial information in hand, the flash drive, and my computer. Every piece is just as important as the other.

Collings spoke up, "My favorite hangout for officers is where we are going. We will go there with a small army of officers for breakfast. I have called ahead for their staff to be ready."

Every pivot point in the hotel, to the S.U.V., and even through the streets, our path was carefully choreographed. They left nothing to chance and verified anyone or any vehicle as we traveled. Once we arrived at the restaurant, we had to wait until they searched every exit, alley, dumpster. It was quite the ordeal just to get out of the S.U.V. and into the restaurant. It also felt like everyone was extremely nervous, as their eyes shifted constantly. It wasn't just Collings either. It was every officer. They acted like we were about to be overrun with terrorists.

"Everyone seems on edge."

"Yea, the Police Chief said some of our undercover people are hearing of a major event in the city where the cartel was calling in every possible person to be a part. It was the very thing we wanted, and I feel like they bought it. We just have to be sure the event occurs in the place of our choosing."

We ordered breakfast and pretty much drank coffee and said nothing. Collings didn't bring up the "dossier" either, likely because he was so concerned about what could happen in the restaurant. When breakfast arrived, I prayed over it and the day. I prayed for safety for all involved and for the apprehension of all who meant us harm. After breakfast, they gave us a car to drive to the dealership. I put the address into my G.P.S., and the escort around us was impressive. We had all types of vehicles coming, going, beside us, behind us, in front of us, turning left and right, only to rejoin us on the route. Two helicopters were monitoring us as well, one unmarked and one a news chopper that typically monitors traffic and important news stories. We briefly took the interstate for one exit, and then we were on a five-lane highway to the dealership. It was just off the interstate.

We pulled up to the doors to the dealership and exited the car we were driving. The dealership was on alert as well, and the manager walked up to Amanda and me and said, "The salesperson you talked to yesterday called in sick. He is terrified. So, I will handle your sale. Let's go inside to do a preliminary workup on the sale. We walked into his office, and there was a plainclothes officer inside the office, waiting on us.

"The plan, on my part, is to do the workup of the sale now, go out and talk about the car, and then you take it on a test drive. We are doing it so I can get out of the way as soon as possible."

"That sounds good. Thank you for meeting us here today. My prayer is this morning is for everyone's safety and that the officers can apprehend those who mean to do us harm."

"Have a seat. Let's get you a car."

He began going over the costs, finance options, and extended warranty options as an average salesman would, and I stopped him. "We are here to buy a car. List price, no extended warranty, only a car. Write it up as-is, and I will give you the routing and account number so we can buy the car."

"That was easy. I will need insurance information."

I called Josiah. "Who is your car insurance company?"

He asked why I needed the info, and I told him to trust me. He told me, and I relayed the information to the manager. I told him everything was good and I would talk to him soon.

Once I got off the phone, I told the manager to put the car in Josiah's name, attached to his insurance information. I told him to include the sales tax and all licensing fees in the cost of the sale.

He put the routing and account number into his computer, input some information, and within minutes, we bought the car.

The officer was constantly monitoring his radio and growing increasingly anxious. "Are you almost done? There are a lot of things happening outside."

The manager said, "Yes, let me grab the temporary tags."

He left and returned with the keys, all the documents, and the temp tags for Josiah. The car is in front. I think you parked near it.

CHAPTER THIRTY-FOUR

The officer in the room radioed that we were on our way out. When we walked outside, a helicopter was coming in at a steep angle. Suddenly, officers began firing on the helicopter as it pulled away to do another sweep, and a S.W.A.T.-type truck hit some parked cars on its way into the parking lot. "Those are not ours, get in the car and go," the officer screamed.

Amanda jumped in the passenger seat while I jumped in to drive. I started it and began to pull away with a hail of gunshots everywhere. The local S.W.A.T. team was there, engaging with the S.W.A.T.-type truck that had arrived. I pulled out onto the five-lane highway and punched it. The car was turbocharged, and while the motor was not that big, it had a little bit of power. I pushed it to the limit. We quickly got on the interstate north and drove as fast as we could. Traffic was somewhat heavy, and the cartel's helicopter was following. There were also cars around us that we thought were officers. Collings called my cell phone, "Jack Cash, the cartel is pursuing you. We need for you to return to the dealership for your safety."

"I am surrounded by officers right now. I am safe."

"Those are not our officers. They are with the cartel."

"They have boxed us in. I can't get off the interstate."

The box I was in started slowing down, with cars whizzing by, honking, and several helicopters hovering near. The traffic came to a stop. When it did, several men got out of the vehicles and started towards us. There was barely enough room to squeeze through the cars, and I took off. They were unprepared for my speedy departure and quickly got in their cars. I was a few cars ahead of them by this time, weaving in and out of traffic. I wasn't trained to do this but thought if I weaved in and out, I would keep from being boxed in again.

Amanda was keeping an eye out. The helicopters were following us when Amanda said, "Hey, let's go to the tunnel."

The Miami tunnel was just ahead and would afford us a chance to ditch the helicopters for a minute or two.

We took the exit and continued to the tunnel. Traffic was just as heavy going to the tunnel as the interstate, as it was the time when passengers were on their way to the cruise ships. It was also when cruise ships were coming in, so the flow in and out was filled with cars. Once through, we found a parking lot where cars were exiting and joined the line leaving the parking lot. It was hard to know if we successfully got rid of our followers until we went through the tunnel again.

Once on the other side of the tunnel, we got back on the northbound interstate when Amanda started screaming, "There they are," just ahead, there was a blue Honda civic they had boxed in, just like we had been earlier. This time, though, the helicopter was landing in front of it. Cars were trying to get around it, honking their horns, slowly creeping around it, so we jumped off of the exit nearest to us. They had boxed in the wrong Honda Civic. Amanda was delighted.

Once off of the interstate, we took a side street and found a parking garage. Once we turned, Amanda couldn't see anyone following us. My phone rang, it was Collings.

"Jack, where are you?"

"We found a hiding place."

"Whew, I was afraid you were the ones boxed in. They have a car they have stopped and are trying to figure out who is in it. We are converging on them now. Stay where you are!"

"Ok, we will stay put," Collings hung up. We pulled into a space and parked. Amanda got out of the car and to look for anyone following us, and we were safe for now.

My Sheriff friend, called me, "Jack, are you ok?"

I told him about all we had just encountered.

He said, "I am afraid you can expect this until you turn over what you have to someone who will do something with it. Can you access the information now?"

"Yes," I turned and took the computer out and booted it up.

"Do you think the information is complete?"

"I have no idea."

"My friend in Albuquerque still has friends on the force. He also knows the Miami-Dade assistant prosecuting attorney really well and dated her once. Anyway, she is happily married and so is my friend, but they are still friends. If her name is not on the list, she would be a good person to call. She has friends in higher places, too, and she is a committed Christian. I think you can trust her but check her name anyway. It is Jenny McCann."

After it booted, I pulled up the massive spreadsheet. I put 'Jenny McCann' in the search bar. There was nothing.

"I have her cell number. Call her in fifteen minutes. I will have my friend call her first."

I wrote the number down, and we waited. Amanda walked over to the car, kissed me, and then walked back for overwatch, over and over again. I was glad she was on alert but keeping me from losing my mind too.

About fifteen minutes later, I called the number, "Hello, this is Jenny McCann, Deputy Prosecuting Attorney."

"Ms. MaCann, my name is Jack Cash."

"Yes, sir, I have already been briefed. Your life is in extreme danger, and now, so is mine. Let's be very clear, Mr. Cash. We have to meet as quickly as possible, and I have to see what you have immediately. My office is waiting on dozens, if not hundreds, of participants in today's sting. It is massive. Your information will close the loop if it is what we think it is. Where are you?"

"Ma'am, I think it would be best to find out where you want to meet because I am not confident we will be safe if I divulge my location."

"Fair enough. Let's meet at the Federal Building downtown. They have security, and we can meet upstairs near the federal prosecutor's office, he is a friend of mine."

"What is the person's name?"

"We go back to our days at law school. His name is 'William Bonfiglio.'"

I searched his name in the files and found nothing.

"Ok, when do you want to meet?"

"We have to do it now. The caseload is about to get extremely heavy."

"Ms. McCann, please do not tell anyone where you are going or who you are meeting. The list of people involved is massive. The wrong person will jeopardize everything."

"Copy that. I will head that way now. Meet me at the entrance. I will have Bill escort us up. That way, we can bypass the line."

I called out to Amanda, "Let's go. We are going to the Federal Building."

She got in, and we inserted the address into the G.P.S. It was only ten minutes away. "We are close; do you want to walk?"

"Let's drive. We might need a getaway car close."

We drove to the address, and there was a massive line outside. We parked, I gathered my computer, and we walked to the door, where a man in a suit and a name badge, William Bonfiglio, was waiting. I told him I was the man he was waiting for, and within a minute, Jenny McCann arrived. He walked us in, to the protests of those in line and took us upstairs to the seventh floor and his office.

Jenny told him the story she knew, and then he looked at me, "Well, Jack Cash, what do you have is worth people killing people over?"

I was so tired of figuring out who was trying to kill me and who wasn't I didn't care if he was with the cartel. I had to get rid of the information. I looked at Jenny and said, "You come highly recommended. How do I know I can trust Mr. Bonfiglio?"

"Well," Jenny said, "You can trust me. If I see something, I will do something. You have my word. All of us are in grave danger just by knowing what we know, so believe me, you can trust Bill and me."

I sighed and booted up my computer. I pulled the file up and showed the massive spreadsheet to Jenny and William. He clicked through a few names, hyperlinks, read a few items, and then found some paper trails embedded in the spreadsheet.

"Do you know what you have here, Mr. Cash?"

"I have an idea, based on the energy used to find me."

"You have no... It's bigger than..." William looked at Jenny, and both of them said, "Wow, just wow."

"I need to download this file, and Jenny needs a copy too. This information is a career-maker and a life-destroyer all in one. There are names of people everywhere attached to this file and events that are actionable. We will have to hire help to dig through it all. Mr. Cash, your life is in grave danger."

"I have heard this over and over again, and people have proved it by their actions, so I believe it."

They both looked at Amanda and said, "Your life is in danger as well."

"I know."

William jumped up and went to a filing cabinet, pulled out two jump drives, and proceeded to download copies of the files for himself and Jenny. After he finished downloading it, he searched for anyone in his office named in the file. No one in his office was named, so he proceeded to call everyone in for an emergency staff meeting. We were allowed to attend so his staff could ask us questions.

There were roughly a dozen people present. William opened his computer and cast the information to a large screen television in their staff room. As he did, he prefaced his presentation with a lot of legal talk that I didn't understand and words like "indictment," "grand jury," "R.I.C.O.," and more. With every click, it was like a vortex of criminal activity was uncovered.

He looked at me, "Where did you get this information?"

"I am not sure who all compiled it, but my former brother-in-law left it to me after his murder. His name was Paddy Gypsy."

Someone spoke up, "Is that Veronica's brother?"

"Yes," I replied, "I was married to Veronica after her dealings with the cartel."

Someone else spoke up, "I heard she came into a lot of money after the cartel dealings."

"She never told me about it, someone murdered her a few years ago."

"I heard she overdosed," he replied.

"You will see her killer is named in the files here. She did not overdose. Kim murdered her."

Someone spoke up and said, "This is big. This information is bigger than any case ever."

"Time is of the essence. No one goes home. We need to sift through this information today, tonight, and tomorrow. We need to determine what we can bring immediately to the grand jury and convene them tomorrow afternoon. We have to start immediately because of the danger on Jack Cash's life."

He assigned teams to determine the highest and lowest players, believing if they indicted a few well-placed high-ranking members and a few low-ranking members, they would stand a greater chance of squeezing the middle. By his estimation, there was enough information to indict several high-ranking individuals immediately.

They began work, and he led us out of the building.

"Mr. Cash, I believe we can seat a grand jury quickly. Once we do, and if they move to indict, the pressure will be off you. Until then, we will provide a security detail for you. They will be people who we have vetted for this purpose, although they may not be familiar with your case."

"I have had such detail before, but it always ended with an attempt to detain me, trick me into giving up the files I turned over to you, or kill me. Some of them were with the US Marshal's office."

"This time is different. Now we have the information and as you have seen, so does an entire team of investigative attorneys. They will not stop until every "i" is dotted, and every "t" is crossed."

Amanda hadn't said much until we walked outside. "I have never felt so relieved and burdened at the same time, in my life."

"What do you mean?"

"Relieved that we no longer have responsibility for that file, and burdened. Burdened that we had a file about to destroy a lot of futures."

"Well, I feel relieved but won't feel completely free until they start indicting people. From the way they talked, it was bigger than I knew. I think I know now why so many people have chased me."

William spoke up, "Your security team should be here any minute. They will guard you until indictments start, and then the government will offer you a protection package that will continue as long as you wish. If what you think is true, the information you have brought to us is truly a once in a lifetime get for any federal prosecutor."

In the silence of the moment, Amanda took my arm into hers and pulled me close, whispering, "Jack Cash, I love you. I want to go with you, I want to be with you, I can't imagine life without..." and in the middle of her words, I pulled her in for the passionate kiss she deserved. I had fallen for her, and whether it was love on the run, or the respect she gave me, adrenalin or whatever, it just seemed right, and she was exactly who I needed. If a symphony were playing at this point, the build of the arrangement would have met the crescendo.

William, uncomfortable with the public display of our affection, excused himself to the office building, mumbling, "Your security detail will be here soon."

Amanda giggled. I looked into her eyes and she said, "I know I am coming off of an adrenalin high after being chased by the world, but I want to run away with you. Let's run away."

Amanda kissed me passionately for the longest time.

At that moment, a familiar but ominous voice interrupted our joy, "who is this harlot?"

I pulled away from Amanda's embrace, turned and looked behind me. It was Kim.

"So, do you think you are going to run away with her? Over my dead body, you will."

I panicked, looking around for anyone to help, for a police officer, for our security detail, for someone who would call 911 for us, but it was like we were the only people on the planet.

"You just can't be alone for a minute, can you, Jack Cash? I thought you would at least have given sometime between your first wife and Tamera, but you were hitting on Tamera on the beach just a few months after Mandy's funeral. I know because I was there. I was sitting next to you, feeling sorry for you, hoping to console you, talk to you, waiting for the right moment, but no, you had to invite the bookworm to dinner. My heart broke, it broke! I came all that way to see you and meet you again. You didn't pay any attention to me in school, but since Mandy died, I thought, now is my chance, but you had to start chasing the woman chasing her hat down the beach."

The level of Kim's stalking became clear. She continued, "so, I had the slut killed. The guy who shot her was already an abuser, so I told him his wife would run away with his kids and worked on him for a few weeks, even bailed him out of jail. I told him stories that just cranked him up, making him angry at his wife, and Tamera. He was ready to kill anyone who stood in his way. I blamed Tamera for all his problems, and after a little persuasion, the murder of your second wife was complete."

"Then, like an idiot, you ran off to the beach because it was some kind of therapy for you, and I was ok with it and followed you down to see how I could insert myself into your life. But you had to go to the seashell shop and meet drug addict Veronica. I thought I would come inside and "meet" you there, but then I saw you and Veronica hugging. You just met her and just like that you were making out. Probably kissing to throw people off, that's how you say it, right? I missed my opportunity. I was so depressed. I even thought about suicide but talked to my sister, and she encouraged me to take care of Veronica myself."

"No one would suspect murder when a former drug addict overdosed except her brother and you. You stopped asking questions, but her brother wouldn't stop. He even called Monica, your fourth wife, the F.B.I. vixen in, to investigate. You fell for her. Jack Cash fell for the police chick, because he can't be alone for a second and he falls for anything in a skirt, or a government pantsuit and now I had to figure out how to stop her investigation and get to you before you asked her to marry you."

"I was too late. You fell for a g-woman, because..." then looking at Amanda, "honey, he can't be by himself for a minute until he is picking up another woman."

Her rant continued, "I thought it would pass but no, he had to marry her. She had to keep her investigation going. And I didn't know enough about Veronica, but she was famous because of her past dealing with the cartel. I thought, 'I can kill her,' but then, snoopy Monica had to go."

"So, I staked out Jack Cash's house. When I saw Monica leaving for training, I followed her. I couldn't shoot her. I had to do something untraceable. So, I followed her to a coffee shop and got her coffee when no one was looking. I poured eye drops into her coffee, and it killed her."

"You killed Monica too?" I asked.

"Ding, ding, ding, ding, you are not very bright, are you Jack Cash? I don't know why I thought you were so smart. I killed them all, all except Mandy. Yes, she died on her own, and I didn't feel like I would have to compete with a dying cancer patient."

"I was the one who poisoned Cybil, the crazy woman with a thousand alias and voices. When I confronted her about you, after you and queen crazy had been married for a while, she used a different voice than she used with you. It was easy to get rid of her. She was crazy."

"I thought, Jack Cash is going to take a break, a break from meeting women, and you did, for a very short time. That's when the missionary big foot called you. Do you know on the day she came to speak, I just so happened to be at church that week? You didn't even notice me. I was a visitor, so I kind of blended in with the crowd, hoping you would come to meet the visitor who came when a missionary visited. But no, Jack Cash couldn't keep his eyes off Amazon woman. Before I knew it, you were dating her, literally that week, running off to the beach with her, sleeping with her, I know, you don't sleep with women, you S.L.E.E.P. You sleep. Even when women show up with sheer lingerie, showing every glorious erotic feature. Who does that? I will tell you, JACK CASH does ..." Amanda pulled me closer.

"So, you ran off and married big foot, so I had to kill her too. I learned how to hit a car and turn it over pretty well, don't you think? I found out bigfoot had a little foot, a little bit of Jack Cash seed in her. Sorry for your loss."

"I laid low for a while, it was good I thought, because Jack Cash was depressed. Needing counseling and consoling. I waited for just the opportune time. And then, you ran off to the beach again. AGAIN!!!! You were so depressed. I thought I could drop in and sweep you off your feet. I even got a condo near you at the very last minute, and I saw you sleeping when the storm blew up. I got my shoes on to come to warn you. I was running out to the cabana! Running!!! I fell down on my way to rescue you and then the sex crazed Marie who has some angelic idea of rescuing girls in sex trafficking, yada, yada, yada, beat me out to the cabana. She warned you, warmed you, took you in! She chased little girls and then took my JACK CASH away from me."

"I just couldn't understand why every time I turned around, Jack Cash was meeting another woman. Most of your previous wives weren't in the ground long enough for the flowers to wilt, and you were cavorting around with another chick. So, I found Marie at her usual place at 3 a.m. waiting for girls to come out of the strip joint. I killed her and killed her stupid friend too, chased down and killed the girl she came to rescue. Then threw her body in a dumpster, all so I could be with Jack Cash. This time I got paid for it too."

"You are so predictable, Jack Cash, same place, same forlorn look, same sad face, so after Marie died, I knew exactly where to find you. I also knew the cartel was hunting you, so I arranged our meeting."

I stood there dumbfounded.

"I found you on the beach before another vixen could put their hooks into you. I arranged everything perfectly. I had to arrange Paddy's murder because he was getting too close to finding out who was behind it all. He tried to warn you, but not before my sister and her husband killed him. So, I found you on the beach, and you were like putty in my hands buying the "pastor's wife" bit. You were so gullible. I was never a pastor's wife. I wanted to be Jack Cash's wife."

It was then I understood all the heavy seduction she tried.

"I didn't care about any of that other stuff. I had to have Jack Cash, so I tried to lure you into sex, but Mr. 'I only S.L.E.E.P.' with women. I don't sleep with them' wouldn't fall for it. I tried every way to get you to marry me, Jack Cash, but no, you refused. Now I find you making out with this skank you met two days ago. You are pathetic. You are worthless!"

Amanda couldn't take it any longer, "you are pathetic. You murder because you can't get a man on your own. You have to maneuver and plot and plan your way into his life, but even then, you meet a man of integrity and can't do that. Can you? Can you??? Jack Cash has integrity and honor," Amanda stepped in front of me, "you can't have Jack Cash, and if you want him, you will have to go through me."

"Amanda, Kim is wrapped up in crazy clothes, get behind me." She did. She took my phone out of my back pocket and texted William telling him of our danger.

"Kim, are you with the cartel?"

"Hahahahahhahahha, heaven's no. I gave Juan Carlos my sister's number to use if needed months ago. I knew my attempt to get you to marry me wasn't working. I mean, who in their right mind would turn this down," Kim said as she motioned to her own body, "but you did, time and time again, I was beginning to think you were gay, but then I saw you with pretty little whore here and thought well, at least he is sleeping with someone. Anyway, I met up with Juan on our way back to Miami, and yes, we had glorious sex, Jack Cash, because someone appreciates my body, and he brought me to the U.S. from the cruise lines island. He also has been tracking you! He was tracking you through my phone. I never got rid of it. I only got rid of your phone, he told me you would be here."

"He knows we are here?"

"Yes, and his crew is on its way here. This whole block will be carteled (is that a word) hahahahaha, and they will level this block. You are going to die, Jack Cash, die, you and your pretty little toy."

I moved Amanda behind me, "Stay behind me."

Kim pulled out a handgun and shot one shot. BANG. I shuddered expecting pain, but she missed me. Then all of the sudden a strange peace came over me. People were running, shouting, and shots rang out from somewhere in the distance.

"Well, Jack Cash, this is the end of the line. If I can't have you, nobody can have you.

Bang, Bang, Bang, I thought Kim shot at me, but Federal agents had emerged from the building, shooting Kim. One hit her.

Kim fell to the ground, dazed and bleeding profusely. She was still alive, still aiming her gun my way and said, "if I can't have you, Jack Cash, no one can."

She shot one more time, BANG! Then she fell back lifeless.

I felt hot blood on my back, as though I had been shot, but couldn't feel anything. I turned around to Amanda. Blood was pouring from her shoulder, "she shot me," she said as she crumbled into my arms. I caught her and held her close, wrapping my arms around her and gently lowering her to the ground. I pressed my hand against her wound, trying to stop the profuse bleeding.

Gun shots in the distance grew louder, now the federal agents who came to our aid were engaged in a fire fight with a large contingent heading our way. The federal building was under assault. Helicopters with men in military gear were rappelling to the roof, others were breaching from the ground floor. People were shooting and sirens were sounding everywhere.

I cried out, "hold on Amanda, I will get you to the hospital!"

She just smiled the surreal smile as if some kind of crazy peace had just drenched her spirit, "I know, Jack Cash, I know!"

Someone grabbed my arm and began pulling, "Jack Cash, you need to come with me. NOW!" a female voice with authority screamed. I was blinded as the sun stood directly above her head. "Someone will take good care of her. Someone will take care of both of them. We've got to go...we've got to go now!"

She jerked me to stand, and then began to pull me to places unknown. I went along because by this time, I was a grieving, sleep deprived fugitive and I was ready to give up and give in. The dossier and the money were all a trap, and I was sure that I was finally caught. I could only hope for a swift end. But that was only the beginning.